THE DARK STAR WAR

BOOK THREE OF THE CODEX REGIUS

Chris Kennedy

Chris Kennedy Publishing
Virginia Beach, VA

Chris Kennedy/Chris Kennedy Publishing
2052 Bierce Dr.
Virginia Beach, VA 23454
http://chriskennedypublishing.com/

Publisher's Note: This is a work of fiction. Names, characters, places, and incidents are a product of the author's imagination. Locales and public names are sometimes used for atmospheric purposes. Any resemblance to actual people, living or dead, or to businesses, companies, events, institutions, or locales is completely coincidental.

Ordering Information:
Quantity sales. Special discounts are available on quantity purchases by corporations, associations, and others. For details, contact the "Special Sales Department" at the address above.

The Dark Star War/ Chris Kennedy. -- 1st ed.
ISBN 978-1942936183

Praise for "The Search for Gram" by Chris Kennedy:

"Chris Kennedy's Search for Gram takes humanity, the most recent newcomers to interstellar space -- and the reader -- on a roller coaster exploration of alien cultures with ancient animosities and startling technologies. There's action and skullduggery in plenty, and along the way Kennedy gives the reader a look inside questions of morality, ethics, and the true meaning of personal responsibility, not simply to others, but to one's self."

> - David Weber
> Author of the Honorverse
> and Safehold Series

As always, this book is for my wife and children. I would like to thank Linda, Beth and Dan, who took the time to critically read the work and make it better. Any mistakes that remain are my own. I would like to thank my mother, without whose steadfast belief in me, I would not be where I am today. Thank you.

I would also like to thank Jim Beall for his assistance with several aspects of the physics in "The Dark Star War." Any remaining errors are mine, in spite of his expert aid.

Author's Note

When more than one race refers to a planet or star, the same name is used by both races in order to prevent confusion. Also on the topic of planet naming, the normal convention for planets is to add a lower case letter to the name of the parent star (i.e., Tau Ceti 'b'). The first planet discovered in a system is usually given the designation 'b,' and later planets are given subsequent letters as they are found. In order to prevent confusion in this book, the closest planet to the star in a star system is given the letter 'a,' with the rest of the planets given subsequent letters in order of their proximity to the star.

"Take time to deliberate, but when the time for action has arrived, stop thinking and go in."

— *Napoleon Bonaparte*

Prologue

Throne Room, Planet Utopia, MOA-2007-BLG-192L
System, December 15, 2021

"Admiral, I don't understand," High Lord Sarpedon said. "We had the Terrans outnumbered, but our fleet commander chose not to attack? How can this be when I *specifically* told you to destroy the Terrans? Did I somehow fail to communicate my intentions clearly? When I said, 'Destroy the Terrans,' did I leave room for interpretation on how and when this was to be accomplished? I meant *immediately!*"

"No, my lord, and I was equally clear in my instructions to the fleet," Admiral Rhadamanthus replied. "I told them to seek out every opportunity to destroy the Terrans, wherever they could be found, and to annihilate them."

"So explain to me why we had four ships in the same system as the Terran ship *Vella Gulf,* and none attacked it? The only reason the crew of the *Agnosios* fought the Terrans was the *Vella Gulf* attacked *them,* and they had no choice!"

"At the time the *Agnosios* was attacked, the other ships were destroying much larger Terran vessels. Even if they *had* known the *Vella Gulf* was there, they probably wouldn't have attacked it; they were busy destroying the Terrans' battleships. Then, when they were finished with the battleships, they were concerned about the *Vella Gulf's* ability to jump between the universes."

"Did you just say my commanding officers were...scared?"

The high lord's voice had fallen to not much more than a whisper; the admiral knew that was *not* a good sign. "No my lord, I did not say that. The commanding officers were unprepared for a ship that could jump between universes and sneak up on the *Agnosios* like it did; since they didn't have tactics to fight these new capabilities, they withdrew rather than lose any more of your ships."

"The *Vella Gulf* has now been responsible for the annihilation of two of my ships. *I want it destroyed!* At all costs! As soon as possible!" All four of his eyes spun to glare at the admiral. "Am I making myself clear?"

"Abundantly, High Lord," Admiral Rhadamanthus said. "I will make sure all our ships' captains know the *Vella Gulf* is to be destroyed on sight. It will *not* escape again."

"It better not, admiral…or you will be the next to die."

"Yes, my lord," the admiral said with a bow.

High Lord Sarpedon turned to the Jotunn ambassador. "Now, what is this 'shield technology' everyone except us seems to have?" he asked. "Why have you failed to make us aware of it? Are you intentionally limiting our capabilities?"

"Not at all," replied the giant, "although the same could be said about your failure to share the technology needed to jump between our universes. We have asked for it on many occasions, and you have yet to make the secret known to us. If the Terrans now have it, they will be difficult for us to defeat, just as your ships are for everyone in our universe."

"You have let us down on too many occasions to entrust you with the secrets of piercing the shroud of the universe. Besides, we have developed shield technology on our own. You also never told us about replicators, and they are quite amazing things…"

Chapter One

Bridge, *Harvest of Flesh*, Sssellississ System, December 12, 2021

All eyes turned toward Calvin as he strode onto the bridge of the Ssselipssssiss ship. Although he'd been onboard for over a week, Terran time, it was the first time he'd been allowed on the bridge. Or pretty much anywhere else. Considering the lizard-like creatures had invited, no, demanded Calvin come with them, they really weren't making him feel very welcome. None of the Ssselipssssiss said a word; the only sound was a hiss from the lizard sitting in the central chair.

Calvin's only companion during the journey had been the Aesir Farhome, with infrequent visits from Ssselipssssiss Ambassador Gresss. The elf-like Farhome was only partly sane, on a good day; he was not the best traveling companion. After a week, Calvin was starting to doubt his own sanity.

Lieutenant Commander Shawn Hobbs, or 'Calvin' to his friends, still wasn't sure why he was even on the disgustingly-named battleship. Certainly, he was a hostage the Ssselipssssiss were using to make sure the crew of Calvin's ship, the Terran Space Ship (TSS) *Vella Gulf*, didn't bring a Mrowry invasion force with them when they returned. The lizards had already lost most of their territory in the current war, including their capital, and they were desperately clinging to their last few systems. A Mrowry invasion would have wiped them out.

Based on what Calvin had seen so far, though, it didn't look like the Ssselipsssiss would be able to hold their remaining systems without outside help. Given that they'd fired on the Terrans unprovoked the first time the two races met, Calvin wasn't sure that their annihilation was such a bad idea.

Unless their enemy was worse and, in this case, it looked like it was.

Based on the enemy's tactics, it appeared the Ssselipsssiss were fighting the same alien race, the Shaitans, that the Terrans were. If so, the Ssselipsssiss could almost be seen as Terra's friends. Well, probably not 'friends,' but maybe they could be considered allies…at least until their war with the Shaitans ended.

The Terrans and the Ssselipsssiss would probably have to redefine their relationship after the war, assuming they were both still around. That appeared unlikely, as no one had been able to stop the Shaitans' advance; so far, the best the Terrans had been able to achieve was a stalemate with them in the Aesir's home system.

The Shaitan race lived in another universe and only jumped into the Terran universe to fight. The ability to jump back to their own universe made them hard to fight, because the Shaitans could determine where and when to accept battle. The fact that they had weapons which distorted time also caused…issues.

"I think what Captain Skrelleth meant," Ambassador Gresss said, "was, 'Welcome to the bridge.'" At seven and a half feet tall, the ambassador was an impressive sight. Maroon in color, the bipedal lizard wore a red velvet robe with black trim, along with what looked like black stretch pants. The robe had a small golden patch on the left side that announced his ambassadorial rank, as well as a large amount of gold jewelry around his neck and wrists.

The ship's captain turned to glare at Calvin, his eyes glowing like the ends of two lit cigarettes. He hissed again and said, "What the captain really meant was, 'Your presence pollutes the sanctity of my vessel and is an affront to everything I feel is good and holy.'"

"Out of curiosity, Captain Skrelleth, how many times have you fought the enemy?" Calvin asked.

"I have fought them twice," the captain replied.

"I see," Calvin said. "And how many of their ships did you destroy in those encounters?"

"We haven't been able to destroy any of them," Captain Skrelleth admitted, "although we did get a couple of laser hits on one last time. We were close to destroying it, but then it disappeared."

Calvin nodded. "And during those two battles, how many ships did you lose?"

"We lost nine ships, including four battleships," the captain said.

"And your capital planet?"

"Yesss. It fell in the last battle. Its loss was unavoidable."

"So let me get this straight, captain. You've lost nine ships in two battles, your capital planet has been captured by the enemy and you have only succeeded in hitting an enemy ship twice. You didn't destroy two ships; you just scored two hits on a single enemy ship. Is that correct?"

Captain Skrelleth hissed. "Yesss, that is correct, but that is because they are able to vanish. We can't get them to fight us."

"You want the enemy to fight on your terms, when theirs are working so well?" Calvin asked. He turned to the ambassador. "I think I've found your problem."

"Careful, Terran," the captain warned, jumping from his seat. He was even larger than the ambassador, standing nearly eight feet high.

He pointed a claw at Calvin, his tail twitching. "Another word about me, and I will be forced to kill you, despite what protection the ambassador offers you. Be very careful about what you say next."

Calvin turned back to the ship's commanding officer. "I do not mean to be disrespectful, but my point is, so far, your race is losing this war. Badly. Not only are you losing, you are being systematically eliminated as a race. At the moment, the only way you can stay alive is to run from them; every time you fight you lose."

"What do you expect?" Captain Skrelleth asked. "They can disappear at will and pop up and hit us with weapons we can't defend against. I suppose you can do better against them?"

"Absolutely," Calvin said. "I have fought them twice, and I have destroyed two of their ships. The second time, we boarded the ship and fought them hand-to-hand, prior to setting explosive charges which we detonated once we were clear. Can we do better? We already have."

"You boarded one of their ships?" the CO asked. "I do not see how this is possible."

"Yes, I led a team that boarded one of their vessels. If we are fighting the same enemy, which I think we are, I have not only been aboard one of their ships, but I have fought them up close. I tell you this not to brag, but so you will see me as an asset to use in your fight against the Shaitans and, hopefully, treat me with a little more respect. I can help you, if you will let me."

Captain Skrelleth shook his head, retreated to his command chair and sat down. He turned his gaze to the view screen, which showed a chart of the system. After a few moments, the twitching of his tail slowed. When he spoke, his voice was calm and under control. "I do not like you, nor do I want you onboard my ship," he said; "however, if you have information on how to defeat the enemy, I am willing to listen."

"We could fight them better if my ship were here," Calvin said, "but there are some things I would recommend to help defend this system." He paused to look at the view screen. "Is that status correct?"

"Yesss, that is everything we have in the system, and where it currently is positioned."

Damn; the lizards were even worse off than he had thought. "Is there any reason why all your ships are around the planet?" Calvin asked.

"The enemy could appear anywhere, and we must protect the planet," Captain Skrelleth answered. "We only have three planets left; we cannot afford to lose this one."

"The enemy's forces can't appear anywhere," Calvin corrected; "they have to use the stargate to come into the system. If you position your ships around the stargate, and mine it with everything you've got, you will stand a better chance of keeping them out. If nothing else, at least you will get a chance to shoot at them before they can jump to their own universe."

"Do you know that to be truth, or are you just guessing?" the captain asked. "You are asking me to leave the planet undefended. We cannot lose it."

Calvin paused a few seconds, debating whether to tell his enemies everything he knew. Giving away your own capabilities to a culture that would rather eat you than talk to you was…complicated. He sighed. In for a penny; in for a pound.

"I know this to be true. I have been to their universe; they do not have stargates there."

Captain Skrelleth's eyes snapped around to glare at the ambassador. "The Terran has been to their universe? Why was I not made aware of this?"

Ambassador Gresss made a shooing motion with his hands. "I have told you several times that the Terran had information on the enemy and urged you to talk to him. We would be better prepared right now if you had listened to me."

"You talk too much," Captain Skrelleth replied. "You politicians always talk too much. How was I to know that this time you actually had something useful to say?"

"What's important is I have been to the other universe," Calvin said. "I know they don't have stargates, so they have to use the ones in our universe. When they come through, there will be a few moments while their systems stabilize when you can shoot them. System entry is your best, and probably your only, chance to defeat them. Once they get loose and can jump to their own universe they are very hard to bring to battle...as you have already found out."

The captain scratched a scar on his shoulder while he looked at the display. "Sometime, you will have to tell me how you were able to travel to the universe of the enemy," he said. "I would dearly like to fight there and have the wreckage of their ships fall onto their planets." He turned back to Calvin. "I take it we cannot do it without some sort of equipment that is only aboard your ship?"

"Unfortunately, that is true," Calvin admitted. "I wish we could jump this ship to their universe, but it isn't possible. We will have to fight them here."

"If that is the case, do you have any other suggestions for how to fight them?"

"You have to fight them at the stargate. Move every ship you have to the gate and put every mine you have in front of it, set to detonate automatically when a ship comes within range. You have to stop them there; if you don't, I don't think you can hold this universe against a massed assault."

"Perhaps you are more than just prey, after all," Captain Skrelleth said, his gaze returning to the status display. "I will do as you suggest, Terran, but you better not have lied to me. If I find out you have, I will kill you myself, before the enemy has a chance."

"It's in my own best interest for you to be victorious," said Calvin. "Here are some other things you can do…"

Visitor's Quarters, *Harvest of Flesh*, Sssellississ System, December 12, 2021

"So you finally met our host?" Esdren Farhome asked. The Aesir had the dark hair and pale blue skin typical of a Drow, the belowground-dwelling Aesir. Tall and thin, he also had the pointed ears typical of the elven race.

That was his normal appearance, anyway. Farhome was also an Eco Warrior, an elite soldier who could manipulate matter at the microscopic level using nanobots. His specialty was life, and he could use his nanobots to change a living being's size and shape, including his own.

Although Farhome's sanity was questionable most days, today seemed to be a good day. "Yeah, he's every bit the fun-loving Ssselipsssiss you would expect him to be," Calvin replied. "After he decided he wasn't going to kill me and eat me, he actually listened to some of my advice. They are going to move to the stargate and try to hold there."

"Well, you do have more experience fighting the Shaitans than anyone else," Farhome replied. He cocked his head and added, "On second thought, the Ssselipsssiss may have more experience *fighting* them, but you have more experience actually beating them."

"I'm happy Skrelleth listened to me," Calvin said, "but that doesn't mean we have a chance. I saw their status board. In addition to this battleship, there are only four more ships in the system. They have two battleships, two battlecruisers and a cruiser. That's it."

"That's all they have?" Farhome asked, wonder tinging his voice. "This is the front line. When we left Keppler 62, there were only two cruisers left in the system, and that is their other front line against the Mrowry. If what you say is true, they are down to their final seven ships."

"Yeah, that's it. If they lose this next battle here, they are pretty much done as a race. There won't be anything to keep the Shaitans from rolling up their last couple of systems and exterminating them."

"They need to mine the stargate," Farhome said. "Maybe tow an asteroid or 10 in front of it, too. They can't let the Shaitans into the system." He paused for a second, then asked, "How soon can we expect the *Vella Gulf* to get—"

The door to their room opened, and a low-ranking Ssselipsssiss entered. "It'sss started," he announced. "The enemy isss through the gate. Captain Skrelleth demandsss you attend him on the bridge."

Calvin turned back to Farhome. "Not soon enough."

* * * * *

Chapter Two

Emperor Yazhak turned away from the large bay window. Behind him, a large rock formation could be seen several miles away. The massive sandstone monolith glowed red in the morning sun.

"That is worse than I feared," the large felinoid finally said.

"Why is that?" Captain James Sheppard, the commanding officer of the Terran ship *Vella Gulf*, asked.

"We have guessed for some time the Ssselipsssiss were fighting another race, and they were probably losing. Although we have been at war with them for some time, they recently began pushing us hard. It was like they *had* to break through; there was a desperation we had never seen before. Then, all of a sudden, they stopped. Although a welcome respite, the absence of war was eerie; we wondered what new stratagem they might be working on."

"And now we know they stopped attacking because they're out of ships," Captain Sheppard interjected. When he had taken the *Vella Gulf* into their territory, the lizards only had three ships guarding their side of the stargate...and only one was battleship-sized.

"That worries me even more," the emperor continued. "If their enemy is strong enough to destroy their entire fleet, something we were never able to do, I am worried about who they will attack once

17

they are finished with the Ssselipsssiss. Our territory is next, unless they advance on Terra."

"Which isn't a great choice in my book," Captain Sheppard said.

"Not only has their enemy destroyed the Ssselipsssiss fleet, they also seem to be taking the planets just as fast," Lieutenant Rrower added. The young Mrowry was his civilization's liaison to the *Vella Gulf*. "I saw one of their maps, grandfather, and they have lost their capital planet; they only have three systems remaining."

"Based on your conversation with them, you believe their enemy to be the Shaitans you fought at Golirion?" Emperor Yazhak asked.

"Yes, it sounds like them," Captain Sheppard answered. "Their ships can jump out of our universe, and they use time-based weapons. If it isn't the Shaitans, it is a race nearly identical to them. Personally, I hope it *is* them; I don't think we can afford to be fighting two of them at the same time; one is more than enough!"

"Truth," the emperor agreed. "So, what did the Ssselipsssiss want?"

"They want us to go to the Shaitans' home world and blow it up."

"Well, that seems simple enough," Emperor Yazhak said with a chuckle. "Did they have any information on where this planet might be, and how you were supposed to destroy it?"

"They have an idea where it is," Captain Sheppard replied. "It's a long way behind enemy lines, and getting further as the Shaitans advance. As for how we blow it up, I don't think they care; they just want it done. They are desperate for a little breathing room."

"What did they offer for taking on this mission?"

"They were very vague on what they would, or even what they could, do," Captain Sheppard replied. "We got an awful lot of 'maybes,' but nothing very definite." He shook his head. "We didn't see a replicator in the system where we met with them, and they have lost most of their other systems. Honestly, I don't think they have much to give. Our choice is pretty simple—we can either help them out of the goodness of our hearts, or we can watch them be exterminated."

"A few months ago, I'm not sure I would have minded watching them go," Captain Paul 'Night' Train interjected. The Terran Space Marine captain was the executive officer of the platoon Calvin commanded. "However, the Shaitans are a much worse enemy…and the Ssselipsssiss are holding Lieutenant Commander Hobbs hostage until we return."

"Ah, I see," the emperor said. "I wondered where he was but was afraid to ask in case he'd been killed."

"No, he was fine the last time we saw him," Captain Sheppard explained, "but the Ssselipsssiss held onto him for fear we would return with a large Mrowry fleet and wipe them out. I think they were worried you would attack from this side if you knew how poorly defended their side of the stargate was."

"There is something to be said for that," the emperor replied, scratching his chin. "I certainly would like to get Typhon back from them…Don't worry, I'm not going to," he added when he saw the Terrans bristle. "Calvin has done just as much for us; I am not going to blithely sacrifice him. Besides, you don't win wars by throwing away your hero spirits; you win wars by supporting them. Calvin must have approved of helping them, or he wouldn't have stayed with the Ssselipsssiss?"

"Yes, he did," Captain Sheppard replied. "He also believes the Shaitans are the greater enemy; he stayed both as a hostage and to help the Ssselipsssiss with their defenses. Although the lizzies have been fighting the Shaitans for a while, they don't really have much of a clue as to how to fight them. The enemy is so different from what they're used to, the only thing the Ssselipsssiss have been good at is losing. Calvin is going to try to shore up their defenses; maybe it will buy them some time."

Bridge, *Harvest of Flesh*, Sssellississ System, December 12, 2021

"The enemy is here, Terran," Captain Skrelleth announced as Calvin walked onto the bridge. Calvin had put on his aviator's space suit, but carried the helmet under an arm.

"What is the status, sir?"

"As you indicated would happen, the enemy vessels came through the portal and immediately disappeared."

"Yes sir, they jumped back to their own universe."

"Whatever. The fact remains that they are loose in this system. I have told the other ships' captains to return to orbit. We cannot allow this planet to fall. There are more of my race here than the other two systems combined. We must hold."

"How many enemy ships are there?"

"At least three of the cruiser-sized vessels and four of the destroyer-sized vessels entered the system. I know from experience all of them carry their time-based weapons."

"Damn," Calvin said, shaking his head. "That's more than I've seen at one time. What defenses does the planet have?"

"Not much," Captain Skrelleth said; "however, the moon has both missile and laser systems on its surface. We also have a few orbital missile pods we can use. By pulling all of our forces back to orbit, it will limit the number of directions from which the enemy can attack and will concentrate our defenses to where we can hopefully get some shots at them."

"Gate emergence!" one of the Ssselipsssiss technicians exclaimed. "It is a type of ship I haven't seen before. It is battleship-sized. There is a second one...now a third."

"Images on screen," the captain ordered.

"Coming up now, sir!" the same technician replied.

The front viewer changed to show a shape Calvin recognized. "That isn't a battleship," he advised; "it is a Jotunn *Raptor*-class battlecruiser."

"Jotunn?" Captain Skrelleth asked. "What is a Jotunn and what are the capabilities of their ships?"

"The Jotunn is a race of giant-sized humanoids, nearly three times my size. Their vessels are over-sized, as you can see. They are very strong, and their weapons are quite powerful."

"How will they attack?"

"I have fought a combined battlegroup of Shaitans and Jotunn before. The Jotunn don't believe in finesse; they will come straight at you and try to destroy your biggest vessels first. Meanwhile, the Shaitans will hover on the edges of the battle, picking off your most vulnerable ships. If they can separate a ship from the group, they will destroy it before coming back to pick off another one."

"Just like a pack of colvargs," the captain replied.

"I don't know what those are," Calvin replied, "but their tactics are very effective. It will be difficult to win this fight." Difficult? Calvin shook his head. This battle was unwinnable. After all he'd been through, he was going to die on a lizard ship.

"How can we defeat this joint assault?" Captain Skrelleth asked.

"As much as it hurts me to say it," Calvin said, "you need to write off this planet and pull back to the next one. That way, you can fight them one at a time as they come through the stargate—"

"Unacceptable," Captain Skrelleth interrupted. "The planet must be saved."

"You can't win this battle!" Calvin exclaimed. "You may destroy some of their ships, but you are outclassed; in the end, your ships will be destroyed, and the remaining enemy ships will have free rein to do whatever they wish with the planet. The only chance you have is to save the two planets you have remaining. Perhaps some of the civilians there can be pulled back to a Terran or Mrowry planet and resettled there, ensuring the continuity of your race. Whatever you do, though, you've *got* to withdraw. *You can't win this fight!*"

"If this fight is unwinnable, then we will die," the captain said. "This ship was built on the planet below, and most of us have families there. *We will not leave them behind.* We will stand and fight, dying if we must, but we *will* win in the end. We have to; our families are counting on us, and we can do no lessss." He pushed a button and the tactical plot reappeared on the front screen. "We will stand and fight."

* * * * *

Chapter Three

The Jotunn vessels continued toward the Ssselipsssiss at 2/3 of their full acceleration. The other ships in the group led them onward, popping in and out of the universe periodically.

"We have an image of one of their jumping ships," a technician reported.

"Put it on the display," Captain Skrelleth ordered.

"Yes sir. Coming up now."

The picture flashed onto the screen, and Calvin's heart sank; it was a Shaitan destroyer.

"Is that their top speed?" asked Captain Skrelleth, changing the screen back to the plot.

"No," Calvin replied. "They can go a lot faster. They must be taking their time so their allies can get into position."

"I thought you said they would come straight for us."

"Has their course deviated since they found us?" Calvin asked. "They are coming, and they will continue to do so. I said they don't believe in finesse, not that they were stupid. They have a plan, and I'm sure it involves letting their allies get a few shots in first."

"That makes sense," Captain Skrelleth said. "Their torpedoes are very powerful—they disintegrate whatever they hit."

"It isn't a disintegration effect," Calvin replied; "the torpedoes actually cause a time bubble. Anything in the area of effect is knocked backward in time about 10 seconds. As ships are usually in motion, it has the effect of carving out portions of the ship."

"So that's what happens…we didn't know. How does it work?"

"We still don't know *how* it works," Calvin said with a shrug; "we just know that it does. I'd love to get my hands on one to figure it out."

"Sir! One of the Jotunn vessels is hailing us," a technician announced.

"I forgot to mention," Calvin said. "They also like to taunt their foes."

"Can they be bribed?" Captain Skrelleth asked. "If we could get them to change sides, it would vastly improve our odds."

"It would indeed," Calvin agreed; "however, they are usually true to their word. If they agreed to attack you, they probably will, regardless of how much you offer them."

"When faced with the destruction of your civilization, it is worth a try," the captain said. "Put them on screen."

The front screen switched to show one of the massive Jotunn. Dressed in blue-striped pelts, the Jotunn had a chain-metal shirt over his torso. White hair flowed from under an enormous helmet with immense horns.

"Greetings, puny ones," the giant said. "I am Oleif Magnusson, captain of the Jotunn ship *Falcon*. I thought I would introduce myself so you'd know who killed you." He laughed a couple of times and added, "Of course, if you would like to surrender now, I could probably use some of you in my zoo."

Captain Skrelleth hissed. "I had hoped we could work out a deal, but I can tell the only thing you'll understand is a laser bolt through your head."

"Ho, ho ho," the Jotunn replied. "Meaningless threats don't scare me. Besides, why would we want to deal with you? We are already on the winning side."

"Have you no honor?" Calvin asked. "You would help the Shaitans wipe out this race?"

"Yes, I have my honor," Captain Magnusson replied. "I have given my word to help my allies capture this system. What they do with it is up to them; I care not. I am curious, though; who are you, and how do you know our allies?"

"I am Lieutenant Commander Shawn Hobbs of the Terran ship *Vella Gulf*," Calvin said. "When the *Gulf* shows up to destroy your ship, just remember we gave you a chance to surrender."

"A Terran, eh?" the Jotunn asked, looking thoughtful. "And from the *Vella Gulf*? Where is your ship?"

"It is where it needs to be," Calvin replied. "Why do you care?"

"Ho, ho, ho," Captain Magnusson said, turning to share a laugh with his bridge crew. "The insignificant one is lippy, isn't he?" He turned back to Calvin. "I care, because there is a reward for destroying Terran ships. If yours isn't here, I guess you will have to do. Maybe there will be a reward for killing Terrans, as well as their ships."

"A reward from whom?" Calvin asked.

"We all have our secrets today, don't we?" the giant asked. "Good bye, Terran; it is time for you to die." The connection ended.

Captain Skrelleth turned to look at Calvin and cocked his head. "It appears I may have misjudged you. If there is a bounty on your ships, you must have gone out of your way to annoy them. I like that; it is too bad I didn't lisssten to you earlier. Perhaps we could have stopped them at the stargate."

Calvin shrugged. "It's too late to worry about it now. What are the ranges of your weapons?"

"Our missiles have a range of about 13 million miles, and our lasers can fire about 600,000 miles. Why?"

"The range of the Shaitan torpedo is about 800,000 miles," Calvin said. "I was hoping they would have to come within range of your energy weapons to fire."

"That is the problem we have with fighting them," the Ssselipsssiss officer said. "They stay just outside the range of our lasers and disappear when we try to hit them with missiles."

"Well, we're going to need to do something about that if we're going to have a chance. Where are your missile pods?"

Emperor Yazhak the Third's Estate, Grrrnow, 61 Virginis, December 12, 2021

"So what are your recommendations?" Emperor Yazhak asked.

"Despite the Ssselipsssiss warnings to the contrary, I think you should bring all the ships you can spare to the border. One of two things is going to happen. Either the Ssselipsssiss are going to be overrun in short order, and you will need them there to defend yourselves, or the situation will become so dire for the lizards that they will ask for your help. I think they're probably very close to that now. Asking for our help is probably a pretty good indicator things may already be beyond 'dire' for them."

"That is sound advice," the emperor agreed, "and it was my intention to do so. Anything else?"

"Yes sir," Captain Sheppard replied. "I know it isn't my place to tell you, but I think you should send word to the Archons. The Aesir need help, and they're the only ones who might be able to assist. It's in their best interest to do so; if the Aesir are destroyed, the Archons will be next in the Shaitans' advance down that stargate chain. I'm sure the Archons would rather fight as far away from their own borders as possible."

"What are your intentions?" the emperor asked.

"Even though I doubt the Ssselipsssiss are going to come up with anything to make it worth our while, I think we ought to see if we can find the Dark Planet the Ssselipsssiss want us to look for. The *Vella Gulf* is the best reconnaissance ship we have, and the one most likely to make it there and back. We are the most experienced with fighting the Shaitans, and we have the ability to jump back and forth with them. We're the best qualified for the job."

"And what are your intentions if you find the Dark Planet?"

"I've never been a fan of genocide," Captain Sheppard said, "so it isn't my intention to destroy the planet. That being said, the Shaitans have given no indication they'd discuss peace with us. Ever. My goal is to bring them to the negotiating table; failing that, I'll give them a demonstration that will."

"What can I do to assist in this?"

"Well, we're sort of short on space fighters again. If you have five we could borrow, I could certainly use them. Also, on your next courier run to Terra, could you please take back word of our intentions to Fleet Command?"

"I would be happy to," Emperor Yazhak replied. "Before you leave, though, I was wondering if you would do one thing for me first..."

Bridge, *Harvest of Flesh*, Sssellississ System, December 12, 2021

"The Jotunn are in range," the missile technician advised.

"Fire!" Captain Skrelleth ordered.

The two battleships and the missile base on the moon launched at the same time as the three Jotunn battlecruisers. As expected, all three enemy ships targeted the flagship, *Harvest of Flesh*, although Calvin didn't know whether that was because the Jotunn were trying to kill the ship or the Terran aboard it.

Either way, he approved of the way Captain Skrelleth had positioned his forces. The *Harvest of Flesh* was in the center of the formation facing the Jotunn vessels. The other battleship, the *Blood Drinker,* was 100,000 miles 'above' the flagship. The two battlecruisers, the *Dagger* and the *Knife,* were a similar distance to the sides and the cruiser *Reaper* the same distance 'below.' All five ships were broadside to the giants' ships and were able to provide mutual defense.

The giants' initial salvo was destroyed.

"Pop-up target, sir!" the sensor technician said. "It is on the far side of the *Knife.*"

Calvin heard a small hiss from the captain; the missile pods were on the opposite side of the formation. "Understood," the captain said after a second. "Have the *Knife* maintain position."

"Another pop-up," the sensor tech said. "Opposite side of the *Dagger*. Both are preparing to launch torpedoes."

"Have them both fire, *now!*" the captain ordered. "When the Shaitans disappear, activate the missile pod by the *Dagger!*"

"Missiles away!" the missile tech acknowledged. "The Jotunn vessels are firing again."

"Understood; continue firing at the Jotunn vessels and defend the ship."

"The two Shaitan vessels disappeared again," said the missile tech. "Launching the *Dagger's* pods."

"Do you think this will work?" Captain Skrelleth asked.

"I don't know," Calvin admitted. "I hope so. If the Shaitan ship pops back like normal, the missiles from the pod should be right on top of it…"

"Pop-ups!" the sensor tech called. "Same two! *Hit!* At least four hits on the Shaitan opposite the *Dagger,* with secondary explosions from its torpedoes! *That ship is destroyed!* The other Shaitan vessel is launching at the *Knife.*"

"Sir, the *Knife* is using its missiles to defend itself," the missile technician said. "Without its defensive fire, some of the Jotunn missiles will probably get through to us."

"I am aware," Captain Skrelleth replied. "Keep firing."

Calvin felt the ship shudder as the first Jotunn missile detonated on the *Harvest's* shields. The Jotunn missiles were huge; it wouldn't be long until the shields failed.

Emperor Yazhak the Third's Estate, Grrrnow, 61 Virginis,
December 12, 2021

"It seems every system that is inhabited in this universe is also inhabited in the other," the emperor said. "I would like it if you could tell me if my planet is inhabited in the other universe, and if so, what race or races are living on it. I heard about what happened on Terra, and I would greatly like to avoid that here."

"Did you want the *Vella Gulf* to jump to the other universe and see if the planet is inhabited," Captain Sheppard asked, "or for us to send some people across from here on the planet?"

"If possible, I would like them not to know we're doing it," the emperor answered.

"We'd be happy to do that for you," Captain Sheppard replied, "but there are some considerations you should be aware of. First, it is more likely we will be seen in the *Vella Gulf* than if we just send some people over on the surface of the planet. We will go over stealthed, but it is always possible the stealth module could break or that they might have something which can see through the stealth. If so, it's going to be hard to miss something the size of the *Vella Gulf*."

"On the other hand," he continued, "we haven't surveyed the planet in the other universe; my men and women would be jumping in blind. They might jump in where there is a house or a tree or something, which would be fatal. Jumping in the *Vella Gulf* runs the same risks, of course, but there are less likely to be obstructions in space. Not impossible; just less probable."

"So what would you recommend?" the emperor asked.

"I would rather jump over with the *Gulf*," Captain Sheppard replied. "I can do it with less risk; losing someone to an unsurveyed jump would be both wasteful and unnecessary. After we take a look, we can come back and let you know what we found. I don't mind taking a quick look, but an extended survey will have to wait. I want to get Calvin from the Ssselipsssiss as soon as possible. I don't think the lizards will last much longer, and I'd hate to leave him hanging in the wind."

* * * * *

Chapter Four

"The *Reaper* has been destroyed," the sensor tech reported.

The battle had gone almost exactly the way Calvin had imagined. The missile pods had closed some of the technological gap between the Shaitans and the Ssselipsssiss, but now their pods were out of missiles, and the Shaitans weren't out of ships. And the Jotunn battlecruisers continued to wear away the Ssselipsssiss ships.

In addition to the *Reaper*, both the *Knife* and the *Dagger* had been destroyed, and the *Harvest* and *Drinker* were both heavily damaged. On the good side, they had destroyed one of the Jotunn battlecruisers, and had damaged the *Falcon*, but the others continued to bear down on the Ssselipsssiss battleships. The lizards had to defend themselves from the Jotunn…which let the Shaitans get undefended shots from the flanks.

"Pop-up behind us!" called the sensor tech. "Cruiser size. It's getting ready to fire."

"Rotate the ship," Captain Skrelleth ordered. "Head straight for the cruiser."

"Some of the Jotunn missiles are going to get through if you do that, sir," the missile tech advised. "I can't stop them all with anything short of a full broadside."

"Understood," Captain Skrelleth said. "We can't let the Shaitans hit our engines."

"The cruiser is firing," the sensor tech called.

"Head straight for the torpedoes," the captain ordered.

The ship rocked. "Missile strikes aft, sir! At least three hits. Damage repair technicians are responding."

"Torpedo impacts in three...two...one..." The ship buffeted slightly.

"That felt...weird," Calvin said. "Did we get hit by the torpedoes?"

"Yes and no," replied Captain Skrelleth. "About the only thing we've been able to learn in this war is how to take the first hit. The bows on all of our ships have a gigantic metal plate welded to a 200-foot spar. By turning into the missiles, we present a much smaller target and the missiles draw close to each other as they near the ship. Most of the time, we can catch at least one of them on the plate, and when it detonates, it usually destroys the others. We lose the pole but can sometimes weather a volley without taking a single hit."

"That's a great idea," Calvin said.

"Unfortunately, it only works once. There are still four Shaitan ships remaining."

"Pop-up target on the port bow!"

Bridge, TSS *Vella Gulf*, 61 Virginis, December 12, 2021

"All hands, this is the captain," Captain Sheppard said over the public address system. "In five minutes, we are going to jump to the other universe. It is my intention to activate our stealth system before we jump and avoid contact with any inhabitants we might find there. Prudence dictates, however, that we be prepared for any eventuality, so we'll be going to General Quarters prior to making the jump. Once all of our weapons are manned, we'll make the jump, survey the planet quickly then return. Stand by for GQ; that is all."

Captain Sheppard's eyes scanned the bridge. His crew had made the jump on many occasions, including a number of combat jumps; they were focused, but loose and ready. "Here we go, folks," he said. "Set General Quarters! Stand by to jump to the Jinn universe."

Bridge, *Harvest of Flesh*, Sssellississ System, December 12, 2021

"The ship is lost," Captain Skrelleth announced. "Abandon ship!"

Yellow lights began strobing across the bridge, and an ear-splitting siren sounded for five seconds. When it ended, a voice ordered, "Abandon ship! Abandon ship! All hands, abandon ship!"

The ship rocked with the impact of another Jotunn missile, and Calvin was thrown to the deck, slamming his head into the steel surface. The ship's lights went out. Everything went fuzzy, and Calvin decided the momentary silence and darkness were pleasant. Maybe he would take a nap, and things would be better when he awoke. The cool steel felt nice under his cheek.

Bright green lights snapped on, and the voice returned, "Abandon ship!"

Calvin had just decided a nap would be more fun than abandoning a perfectly good ship when a claw grabbed the back of his suit, nails raking his back. He was lifted from the deck, and another claw grabbed his shoulder, its nails piercing deeply into his flesh.

"*Let's go, Terran!*" Captain Skrelleth bellowed. "We're leaving!"

Calvin found himself placed on his feet. The lights had dimmed again and were barely bright enough for him to see by, although a fire at one of the consoles provided a little extra illumination. Shadows danced across the bridge as the flames flicked across the display.

The pain of the nails in Calvin's shoulder was excruciating but helped him focus. The claw began dragging him along.

"Wait…" he muttered. "Need…my helmet…"

"We don't have time!" Captain Skrelleth shouted. "Let's go."

Calvin dug in his heels. "Need…helmet."

"By the 15th level of hell," the captain hissed. The pressure on his shoulder disappeared, and Calvin's helmet was slammed over his head. The enormous Ssselipsssiss grabbed Calvin by the shoulder again and began dragging him off the bridge.

Calvin reached up and seated the helmet, and the space suit activated. The miniature artificial intelligence (AI) determined his status ("heavily damaged") and began injecting him with a variety of pain killers and stimulants. The suit also sprayed his face with a nanobot wash as it worked to simultaneously repair the damage caused by Captain Skrelleth's claws and getting slammed to the deck. The miniature machines cleaned the blood from his eye and began closing the wound on his scalp. Slowly he regained some equilibrium and was able to walk on his own.

"Here," the captain said after 15 seconds of forced marching down the passageway. He pushed a button, and a panel slid open, revealing the access tube to a two-seat cockpit. The Ssselipsssiss shoved Calvin into the back seat, leaving the Terran to deal with the oversized straps, while he vaulted into the front. As Calvin's backside hit the seat, the canopy began closing.

Calvin barely heard Captain Skrelleth yell, "Hold on!" before the small craft detached from the battleship in a flash of rocket fire. Clear of the surrounding structure, Calvin could see the craft was a small two-person transport, probably used to ferry the captain to other ships.

As the transport dropped away, Calvin could see a portion of the destruction inflicted on the warship. Huge gaps were missing where the Shaitan torpedoes and Jotunn missiles had hit. The first left smooth edges where the time bubbles had carved away sections; the missiles left jagged-edged holes. The *Harvest of Flesh* looked like an overgrown metallic Swiss cheese. The captain spun the transport down and away from the battleship, and Calvin lost sight of it as the planet came into view.

Red in color, the planet only had a few small seas; there weren't any ocean-like bodies of water to be seen. It appeared Captain Skrelleth either knew where he was going or had a navigation system in the front cockpit; the ship turned and oriented itself to a spot on the planet and accelerated in a straight line toward it. Wherever they were headed, they were going to get there quickly.

* * * * *

Chapter Five

Bridge, TSS *Vella Gulf*, 61 Virginis, December 12, 2021

"Stealth?" Captain Sheppard asked.

"On and operational," the duty engineer replied.

"Solomon, are you ready for the jump?"

"Yes, Captain Sheppard, I am ready," the ship's AI replied. "All systems are operational."

"On my mark, then," Captain Sheppard commanded. "Three…two…one…mark."

Everything flashed although the view on the front screen remained the same.

"We have made the jump into the Jinn Universe," Solomon noted.

"You're sure?" the CO asked.

"I cannot know for sure whether this is the Jinn Universe without additional information, but I can confirm we are somewhere else. There is a solar power facility on the moon, which does not exist in our universe."

"A solar power station?" Captain Sheppard asked.

"Calling it a station is deceptive as it's not actually a station, but a 250-mile-wide band of solar receivers that completely encircles the moon. The power generated through the receiver array is transferred to laser power-transmission antennas, which in turn beam it to receiving stations on the planet."

"What about ships or space-based defenses?"

"I have two destroyer-sized ships in planetary orbit," Steropes said from the sensor station. "They do not seem to have noticed our entrance into this universe. There is also a considerable presence on the planet. The technology level is somewhat higher than Terra's was prior to our intervention."

"How much further advanced?"

"It is difficult to postulate how quickly Terran civilization would have advanced; however, it is probably on the order of at least 100 years. The access to cheap energy gives them a great advantage over your civilization."

"How much energy are we talking about?" Captain Sheppard asked.

"The lunar production facilities are beaming back a steady stream of almost 14,000 terawatts of power. To put that into perspective, all of Terra only generated about 25 terawatts before we made ourselves known to you. They are producing several orders of magnitude more than you did, and this energy resource is transformative for a civilization. To put it another way, they are a Type I civilization on the Kardashev scale of technological development; Terra was a Type 0 before our assistance. Although Terra is further along than they are now, you would not have been without our intervention."

"Can you determine what race inhabits this planet?" the captain asked.

"It appears to be an offshoot of the Sila race. Of note, I do not see any evidence of Efreeti interaction. It appears that this planet was spared for some reason."

"I think we've seen all we need to," Captain Sheppard announced. "Solomon, please take us back to our universe; we have a crew member to pick up."

Cockpit, Transport Craft, Sssellississ, December 13, 2021

The escape ship angled downward in a steep descent. From his seat in the aft cockpit, all Calvin could see was the red soil of the planet, and a lot of it, as the transport dove toward its impending crash. Calvin hoped Captain Skrelleth knew what he was doing; if he didn't pull the craft out of the dive soon, they were headed for a fiery impact with the planet.

"Are you strapped in?" the Ssselipsssiss captain yelled from the front seat.

"No!" Calvin yelled back. "My suit isn't compatible with the fittings in this cockpit!"

"Hold on, then!"

Calvin scanned the cockpit, looking for something to tie into. Just like his F/A-18 fighter, everything was utilitarian; there weren't a lot of extra things available to hold onto. To his right, he saw a handhold, or actually a clawhold, and he grabbed onto it with both hands although he suspected his grasp wouldn't survive a crash. He finally figured out which gauge was the altimeter as it spun through the equivalent of 1,000 feet.

The transport exploded in a burst of flames and black smoke.

As the smoke cleared, Calvin realized the transport hadn't been destroyed; instead, his pilot had ejected them from the craft, but instead of the individual ejection seats he was used to, the entire cockpit had come out in a single bathtub-like capsule.

With a tremendous jerk, their forward motion ceased as a number of parachutes deployed. The escape module swung twice under its canopy of scarlet and gold then slammed into the ground.

Calvin lost his grip, and his head smashed into the instrument panel. Although his helmet and visor absorbed most of the blow, Calvin was still stunned by the impact.

With another flash of flames and a loud "*chunk!*" the canopy blew off.

"Come, human," Captain Skrelleth urged as he exited the remains of the craft. "We must get out of here before the demons come. This planet will soon be swarming with them; we don't have long."

Calvin heard the words, but they were slow to register through the fog filling his brain. Seeing the Terran unmoving yet again, the Ssselipsssiss officer reached down, grabbed him by both shoulders and lifted him from the capsule.

"Here," Captain Skrelleth said, thrusting a laser rifle into Calvin's chest.

"Uh, thanks," Calvin said. His suit went to work fixing the new damage caused by the lizard's claws. Several red lights illuminated in his heads-up display as pharmacopeia and nanobot levels dropped into the critical.

The captain removed a second rifle from the cockpit, slung it over his shoulder and took several steps away from the craft before turning and waving Calvin forward.

"Let's *go!*" he urged. "I may have given us a little time; hopefully, they will think we were in the shuttle when it crashed. If they come down and look for us, though, it won't take them long to figure out where we went."

"I'm coming," Calvin replied as he clambered from the cockpit to join the Ssselipsssiss. "Do you know if Farhome made it?"

"Farhome?"

"The Aesir who was traveling with me."

"Your care for your mate is touching, but it is out of place at the moment. I do not know if he made it off the ship, but I would assume he did not. It exploded soon after we departed."

"Mate?" Calvin said, stopping to turn toward the Ssselipsssiss. "He's not my mate. He's a…well, he's a friend, I guess. Sort of. Kind of a protector, too, I suppose. But mate? Definitely not."

"Fine; he's not your mate. You Terrans talk too much. Can you focus? *Let's go!* We have to get away from here before they come looking for us." He turned and began jogging away from the wreckage of the capsule toward a tall cliff several miles away; Calvin was forced to a full run to keep from getting left behind. Overtaking the Ssselipsssiss was not an option.

"Wait!" Calvin called after a couple of minutes when he could see he wasn't going to be able to keep up. "Where are you going?"

Captain Skrelleth stopped and turned around. "Isn't it obvious?" he asked. He motioned toward the face of the cliff. "On top of that cliff is a spaceport. Hopefully, there is still a ship there we can use to escape. Less talking; more running." He turned and began running toward the cliff again.

"Could you…" Calvin puffed, "just slow down…a little? Your legs are…lot longer…than mine."

The Ssselipsssiss slowed marginally, enabling Calvin to keep up, and they quickly covered the remaining two miles. The captain stopped as he reached the side of the sheer cliff, which rose over 1,000 feet above them.

"We are almost to my home," Captain Skrelleth said.

"We've got to climb this?" Calvin asked, gazing at the face of the cliff. It was nearly vertical, with little in the way of handholds to be seen.

"Don't worry," the Ssselipsssiss said. "It's easy."

"Are you sure, captain?" Calvin asked. "It doesn't look like an easy climb to me."

Without warning, the lizard turned and hit him in the face with a closed claw, knocking him to the ground.

Calvin lay on his back, rubbing his jaw. It didn't seem broken, but hurt like hell. He was in no hurry to get up for more. "What was that for?"

"In our culture, if we lose a ship, we lose our rank. I am no longer Captain Skrelleth. I am now just Salissessolliss."

"So you had to hit me?"

"I went easy on you. If any of my people had dishonored me so, I would have killed them."

"Well, thanks for just punching me then," Calvin replied; "however, if we're going to work together, maybe next time you could warn me if I violate one of your moral codes, rather than resorting to violence from the start? It might help our working relationship. Like, a lot."

"I will think about it, but will not make any promises."

"Don't do me any favors. What did you say I'm supposed to call you?"

"Salissessolliss. It is my name."

"In the interests of time, like if an enemy is about to shoot at you, can I just call you 'Sal?' That way, I don't mispronounce your name and cause some other grave insult?"

"Shortening my name is an insult."

"I'm not sure I can pronounce the whole thing."

The lizard hissed. "Well then, just call me Sal. It is probably better that way. The less I have to hear you speak my language, the greater I will like it."

"The feeling is mutual," Calvin muttered. Looking at the bluff from his back, he didn't see any openings or doors…or anything which would indicate the cliff was populated. "So where is the city?"

"Right here." The captain pushed a black rock jutting out from the cliff face and Calvin heard a 'click.' The outline of a door became visible. "It's inside the hill." Captain Skrelleth took hold of the rock and pulled open the door. "After you."

* * * * *

Chapter Six

Emperor Yazhak the Third's Estate, Grrrnow, 61 Virginis, December 12, 2021

"There was a civilization on the planet, which appeared to be Sila," Captain Sheppard said. "As you requested, we did not interact with them. Of note, this is the first time we've found a Sila civilization where we didn't see any evidence of the Efreet. This appears to have allowed the Sila to progress into the space age. They had at least two destroyer-sized ships, as well as a solar collection facility on the moon."

"Thank you for doing that," Emperor Yazhak replied; "I will sleep better at night knowing the Efreet or Shaitans aren't going to pop in and start bombing my cities. I would like to open up relations with the civilization, but I am willing to wait until you return for that."

"You're welcome," Captain Sheppard said. "We will be happy to make contact with them the next time we're here, but for now, we have a dark planet to find and a crewman to recover."

Passages, Sssorowyn, Sssellississ, December 13, 2021

The doorway opened into a passage that led deeper into the cliff. Sal hadn't been kidding, Calvin realized; there was an entire city inside the hill. He followed the Ssselipsssiss through a warren of passageways, with tunnels branching off in every direction. The passages were a three-dimensional maze; they would climb several flights of stairs only to go back down again, even further, a few minutes later.

Complicating things, Ssselipssssiss were running everywhere. Big ones, small ones; all were running somewhere. Calvin was jostled, bumped and, on two occasions, slammed into the wall. Within minutes, Calvin was hopelessly lost and couldn't have found his way back out if his life depended on it. And looking at the situation, it soon might.

After another few minutes of being banged around by creatures larger than himself, Calvin finally had to ask, "So, where did you say we were going?"

"We're almost there," Sal replied over his shoulder. He turned back just in time to crash into another Ssselipsssiss, and he pushed it away. The unfortunate lizard bounced off the opposite wall, tripped and went headlong into Calvin's knees, cutting his legs out from under him. Calvin went down in a heap, his helmet flying forward to bounce off Sal's back.

Sal turned with the hiss of steam escaping a broken boiler and grabbed Calvin's shoulder again to lift him upright. Calvin saw stars and was momentarily dazed. Until Sal slammed Calvin's helmet into his stomach, nearly knocking the wind out of him.

"Come *on!*" Sal urged. "We are almost there."

"Almost there" really meant five more minutes of travel at a forced march; the last two of which were climbing stairs. Up, the entire way.

"We are here, finally," Sal said. He stopped next to a door that looked just like the others they had passed. The Ssselipsssiss surveyed the hall and slid the door to the side.

Calvin started to enter, but Sal grabbed his arm. "Let me go first," he said. "We're liable to have fewer problems that way."

Calvin wasn't sure what he meant, as the room appeared empty, but he moved to the side and let Sal slide past him. Sal took three steps into the room, stopped and emitted an ear-piercing whistle.

At the sound, a group of smaller Ssselipsssiss exploded from the places they'd been hiding. One even dropped from a vent in the ceiling. The four were all about five feet tall, and they were armed to the teeth; each had at least one wicked-looking blade and a laser pistol. They came running toward Sal, but stopped when they saw he had someone with him.

"These five are the children from my last, and best, brood. Their mother was a warrior beyond compare." He indicated the tallest of the group. "This is Reyl. He is the first-hatched and extremely smart although often more generous than is appropriate. He'll give you the shirt off his back without a thought to his own need."

The second lizard stepped forward. "This is Syrusss. He is also very smart but tends to the sly. You'll never see his revenge coming and usually won't know that he's gotten even until long after it's done."

The third Ssselipsssiss wasn't as tall as the first two but was built like a tank. Calvin couldn't remember ever seeing a lizard with bulging muscles, but this child had them. "This is Karver. Don't let the muscles deceive you; he is almost as smart as his brothers."

"The smallest one is Paxton. He is the runt of the litter but mean as all hells. If you ever wrong him, you'd better kill him because he *always* gets even. He'll start a fight between his brothers then walk away laughing."

"I thought you said there were five," Calvin said. "I only see four."

"Turn around."

Calvin turned to find the muzzle of a laser pistol several inches from his right eye. Her other hand held a knife at stomach level, ready to eviscerate him.

"That's their sister, Burkuri. She's the leader and most dangerous one of the bunch."

"I see," Calvin said. He reached up and pushed the barrel of the pistol away from his face. "I'm a friend," he added.

"Is he really a friend, father?" Burkuri asked, moving to block the doorway. "Or can we kill him and eat him? He looks tasty."

Calvin tensed, ready to attack the young Ssselipsssiss, but Sal intervened.

"Yes, he is a friend," Sal said. "If not a friend, he is at least an ally against the demons. If you kill him, you will deprive our civilization of his experience."

"As you wish, father," Burkuri said, spinning the pistol around her finger once before sliding it into the holster. She did the same with the knife in her other hand before sheathing it. "I still say he looks tasty, and meat *has* been in short supply."

"Maybe another time," Sal said, which didn't boost Calvin's confidence. "Right now, though, we need him. Everyone grab their packs; we're leaving."

Within 10 seconds, the five children were back with their packs. "Ready, father," Burkuri said.

Sal drew Burkuri aside and said something to her Calvin couldn't hear, although he could see she wasn't pleased by it. He said something else and then returned to where Calvin was waiting.

"Let's go," Sal said, then he turned and led the group into the tunnel system. This time they went up, staircase after staircase, and it wasn't long until Calvin's legs were burning again with the effort. Finally, Sal stopped.

"There is a cave mouth nearby that overlooks the spaceport," Sal said. "Children, I want you to stay here while the Terran and I take a look."

"But, father, if we do not also look, how will we be able to assist you in the planning?" Reyl protested.

"I want you to stay here and guard our backs," Sal replied. "The enemy will be here soon, if they haven't already landed. Two of you on each side of the passageway, with Burkuri on overwatch. Do it!"

"Yes, father," five voices chorused, and they scampered off to take their positions.

"Quietly," Sal said, turning back to Calvin. "If they are at the spaceport, they will hear you."

He pulled open a door and lay down to slide out on his belly. Calvin also got down on his stomach and followed. Beyond the door was a small overhang that opened out from the hill above the spaceport. The complex was in a circular depression about three miles in diameter at the top of the plateau.

Sal crawled to the edge and peered down for a moment before sliding back away from the lip. "The enemy approaches," Sal whispered.

Calvin let the lizard slide past him and took his place. The narrow ledge overlooked the spaceport from about 25 feet above it. He froze as he saw a number of creatures going by below, then slid forward to get a better look at the procession after it passed. Four centaur-like beings herded three of Sal's countrymen with some sort of electric prod, laughing as they used it on the helpless lizards at will. The creatures looked like what you'd get if you crossed a longhorn steer with a four-armed man and then added an extra pair of eyes on antennas. They were the creatures from his nightmares.

Shaitans.

He pushed himself backward before one of the Shaitans could look up and see him.

"Yeah, that's our enemy too," he whispered. "Those are Shaitans, and it looks like they captured three of your people. We've got to find a way to free them."

"They are as good as dead," Sal said, "just like the rest of this planet. It is more important to find a way off-planet and take the word back to my people."

"What are your people going to do with the information?" Calvin asked. "Just knowing the name of the race you're fighting isn't going to help defeat them."

Sal hissed, his annoyance evident.

"It doesn't matter whether you like it or not," Calvin argued; "it's the truth. We have the same problem. We know *who* we're fighting, but we don't know where their home planet is, or anything else about them. All we know is they have at least a limited mastery over time because they use it as a weapon. If they can do other things with it…more powerful things…then we are well and truly screwed."

"My race is already, as you say, 'screwed,'" Sal replied. "They have taken most of our planets, including our capital, and now my world. If we don't find a way to stop them, and soon, we will be annihilated."

Having fought the Ssselipsssiss, Calvin wasn't sure the loss of the race was something the galaxy would mourn, but he shrugged internally. Better the enemy you know than the one you don't.

"If nothing else," Calvin said, "at least we now know we're fighting a common enemy. If we can put pressure on them in another place, maybe that will help your race to hold on to what you still have. To do that, though, we have to get the word back to *my* people."

"Agreed. How do you suggest we do that?"

"I don't know," admitted Calvin. "Maybe we can hold out here. Do you think your people will come looking for you?"

"No," Sal replied, with another hiss. "With the loss of my fleet, our entire navy consists of just two cruisers. They will not send an offensive expedition to look for us; we don't have one. What about your people?"

"We are almost as bad off," Calvin replied. "We just lost our only super dreadnought fighting the Shaitans and the Jotunn, as well as two battleships. Unless we've built a lot more while I was gone, that only leaves us with a cruiser and a couple of battleships."

"That's all?" Sal asked. "You are even worse allies than I thought. I knew allying with you was a mistake. We should have just fallen back on your planets and taken them as our own."

"You would turn your back on our agreement? That quickly?"

"No one is altruistic with the fate of their civilization at stake. Yes, I would happily turn my back on the agreement if it saved my race. Faster than I could kill you."

"Well, happily for Terra, then, you're marooned here with me, and that knowledge won't make it back to your people if we don't get off this planet."

Sal hissed again.

"You know, you hiss a lot," Calvin noted.

"We do that to show anger or frustration."

"We do something we call sighing," Calvin said. "I'm told I do that a lot, too. If nothing else, at least we have that in common, just like the fact that both our nations need us to make it back with the information we have." He held out a hand to the Ssselipsssiss. "Truce. At least until we make it out of here."

Sal looked at his hand for a few seconds, causing Calvin to wonder if he would take it or bite it. As the alien had a mouthful of extremely sharp teeth, Calvin hoped for the former.

"Truce," Sal said finally, taking Calvin's hand in a claw-to-forearm grip. "At least until we get back."

"Fair enough. Now let's go see if we can figure out a way off this rock."

* * * * *

Chapter Seven

Sal and Calvin slid back onto the ledge and surveyed the spaceport. A disassembled engine sat next to a destroyer on the left side; most of the rest of the field was covered by some type of assault/shuttle craft. There were over 100, parked in neat rows.

"That's a lot of crap out there," Calvin said. "Are those your shuttles, or is it the invasion force?"

"Unfortunately, only the destroyer is ours," Sal replied. "It had a broken motor and couldn't join us for battle…not that it would have made any difference. The rest are invaders. With that many craft, there have to be thousands of Shaitans in the city."

"Don't move," Calvin said, catching a flash out of the corner of his eye as another shuttle landed next to the destroyer. This one was different; it was about triple the size of the earlier shuttles. While they watched, the shuttle's ramp came down and a platoon of armored Jotunn marched out with laser rifles at the ready.

A Shaitan galloped up and pointed with both right arms, and the Jotunn jogged off in the direction indicated.

"Is there any chance of getting the destroyer off the ground?" Calvin asked. "That's the only thing out there able to go through the stargate."

"No, it needed a part we couldn't replicate," Sal replied. "Only one of its motors works; it would be suicide to try to take that past the fleet in orbit." He paused, then asked, "Do you think you could fly one of the Shaitan shuttles?"

"I don't know," Calvin replied. "I flew one of their ally's shuttles and was able to get around in it; however, these look different. If everything is labeled in Shaitan, probably not. I don't speak Shaitan, nor does my suit know enough to attempt a translation."

"What about the giant's shuttle?"

"I could probably decipher the instruments on the Jotunn shuttle, but I doubt I could reach everything I needed at the same time."

"Well, we need to get off the planet before the city falls and we get captured," Sal said. "If we get caught, we're dead."

"I agree," Calvin said. "So what are our options?"

"We can't take the destroyer; it's hard down."

"I doubt I can read the instrumentation in the Shaitan shuttles," Calvin said.

"So, it's going to have to be the Jotunn shuttle. You'll have to take off and either find somewhere to hide, or wait until the Shaitans leave and come back here. Eventually, your people will come and hopefully they will find you. It's not a great chance, but it's better than the one we have right now."

"What do you mean 'I' have to do all those things?" Calvin asked. "Don't you mean, 'we'?"

"No, I meant 'you' will have to do them," Sal replied. "You and my children."

"What are you going to do?"

"I'm going to provide cover to get you out of here."

"How are you going to do that?"

"With the destroyer."

"I thought you said it was broken."

"I said one of the motors was broken. The other one is operational, and if I can get it running, I can use its weapons to clear the spaceport of resistance."

"And how are you going to do that?"

"See the tube going from the ground to the ship?"

"Yes. What is it?"

"We use it to load water. I'm going to swim up through that, get into the destroyer, turn it on and provide cover for you."

"You can do all that?"

"If I can't, no one can," Sal replied. "Hopefully, the ship will still think I'm Captain Skrelleth and follow my orders. There isn't anyone else the ship will recognize as a proper authority."

"So, how will we know when it's time?"

"I will have the kids take you to the loading bay. When you hear things exploding, it's time."

"That's a sucky plan," Calvin said.

"Do you have something better?"

"No. I wish I did...but no." Calvin sighed. "What do you want me to do with your kids?"

"If you can resettle them on a Ssselipsssiss planet, do that; otherwise, adopt them into your family so you can get them into your navy. That way, they can avenge me."

"I will do it," Calvin said. He didn't think the Terran Navy would take the children, but the odds they would survive the next few hours made the question pretty much moot.

They slid back from the cave mouth and rejoined the children.

"This is what is going to happen," Sal said. "I am going to provide covering fire so you can escape with Lieutenant Commander Hobbs. He will be your new father. That means you are to do what he says. It also means you are not to eat him. Burkuri, got that?"

"Yes, father."

"Any questions?"

"Will we see you again?" Paxton asked.

"It is unlikely in this lifetime," Sal said. "Avenge me!"

"We will, father," the five children chorused. A single tear rolled down Paxton's face; he wiped it away and drew his laser pistol. "You can count on it," he added.

"Good," Sal said. "Take the Terran to Loading Bay Five and wait there. I won't be long."

Approaching Loading Bay #5, Sssorowyn, Sssellississ, December 13, 2021

Getting to the spaceport's loading bay wasn't as easy as it sounded; the entire complex was in chaos. As the group turned a corner, a Ssselipsssiss ran full speed into Calvin, and both went down. Calvin threw an arm over his face to protect himself from the flurry of claw strikes and tail whips the lizard unleashed in its panic.

After a few seconds the Ssselipsssiss' struggles ceased, and Calvin cautiously peeked out from under his arm. Karver had the much larger lizard in a choke hold from behind. The Ssselipsssiss was no longer struggling, and his face was much paler. Reyl and Syrusss had also taken the opportunity to bend his arms into creative positions that probably hurt. A lot. He couldn't see the Ssselipsssiss' face very well, though, because Paxton was standing in front of him, holding the point of a knife in front of one of the lizard's eyes. Paxton appeared to have the lizard's complete attention.

"Give him a little air," Calvin said. "He's obviously running from something; I'd like to know what."

Karver loosened his grip, and the Ssselipsssiss took a deep breath, careful not to lean forward into the knife.

"What's going on?" Calvin asked.

"The enemy has landed and controls the spaceport," their captive reported. "We've got to flee!"

"Do they hold the loading bays, too?" Calvin asked.

"Yes!" he screamed. "They have it all. Not only are the demons gathering up everyone they find, there are creatures three times your size! If anyone resists, the giants tear them apart! It's a slaughter! We have to flee!"

"Let him go, boys," Calvin said. "We'll have to find another way into the loading bay."

"You there!" a voice called. "Wait!"

Calvin turned to find a Ssselipsssiss running toward them, cradling an enormous laser rifle in his arms.

Calvin grabbed his rifle from where it had fallen in the struggle and turned to find all five children holding laser pistols on the newcomer.

"Oh, hee, hee, I forgot," the lizard said, setting down the rifle. He started laughing.

"Come on, kids," Calvin said. "This one has obviously lost his mind."

"Heeheehee, sorry about that," the lizard said. "I can't help it. It seems we have been under some stress recently, and it brings out the worst in us."

The lizard's features began to change, and his tail dissolved into his torso. His coloring also changed and within seconds, Calvin recognized the face.

Farhome.

"Sorry," the Aesir said, "I had to become a Ssselipsssiss to blend in. I don't have enough mass to be a cowtaur, not that I really wanted to look like one of those disgusting creatures. So, heehee, what's the plan?"

"Do you know this…this…thing?" Burkuri asked, looking at Calvin with one eye. Her pistol and the other eye never flinched from the Aesir. "Or can we just kill it and be done with it?"

"Yes, I know him," Calvin said. "And no, you can't kill him. He has some skills that may be valuable for our escape."

Burkuri turned back to Farhome, spun the pistol once and holstered it. "I won't kill you because he said not to, but my eyes are on you. Just give me a reason…"

"Nice friends you've got here," Farhome noted. "We are about to be overrun; can we leave? It will be much easier to protect you if we do."

"We are supposed to be going to Loading Bay Five," Calvin said. "The *Harvest of Flesh's* CO is going to fire up the destroyer sitting on the pad outside and provide cover while we steal the Jotunn shuttle."

"Then what are we going to do?"

"I don't know; I haven't figured that out yet," Calvin admitted. "All I know is we've got to get out of here before the Shaitans find us."

"The air ducts," Paxton said. "If you want to get to the field without being seen, we need to use the air ducts."

Calvin looked up. Sure enough, there was a vent on the ceiling a few feet from where he was standing.

"Will we fit into them?" Calvin asked.

"My siblings and I will fit with no problem," Paxton said. "I am used to being in them; I do it all the time. Your…friend…will probably be okay too. You'll be tight but ought to be able to make it. It's the only way."

"Okay, let's go!" Calvin exclaimed. "Quickly!" He boosted Paxton up, and the lizard pulled a tool out of his belt and opened the access panel. He scurried up, followed by his siblings and Farhome.

"Krrreeplrt!" a voice yelled. Looking down, Calvin saw a Shaitan coming up the passage toward him. The cowtaur had a rifle pointed at him, and Calvin's was slung on his back. He put his hands up in surrender.

A laser bolt lanced out from above, striking the Shaitan in the lower right eye; the creature screamed and put both of its upper hands over the wounded eye. The tentacle eyes looked up and the lower set of arms started to raise the rifle as a grenade bounced to a stop under the belly of the beast.

"Look out!" Burkuri yelled. Calvin dove away from the creature as the blast tore it open from underneath. It screamed again as its blood sprayed out to cover the passageway in purple polka dots.

Calvin unslung his rifle and shot the creature through the head. Its screaming and thrashing ceased.

"Hurry!" Farhome urged from the vent, holding down a hand. "With all that screaming, more will be here soon."

Calvin slung his rifle, ran up and jumped. Farhome reached down and grabbed one of his hands, and the Aesir pulled him into the shaft.

"Go," Burkuri said. "I'll close the shaft and follow you."

Calvin turned and followed Farhome down the shaft after the male Ssselipsssiss. There was just enough width for his shoulders to fit, but it wasn't tall enough for him to crawl on all fours. He was forced to drag himself along with his elbows, and his arms and shoulders were burning in no time.

Bridge, *Rapacious*, Sssorowyn, Sssellississ, December 13, 2021

Sal stopped as he entered the bridge of the destroyer and stood dripping while he surveyed his final command. He didn't deserve a second chance at command, having lost his entire fleet in his first opportunity, but he *would* make the most of it.

And he would get to kill a few more Shaitans, too.

He strode to the captain's chair and sat.

"AI, what is the status of the ship."

"Person on the bridge, state your name and rank for authorization, or you will be destroyed," the ship's artificial intelligence challenged.

"My name is Salissessolliss Skrelleth, Captain, Ssselipsssiss Navy, Identification Number 567G&#21."

"Welcome Captain Skrelleth. My logs do not list you as the commanding officer for this vessel. Please state your intentions."

"The planet has been overrun by our enemy, the Shaitans. I am using my rank to commandeer this vessel due to the needs of the ongoing situation. How long will it take you to bring your weapons systems online?"

"It will depend on what you intend to do with them," replied the AI. "I am on shore power, and would not have enough energy available to power all of the laser, graser and missile systems. In order to do that, I would need to start at least one motor. Two motors would be preferable, but my second engine is currently disassembled due to a broken space modulator."

"What if I only wanted to fire the port grasers?" Captain Skrelleth asked. "Do you have enough power to do that?"

"Between the shore power and what I have stored in my batteries, I can fire a little more than a salvo; to do more will entail starting my remaining engine."

"When I give the order to fire, I want you to simultaneously start the motor. Once it is online, continue firing as targets present themselves. Do not allow any further personnel to board the ship. Do you understand?"

"Yes, Captain Skrelleth. When you give the order, I will begin firing my port grasers and will start the Number One engine. I will not allow anyone else entry into the *Rapacious*. What is my target?"

"Can you see the craft on the spaceport landing area?"

"Yes, I have a variety of cameras and other sensors at my disposal," the AI replied.

"There is one shuttle larger than the rest. Do not destroy that ship nor hit it with flying debris if possible. Every other ship is a valid target, and I want you to destroy as many as you can. There will be a group of young Ssselipsssiss, along with a Terran, who will transit from inside the loading bay to the shuttle I told you not to destroy. Do not shoot them or impede their progress; however, you are cleared to destroy any enemy you see. One race has four arms; the other is 15 feet tall. Kill any of these races you see."

"Understood," the AI confirmed. "The defense net shows enemy vessels in orbit above us. When we begin firing on their troops, it is likely we will be targeted by them, and I am unable to bring my weapons to bear. I estimate, with a near-certain likelihood, that we will be destroyed if we undertake this action. Are you aware of the consequences of proceeding?"

"I am aware. The purpose of this attack is to allow the escape of high-value personnel on the shuttle. If we can do that, the destruction of this vessel is acceptable."

"Understood, although I do not see how they will make it past the ships in orbit without outside intervention."

Captain Skrelleth looked at his personal chronometer. They were running out of time.

"Don't worry about it," the captain said. "It will all be taken care of. Are you ready?"

"I am," replied the AI.

"Proceed."

Loading Bay #5, Sssorowyn, Sssellississ, December 13, 2021

The destroyer continued firing outside, and the ground shook as explosion after explosion rocked the spaceport. Dust trickled down in mini rainstorms inside the ducting, tickling Calvin's nose. "Can we go yet?" he whispered, fighting back a sneeze.

"Not yet," whispered Paxton. "There are still two enemy below us."

"We don't have much time," Calvin whispered back. "Eventually, they will get something into place that will destroy your father's ship."

Paxton hissed in annoyance, the sound reminding Calvin of the boy's father.

"Give me your grenades," Paxton said, and the other boys each pulled a grenade from their packs and sent them forward.

"Hold the grate up," Paxton said to Reyl. He took a grenade in each hand and tore off the retaining straps with his teeth. Shrugging his shoulders to loosen them, he nodded to his older brother.

Reyl threw the grate to the side and Paxton lobbed his grenades toward the two Shaitans. One ended up under its target; the other passed under and stopped within a few feet of the second Shaitan. The grenades detonated, knocking the enemy troopers off their feet. They kicked a couple of times then ceased moving.

Reyl dropped through the opening, pistol at the ready. He hit and used his tail to brace himself as he spun around to look behind him. Clear. A Shaitan twitched, and he shot it in the head. It stilled.

The rest of the boys dropped down, setting up a perimeter, then Farhome, Calvin and Burkuri followed.

Calvin looked out the window across the starport. There must have been a number of Shaitans in the bay who had run outside when the firing started. What was left of them wasn't pretty. Even though the destroyer was 'small' as far as warships go, its weapons were meant to go up against armored spaceships; they were devastating on unprotected flesh. Even Shaitans, much larger and bulkier than humans, were turned to purple goo as the grasers passed through them.

"It's the shuttle by the destroyer," Calvin yelled. "Follow me!" He sprinted across the ferro-crete with the rest close behind. The destroyer's grasers fired all around them, lancing out to wreck landing craft after landing craft. The targeting was superior; Calvin only ducked inadvertently a couple of times as ships blew up nearby. Free of pursuit, the group charged up the boarding ramp at the back of the Jotunn shuttle.

Calvin drew up at the enormity of the cargo bay. "Here's where it gets interesting," he said, scanning the interior of the shuttle; it was so large he almost expected his words to echo.

With a squeal, the ramp began closing.

Calvin turned to Farhome. "Did you do that?"

"Not me," the Aesir replied.

"Did any of you do that?" Calvin asked the Ssselipsssiss.

"No, we didn't," Burkuri said.

"Damn," Calvin said under his breath. Louder, he added, "We're not alone. There must be a pilot or two in the cockpit."

In confirmation, one of the engines roared to life.

"What do you want to do?" Farhome asked as the ramp sealed. "Find a way out or stay?"

"This is still our best chance to get off the planet," Calvin replied. "If it were me up front, I'd be trying to get the heck out of here. I don't know whether the pilot will take us up to the mother ship or if he'll just go somewhere else and then return."

The second motor ignited, making normal speech difficult.

"I'm betting he's going to go back to the mother ship," Calvin decided, "which is probably where we want to go. We definitely don't want to stay on the planet and be captured by the Shaitans. We also don't want to end up on one of their ships. We have more opportunities with the Jotunn."

"Opportunities for what?" Farhome asked.

"To stay alive, for a start."

"And then what?"

"As soon as I figure it out," Calvin replied, "you'll be the first person I tell."

* * * * *

Chapter Eight

Bridge, TSS *Vella Gulf*, 61 Virginis, December 13, 2021

"Captain Sheppard, I am getting a transmission from the planet," the communications officer said. "There is someone who wants to beam up."

"Aren't we about out of range for that?" Captain Sheppard asked.

"Yes sir, we are," Steropes replied. "Whoever is coming is taking a risk this far out; they could easily be disassembled."

"Did they say who it was?" Captain Sheppard asked.

"No sir," the communications officer replied. "I asked and they refused to say."

Captain Sheppard looked to his left. "Night, would you go meet our guest in the Transporter Room?"

Night nodded. "This is kind of irregular, sir."

"It is," Captain Sheppard agreed. "Why don't you take several of your troops as an honor guard? Have them armed, but don't be obvious about it."

"Yes sir," Night replied. He commed the duty officer on his way to the transporters, and Sergeants Brian Mchugh and Steph Taylor met him there. Both had laser rifles; Sergeant Mchugh had two.

"Here you go," Mchugh said, handing one to Night.

"Thanks," Night said. He nodded to the transporter technician. "Beam 'em up."

A dark smear appeared above one of the pads, coalescing into a large, black Mrowry holding a rolled up piece of paper.

"Present arms!" Night ordered. "Welcome to the *Vella Gulf,* Your Highness!"

"Thank you," Emperor Yazhak said. "I would prefer, however, if you didn't emphasize my presence. Is it possible to meet your commanding officer somewhere private?"

"He will meet you in his conference room," Night replied after a quick call.

Cargo Bay, Jotunn Shuttle, Sssellississ, December 13, 2021

The shuttle lifted and lurched to the side, throwing everyone from their feet.

Calvin ran to one of the window seats and clambered onto it so he could look out.

"What was that?" Farhome asked. "Are we hit?"

"No," Calvin replied, his voice low enough only Farhome could hear. "The Shaitans hit the destroyer with something big, probably something from orbit. It's *gone.*" He climbed down from the seat.

"Hee, hee, hee, I'll say one thing," Farhome commented; "being around you is never dull."

"Yeah, sometimes I wish my life wasn't *quite* so exciting." Calvin replied, waving a hand to indicate their surroundings.

"So what are we going to do now?"

Calvin looked back up at the window. The sky outside was turning black as the shuttle continued to climb.

"Well, it looks like we're headed to the Jotunn mother ship, and when we get there, I suspect this shuttle isn't going to fly again until it gets inspected. I think we should find some good hiding places and see what happens once we get there. Maybe an opportunity will present itself—" He stopped suddenly. "Hey, where did the kids go?"

"Ha, ha, ha, where do kids normally go?" Farhome asked. "To get in trouble someplace, I'm sure!" He giggled again and added, "It's what kids do best."

"Yeah," Calvin replied; "that's what I'm worried about."

Calvin led Farhome toward the forward end of the cargo bay, worried that the youths had gone to the cockpit and been seen, but saw them returning from different directions to gather at the front of the cargo bay. He jogged the rest of the way to meet them.

"Where did you go?" Calvin asked.

"I sent the males to see what they could find," Burkuri explained. "I told them to stay out of the cockpit, but to look for hiding places everywhere else. I also had them look for weapons or anything else useful."

"What did you guys find?" Calvin asked.

"I searched the weapons lockers," Reyl reported. "Unfortunately, all their weapons are too large for us to use. Even their smallest ones would have to be crew-served although there were two grenades we could probably make small bombs out of."

"Crew-served weapons?" Calvin asked. "Making bombs? How old *are* you kids, anyway?"

"We are only a few weeks from adulthood," Burkuri said. "We have already completed our fleet apprenticeship training schools and been given our orders. We were just waiting for our final shedding prior to shipping out."

"Yeah, shedding is nasty enough to do on-planet," Syrusss explained. "I wouldn't want to shed in space. It would clog up a spacesuit something awful."

"You've already been through space training?" Calvin repeated incredulously. "As kids? What did you train as?"

"We are a...um...team," Burkuri said looking at the deck.

"What kind of a team?" Calvin asked.

"We're a—" Reyl said.

"He wouldn't understand," Burkuri interjected, cutting her brother off. "Father said not to talk about it with him."

"What wouldn't I understand?"

"It's nothing," Burkuri said. "Our societies are very different, and we do things Father said you wouldn't be comfortable with."

"Wait a minute!" Calvin exclaimed. "Your father said you were my responsibility now, and that you were supposed to listen to me. What kind of a team are you?"

"It doesn't matter," Burkuri said. "Can't you just leave it alone?"

"No I can't," Calvin replied after considering it for a few moments. "I'm the military leader here. I can't effectively use your training and skills if I don't know what they are." He paused, but Burkuri remained silent. "Tell me!" he ordered.

Burkuri hissed. "Remember, you wanted to know," she said. "We're an Urban Pacification and Control Team."

"Okay," Calvin said. "And what does one of those do?"

"We go into unprepared locations and take charge of the local population."

"And what skills do you have for that?"

Burkuri hissed again, her dismay evident. Finally she shook her head and commanded, "Team, atten-*hut!*" The brothers came to positions of attention. "Sound off!"

"I am the team executive officer and explosives expert," Reyl said. "I also handle psychological operations."

"I take care of communications and information technology," said Syrusss, "as well as the exploitation of same."

"I'm the heavy weapons expert," Karver said, flexing his muscles.

"I handle intel and reconnaissance," Paxton said. "I go places no one else can."

"And I am the team lead," Burkuri said; "I handle selection and command and control. All of us also have certain other scavenging and reclamation skills, and we are trained to use most light weapons."

"Wait a minute," Calvin broke in as he processed what he had heard. "Take charge of the local population? What does that mean?"

"We prepare them for processing," Burkuri replied. "You asked for our skills and training, and we have given them to you. Father told me not to tell you any more than that. He said you would be happier not knowing."

Calvin had a bad feeling, but he had to know. "What do you mean by, 'Prepare them for processing'?"

Burkuri cocked her head and stared at Calvin for a few seconds before answering. "Remember, you wanted to know." Her head came back to vertical. "We are trained to go to recently captured planets and interact with the local population. We find out who the troublemakers are and kill them. This makes the rest of the population easier to herd. We deal with insurgents. Permanently. We also select who will be turned into food first, so the remaining ones will be easier to handle. We are the choosers of the slain."

Chapter Nine

"Welcome aboard," Captain Sheppard said as the emperor strode into the conference room.

The Mrowry looked back through the doorway and waved for Lieutenant Rrower to join them. The younger Mrowry entered, and Night closed the door, waiting outside with the troopers.

"What can I do for you?" Captain Sheppard asked.

"I have two reasons for coming to the *Vella Gulf*," the emperor said. He turned to Lieutenant Rrower. "The first is a word of guidance for my grandson." He stared at the younger Mrowry as if taking his measure. Lieutenant Rrower withstood the gaze, unflinching. After several long seconds, the emperor seemed to see what he was looking for.

"You are headed to the border between our systems and the Ssselipsssiss," the emperor continued, "and I do not know what you will find there. I wish it were possible for me to come as well, but my place is here. Depending on what is happening there, decisions affecting the empire will have to be made. You alone of the Mrowry have seen enough of the enemy to take their measure and know what must be done." He held out the roll of paper he carried to his grandson.

"As a member of my household, you have always had the ability to take charge of a single ship if required by the circumstances. This writ allows you to take charge of the fleet, on a temporary basis, if you find it necessary to support the Terran's hero. Do not abuse this privilege or take it lightly, as I will require a complete accounting when you return. Do you understand?"

"Yes, grandfather, I understand," Lieutenant Rrower replied. "I will use it only if necessary."

"See that you do." The emperor stared at his grandson for a few moments longer, as if to impress upon him the gravity of the situation, then turned to Captain Sheppard.

"My other reason for coming is of even greater importance and sensitivity," the emperor said. "I have given it a lot of thought since we spoke, and I have come to ask for the secret of the jump modules."

"I see..." Captain Sheppard replied. "I figured your visit had to be something of great importance for you to transport this far out."

"I know how much of a favor it is to ask for the secret of the modules," the emperor admitted; "if my race were to conduct a technology transfer of this magnitude, it would require my personal approval. I'm sure you would normally have to receive permission from Terra to give it to us; however, the times we find ourselves in are anything but normal. The Aesir are being overrun by the Jotunn and the Shaitans; the Ssselipsssiss also appear to be victims of the Shaitans. Every day brings them closer to my border, and I can't be sure when you'll be back."

The emperor said "when," not "if," but the word hung in the air nonetheless.

THE DARK STAR WAR | 77

"The Ssselipsssiss are being driven back into our systems," the emperor continued; "it is likely their enemy will wipe them out soon, and then the enemy will be on our borders. If we don't have the technology to fight them, you may return from your mission to the Dark Star to find us overrun, as well. In fact, I find this outcome fairly likely."

"You're right about a couple of things," Captain Sheppard replied after thinking a few seconds; "permission for such a transfer would normally have to come from Terra. Normally. You're also right about the times not being normal."

The CO nodded once. "I will give you the replicator blueprints for the jump modules. Hopefully, Fleet Command won't throw me in the brig for it." He smiled. "Just don't pass them on to anyone else, okay?"

Cargo Bay, Jotunn Shuttle, Sssellississs Orbit, December 13, 2021

Calvin's jaw dropped, and he paused, unable to speak. The 'children' were trained to kill people like himself on any planet the Ssselipsssiss invaded. Kill them and send them to the butcher to be turned into food. He could feel himself going green and his stomach revolting at the thought.

"Nice kids you've got there," Farhome said. "Hee, hee, Captain Skrelleth's spaceship probably had a sticker on it that said, 'My kids chose your honor student to eat first.' This is going to be *way* more fun than falling into a super nova." He doubled up in laughter.

Calvin took a deep breath and let it out slowly. Farhome's reaction wasn't helping. All five Ssselipsssiss still stood at attention, looking at him. They looked tense…probably getting ready to kill him if he took their revelation poorly. Their father had told them not to eat Calvin; he hoped they still remembered that.

"At ease," Calvin said, and they relaxed a little. A very little. "We're not going to have any problems," Calvin continued," although your father was right; I didn't want to know that, nor will any others of my kind, should we make it back to civilization. Still, you have a broad range of skills; you're almost your own little special forces team. Not only will we be able to put your skills to good use, but those skills are also the ones we happen to need at the moment."

"What can we do to help?" Burkuri asked.

"First off, remember that having an education isn't the same as having experience," Calvin warned. "Don't try to do too much, too fast. There aren't many of us, and we're all important."

The Ssselipsssiss gave short hisses of agreement.

"Here's what I'm expecting," Calvin explained. "I think we're going back to the Jotunn mother ship, which is probably one of the battlecruisers. Since this shuttle was close to a number of explosions, they will probably want to shut it down and check for battle damage. The pilot won't do it; some of their maintenance technicians will. The pilot will probably just leave and turn the craft over to maintenance to get it checked and serviced. So, the first objective is to hide so we don't get seen by the pilot."

Calvin looked at the group and couldn't tell whether they understood or not. "I don't know Ssselipsssiss body language very well," Calvin said, "so if you understand and agree, do this." He nodded. All five nodded back at him.

The shuttle jerked suddenly.

"Okay, we don't have much time," Calvin noted. "That was probably the tractor beam which will pull us aboard. So, we will hide until the pilot leaves, then we will meet back up. After that, we'll try to find a place to hide on the mother ship while we figure out what to do next."

"Air ducts are great for moving around unseen," said Paxton, "and if everything on the mother ship is oversized like it is on this shuttle, we shouldn't have any problems moving around in them."

"Yeah, they would work well," Calvin agreed; "however, you have to remember the ceilings onboard the ship are going to be about 20 feet high." He looked up at the overhead. "They are going to be difficult to get to."

The shuttle bumped as it touched down.

"Okay we're here, and we're out of time. Everyone, go hide. We'll meet back here after the pilot leaves."

Cargo Bay, Jotunn Shuttle, Sssellississ Orbit, December 13, 2021

Calvin peered out the shuttle's cargo bay. The pilot had turned the craft around prior to landing, so he had a view of the interior of the ship, not space.

It looked like any hangar he had ever been in, only on a much grander scale. Spare parts were stacked in enormous piles, oversized crates sat against the towering bulkheads and massive ground vehicles drove back and forth carrying gigantic gear from place to place. Calvin would have felt at home…if everything didn't make him feel so small.

Finally, he saw what he was looking for and returned to the forward part of the cargo bay where everyone was waiting for him.

"I've got some good news, and I've got some bad news," he whispered.

"Ooooh! I love this game!" Farhome exclaimed. "Give us the good news first!" His voice had a new tone Calvin had never heard before. It was thin and reedy, as if missing something. No; Calvin realized with horror he *had* heard Farhome's voice like this before—the first time Calvin had met him...right before Farhome had tried to kill him. It was the fully-crazed Farhome talking.

"I found a vent," Calvin reported; "it's to the left as you come down the ramp, next to a pile of crates."

"Now wreck our hopes with the bad news," Farhome urged. He looked at the Ssselipsssiss, shivering in anticipation, and added, "This is my favorite part."

"As I expected, it's about 18 feet up," Calvin continued, ignoring Farhome.

"Sounds like fun," Farhome said. "Let me look."

Farhome crept to the aft of the shuttle and returned after looking out the hatch for a few seconds.

"I can do it," Farhome said. "I think. Well, I'm actually pretty sure I can. Most of me says 'yes.' It's just the smallest part of me that says 'no,' and he's usually wrong. Too defeatist, you know? Overall, though, most of me thinks it can be done. I'm pretty sure, anyway. Certainly, the biggest part of me says 'yes.'"

Calvin's eyebrows narrowed. It sounded like Farhome had lost it. "Umm...how many people are in your head?"

"You mean right now?" Farhome asked. Seeing Calvin nod, Farhome shrugged. "I don't know; I quit counting. There were too many, and they all kept shifting around, and some played hide-and-seek. It got to be really frustrating, so I quit." He paused, then asked, "Want to hear a poem?"

"*Now?*" Calvin asked. "Do you really think *now* is a good time?"

"Absolutely!" Farhome exclaimed. "I'm glad you asked. There's always time for poetry." He smiled. "I borrowed this from some Terran poetry I heard. Here goes:

Roses are red,
Violets are blue,
I'm a schizophrenic,
And so am I."

"Isn't that a good one?" Farhome giggled. "It's one of my favorites." He smiled, obviously pleased with himself.

"Now you're scaring me," Calvin said. He glanced at the Ssselipsssiss and saw them gesturing at each other in some kind of sign language. He couldn't read their expressions, but he didn't have to; he was confident he knew what they were thinking, because he was thinking it himself.

"I need you to focus," Calvin said. "Can you do that?"

"Yes," Farhome said. "I can do that. Or not. Actually, I'm pretty sure I can pull all of me together...unless I fail."

"Damn it!" Calvin exclaimed. "We may only get one shot at this. Are you with us or not?"

Farhome took a deep breath before speaking; Calvin couldn't tell if he was gathering his thoughts or his personalities.

"Yes," Farhome repeated, "I can do it." His voice sounded more normal and more...fuller, somehow.

"Great," Calvin said. "So how are you going to get us to the grate?" He wasn't ready to put all their lives in the hands of a crazy man without a little more info.

"Well, *I* can't actually do *that*," Farhome said.

"Wait; I thought you said you could," Calvin said. He noticed the Ssselipsssiss were gesturing at each other again. Not good.

"*I* can't do it," Farhome explained, "but Max can."

"Who's Max, dammit?" Calvin asked, tired of playing games.

"Maximus is the 10-foot version of me," Farhome replied. "He can climb the stack of boxes next to the vent, then lean over and grab hold of the grate. After that, one of the Ssselipsssiss can climb over me like a bridge and open it. I would recommend Paxton, as he's the reconnaissance operative. Once he has the grate open, we all go in. Piece of biscuit."

"Hmm…" Calvin said, trying to picture it in his head; "that might work."

"Excuse me," Burkuri interjected, "but we don't understand what the crazy man is saying. Who is this 'Max' person? How is he going to bridge a 10-foot gap?"

"Just like you five are more than you first seemed, Farhome is too," Calvin said. "He has the ability to stretch himself and become 10 feet tall."

"How does he do that?"

"I'm not really sure," Calvin admitted. "Every time I've been around him when he's done it, someone's been trying to kill me…including Farhome himself, one time."

"But I thought you were friends!" Burkuri protested.

"Our relationship is…complicated," Calvin replied. Farhome just smiled beatifically. Calvin put his hands up to forestall any further questions. "Don't worry about it; just accept that he *can* actually do it."

Burkuri didn't say anything, which Calvin was willing to take as concurrence.

"Okay," Calvin continued after a moment; "here's the plan. When we think the hangar is clear, we'll run to the crates by the wall. Farhome will grow and lean over to the grate. When he's in place, Paxton will cross over him, remove the cover and go inside. Then the rest of us will follow. Any questions?"

"I have a question," Paxton said. "Before we go, would you like me to surveil the hangar?"

"You can do that?" Calvin asked. "Without being seen?"

"Of course," Paxton replied; "I'm the recon expert, remember?"

Paxton dug into his pack for a moment and pulled out a box. He opened it up and removed what looked like a six-inch-long salamander.

"Is that a robot?" Calvin asked.

"No, it's a live risst," Paxton replied. "They are native to my planet. Even if the Jotunn see it, they will just think it crawled into the shuttle when it was on the planet. There is a small transmitter and muscle control interface in the risst. Don't worry about the Jotunn intercepting the transmission; it is so low power it can't be traced beyond about 10 feet."

He carried the creature to the back of the cargo bay and set it on the deck. It scampered to the ramp and then slowly slithered down.

"Now we do what all good reconnaissance people do," Paxton said.

"What's that?" Calvin asked.

"We wait."

* * * * *

Chapter Ten

The group had to hide two more times over the next three hours as Jotunn ground crew inspected the shuttle and made minor repairs. Shortly after the repair crews left, the lights in the cargo bay dimmed, signifying "night" had fallen for the ship.

"Okay, the lights just went out in the maintenance spaces," Paxton noted. He had been keeping one of the lizard's eyes on the door where the ground maintenance personnel had gone.

"This is our chance," Calvin said. "We need to hurry before the next shift gets here."

The group ran down the shuttle's ramp and over to the boxes stacked near the vent. Paxton grabbed his lizard as he passed.

"Maximus," Farhome said, and he grew to nearly 10 feet tall. He began climbing the seven-foot-tall crates by himself while the rest of the group helped each other up.

Farhome held up his hands, and the group watched as his fingers elongated and thinned. He judged the distance he had to cover and leaned over, sliding his fingers through the gaps in the ventilation grating to get a grip.

"I've got it," Farhome whispered. "Go!"

Calvin lifted Paxton, who climbed the Aesir like a tree and opened the clips holding the grate closed.

"Got it," Paxton reported.

"Just a second," Farhome said. He readjusted his grip. "Go!"

Paxton opened the screen and climbed in. Reyl climbed the Aesir next. He had barely made it into the shaft when he turned and started gesturing to Burkuri, who was standing next to Calvin.

"Paxton says he's not alone in the shaft," she translated.

"*What?*" Calvin asked. "What does he mean he's not alone?"

"He said something just ate his risst. He didn't get a good look—" she paused, then added, "A big bug just walked up and is looking at him. He says you better get up there…now!"

"On my way!" Syrusss stepped aside so Calvin could climb up next, and gave him a boost onto Farhome's shoulders. Calvin slipped inside the vent and crawled forward. Like everything else on the ship, the shaft was oversized, nearly four feet high and wide, so he could almost crouch and duck walk, but decided it was easier to crawl.

He was brought up short as he reached Paxton, and the…creature…watching him. It wasn't just a 'big bug;' *it was an enormous bug!* It had 10 legs, stood over three feet high and was at least three feet wide. From what Calvin could see, it was probably five feet long. The most disturbing part wasn't its size, but the fact that it looked like a giant cockroach, with four massive, jagged-edged mandibles surrounding an enormous mouth. Calvin's whole arm would fit inside it with room to spare. The bug blocked the passageway; there was no getting past it.

"No…sudden…moves," Paxton whispered. "It reacts poorly to them. It ate the risst when it tried to run." He was sitting to the side of the passage, and Calvin had to move carefully so he didn't kneel on Paxton's tail as he passed. Calvin sat down next to Paxton.

"What's going on?" he asked out of the corner of his mouth, keeping both eyes on the bug.

"Nothing, since I sat down and put my pistol away," Paxton said. "You may not believe this, but I think it's intelligent."

"Why do you say that?"

"It keeps motioning to me, but has neither tried to attack, nor flee. If it ran, it could easily get away from me, but it hasn't. The fact it's just watching us tells me it can think."

"Have you tried to talk to it?"

"Yes, but it didn't react to anything I said."

The creature tapped the floor of the shaft several times with a front leg. Calvin looked at the bug's foot and saw it was more like a talon; two sharp claws extended from both the front and back of its two front legs. Calvin sensed impatience from the creature; he knew he needed to do something before it made up its mind to attack.

"Maybe it doesn't speak Ssselipsssiss," Calvin said. "Have you tried any other languages?"

"No," Paxton replied. "I would try Jotunn, since this is a Jotunn ship, but I don't know any."

"I have a full download," Calvin said. "Let me try."

Calvin slid forward a little, and the creature backed up an equal amount, raising its front claws and clicking them in apparent warning.

"See?" Paxton asked. "You need to move slowly."

Calvin put both hands up, slowly, and the creature put its claws down.

"Do you understand me?" Calvin asked in Jotunn. The question had an obvious effect as the creature started clacking its mandibles and bobbing up and down.

"I think you're onto something, sir," Paxton said. "Wait…I've got just the—" He pulled his pack off his back.

Faster than Calvin would have thought possible, the alien creature reached up to its back with its front claws and pulled out two objects from under its carapace.

"Don't move!" Calvin ordered in Ssselipsssiss, his eyes focused on the muzzle of the pistol pointed at his face from less than two feet away.

Paxton looked up and froze; a second pistol was aimed at him. He slowly withdrew his hands from his pack and held them out to show they were empty.

"Let's try to move *really* slowly," Calvin suggested.

"Sorry," the Ssselipsssiss said; "I got excited and forgot."

"Well, I think we've confirmed its intelligence, if nothing else," Calvin noted.

"I think it answered you when you spoke to it," Paxton said. "I have a language analysis device in my pack. That is what I was trying to get."

"I didn't hear it say anything."

"It was extremely high-frequency," Paxton replied; "it might be above what Terrans can hear." After a couple of seconds, he added, "Maybe you could ask it to lower its weapons so I can get my equipment out…it might help."

Calvin switched to Jotunn. "My friend has a machine in his pack which will help us communicate with you. If you would lower your weapons, he will *slowly* get it out. We mean you no harm and are only trying to hide from the giants."

Calvin couldn't tell if his words were understood; the giant bug didn't move, and it was impossible to tell where its multi-faceted eyes were looking. After a moment, though, it lowered its weapons.

"Slowly get out your equipment," Calvin said. "And I do mean *slowly*. My friends would never let me hear the end of it if I got shot by a giant roach."

Bridge, TSS *Vella Gulf*, 83 Leonis System, December 14, 2021

"I've got stargate emergence," the Defensive Systems Officer (DSO) announced.

"Which stargate?" Captain Sheppard asked.

"The stargate that leads toward home, sir," the DSO replied. "The ship is cruiser-sized, but I don't recognize—"

"Sir, we're being hailed by a ship calling itself the TSS *Remurn*," the comms officer said.

"Must be a Domus ship," Captain Sheppard said. "On screen."

His guess was confirmed as the front view screen switched to the image of a Kuji, one of the allied races from the planet Domus, wearing a Terran Federation captain's uniform. Reptilian, the race looked like six-foot-tall tyrannosaurus rexes. Captain Sheppard could see several other Kuji behind him, as well as a few of the humanoid race that was also indigenous to Domus.

"Greetings," the Kuji said. "I'm Captain Skadolisses of the *Remurn*. We are on a diplomatic voyage to Archonis."

"Greetings," the CO replied. "I'm Captain Sheppard of the *Vella Gulf*. What's happening on Archonis?"

"I'm carrying the new ambassador," Captain Skadolisses replied. "The Federation is hoping to get them involved in the war."

"Good luck with that," Captain Sheppard said. "I've been there, and the Archons can be…difficult…to negotiate with."

"So I've heard. Happily, I don't have to bargain with them; I just have to transport the ambassador so *she* can talk to them."

"Hey sir," Night said in a stage whisper from the right of the CO. "Do you suppose they might have a few troops they can loan us? I'm down 12, and if we're going to go behind enemy lines, I'd feel better with a full platoon."

"I wouldn't mind a few crews either, if they had them," added Commander Sarah 'Lights' Brighton, the acting CO of the space fighter squadron. "I'm down five and a shuttle."

"I do not have an air wing like you do," Captain Skadolisses said, overhearing the requests; "I only have two shuttles and a handful of pilots. I can probably spare a couple of crews and a few of my ground troops, but I need to keep the shuttles for my diplomatic mission."

"I understand completely," Captain Sheppard replied. "We'll take whatever you can spare. We intend to go up the Ssselipsssiss star chain looking for the Shaitan home world."

"I will send you what I can. I also have a few Terrans aboard functioning as trainers; I can return them to you as well. Good luck and safe journey!"

* * * * *

Chapter Eleven

Ducts, Jotunn Ship, Sssellississ Orbit, December 13, 2021

Calvin looked at his watch and unplugged from the Ssselipsssiss translation box. It had taken a couple of hours for Paxton to fashion a plug that would fit into the upload/download jack in the back of Calvin's neck, and then another 30 minutes to download all the Jotunn language in his implants. They had been at it for more than three hours since then and were finally starting to make some real progress.

Calvin turned around to address the rest of his group and found them staring in rapt attention. He didn't know how they did it; he would have been bored long before now if he'd been the one watching. He slid over to where the group was waiting.

"What's the creepie crawlie saying?" Farhome asked.

"Careful," Calvin cautioned, his voice low. "They're very smart and have been picking up our language almost as fast as I could pick up theirs with the translation box."

"They?"

"Yeah, you can't see them, but there is a big group just around the next bend in the duct. If we'd done anything aggressive, they would have overrun us."

"How big a group?"

"No idea. It's dark back there, and they're moving around a lot. I got the feeling there were a lot of them."

"Like 10 or 12?"

"No," Calvin said. "Hundreds. The ducts are their home, and there is apparently a whole colony here."

"Ewww!" Farhome exclaimed. "That's nasty."

"Yeah. Happily, they're intelligent and decided to talk to us first."

"First? Before what?"

"Before they ate us," Calvin explained.

Farhome sat up, bumping his head on the ceiling. "Wait!" he screeched. "They were going to eat us?" He peered at the oversized insectoid talking with Paxton. "Do you suppose they'd want to eat all of me, or would they be happy with just Minimus?"

"I don't think they've decided what to do with us yet, but there are an awful lot of them; if they make up their minds to do it, I think they'll eat all of you."

"Over my dead bodies."

"I don't think it matters. They're scavengers; they'll eat you dead or alive."

"More to the point," Burkuri interjected, "what are *you* doing to keep them from eating us?"

"We're still trying to translate enough words so we can communicate. Their speech is too high-pitched for me to even hear most of it; I'm relying on Paxton's box to capture what Zeeelbit is saying and translate it for me."

"That's a handy box," Farhome said. "What is it?"

"It's an interrogation tool," Burkuri answered. "After it has learned the nuances of a race's speech, it can also determine with a good degree of accuracy whether the subject is lying or not. If we had a power source, it could also be used for stimulating the subject."

"Stimulating the subject?" Calvin asked.

"Yes," Burkuri said. "There are leads that can deliver an electrical shock to whoever is being interrogated. Depending on the race, it can be set high enough to kill, if desired."

"Nice kids you've got there," Farhome said, looking at Calvin.

Calvin ignored him and continued, "So far we've learned the creatures live here in the ducts. The Jotunn generally ignore them unless too many get caught out in the open, in which case the giants try to kill them."

"Do they fight back?" Reyl asked.

"I asked the same question," Calvin replied. "The answer was 'no;' they don't fight back."

"Why not?" Burkuri asked.

"Because they realize that no matter what happens, they lose. If they become big enough nuisances that the Jotunn decided to exterminate them, they'd all be dead. If they were to fight back and kill all the Jotunn, they would eventually starve to death after they ate all the bodies. It would take a while, but they can't fly the ship. They'd lose either way."

"So, they just live here in the ducts?" Burkuri asked. "How do they get food and water?"

"They clean up whatever the Jotunn leave out or spill. Apparently, the Jotunn don't ever clean up after themselves, so there is a lot to eat."

"That makes sense," Farhome said. "The Jotunn are warriors; cleaning is beneath them. They probably allow the bugs to live in the ducts in some sort of weird symbiotic arrangement so they don't have to clean up after themselves. As long as the bugs don't make pests of themselves, they're happy to have them aboard to do the menial work." He giggled. "I made a pun."

"That must be it," Calvin agreed, ignoring Farhome's last comment. "I wondered why the Jotunn didn't kill them off."

"So the bugs are happy here?" Burkuri asked.

"No, they're not," Paxton said, joining the group. "Zeeelbit says they'd like to get off the ship. They have some racial memory of being on a green planet. He said they won't kill us if we can get them off this ship and onto a planet."

"Well, tell them we'd be happy to do that," Calvin said.

"How are you going to get them off the ship?" Farhome asked. "Better yet, how are you going to get *us* off? Max doesn't like the ducts; they're too small for him."

"I don't know," Calvin replied. "Yet."

Bridge, TSS *Vella Gulf*, 83 Leonis System, December 14, 2021

"Squadron maintenance just said that all the people from the *Remurn* are aboard, sir," Lights reported.

"Understood," Captain Sheppard said. "What did we end up with?"

"It looks like we got six troopers, four pilots and four weapon systems officers," Lights replied. "Most of the troopers are Terrans; the aviators are split between Terrans and Kuji." She paused, then added, "The shuttle has detached and is returning to the *Remurn*."

"Thank you," Captain Sheppard replied. He turned toward the front table. "Full speed to the stargate," he ordered. "We've been gone too long."

Ducts, Jotunn Ship, Sssellississ Orbit, December 14, 2021

Calvin took one last scan of the bridge before sliding away from the grate he had been watching the bridge crew through. He crawled along the passageway to the intersection where Farhome, the Ssselipsssiss and three of the bugs waited patiently. Their race had a name, but it was unpronounceable. Not only was it long and full of consonant-like sounds, it also involved stomping your fifth and sixth feet halfway through, which was problematic for a race that didn't have them. They had finally settled on the abbreviation 'S'nark.'

Communications with them had improved, although it still required Paxton's interrogation box. The bugs had promised Calvin they wouldn't eat his group, for the moment, if he would help get them to a planet. They had, however, made it clear the ductwork was their territory, and they would only suffer the presence of Calvin's group for a short while before 'something would have to be done with them.' Calvin didn't want to find out what the 'something' was; he had to come up with a plan…or at least enough of a plan to buy some more time.

"Did you learn anything?" Burkuri asked.

"No," Calvin whispered, his voice grim. "I wasn't able to find out much about the giants' plans."

"That's unfortunate," Burkuri said.

"I may not have come up with a way off the ship yet," Calvin said, "but at least I know where we are now."

"Where's that?" Farhome replied.

"We're on the Jotunn ship *Falcon*," Calvin replied. "I recognized Oleif Magnusson, the captain."

"We're on a Jotunn ship?" Farhome asked. "Wow! I never would have guessed. What gave it away? The giants?"

"I don't—" Calvin started, but then everything expanded into infinity…before going black…then sideways…then green…then salty…

CO's Conference Room, TSS *Vella Gulf*, HD 40307 System, December 16, 2021

"I called this meeting to talk to everyone before we transit back into Ssselipsssiss space," Captain Sheppard announced. "I wanted to make sure we're as ready as we can be, given the nature of our voyage."

"Are you expecting trouble from the Ssselipsssiss?" Night asked.

"Expecting trouble? No. But do I trust the Ssselipsssiss to honor their word? Also 'no.' In fact, I trust them to honor their word far less than most other races, so I want to be ready for anything, just in case."

"You don't think we need to go in with grasers blazing, do you?" the *Vella Gulf's* executive officer, Commander Russ Clayton, asked.

"No, I don't want to provoke a confrontation with the Ssselipsssiss, especially while they have one of our folks," Captain Sheppard replied. "I do, however, want to be ready in case *they* start one. I want to make sure we have our stealth modules up, and we're prepared to jump to the Jinn Universe at a moment's notice if needed."

"Do we need the stealth modules, sir?" the operations officer, Commander Dan Dacy, asked. "The Ssselipsssiss can't follow us if we jump to the other universe. Having the stealth modules installed will take away a lot of our combat capability."

"I'm aware of that," Captain Sheppard said. "The problem is, I'm less worried about the Ssselipsssiss than I am our other enemies. If it were just a matter of fighting the Ssselipsssiss, we could jump back and forth between universes and take care of them. But what happens if we jump into the next system and find the Shaitans have arrived? I would hate to find us outnumbered and facing enemies we couldn't get away from. Having the stealth modules installed gives us options…and I want options when facing the unknown."

"Makes sense to me," Night said. "I'll have the platoon standing by in case they're holding Lieutenant Commander Hobbs somewhere, and we need to go bring him back."

"Thanks," Captain Sheppard replied. "Hopefully, the Ssselipsssiss will be true to their word…but I'd like them standing by just in case."

"Options," Night noted.

"Exactly," Captain Sheppard agreed. "How are the new troops fitting in?"

"They're doing well, sir. Most are combat veterans and experts in their field, which is why they were selected to train the Doman forces. We've been running them through the simulators, and they're adjusting to our platoon's tactics."

"The new pilots are doing equally well," Lights added. "We're seeing the same thing with them; they're also experts."

"Good," Captain Sheppard replied. "I don't *think* we'll need them, but…"

"Options."

"Right. Okay, that does it for now. I'd like everyone to make sure your departments are fully ready for combat. Even if it doesn't happen when we make our jump into the Kepler-62 system, it will be hard to avoid as we press on toward the Dark Star. Meeting adjourned."

The assembled staff began dispersing to attend to their tasks.

"Father Zuhlsdorf, would you stay a moment longer?" Captain Sheppard asked. Once the room had cleared, he continued. "Father, I'm sure you're wondering why I asked you to attend the staff meeting."

"My presence was somewhat…out of the ordinary," the priest replied. "Although it was interesting to find out some of the specifics of our mission, the details are, however, somewhat daunting. Going 10 systems up an unexplored stargate chain to find our enemy's home planet is further than any missionary has ever gone, I believe."

"That's what I wanted to talk with you about," Captain Sheppard said. "The enemy's home planet."

"I doubt you want my advice on military planning. Although I have a small amount of hand-to-hand combat experience, ship-to-ship warfare is certainly not my forte."

"No, I wanted to talk about what we're going to do once we get there. If we somehow make it to the Dark Star and find the Shaitans' home world, the Ssselipsssiss have asked us to destroy it. I've given the situation a lot of thought, and I'm having a hard time convincing myself that destroying an entire world is the proper course of action."

"Despite the fact you've already done it once?"

"I never intended to destroy the Psiclopes' home world," Captain Sheppard replied; "in fact, I specifically ordered the troops *not* to turn it into a black hole. This time is different, though. I'm actively contemplating the obliteration of a world and potentially billions of lives. Even though they're aliens, they're still conscious beings."

"So, you are wondering about the morality of the action, not the strategic implications?"

"Exactly. I know the Ssselipsssiss will approve of annihilating the planet, and I expect even the Mrowry would turn a blind eye as it would help secure their borders. Fleet Command would also probably be okay with it, especially if I do it on my own, and they don't have to take responsibility." He sighed and shook his head. "The truth is, assuming we can do it, wiping out their home world, and any facilities there, is also probably our best opportunity to end this war without any further loss of allied lives. But is obliterating an entire planet's worth of sapient beings the right choice, even if they are all evil?"

"That is a good question," Father Zuhlsdorf replied, "and I am reminded of how Abraham bargained with God in Genesis, Chapter 18: *Then Abraham drew near, and said, 'Wilt thou indeed destroy the righteous with the wicked? Suppose there are fifty righteous within the city; wilt thou then destroy the place and not spare it for the fifty righteous who are in it?'*"

Father Zuhlsdorf smiled. "Abraham got God to reduce the number all the way down to 10 righteous men, but God destroyed Sodom anyway. He makes His own decisions." Father Zuhlsdorf paused, then asked, "My question would be, how do *you* know they are all evil? I have faith that the Good Lord must have put the Shaitans here for a reason. For the life of me, I can't think of what that might be except to test us, but it is not up to me to determine or judge."

"What if our God, the God who I believe created our universe, doesn't exist in *their* universe?" Captain Sheppard asked. "What if there is a separate god who rules it? What then? Maybe the reason the Shaitans are bent on exterminating us is they think that's the reason their god created them?"

"That is an interesting premise," Father Zuhlsdorf replied. He thought for a moment. "Here's another quote from the Book of Genesis: *God made the two great lights—the greater light to rule the day, and the lesser light to rule the night—and the stars. He set them in the dome of the sky to give light upon the earth, to rule over the day and the night, and to separate the light from the darkness.*"

"Nowhere does it say He also created alternate universes," Captain Sheppard noted.

"Nor would it," Father Zuhlsdorf replied. "Alternate universes would have been as far beyond the people who originally wrote the Book of Genesis as stargate mechanics were to us before the Psiclopes arrived. The authors were struggling with the creation of our own universe; they would not have been able to even conceptualize the existence of another one."

"And I'm guessing the Church doesn't have any teaching on going to new universes and wiping out the creatures there?"

"While I'm sure the Church is working to understand the implications of the Jinn Universe, the Pope hasn't shared his thoughts with me yet, so I'm afraid I am somewhat handicapped in my ability to advise you. What I do know for certain is that life, all life, is precious. I think you have to make your decision with that in mind."

"Not only do I have to balance the lives of the Shaitans I may take, I also have to consider how many people they're going to kill if this war continues. The dilemma is somewhat like the choice to use nuclear weapons on Japan at the end of World War II. Our leaders knew there would be horrific casualties if they used them, but they knew there would be even greater destruction if we were forced to invade Japan. The only difference is this war appears to be a war of extinction. If given the opportunity, I don't believe the Shaitans would think twice about coming to Terra and destroying all of us. We'd all be dead as soon as they arrived."

"Do you know that to be certain? That *every single Shaitan* would kill every single human if it were possible? Or are you merely guessing it to be true?"

"Well, I can't say I've spoken with every Shaitan, so I guess it is within the realm of possibility that some Shaitans may exist who don't want to kill all of us, but recent evidence seems to point in the other direction."

"Although I do not discount that there are conditions where war may be the right choice, judging the actions of all, based on the actions of a few commanders already at war, is an unsatisfactory argument to me. I am mindful of 'jus ad bellum' or the 'Just War Theory.' While the Church teaches the use of deadly force can be justified in self-defense or when there are no other options, it cannot be used indiscriminately, such as in the case of genocide. The use of force must cease when the threat no longer exists."

"How am I supposed to know when the threat is over?"

"Unfortunately, there is no 'right' answer for all cases. It is, and must be, situationally dependent. Say you are a trained carrier of a concealed handgun, and you are threatened with the loss of your life. If you cannot flee or deescalate the threat, you have the right to defend yourself and others, even with deadly force. So you shoot the attacker. He keeps coming, so you shoot him again. Still, he keeps coming, so you continue shooting…but only until he stops. You don't keep shooting after the threat is over. You shoot to stop the threat; you don't shoot to kill."

"War is the same way," Father Zuhlsdorf continued. "If, in righteous anger and with grave cause, we wear down the unjust aggressor to the point where he ceases to be an existential threat, then the use of deadly force has to stop. If we are unjustly attacked, we defend ourselves and stop the existential threat our opponent is manifesting, but we are required to stop when the threat is over. Right now, we don't know enough to say the entire species is wholly evil or immoral, so we can't simply destroy them. Just War requires us to stop the existential threat by reducing the Shaitans' capacity to harm us, at which point we *must* stop using lethal force. Killing anyone is a last resort; killing all of them, just because you can, is reprehensible."

"I was afraid you'd say something like that," Captain Sheppard replied, "because I'm afraid I'll only have two options. Either I wipe them out, or I run the risk they will somehow make it to our planet and wipe out all of us. I don't like either of those choices."

"Neither do I," the chaplain replied. "I guess you'll have to find another way."

* * * * *

Chapter Twelve

Ducts, Jotunn Ship _Falcon_, Unknown System, December 14, 2021

"That's funny," Farhome said with a giggle. "You said you knew where we were, but now you don't anymore."

Calvin had been through enough stargate jumps he barely noticed anymore when they occurred…but he still was able to tell it had happened. "Okay, I know what ship we're on," he whispered. "And now, we're either one system closer to home…or farther away."

"Which do you think it is?" Farhome asked. Another giggle escaped. "Do you think there's a supernova we can fall into here?"

"I don't know what your fascination is with supernovas," Calvin said, "but I wish you'd stop it." He thought for a moment. "The ship hasn't taken _that_ much battle damage. I'm guessing we've moved one system closer to Terra. We're going to assault the next system."

Calvin looked down the duct to where the Ssselipssssiss had retreated after the jump. One system closer to home meant one system fewer the Ssselipssssiss had until their annihilation. He could tell from their agitation as they communicated in hand signals that they were aware of the fact too. If this system fell, they'd be down to only one. Even if the _Vella Gulf_ showed up now, the Terrans still probably wouldn't be able to stop the extinction of the Ssselipssssiss.

Now that he had come to know some of the saurian race, he found that he wasn't ready for that to happen. A couple of months ago, he wouldn't have given it a second thought, but now that he had a relationship with them…

The Jotunn/Shaitan alliance had to be stopped.

He just had no idea how.

He crawled along the duct to join the Ssselipsssiss, and found they were all bleeding from gashes down their arms.

"Crap!" Calvin exclaimed. "What happened?"

"We are mourning the loss of our world," Burkuri said. "Soon, it will be the loss of our entire race. There is nothing we can do to stop it. Worse, we will be forced to endure watching it happen."

"The gods hate us!" Reyl cried.

"The gods hate us!" the group chorused.

"So that's it?" Calvin asked. "You're giving up? What? Are you going to kill yourselves rather than fight to the end?"

"I would rather fight," Karver replied, "but there is nothing we can do. We could wage a guerilla war from the ducts. We could probably kill a number of them before they killed us. If you and the pointy-eared giggler joined us, we might kill an additional two or three Jotunn before they killed us. But kill us they would, and we would only help end our race that much sooner."

"Well, what if I were able to get the bugs to join us in the fight?" Calvin asked. "We might be able to overwhelm them if we attacked by surprise."

"What good would that do?" asked Syrusss. "Even if all ten gods smiled on us at once, and we killed all the Jotunn on this ship, we couldn't fly it or fight it. As soon as the other Jotunn saw we had killed the crew, they would destroy us. Even *if* Paxton or I were able to rewire the ship's AI and get it to help us, the Shaitans would use their weapons to destroy us, and there would be nothing we could do about it. The gods hate us."

"The gods hate us!" the group chorused.

"Okay, I can see that," Calvin replied. "Still, there's got to be a way…we need to do something to stop the Jotunn. If we could get them to leave, the Shaitans might call off their attack. The *Vella Gulf* will be back before too much longer, and the *Gulf* is able to fight the Shaitans in their own universe."

"But that ship is just a cruiser, right?" Burkuri asked. "Assuming your ship kills the Shaitans, which is unlikely, what is it going to do against this ship and the others of the Jotunn fleet?"

"Well, the *Gulf's* crew can launch and then jump to the Shaitans' universe," Calvin said. "The Jotunn won't be able to target them. Perhaps the giants will get frustrated and call off the attack." Calvin's eyes swept the Ssselipsssiss. They were all staring at him, but he couldn't tell if their looks were hope or disbelief. "Honestly, it happened once before. The Jotunn left when they weren't able to attack the *Vella Gulf*."

"Or, they could bomb our next-to-last system to dust while they wait for your ship to come back and battle them," Burkuri said. "Then they could go through the next stargate and destroy our last system. Our fleet has been destroyed. What is there to stop it from happening?"

The Ssselipsssiss looks were disbelief, then. Calvin had to find a way to give them hope, if even a little. But he didn't have any to share. He knew as well as they did, if not better, how small the *Vella Gulf's* chances were against the combined Shaitan/Jotunn battle fleet. The *Gulf* could probably hold its own against the Shaitans, but there was no way they were going to beat the Jotunn. All the missiles the

Gulf carried weren't enough to destroy the giants' enormous battle-cruisers.

They were screwed. The Ssselipsssiss were going to be annihilated.

He hit the side of the duct in frustration, striking one of the cabling runs. "*Bitch!*" he exclaimed under his breath, his hand throbbing.

He looked at the cables a moment longer, then his hands fell to his sides and his mouth dropped open. He turned to face the Ssselipsssiss, a smile starting to show on his face.

"I know what we can do," Calvin said.

"To help the bugs or preserve our race?" Burkuri asked.

"Both."

Bridge, TSS *Vella Gulf*, Kepler-62 System, December 16, 2021

"Entry into the Keppler-62 system and Ssselipsssiss-controlled territory," Steropes said. After a pause he added, "Captain Sheppard, I don't see any of the Ssselipsssiss warships that were here on our last visit."

"What do you mean you don't see them?" asked the CO. "Have they landed somewhere? Where did they go?"

"It is unknown," Steropes replied. "I don't have any indication of communications or ship drive signatures. It appears they left."

"Why would they leave?" mused the duty engineer. "Who's holding the border against the Mrowry?"

"It doesn't appear anyone is," Steropes replied. "Not only are the ships missing from the system, it appears most of the mines were removed from the stargate, as well."

"That can't be good," Captain Sheppard noted. "The only reason they'd do that…"

"Was if they needed them for a last-ditch defense," Steropes said.

"Maybe Calvin convinced them the Shaitans were the real threat, and they didn't have to worry about the Mrowry," Lights said. "If so, he might have also convinced them to move the mines to another system to help in its defense."

"That assumes three things," said Lieutenant O'Leary. "First, it assumes they actually kept him because they wanted to see what he thought. Second, it assumes they actually took him somewhere to look at the defenses, and he found they were insufficient. Finally, it assumes he was not only an excellent strategist but politician and speaker, too, as he convinced their entire military command to strip all their defenses from their border with a race they've been fighting for decades. It *might* have happened that way…but I ain't buying it."

"Oh?" Captain Sheppard asked. "What do you think happened?"

"I think they're getting their asses kicked somewhere else and needed the ships for a last-ditch defense. And, if past history is any sort of guide, our beloved Lieutenant Commander is probably right there alongside them with a ringside seat to the destruction of the lizzie civilization. There's some razor saying that if you've got a bunch of possible options, you should go with the one that has the least assumptions."

"Occam's Razor," Steropes interjected.

"Yeah, whatever," Lieutenant O'Leary said. "Honestly, I don't give a shit about whose damn razor it was; all I know is the lizzies are probably getting their asses handed to them somewhere, and I will bet you any amount of money that Lieutenant Commander Hobbs is right in the middle of it."

Captain Sheppard nodded. "Unfortunately, that is probably true."

"Sir!" the communications officer called. "We're being hailed from the planet."

"Contact!" the DSO announced. "There's a shuttle that just lifted from the planet."

"Put the call on screen," Captain Sheppard ordered.

"I'm unable," the communications officer replied. "They gave me a message then signed off and are no longer replying to my hails."

"What was the message?"

"That the ambassador is coming for a meeting."

"Did they say why?"

"No sir," the communications officer answered. "They didn't say or give me any other information."

"Ask them again," the Captain said.

"They aren't answering."

"They're in a big hurry," Steropes reported. "The shuttle is coming at better than its best speed."

"Huh," the CO grunted. "Whatever it is, it must be important. Still, I don't like all the secrecy. Night, Lieutenant O'Leary, please meet our guests at the shuttle and bring them to my conference room. Oh, and please meet them armed. You can be as obvious as you'd like."

"Yes, sir," Night said. "It would be my pleasure." The two troopers left the bridge at a run.

Ducts, Jotunn Ship *Falcon*, Unknown System, December 14, 2021

"What is your idea?" Syrusss asked.

"This is my idea, right here," Calvin said, patting the side of the duct.

"The ducting?" Karver asked. "What are we supposed to do? Cut it apart and use it for weapons? Without a shop to fashion points, I don't see how it'll be very effective."

"No," Calvin explained, "I don't want to use the ducting, but the cables running along it."

"I guess we could make nooses out of the cables," Syrusss said, "but I'm not sure we will be able to pull the Jotunn up off their feet to strangle them; they look awfully heavy."

"No, that's not what I mean, either," Calvin said.

"I see—" Reyl started.

"Shut up, all of you," Burkuri ordered, cutting him off. "Dad will tell us if you'll. Just. Shut. Up." She hissed in frustration. "Males."

Calvin smiled. Some things were universal. He coughed to cover a laugh.

"No, what I meant is that we have access to a lot of their systems' cables. If we found the cable runs for some of their more important systems and started inducing failures, we might be able to get them to leave here and return to their home planet…or at least their closest base."

"That's just this one ship, though," Burkuri said. "How do we get the other Jotunn ship to leave, too?"

"We need a failure that will make this ship's commanding officer want the other ship's support," Calvin said. "Hmm…if I were the CO, what would I want support with? Definitely my engines, as I don't want to get stranded somewhere out in space. Oh, yeah, life support would be good, too. If we can find the cables for those systems and a way to make them fail, I think we might be able to get the Jotunn to leave."

"So how do we find those cables?" Paxton asked.

"We just have to look," Calvin said, excited to get started on his plan. "I'm sure the cables will all be labeled; I know they are in our ships. We can split up; that way we can get it done faster. Let's get going!"

"Umm…that won't work," Paxton said. "None of us speak Jotunn, nor can we read it. I bet the bugs can't read it, either. That's a problem."

"Well, I'll write it down and you can compare it to the markings on the cabling as you go along," Calvin said. "Who has some paper?"

The five Ssselipsssiss looked at him, unmoving.

"Really?" Calvin asked. "With everything you've got in your packs, no one has any paper?" He turned to Farhome. "I don't suppose you have any paper?"

"You could write on our other tunic if you'd like," the Aesir said. "We don't mind."

Calvin sighed. "Let's go ask the bugs."

Shuttle Docking Port, TSS *Vella Gulf*, Kepler-62 System, December 16, 2021

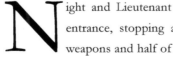ight and Lieutenant O'Leary hurried to the shuttle entrance, stopping at the armory to pick up their weapons and half of First Squad along the way. They

didn't have long to wait before the shuttle arrived, and a single Ssselipsssiss debarked.

"*Sir, we've got a problem,*" Night commed. "*The ambassador is armed with a sword.*"

"*Solomon, does he have anything else?*" Captain Sheppard queried.

"*I do not detect any other weapons,*" the AI replied.

"*Let him keep it, but stay alert,*" the CO ordered.

"*By the way,*" Night said, "*this is the Ssselipsssiss who was the assistant ambassador the last time we were here. I don't see the original ambassador; there is no one else with him.*"

"*Understood,*" Captain Sheppard acknowledged. "*Bring him to my conference room.*"

"*On our way.*"

The troops escorted the ambassador through the ship. The Ssselipsssiss didn't speak to them; although his head was down and his shoulders slumped, he walked with a purpose, stepping on the soldiers' feet in front of him on several occasions as if he wanted them to go faster.

The procession arrived at the conference room and several soldiers preceded the ambassador into the room, keeping him in view at all times. Captain Sheppard was waiting but kept the conference room's table between them rather than coming to formally greet the ambassador.

Without uttering a word, the ambassador drew his sword.

"Don't move!" Night yelled, as the nine soldiers aimed their weapons.

The ambassador took his sword in both hands and laid it on the table. "I don't know what your custom is for such a disgrace," the ambassador said, "but I surrender all the forces in this system to you, as well as any additional forces still remaining under my command. I would only ask that you transport the civilians to a place of safety somewhere in your territory before our enemy gets here."

"Uh, I've never had anyone surrender to me before, so I don't actually know the protocol," Captain Sheppard said, "but I think this will do all right. I take it things have changed greatly since we were here last. My biggest question is, where is our crewman?"

"Gone…" the ambassador said. He sat down heavily on one of the chairs, keeping to the front so his tail would fit. "He's gone, the fleet's gone, they're all…gone. If you do not help us, our race will perish."

"What happened?" Captain Sheppard asked.

"After you left, the fleet went to assess our defenses two star-gates over. While there, a combined fleet of the enemy and their allies arrived. Our forces fought better than they ever have…they even destroyed some of the enemy's ships…but ultimately all were lost, and the planet was taken."

"Was our crewman with the fleet?"

"Yessss…" The word hung in the air a long time as a silence came over the group.

"No one made it out?" Captain Sheppard asked.

"None," the ambassador replied. "When nothing was heard, our last two cruisers entered the system to find the rape of the planet already in progress. The captain in charge immediately returned with the news and said there would be no survivors…in space or on the planet below. He started shuttling people from the next system over to this one, trying to save as many as he could…but he is now…overdue. I suspect…the invasion…next system…already begun." His voice grew weaker while he was speaking, and he seemed to run down. "The gods hate us. It is…ended." He leaned forward onto the table, his head on his arms.

"Can you at least tell us about the enemy's fleet?" Captain Sheppard asked. "What are the forces we have to face?"

The ambassador raised his head enough to peer over an arm. "They are too many for this ship," he said. Without another word, he grabbed his sword from the table and drove it through his chest. He collapsed, falling to the deck. "The Ssselipsssiss are through," he wheezed, then stilled.

Night slung his rifle and sprang forward to the motionless Ssselipsssiss. He knelt down and felt around his arm, looking for a pulse. After a few seconds, he looked back up at the CO. "I'm not real sure what to do for him," he said. "Or with him." He looked up at the overhead and asked, "Hey, Solomon, can you tell if the ambassador is still living?"

"No sir, he is not," the AI replied.

"Well…shit."

* * * * *

Chapter Thirteen

CO's Conference Room, TSS *Vella Gulf*, Kepler-62 System, December 16, 2021

"Even though he said Calvin's dead, we still need to find out for ourselves," Lieutenant O'Leary said. "He's lived through too many other things not to at least take a look."

"I agree," Captain Sheppard said, "but we've got to do something to help the Ssselipsssiss in this system first. If the Shaitans come and wipe them out here, the race will perish."

"And that's a bad thing, why?" Night asked. "What have they ever done for us? I'm finding it hard to see a reason for any allegiance to them when they would just as soon eat us as look at us."

"I'm not going to let the Shaitans finish them off on my watch," Captain Sheppard said. "We're going to have to go back and call up the Mrowry fleet to defend this system. Maybe we can convince them to move forward to the next system with us and take on the Shaitans there; that way, we don't have to worry about the planet being bombed in the course of a Shaitan invasion of this system."

"I do not know if the fleet commander will be as willing to defend the Ssselipsssiss as you are," Lieutenant Rrower said. "We have been at war with them for a long time, and there is a considerable amount of hatred between our races. Most of my people will see the question the same way Captain Train did, and they will be willing to allow the Shaitans and Ssselipsssiss to destroy as much of each other as possible, prior to engaging whoever's left afterwards."

"Can't you use your writ?"

"I could try," the Mrowry officer said, "but there are a couple of reasons why it would be difficult. First, I'm not even sure I want to. I have to look at the situation from the viewpoint of what's best for my civilization. Not only am I *not* convinced of the need to save the Ssselipsssiss, there is also the tactical situation to look at. Currently, our fleet is on the other side of a stargate, where their position is well defended. Not only will an invading force have to get past the fleet, they will also have to break through the minefield and other defenses that await them in the HD 40307 system. Calling them forward to defend this system exposes them to additional, and perhaps unnecessary, risk. To assault through the stargate here into the next system will add on an enormous amount of risk, as they have never fought the Shaitans and do not have the ability to jump with them into their universe. If it were simply a matter of normal fleet-versus-fleet combat, I would be in favor of them moving forward to reclaim this system and as much of the former Ssselipsssiss empire as possible. As it is…I don't know."

"I know making that decision is a lot to put on a Lieutenant," Captain Sheppard said, "even one as well-travelled as you, but would you at least be willing to discuss it with the fleet commander if we go back to HD 40307? I want to go look for Calvin, but the continuity of the Ssselipsssiss race has to take priority."

"That brings us to the second reason why it will be difficult. The commander of the fleet in HD 40307 is my father, Admiral Krrower. He will be…reluctant…to have me tell him what to do. As he is also a member of the royalty, the writ will not work as well on him, as he could, theoretically, override me. I will talk to him…" Lieutenant Rrower finally agreed, "but I am still not sure what I will say, or if he will listen."

Ducts, Jotunn Ship *Falcon*, Unknown System, December 17, 2021

"This isn't working," Calvin said.

"If your plan was to give us a lot of busy work to distract us, it's working perfectly," Farhome replied. "We've wasted a couple of days on it, and no one has talked about killing themselves or eating us during that entire time." He giggled. "I would have thought you'd be happy with that."

"Well, I'm happy with the other stuff, but I really wanted to find the cabling," Calvin said. "I guess it's not surprising we didn't find any cable runs we could use around the engineering spaces. All the power generation and engine control cabling must be inside the engine rooms. I'm disappointed we haven't found any communications circuits. We've been all around the bridge, and they just don't seem to exist."

"Or they go through the walls or floors or ceilings, rather than the ducts," said Burkuri. "I personally went around the bridge twice, and there's nothing like this to be found." She held out the piece of paper one of the bugs had 'requisitioned' from an empty stateroom. It held the Jotunn words for the systems they were looking for. "They either don't exist in the ductwork, or they're unlabeled."

"Unlabeled?" Calvin asked.

"Yes, some of the cables are unlabeled," Burkuri said. "Maybe it's one of them."

"I guess it could be…" Calvin said, shaking his head, "but it's really going to suck if we have to figure out which one it might be." He sighed. "I'm not really sure how we'd even go about doing that…" His idea, which had seemed great at the start, was fading fast.

"Well, there wouldn't be *that* many we'd have to try," Paxton said. "I was with her, and most of the cables coming from the bridge *are* labeled. There's only a few that aren't." He held up his paper, showing the words they were looking for, then turned it over. "I wrote down the ones that weren't on the list."

"Can I see them?" Calvin asked, a tinge of excitement in his voice. "Maybe I used a wrong word, like 'comms' instead of 'radio,' or something." He took Paxton's list and quickly scanned it, but his hopes were dashed once again. "Nope, nothing here. Nothing we can use, either." He sighed again.

"What about these other two?" Paxton asked. "I ran out of room and had to put two on the back."

Calvin flipped the paper over and looked at the final two entries. A triumphant smile grew across his face.

"Is one of them the radio cable?" Paxton asked.

"No," said Calvin. "It's even better." He pointed to the final entry. "This one is for the shield generators."

Conference Room, Mrowry Ship *Night Hunter*, HD 40307 System, December 17, 2021

"Thank you very much for meeting with us, Admiral Krrower," Captain Sheppard said to the large, all-black Mrowry sitting at the head of the table. In addition to the admiral who commanded the fleet, the commanding officer of the dreadnought *Night Hunter* and the three battleship captains were also in attendance. Captain Sheppard was joined at his end of the table by Night, Lieutenant Commander Brighton and Lieutenant Rrower.

"You're welcome," the admiral replied, "although I am afraid your journey has been for naught. My son tells me you want us to move forward to protect the remaining Ssselipsssiss; that isn't going to happen."

"May I ask why, sir, since you haven't even heard my reasoning as to why I think that course of action makes the most sense?"

"The Ssselipsssiss are our enemies. I have lost too many of my brothers and sisters to even consider providing them aid against their new enemy."

"The admiral's right," one of the battleship captains agreed. "Let them bleed each other to the end; that way, there are fewer for us to have to fight." The other captains signaled their approval by banging their fists on the table.

"As you can see," the admiral noted, "there is very little love lost between our societies. It is survival of the fittest...and they were obviously not worthy of survival."

"What if the roles were reversed?" Captain Sheppard asked. "What if your civilization was about to be wiped out, and the Ssselipsssiss were the only ones who could offer you aid? Wouldn't you go to them if the survival of your race was at stake?"

"I would not!" Admiral Krrower stated. "I am fully aware of the consequences of such an action. The Ssselipsssiss would betray us at the first opportunity, which would result in the destruction of the Mrowry even sooner than if we didn't have their 'help.' No thank you. I would not ask for their aid, nor do I intend to give them mine. This ship was built to destroy Ssselipsssiss, not protect them."

"I understand," Captain Sheppard said. Realizing there was no use pursuing that line of argument, he tried another tact. "My real question is less about the Ssselipsssiss than it is about the future of the Mrowry."

"We have a great future," Captain Twanx, the CO of the *Night Hunter*, interjected. "Our enemy is being wiped out for us. We are secure in our defenses, and we don't have to lift a paw to help."

"If only that were true," Captain Sheppard said.

"What do you mean?" Admiral Krrower asked.

"I mean you have to look at recent history. The Mrowry and the Ssselipsssiss were enemies who fought their way to a draw after decades of fighting. You have similar technology and were equally matched; a stalemate existed between your civilizations prior to the advent of the Shaitans."

"So?"

"So? The Shaitans came, and they rolled up the entire Ssselipsssiss Empire in just a few years. They succeeded where you couldn't, and they did so completely and expeditiously. The Ssselipsssiss were barely a speedbump in the road."

"I'm sorry, that word didn't translate," Captain Twanx interrupted. "What is a 'speedbump'?"

"A speedbump is a Terran device to slow down a vehicle driving on the surface of a planet. The Ssselipsssiss didn't slow down the Shaitans at all; the Shaitans drove right through the Ssselipsssiss Empire from one end to the other, without ever being stopped. Until their final battle, *the lizards hadn't even destroyed a single Shaitan ship!*"

"That won't happen to us, though," Admiral Krrower said. "Our defenses here are strong."

"I'm sorry, father, but I must respectfully disagree," Lieutenant Rrower said. "I have seen the Shaitans in battle. A combination Shaitan/Jotunn fleet blew through Aesir defenses much stronger than the ones here, as if they were only cubs' toys, not ships of war. The Shaitans are able to jump back and forth to the universe from which they hail; they are nearly impossible to destroy and have nearly unstoppable weapons. If they can do it against the Ssselipsssiss, the Shaitans stand a good chance of being able to do it to us, too."

"And without much of a buffer zone," Captain Sheppard added, "the Shaitans will be within range of your populated planets in no time."

"Son, no disrespect intended, but if the Shaitans were so overwhelmingly powerful, how is it you were able to survive? Did you run from them?"

"No, father, the Terrans fought alongside the Aesir although their fleet was destroyed as thoroughly as the Aesir's. The only ship that survived was the *Vella Gulf*, and only because it is able to jump between the universes like the Shaitans. Were it not for the Terrans, the Aesir civilization would have been destroyed."

The admiral turned to stare at Captain Sheppard. "We need this technology that allows you to jump between the universes," he said.

"I have already given it to your emperor," Captain Sheppard replied. "You'll have ships that can go up against the Shaitans, but you need to give your shipbuilding industry time to produce them. In addition to the technology, you also need metal from the other universe to make the jump modules work. Your emperor has sent a ship to Terra to get some, but that will take time, too. You have to give the emperor the time he needs."

"And how do you suggest I do that?" the admiral asked. "You just said my ships and defenses here are worthless; what would you recommend I do to delay the Shaitans?"

"You need to take the fight to the enemy," Captain Sheppard said. "Your forces need to advance into Ssselipssssiss territory and provide the speedbump the Ssselipsssiss couldn't. The longer you delay them, the more prepared your fleet will be when they arrive in force."

"I don't understand your logic, Terran," the admiral replied. "How will advancing into the lizards' territory to throw away our fleet sooner help us delay them? If my fleet is destroyed, there is little to stand in the Shaitans' way until we can bring forward or redistribute other units of our fleet. What do you know that will help us make the loss of my fleet a worthwhile sacrifice?"

"I know that we will be right there alongside you. Your fleet is big enough to take on any conventional fleet, and we'll handle the Shaitans. By pushing the boundaries of Mrowry space forward, we can buy your emperor the time he needs."

"You will fight with us?" the admiral asked. "To the death?"

Captain Sheppard could feel the tide turn, but there wasn't time to contact Fleet Command for authorization. The choice was his. But then again, there really *wasn't* any choice. "Yes, we will," he said, standing up. "We *will* stand by you in the battle to come. To the death if necessary."

The admiral also stood and crossed to Captain Sheppard, drawing a small knife as he approached. He cut a three-inch slice in the side of his arm and then drew the blade across the palm of his paw without flinching. The Mrowry spun the knife in its paw and handed it to Captain Sheppard, butt-first.

Gritting his teeth, the *Vella Gulf's* CO made the same cuts, and the Mrowry reached out to take the Terran's arm in a hand-to-forearm grip. "You are blood of my blood," the admiral intoned. "We are brothers and will stand together. Should you fall, my claws will defend you until you can rise; should you not rise, I will avenge you to my last breath. To the end!"

Captain Sheppard nodded. "To the end."

Ducts, Jotunn Ship *Falcon*, Unknown System, December 17, 2021

"There it is," Paxton said, pointing at a thin cable that ran from the bridge below them toward the bow of the ship.

"That's even better than I hoped," Calvin said. "That's the control cable for turning the shields on and off, not the power cable. If it were the power cable, it would have been a lot bigger and harder to work with, to say nothing about how dangerous it would have been if we'd had to cut it. But this? This is going to work nicely."

"Are you going to cut it?" Burkuri asked.

"No," Calvin said. "They may have some sort of maintenance robot they can send down the cable runs. We have to make it look accidental in case they come looking. Let's see if we can find a junction box we can pull the wire out of. We can make it look like it fell out."

"But if they have a robot that can fix it, won't they send the robot? Then, once it's fixed, the Jotunn won't have a reason to leave the system, right? Isn't that the whole idea?"

"Well, yeah, it is, but maybe they won't have a robot."

"Okay…" Burkuri didn't sound convinced.

Calvin wasn't convinced, either, but wasn't going to say so. "So let's see if there's a junction box."

Three hours later, they hadn't found a junction box for either that cable or the other forward shield control cable they found.

"So, what now?" Burkuri asked.

"Paxton, do you have another one of those little animals? We could have it gnaw through the cable, and it would look like a mouse chewed its way through. That's better than just cutting it."

"No, I only had the one risst, and the bug ate it."

"Damn." This was getting harder and harder.

"I have a small set of clippers I can use to make it *look* like something ate the wire if you'd like," Paxton said. "If I do it right, it will look like a number of small bites were taken out of the cable."

"Well, why didn't you say so?"

"You never asked."

Calvin sighed. "Yes, I would like you to do that. Please."

"Before he does," Burkuri said, "what if a maintenance robot shows up? We can't let it see us, or they're going to know we're up here in the ducting and come looking for us. Also, what if it fixes the wire? We're back where we started."

"We need something that's going to trap and destroy any maintenance robots the Jotunn send," Calvin said. "But it has to be disguised so they can't tell what happened."

"If you let me have the battery from your space suit, I can do that," Syrusss said. "Nothing could be easier."

* * * * *

Chapter Fourteen

Ducts, Jotunn Ship *Falcon*, Unknown System, December 17, 2021

"That's it," Syrusss said. "One robot trap, ready to go."

Calvin looked down the duct and shook his head. "I don't get it," he said. "I see the wire hanging from the ceiling, but even if there's current running through it, it's never going to work; any robot is going to see it sticking out a long time before it runs into it."

"It's supposed to see that wire," Syrusss said. "The real wires are disguised on the sides of the duct. See that slightly discolored square of metal?"

Calvin nodded. "Yeah, I didn't notice it before, but I can see it's a little different."

"That's because there's a thin, non-conductive mat there. The robot will see that the wire hanging down has been gnawed before it gets onto the mat. That will give more credibility to the story there's something up here chewing on the cables."

"Nice touch," Calvin said.

"Thanks," Syrusss said with the Ssselipsssiss version of a smile. "As the robot approaches the wire, it hits the trigger in the mat and two leads spring out from the sides of the duct. The robot completes the circuit, and current flows through it. The robot's electronics fry, hopefully enough for a complete mission kill."

"Do you think it will work?"

"If everything works right, the robot is going to get hit with about 100,000 volts. 4,000 volts might be enough to kill it, but we also need enough power to push the current, as a transitory high voltage might not sustain the current enough to burn up a robot. Unfortunately, we don't know how it's designed, so I had to incorporate a couple of extra features."

"Like what?"

"Well, current causes strong magnetic fields, and any decent maintenance robot will have sensors for that. Therefore, I needed to either build a trap where the robot's contact completed the circuit or have a remote initiation of current in a previously dead circuit. Since we couldn't be around, the second option was out."

"That makes sense," Calvin said.

"Second, in addition to the ability to sense current, any good maintenance robot will have internal insulation and a variety of safeties and fail safes. I'm sure the Jotunn don't want to have to climb up here to get a failed robot, so they won't want it to fail. Thus, trying to fry the robot is more difficult than having it simply roll across a metal floor with a big charge applied to it. Its treads are probably nonconductive, so any charge would be unlikely to hurt it; such an event would be likely in its normal duties and its design would take that into account. Therefore, the circuit path across the robot has to include its vital spots, which are probably in its upper housing. Without knowing what the robot looks like, I don't know where those areas are, so I had to guess at what height to set the leads. Hopefully, the trap will work."

"What are the odds it will?"

"Without seeing the robot, I couldn't begin to guess. I don't know how well the Jotunn have hardened its circuits; it's possible it may survive. If it does, though, it's still going to know there are some major stray voltage problems up here. With the failure of the shields, as well…hopefully that will be enough for the Jotunn commander to decide he needs a shipyard to look at it."

"Well done," Calvin said. "How did you put all that together?"

"It was just some equipment I had I could repurpose. Don't ask if you don't want to know."

"Do I want to know?"

"No."

"Okay," Calvin said, "I won't ask. I'm pretty sure I don't want to know why you'd want to deliver a large amount of electricity or have non-conductive padding." He shuddered as he looked around at the assembled group. "Let me tell the bugs to stay away, and we'll get started."

Bridge, TSS *Vella Gulf*, Kepler-62 System, December 18, 2021

"We will go in first, take a look around, and then will return and report," Captain Sheppard said, looking up at the faces of the Mrowry officers on the main viewing screen, "that way you know what you're getting into and don't go charging into something you can't get back out of."

"Very well," Admiral Krrower replied. "We will mine the stargate on this side while we await your return. The more defenses we put into place now, the easier the systems will be to defend if the enemy's forces are too great, and we are forced to retreat."

"A sound plan sir," Captain Sheppard replied. "*Vella Gulf* out." He switched off the display, terminating the transmission, and the view on the screen changed to the emptiness of the stargate, just in front of the ship. He scanned the bridge; everyone seemed ready. "All ahead slow. Once we're on the other side, engage stealth and jump to the Jinn Universe."

"All ahead slow," the helmsman repeated, "and jump to the Jinn Universe once we're on the other side."

"Stealth once we're there," the duty engineer added.

The helmsman looked at his readout. "Stargate in three seconds," he said. "Here we go…"

Overhead the Bridge, Jotunn Ship *Falcon*, Unknown System, December 17, 2021

"We're ready," Syrusss whispered.

Calvin nodded and took a final look down onto the bridge. Everything seemed normal. Most of the crew was watching the front view screen while trying to look like they weren't. Calvin couldn't see what was on the screen from his vantage point, but it was something that had disturbed the battle-hardened Jotunn crew when it first appeared.

Calvin crawled back from the grate to where they could talk without the bridge crew hearing.

"Cut the wire and get out of the way," Calvin ordered. "I'm going to stay and watch their reaction. Whatever you do, *don't* let the Jotunn catch sight of you."

"That shouldn't be a problem," Syrusss replied. "I talked with the bugs, and they can tell when a robot's coming. They'll let me know which way to go."

"They're sure?"

"Yes. They can feel the vibration of the treads long before the robot can see them."

"Okay," Calvin agreed. "Go ahead and cut the wire."

Without a word, the Ssselipsssiss left on his mission. Calvin didn't have to wait long until a Jotunn's head snapped up. Over several days watching, Calvin had determined the position the Jotunn was manning was responsible for operating the vessel's defensive systems.

"Sir!" the operator exclaimed. "We just lost the forward shields on the starboard side. I have tried cycling them, but they remain out."

"Gah," Captain Magnusson said. "Get maintenance to send a robot to track down the cause. We haven't heard anything from the Ssselipsssiss. They may be planning a final counter-offensive. We need to be ready. I want the shields back up *now!*"

* * * * *

Chapter Fifteen

"The second maintenance robot has corrected the problem," the defensive systems operator reported.

The plan had worked as well as Calvin could have hoped. The trap had fried the robot, but the giants had a second robot. The replacement robot had come a different way and avoided the trap, which Syrusss had disassembled and removed when the bug scouts passed the word.

"What was the source of the failure?" asked Captain Magnusson.

"There appears to be an animal in the ducting," the operator replied. "The wire to the shield generator had been chewed through."

"And this creature also disabled the first robot you sent?"

"No sir. That failure seems to be due to stray voltage. The robot didn't show any signs of life forms on its scanners before it stopped working. The second robot brought it back and it is undamaged except for a scorch mark on its side. Whatever is chewing through the wires must have damaged another wire that came in contact with the robot."

A light began flashing on his console, and he spun around and began pushing buttons.

"Is there another problem?" the captain asked.

"I'm not sure…" the operator replied. "A small vessel appeared at the stargate to the next system in our advance, but immediately vanished."

"Was it one of the Shaitan cruisers?"

"No sir; it was a different shape entirely. This ship appeared to have smaller craft mounted on both ends."

Calvin's head snapped up. *That could only be the* Vella Gulf!

"If it wasn't the Shaitans, where did it go?" asked Captain Magnusson. "Unless it immediately jumped back through the stargate, it either had to go into stealth or jump to the other universe. Which was it?"

"Sir, I don't know."

Calvin slid back from the grate to where the Ssselipsssiss were waiting and motioned to Syrusss.

"Quickly!" he ordered. "I need you to cut the second shield cable. Make it look like an animal did it again if you can…but do it quickly. My ship is here!"

Bridge, TSS *Vella Gulf,* Kepler-186 System, December 18, 2021

Captain Sheppard watched the *Vella Gulf* transit into the new system then immediately jump into the Jinn Universe.

"Stable in the anti-Kepler-186 system," the helmsman noted. "No course or speed given."

"We are stealthed," the duty engineer added.

"As indicated on the chart the Ssselipsssiss gave us, the system has an M-class dwarf star with about 4% of Sol's luminosity. There are five planets in the system. The only habitable one is the furthest from the star; it has an orbital period of 129.9 days and orbits at about the same distance as Mercury does from your star. Even that close to the star, Kepler-186e only receives about as much energy as Mars does."

The CO nodded. "We need to find out what the Shaitans are up to and look for Calvin, even though the ambassador said it's a lost cause. Full speed toward the planet that's inhabited in our universe," the CO ordered. "You said that's the fifth one, right?"

"Yes sir," Steropes replied. "The fifth planet is inhabited in our universe and in this one as well. It's too early to identify the civilization, but there are signs of habitation."

"Were there any enemy ships in our universe when we transited through?"

Steropes nodded. "I am still analyzing the data, but there were at least two Shaitan vessels and one I identified as a Jotunn battlecruiser. There may be more, but that is what I have so far."

"That explains how they've been able to kick the Ssselipsssiss' asses so thoroughly," Night said. "Just like when we fought them at Golirion, the Jotunn hold the Ssselipsssiss in place while the Shaitans pick them off with their time-based weapons. It worked well against the Aesir."

"It also worked well against our fleet," Captain Sheppard added. A predator's grin spread across his face. "But we've got them this time. The Mrowry fleet is bigger than the Jotunn's, and I don't think Admiral Krrower will tie us to the fleet like we were at Golirion."

"He will not, if you think it best," Lieutenant Rrower said.

"How can you be sure?"

"You are now brothers of the brood," Lieutenant Rrower replied. "For all matters except succession, you are now a member of my family. He will listen to you as his equal…and in most facets of our law, you now have similar status."

"*What?* Are you saying I'm now Mrowry royalty?"

"That's exactly what I'm saying," Lieutenant Rrower replied. "Didn't you know?"

"No, I didn't know," Captain Sheppard replied. "I'm not familiar with your customs; I didn't know *any* of that. I just thought it was some kind of bonding ritual."

"It's more than that, sir…far more. In our society, that ritual is not only bonding, but adoption. It only happens when a senior elevates someone of lower class to their status. It is usually only done in the peerage, though; it is almost never used by the royal family. There are only a pawful of people who have been adopted into my family throughout all of our recorded history…and none from outside our race. You obviously impressed my father."

Captain Sheppard slumped back into his chair. Royalty? He had only done it as a spur of the moment thing. If he'd known the consequences, he wouldn't…yes, he would. It's good to be king. Apparently, he couldn't be king, but now he was royalty. If only his friends from the ghetto could see him now. He would dwell on it later, but for now he had business to attend to. Energized, he straightened in his chair.

"As I was saying, the Mrowry fleet is bigger than the Jotunn's and we're not going to be tied to the fleet. We can go and hunt the bastards…and this time, *we're* going to kill *them!*"

Overhead the Bridge, Jotunn Ship *Falcon*, Kepler-186, December 18, 2021

"The port forward shield just failed," the defensive systems operator said.

"Odin's beard!" Captain Magnusson swore. "Get it fixed *now!*" He stood up and started pacing. "The ship that entered this system is obviously here to spy, probably in preparation for an invasion."

"My system has analyzed the ship, and there is nothing in the current database which equates to the ship. The only thing that comes close is a 3,000-year-old model from an extinct race."

"Send the info to the Shaitans and see if they can identify it. If the ship has gone to their universe, they will have to be the ones to hunt it down and kill it. If it is here and stealthed, they could take advantage of our shield being down. While a ship that size probably wouldn't be able to critically damage us before we destroyed them, they might damage some of our systems, which would be inconvenient."

"Sir!" the communications operator exclaimed. "The Shaitans have identified the interloper; they say it's the Terran ship *Vella Gulf*, sir. The Shaitans are bringing their ships closer to ours for mutual defense and are sending a shuttle over to discuss the destruction of the Terran ship. Apparently, their ruler has put out an order to destroy it on sight."

Calvin slid back from the grate and crawled over to Paxton.

"Go contact the bugs," Calvin said. "The Shaitans are sending over a delegation. See if they know where a conference is likely to be held and ask them to take me there as soon as possible!"

Bridge, TSS *Vella Gulf*, Anti-Kepler-186 System, December 18, 2021

"It appears the civilization is another Sila outpost," Steropes said. "The buildings look similar to architecture we have seen them use in the past, anyway."

"Understood," the CO replied. "Probably friendly-ish, but we would have to do some diplomacy with them first. If we end up having time, I would like to go down and see if we can round up some of the unobtanium metal needed to make jump modules. Emperor Yazhak was nice enough to restock us with missiles, but without the metal we can't make them jump like the Shaitans' missiles do."

"The Shaitans may be doing the same thing," Steropes said. "There is a destroyer in orbit and a shuttle on the surface."

"Why would they be doing that?"

"The Ssselipsssiss ambassador mentioned there had been several battles since we left; perhaps the Shaitans need to resupply their ships."

"Do you suppose they have replicators that can make replacement missiles?"

"Probably not on the destroyer," Steropes said. "We barely have room for ours, and it can't make missiles. I don't know if the Shaitans have replicator technology, but even if they do, I doubt the destroyer would have one."

"Do you suppose the Jotunn could make missiles for the Shaitans?" Lieutenant Rrower asked.

"Unknown," Steropes replied; "however, it is unlikely the Shaitans would give the Jotunn the unobtanium necessary to make their jumping missiles. If anything, they would probably add it later."

"True," Captain Sheppard agreed. "They haven't given the Jotunn the ability to jump to their universe; giving them the metal would get them one step closer to being able to do it on their own." He thought for a second, then asked, "So, you think they are resupplying?"

"I believe that to be a near certainty," Steropes replied. "In addition to the shuttle, there is also a blast crater in the center of the nearest city to where they landed. It looks like the Shaitans dropped an orbital bombardment round on the city."

"They sure know how to win friends and influence people," Night said. "Hey, sir, if you'd like to take care of the destroyer, I'd be happy to go down to the surface and kick their butts. Maybe the locals would be so thankful they'd give us whatever the Shaitans were stealing."

"While I might want to have whatever the Shaitans are collecting, it would expose us to a lot of unnecessary risk," Captain Sheppard replied. "With most of our weapons ports blocked with stealth modules, we can't be sure we'd destroy it in the first volley."

"True," Night agreed, "but couldn't you bring the ship to point-blank range, like right behind the destroyer, and blast its motors? That way, they couldn't escape. If you had to hit them again, you could."

"Okay, say we disable the destroyer. Then what?"

"While you check out the other universe, we fly down in a shuttle, steal their stuff and wait for you to get back."

"So you're going to steal what they're already stealing? I'm not sure that will endear us to the locals."

"Well, we'll ask nicely," Night said with a grin. "I can be very persuasive when I want to; maybe the Sila would just give it to us if I asked nicely. Even if they don't, that's one less destroyer we have to fight and fewer troopers. In fact, with the shuttle on the planet, the destroyer is probably undermanned at the moment. Besides, there's no way they'd be expecting an attack; they're probably not even at their battle stations."

"Solomon, if we moved behind the Shaitan destroyer, what are the odds you could hit the ship's engines with the first volley of graser fire?"

"If we match their course and speed, I forecast an 87.8 percent probability of hitting their engineering spaces," the AI replied, "with a 63.6 percent chance of totally disabling the destroyer."

"*If* we do this," Captain Sheppard said, "we may be on the run when we come back. You'll need to get down and back *fast*."

"I understand, sir," Night replied. "I think it's a necessary risk; having some unobtanium gives us a big advantage against the Jotunn, and an even bigger edge when we fight the Shaitans."

The captain paused a moment, considering. "Okay," he said finally; "get the platoon ready. We'll send the shuttle down to see what you can forage while we go check out the other system. No delays are to be tolerated, though. I need you to get down there and back ASAP."

"Yes, sir," Night said. "They'll never know we were there."

* * * * *

Chapter Sixteen

"Their leader says this is where they usually bring visitors when they come," Paxton whispered, nodding at the bug that had led them to the vent they were peering through. Calvin had no idea if it actually was Zeeelbit; he couldn't tell them apart and had no idea how the Ssselipsssiss could. The room below them certainly *looked* like a conference room; it held an oversized table and enormous chairs along one side of it.

"Can you record what they say?" Calvin asked.

"Yes sir," Paxton replied. "The quality won't be very good, though."

"That's fine."

Regardless of the position the bug held in its society, Calvin saw it had been correct; two Shaitans were led into the room, followed by Captain Magnusson. This was Calvin's first opportunity to study live Shaitans, and he was struck by how much the epithet 'cowtaur,' fit them. The aliens looked like a cross between a cow and a centaur, with the body of a full-grown bull and an upper half that was somewhat humanoid in appearance, except that they had four arms to go with their four legs. They also had four eyes, with two of them on stalks that protruded from their heads.

Both of the Shaitans wore sashes covered with silvery emblems; one was a pale blue and the other red. The Shaitan in blue introduced himself in Jotunn as Captain Tectamus of the Shaitan ship *Tarachos*; he also introduced the Shaitan in red as Fleet Admiral Zeontes.

"Welcome to the *Falcon*," Captain Magnusson said. "What is so important you needed to come here yourselves?"

"We recognized the pictures of the enemy ship you sent us," Captain Tectamus replied. "We have come to make sure you know how important it is for that ship to be destroyed."

"Why is that?"

"The ship is called the *Vella Gulf*," Captain Tectamus said. "As you are aware, it is a Terran vessel, and our high lord has decreed all Terran vessels must be destroyed. This ship, however, must be destroyed *immediately*, due to crimes its crew committed."

"What crimes are those?"

"That ship can jump between the universes and is responsible for the destruction of several of our ships," Captain Tectamus replied. "I believe it was involved in the destruction of several Jotunn vessels, as well."

"So, it is true," the Jotunn captain said. "There are rumors in our fleet that another race had acquired the ability to jump between universes like you can...an ability that is still denied us."

"Yes, they can," Captain Tectamus said, "and we are unable to determine where it is now. We have a destroyer in the other universe on a resupply mission; it has not seen the ship."

"Then the Terrans also must have the ability to cloak themselves."

"How does a ship cloak itself?"

"With great difficulty," Captain Magnusson replied. "I'm sure we could tell you more if you were to explain to us the secret behind jumping between the two universes."

"The high lord has decreed that technology will not be shared. If you give us the secret of cloaking, however, I will send back to ask for permission to give you the secrets of our jump modules."

"I will consider it," the Jotunn replied, "but my leader has forbidden the transfer of any additional technology until you give us the secret of your jump modules."

"I see," Captain Tectamus said, his eye stalks twitching. "This reluctance to share your knowledge with us will not sit well with the high lord. I suspect several of your planets will suffer because of it."

"If that happens again, there will be war between our civilizations," Captain Magnusson warned. "My leaders will dissolve our alliance."

"That is for our leaders to discuss, I suppose," Captain Tectamus said. "At the moment, I am more worried about finding and destroying the *Vella Gulf.* If we do not, our lives will be forfeit."

"Whose lives?" Captain Magnusson asked.

"If the ship is not destroyed, it will cost the lives of everyone in this system, yours as well as ours. You are now aware of the requirement to destroy the Terran ship; if you fail to do so, the high lord will order your destruction too."

"And how exactly would he be able to carry out such a decree?"

"If you do not assist us, you can be sure that we will destroy your ships ourselves."

"Your three little ships are going to destroy our two battlecruisers?" The Jotunn captain began laughing. When he stopped, he added, "I do not think you have the ability. We are well aware of how you fight."

"Do not test us, Jotunn."

"And do not threaten me, Shaitan."

"You are both missing the point," Admiral Zeontes said, speaking for the first time. "There is an enemy in this system. Regardless of any potential consequences, that enemy *must* be destroyed. Are you able to find the *Vella Gulf* while it is cloaked?"

"Probably not," Captain Magnusson admitted, "but I will go tell my crew to be on the lookout for it." The Jotunn CO left.

The door shut, and Calvin watched as the two Shaitans turned to face each other and began communicating in a far more animated way than they had previously with the Jotunn officer. Whatever they were saying seemed incredibly important.

Unfortunately, they switched back to their own language, and Calvin couldn't understand a thing.

Bridge, TSS *Vella Gulf*, Anti-Kepler-186 System, December 18, 2021

"Stand by to fire," Captain Sheppard said. It had taken time to maneuver into position, but the *Vella Gulf* was finally ready, and the Shaitans had given no indication they knew the Terrans were there. "Let me know when all available weapons are locked onto the destroyer's engineering spaces."

"All available weapons are locked," the Offensive Systems Officer (OSO) announced.

"De-cloak!" the CO ordered. "*Fire all weapons!*"

"De-cloaking!" the duty engineer replied.

"Firing!" the OSO added.

Coherent light and missiles leapt from the *Vella Gulf* to lash the smaller ship. Over half of the *Gulf's* missile and graser ports were blocked by the stealth modules, but it was enough. Three of the ship's grasers drilled eight-foot-wide holes through the destroyer's aft section, followed by four anti-ship missile strikes moments later.

"The Shaitan destroyer has been disabled," Solomon noted.

"Thank you," Captain Sheppard said. "Launch the shuttle while we finish it off."

"Shuttle launching," the squadron duty officer, Lieutenant Mike 'Retro' Burke, confirmed.

"The destroyer has been…well, it's been destroyed," the OSO announced after several more volleys. "Should I slag the shuttle that's down on the surface of the planet?"

"No, we want what they're collecting," the CO replied. "Destroying the shuttle might defeat the whole purpose of the assault. Stealth us up and take us back to our universe."

"Stealth coming…now," the duty engineer replied.

"Back to our universe, aye," the helmsman added. "Here we go!"

Bridge, TSS *Vella Gulf*, Kepler-186 System, December 18, 2021

"System entry back into the Kepler-186 system," Steropes announced.

"Contact!" the defensive systems officer (DSO) called. "I've got a cluster of ships on the far side of the planet."

"Can you tell what they're doing?" Captain Sheppard asked.

"Not from here," the DSO replied. "There is a large amount of activity, though. Both the Jotunn and the Shaitan seem to be dropping orbital bombardment rounds on the planet, but they don't seem to be taking any fire in return. There are a number of shuttles active as well."

"Helm, take us away from the planet and then around to the other side so we can see what's going on. Not too close to any of the Jotunn ships."

"Aye aye, sir!" the helmsman replied. "Further out and then around to the other side, aye!"

"Sir, we're already in range of almost all of their weapons," the DSO said. "If they see us, I won't be able to stop everything they can send our way. Even their light stuff can hit us here. If we get even closer to them..."

"Then the duty engineer better not let the stealth module fail," Captain Sheppard replied. "And the helmsman had better keep us out of the flight paths of any of their shuttles, too."

The color drained from the faces of both junior officers seated at the front table.

"And just in case," Captain Sheppard added, "Solomon, please be ready to jump us back to the other universe at a moment's notice if either of those things looks likely to happen."

Ducting, Jotunn Ship *Falcon*, Kepler-186, December 18, 2021

The Shaitan officers became silent as the Jotunn captain returned to the room.

"I have instructed my crew to watch for the *Vella Gulf*," Captain Magnusson said. "I am, however, somewhat concerned about what its presence portends; a Terran attack may be imminent. We are having problems with our shields, and I do not want to go into battle without them. They are operational at the moment, but have failed twice. We appear to have something in our ducting chewing on the wires. We need to withdraw temporarily to have the ducts cleaned and the shields repaired."

"That is unacceptable," Captain Tectamus replied. "You must remain here and help us destroy the *Vella Gulf*."

"I'm not sure what you intend for us to do," Captain Magnusson said. "We cannot locate them any more than you can; in fact, you can probably do it better. If they have gone to your universe, they are beyond our reach. We can't jump into your universe. Even if we did find the ship, it is unlikely they would fight us; we are much larger and would annihilate them easily. They have to know this."

"If you allow the *Vella Gulf* to escape, the high lord will be angry. Trust me, you do not want the high lord angry at you. He always has his revenge."

"Our Odin has promised our aid to you, but we will be handicapped in an assault if our shields don't work. You can always jump back to your universe and escape. We cannot. We will come back and fight at your side; however, we need to get our shields fixed. We will also return with more ships in case there is an assault. It is only a few days to our home world; we will be back in eight or nine days, and we can finish destroying the Ssselipsssiss then."

"We're screwed," Calvin said, sliding back from the grating.

"Why's that?" Farhome asked.

"We're going further behind enemy lines. The Jotunn are returning to their home world to clean out the ducting. Apparently the plan worked…too well."

"I've never been to Jotunheimr."

"Yeah," Calvin replied, "neither have I. But this isn't how I wanted to get there."

Cockpit, *Shuttle 01*, Anti-Kepler-186 System, December 18, 2021

"Y ou seeing that?" asked the shuttle's pilot, Lieutenant Tom 'Harv' Walsh.

"If you're asking if I see that parts of the city are burning, yeah, I see it," Lieutenant Daniel 'Admiral' Walker replied. "It'd be pretty hard to miss; half the freaking city's on fire."

"Think we ought to tell the guys in back?"

"Yeah, probably." Lieutenant Walker switched to his comm. "*It looks like the Shaitans aren't making any friends on the surface. About half of the nearby city appears to be on fire.*"

"*Anything going on near our landing zone?*" Night asked.

"*Not that we can see from here,*" Lieutenant Walker replied. "*Looks like there may be some fighting to the east, though. One minute 'til touchdown.*"

"*Understood,*" Night replied. "*Land at the shuttle. We'll take it from there.*"

Cargo Bay, *Shuttle 01*, Anti-Kepler-186 System, December 18, 2021

"*L*ooks like things are hot on the surface," Night commed on the platoon frequency. "*The flight crew said the city to the east of our landing zone is on fire. Expect the situation to be fluid; neither side will recognize us, so you can expect both of them to shoot first and ask questions later.*"

"*The locals are fighting back?*" Lieutenant Contreras asked.

"*I don't know for sure, but I can tell you that if some damned cow-looking creatures landed on* my *planet, stole* my *shit and then burned* my *town, they would be on the receiving end of some laser fire.*"

"*Only if my trident ran out of antimatter first,*" Lieutenant O'Leary added.

"*I don't want anyone to take chances,*" Night warned. "*The locals may or may not be friendly to us, but they're probably going to be primed to kill anyone who doesn't look like them. While I'd rather* not *kill them if we didn't have to, I'd rather kill them than lose any of our folks.*"

Night paused to let the guidance sink in, then continued, "*Here's what we're going to do. Lieutenant Contreras, I want you to take the Space Force and seize the Shaitan shuttle. If you can capture any Shaitans, do so, but do not take any casualties. Put them down if they resist.*"

"*It would be my pleasure!*"

"*Once the shuttle is secure, see if they have anything we can use. If so, transport it back to our shuttle.*"

"*Yes sir!*"

"*Lieutenant O'Leary, I want you to take the Ground Force and secure the area to the east of the shuttle. I want to be ready for when the Shaitans return; prepare positions and wipe them out.*"

"*Yes sir. Nothing would make me happier.*"

"*Ten seconds!*" Lieutenant Walker interrupted from the flight deck. The cargo ramp started down.

"*Any questions?*" Night asked as the ground rushed up to meet them. Silence ruled the net.

The shuttle slammed into the ground in a combat touchdown. The struts absorbed some, but not all, of the controlled crash.

"*Go! Go! Go!*" Lieutenant O'Leary yelled as the troops punched their quick release buttons, stood up and charged down the ramp.

Night watched from the shuttle ramp as the Space Force sprinted toward the alien shuttle. It was red and looked like a 200-foot long brick sitting on skids in the forest clearing. The only distinguishing features were some sort of glass-like canopy for the cockpit and a large ramp that extended from its starboard side. They had either caught the Shaitans napping or unaware; four of his soldiers made it onto the ramp before it began closing.

Night could no longer see the Ground Force; they had disappeared into the forest almost immediately. The shuttles rested in a forest clearing little larger than the two shuttles, and Night could almost touch the foliage from the cargo ramp. The trees looked like the vegetation artists drew in dinosaur pictures; huge, frond-like leaves effectively blocked all vision into the forest beyond a few meters. He could still track the troops on his in-head display, though, and they appeared to be maintaining good formation. Everything appeared to be going so well, he wasn't surprised when the comm system came to life.

"*Captain Train, we've got a problem.*"

* * * * *

Chapter Seventeen

Shaitan Shuttle, Anti-Kepler-186 'e', December 18, 2021

*"F*ollow me!*"* Staff Sergeant Alan 'Arty' Isom commed as he raced toward the boarding ramp. Last to load on the Terran shuttle, his fire team was the first out, and the first to reach the alien vessel. Built for Shaitans, the shuttle's boarding ramp was 15 feet wide and less steep than a similar Terran one would have been. And it was still down; maybe they didn't know the Terrans were coming. *"Quickly! Before they raise the ramp!"*

He had no more said it, and the ramp started up, forcing him to grab hold of the side to regain his balance. He checked his in-head display as he continued up the 30-foot ramp; Sergeant Margaret 'Witch' Andrews and Sergeant Austin 'Good Twin' Gordon were right behind, along with Sergeant Steph 'Valkyrie' Taylor from the third fire team. The fire team's cyborg, Sergeant Ken 'Boom' Weinert, hadn't made it to the ramp. Stupid cyborgs were just too darn slow.

He slowed when he reached the top of the ramp and Witch ran into him from behind as the ramp continued to rise behind him.

"Go, mon!" the Jamaican commed on the fire team's net. *"We not be havin' much time."*

Arty looked left and saw the cargo bay, stuffed nearly deck to ceiling with crates and containers. *"To the right!"* he commed. He sprinted up the passage, narrowly avoiding Good Twin and Valkyrie as they were forced to run down the ramp and into the vessel.

The passage turned to the left and Arty scarcely slowed as he negotiated the corner. The natural light was quickly dimming as the ramp shut behind him, and he barely had time to see the Shaitan before he ran into it at full speed.

Although Arty had seen pictures of Shaitans, they didn't do justice to just how enormous the aliens actually were. Especially if you ran into one at full speed. Bigger than a full-grown Hereford bull, the creature massed over 2,000 pounds, and the force of the collision threw Arty sideways to the deck; the alien hardly shuddered.

Witch drew up short, barely avoiding running into the Shaitan. She tried to bring her rifle into line with the enemy, but the Shaitan was just as fast and grabbed the barrel of the rifle with its upper pair of arms. The lower pair of arms reached toward a pair of pistols attached to the harness it was wearing.

Witch screamed as the alien twisted the rifle from her hands. Taller than the Terran by almost two feet, the creature used its leverage to bend her over backward as it twisted, and she could feel herself losing her footing.

The Shaitan's pistols came clear of their holsters.

"Move, damn it!" Good Twin yelled.

Without looking, Witch released the rifle and threw herself to the side. Good Twin fired his rifle at the Shaitan's head, but the creature ducked, and the laser bolt only succeeded in severing one of the alien's eye stalks.

The creature emitted a high-pitched scream, and Good Twin's second shot caught it in the chest as it bucked up off its front legs. If the shot fazed the beast, it wasn't apparent. The Shaitan's front legs landed on the deck and its pistols turned toward its tormentor.

Arty crashed into the creature's arms from the side, and the shots went wide. One shot hit the bulkhead next to Good Twin's head, and the metal sizzled from the plasma's impact.

Good Twin aimed and shot the alien in the head with a long blast. The creature's legs went out from under it, and the Shaitan collapsed onto the deck, its torso coming to rest on top of Arty.

"Let's go, mon," Witch said, taking hold of one of Arty's arms and pulling him out from under the creature.

"I think I'm…done," Arty said. The hole in his chest still smoked from where the plasma burst from the second pistol had hit him. His head rolled to the side.

"He saved my life," Good Twin said, looking down at Arty's body.

The ship vibrated as one of its motors came to life.

"You can thank him later, mon," Witch replied. "Right now, we need to be finding the pilots before they take us to space in 'dis piece of shit."

Bridge, TSS *Vella Gulf*, Kepler-186 System, December 18, 2021

"Oh my," Steropes gasped.

"What is it?" Captain Sheppard asked.

"I think I know what the Shaitans are doing, sir. I believe they are systematically exterminating the Ssselipsssiss."

"What do you mean?"

"Well, they've been dropping a large number of bombardment rounds…"

"Yes," Captain Sheppard replied. "We know that. What makes you think they're exterminating the Ssselipsssiss?"

Steropes pushed a button on his console, and the front screen illuminated to show a picture of the surface of the planet. A dark spot on the planet flashed, and was replaced with a large mushroom cloud. "That was their last bombardment round."

"So?" Captain Sheppard asked.

"Here's the target, under greater magnification." He pushed a button, and the picture on the screen zoomed in on the dark stain. Thousands of Ssselipsssiss milled about inside a pen about 1,500 feet in diameter. Shaitan robots could periodically be seen around the edge of the pen. Not many, but enough to prevent the unarmed lizards from escaping.

The screen flashed again, and a mushroom cloud took the place of the pen.

"That was the second such target I observed," Steropes noted. "I didn't believe it the first time. How can a race be so…unfeeling? It's not like they're harvesting the Ssselipsssiss for some reason…they just seem to be systematically exterminating them. We have counted over 70 bombardment round strikes since we arrived. So many dead…I think I may need a few moments…"

"Damn," Captain Sheppard said under his breath as the screen turned off. "Go ahead and take a break. We'll fill in for you." Captain Sheppard understood Steropes' discomfort. He felt like he was going to throw up. Louder, he added, "Well, if nothing else, that makes the decision of whether or not to destroy their planet a little easier. Suddenly, I don't feel quite so badly about it."

The bridge was silent as the crew tried to rid their minds of what they had just seen.

Captain Sheppard thought for a moment then had a disturbing idea. "I may have made a mistake leaving the platoon in the other universe," he announced. "We need to find out if Lieutenant Commander Hobbs is still alive down there. If so, we're going to have to go back and get Captain Train to put together an assault." He shook his head. What a dumb idea it had been to leave the platoon in the other universe.

"Comms officer, trail a line outside the cloaking field," Captain Sheppard ordered. "I want to transmit a pulse and find out if Lieutenant Commander Hobbs is still alive."

"Streaming a line, sir," the communications officer replied. "When we transmit, there will be a risk of the pulse being intercepted. They may even be able to triangulate where the pulse originated."

"I understand that," the CO replied, "but we have to know. We can't leave him down there to be on the receiving end of one of those rounds."

"Transmitting...now."

Overhead the Bridge, Jotunn Ship *Falcon*, Kepler-186, December 18, 2021

Calvin jumped like he had received an electric shock as his comm set came to life. "*Lieutenant Commander Hobbs, this is the* Vella Gulf. *We are in-system for recovery. Please transmit your location if able.*"

One of the Jotunn below him jumped like he had received the same shock. "Sir! I just received an unknown transmission."

"Did you get a good fix on it?" Captain Magnusson asked. "Pass the coordinates to the weapons operator and fire on it before the ship moves!"

"I'm sorry sir, but it was a burst transmission. Without some other ships to help triangulate it, I won't be able to narrow it down on just the one pulse."

"Watch that frequency then," Captain Magnusson ordered. "If the signal comes back, try to locate its source so we can fire on them. Maybe we'll get lucky and kill their stealth generator. And if the gods really favor us, we'll disable their ability to jump to the other universe to get away from us." He smiled, savoring the chance to kill the untouchable ship...and maybe get a look at whatever machine helped the other races jump between the universes.

"All I got was just that one pulse," the technician replied. "There hasn't been anything else since."

"It is possible they were signaling another ship," the CO mused, "which may indicate a possible counterattack by the Terrans or the Ssselipsssiss." He paused as he considered, then he added, "Hel take the damn Shaitans. I am not going to sit here and let the Ssselipsssiss catch us unprepared. Navigator, set a course for Jotunheimr. Best speed. We're going to go get our shields fixed and come back with additional forces."

Calvin rolled away from the gate, trying to think. He was screwed. The *Gulf* had come back, and it was so close...and yet, so very far away. There was no way they could hope to get close enough to get a shuttle over to him. The *Falcon* would blast it as soon as it became visible. Worse, the *Gulf* wouldn't have any idea he was still alive, and they would go on their way to look for the Dark Star, leaving Calvin to return to the home world of the Jotunn. Where he would be killed by whatever process the giants used to de-louse the ducting.

He was going to die like a roach caught in a bug bomb.

If he only had a way to let the crew of the *Gulf* know he was okay...but he didn't. As soon as he commed back in reply, the Jotunn would realize there was an enemy in the ducting. What they currently saw as a "Get rid of when convenient" problem would become a "Get rid of now" problem, and the Jotunn and their robots would come up into the ducting looking for them. They might be able to hide and escape detection...but probably not.

He needed another plan.

Task Force O'Leary, Anti-Kepler-186 'e', December 18, 2021

"*D*o you see them?" Gunnery Sergeant Jerry 'Wolf' Stasik asked.

Not through this damn forest, Lieutenant O'Leary thought as he ducked under one of the large fern leaves. The foliage had slowed their progress to a crawl; invisibility did you no good if the enemy could see you pushing aside the leaves as you passed. "*Yeah, I see them,*" he commed, coming around a massive trunk. "*Don't get any closer. We don't want to spook them.*"

The locals looked like the other Silas he had seen. They were generally humanoid, but their knees pointed backwards, like birds.

He switched to the command net. "*Captain Train, we've got a problem. I'm looking at about 30 locals in prepared positions.*"

"*Can you take them?*" Night asked.

"*We're behind them, so yeah, we could wipe them all out pretty easily. I doubt any of them would even get a shot off. That's not the problem. What I'm worried about is that they're obviously waiting for the Shaitans to return, and they're armed with what looks like some kind of crossbow. Even though they have good hiding positions overlooking the trail, they're going to get creamed by the Shaitans' plasma weapons."*

"I'm not sure how that affects us. Let them fight it out. If the Shaitans win, kill them. If the locals win, try to negotiate with them afterwards."

"Cap'n, I'm for helping the locals. They're just trying to get some payback for what the Shaitans did to their city. They've got to know that they don't stand a chance, yet they're willing to take the cowtaurs on anyway."

"Have they seen you?"

"No sir, not yet."

"Use your best judgment. I've gotta go—it looks like the Shaitan shuttle is about to take off with some of our troops inside. Train, out."

Okay, he had permission. Now what? How do you tactfully approach a group of civilians who are primed to kill anyone who doesn't look like them without getting shot? He really didn't want to go back to the shuttle looking like a pin cushion.

"Hey, Lieutenant O'Leary," Staff Sergeant Brian 'Huge' Mchugh commed, *"I just saw one of the locals pouring something onto his arrowhead. I think they may be poisoning them."*

"Understood." Great. Becoming a pin cushion was suddenly the least of his worries.

"Wolf, take Fire Team One and go up the trail about a quarter mile so we know when the Shaitans are coming." That way he wouldn't have to dodge plasma at the same time he was avoiding poisoned bolts.

"Yes sir. Are we going to help the locals?" Wolf asked, his tone hopeful.

"Yeah, if I can figure out a way to do it without getting my ass shot off." He surveyed the ambush site again. He didn't know much about how the

Sila reacted to stress, but the ones in the ambush didn't appear to be exhibiting any of the emotions that humans in their place might have. They didn't look scared or act apprehensive; they just appeared focused on what they were doing.

Maybe they were too pissed off to be scared, kind of like what I'd be if someone had just dropped an orbital round on my home town.

He shook his head. Thinking about it any longer wouldn't make it better. There was one a little further back from the rest. Might as well start with the leader. He strode over to stand five feet in front of the Sila. The leader felt or heard something from his passage, and he began to look around wildly.

O'Leary nullified his invisibility and held up his hands. "I'm here to help you in your fight."

The Sila jumped backward, falling to the ground as he tripped over a branch. Hearing O'Leary or the commotion of their leader, the rest of the Sila turned and aimed their weapons at O'Leary, who stood as motionless as he could.

"I'm here to help you," O'Leary repeated. "Can you understand what I'm saying?"

The leader picked himself up off the ground and turned to the Terran. "Your accent is odd, and your appearance sudden, but if you're truly here to help, you are most welcome." He waved at the rest of his men, who lowered their weapons fractionally.

"*Shaitans inbound,*" Wolf commed. "*Looks to be at least 25 of them.*"

Damn. That was more than he'd hoped for. "*Copy. Follow them back so you can hit them from behind when I tell you, but not so close that they hear you.*"

"*We're on 'em. See you soon. Wolf out.*"

"We have to hurry," Lieutenant O'Leary said. "They are almost here."

"You are in that much of a hurry to go to your death?" the Sila asked.

"Not today." He cancelled the squad's invisibility. "Nor are my men." Several of the Sila jumped in surprise as the squad materialized in their midst. "I'm hoping that if we surprise them, we can kill them all without taking any casualties."

A Sila burst out of the forest and dove behind a log. "They come!" he exclaimed.

O'Leary reengaged the Terrans' invisibility as the first Shaitan came pounding down the path.

Ducting, Jotunn Ship *Falcon*, Kepler-186, December 18, 2021

"My ship, the *Vella Gulf*, just contacted me," Calvin said to the assembled group of Farhome, the Ssselipsssiss and Zeeelbit, the leader of the bugs; "they're here, in-system. I need a way to contact them."

"Can't you just contact them the same way they contacted you?" Zeeelbit asked.

"I could," Calvin replied, "but I'm worried the Jotunn would intercept my transmission. While they *probably* couldn't break the encryption on it, they *would* be able to tell the transmission came from this ship, and I'm sure they'd come looking for me. In fact, I doubt they'd stop until they found me. This could have some pretty serious repercussions, not only for us, but for your society as well."

"You're right," Paxton said. "They probably could intercept it; I could, anyway, if I had my normal equipment." He paused, then added, "You need a way of signaling them, without actually signaling them."

"Yeah," Calvin agreed. "Got one of those in your bag of tricks?"

"Sadly, no," the Ssselipsssiss replied. "Standard loadout for a planetary mission would have at least two methods of surreptitious communication, but I don't have a normal loadout. I only have what I could gather from my training equipment."

"Any ideas?"

"We could try a mass assault on the bridge," Burkuri replied. "If we hit them by surprise, we might be able to capture and hold it long enough for your forces to rescue us. It might be possible if the S'nark helped us."

"We might be able to overwhelm the bridge crew," Calvin agreed, "but there's too many variables for what could go wrong after that. What if they can shift control to an auxiliary control station? They just tell the computer to transfer the conn, and then all of a sudden we've got nothing. They can come in and kill us at will. Even if we *could* hold it, my ship is a cruiser, and a Terran one at that. It wouldn't stand a chance against this ship. My CO wouldn't bring the ship into weapons range of this ship unless he absolutely had to; it would be suicide. Even sending a shuttle would be foolish. If I were there, I would have to advise him against it."

"I am against anything that would upset our status quo with the giants," Zeeelbit said. "While our lives are imperfect here, at least the giants tolerate us living above them. It is unacceptable for you to do something which will cause them to attack us."

"I don't get it, then," Burkuri said. "If you would tell your captain not to rescue us, what is the point of contacting him? All we would do is give away our presence. It would be better to remain silent and hope to find a way to escape later."

"That's what I'm saying," Calvin said. "We can't afford to alert the Jotunn we're here."

"So we're still going to Jotunheimr?" Farhome asked, his voice hopeful.

"Not if I can help it," Calvin replied. "The further we go into Jotunn territory, the smaller our chances of being recovered. We need to get a message to the *Gulf*. There has to be a way."

"So how do we do it?" the female Ssselipssssiss asked.

"I don't know," Calvin replied. He sighed. "I just don't know."

"We could turn off their shields again," Karver said. "If we did that, and we assaulted the bridge, maybe they would come close enough for us to steal a shuttle and meet them before the Jotunn could break into the bridge."

"That's stupid," Burkuri said. "How are the people holding the bridge going to escape?"

"I'll hold the bridge, and the rest of you can go without me."

"That'll never work," Burkuri said. "If we're all needed to assault the bridge, who's going to steal the shuttle? Not only that, the Jotunn will destroy the shuttle before it gets 100 kilometers from the ship." She hissed in frustration. "We don't have time for this. What if you just shut up and leave the strategy planning to people who haven't already donated their brains to the repair lab?"

"No," Calvin said; "Karver's right. That's perfect."

"What?" Burkuri asked, stunned. "Stealing a shuttle at the same time everyone's assaulting the bridge?"

"No, you were right; that part will never work. What *will* work is the shield idea. If we do this right, we can use the shield to signal my ship. We'll just need a distraction, but I think it can be done."

Farhome's face fell. "Does that mean we won't be going to Jotunheimr?"

"It's too early to tell," Calvin said, "but I have something for you that might be a lot of fun."

"Better than a trip to Jotunheimr?"

"Absolutely. If nothing else, it will be *very* exciting…"

Bridge, TSS *Vella Gulf,* Kepler-186 System, December 18, 2021

"Huh," the DSO muttered. "That's odd."

"Could you be a little more descriptive?" Captain Sheppard asked. "You know how much I don't like odd things."

"Uh, yes sir. I was watching the enemy ships, and the Jotunn ships just broke orbit. It looks like they're heading out-system."

"They're not just going to a higher orbit?"

"No sir. They're pulling out and away."

"The DSO is correct," Steropes added. "Their engines have come to full power, and their speed continues to build. They are definitely leaving orbit."

"Any idea where they're headed?" Captain Sheppard asked. "Do you suppose they intercepted our transmission and are looking for us?

"If they're looking for us," Steropes replied, "they're going the wrong way; in fact, they are headed in nearly the opposite direction."

"Maybe their direction finding gear is broken," the duty engineer guessed. "I mean, machinery breaks, right? Ours does; theirs must too."

"*If* they intercepted our transmission, which is statistically possible but unlikely, it is even more unlikely they would be looking for us in the direction they are proceeding. The Jotunn are headed at a right angle to the plane of the ecliptic; beyond a comet or two, there isn't anything to be found on that heading. I believe they have other intentions than searching for us."

"Maybe they're afraid of us?" the helmsman asked. "You know, because we can jump back and forth, and they can't? The Jotunn probably heard how we kicked their asses in Golirion and are running from us."

"I rather doubt a ship that size is running from us," the CO replied. "Barring a lucky shot that hits something vital, they could probably absorb everything we shot at them and keep going. All they need is one lucky shot on us, though, and we're done. No; that isn't it. Steropes, got any ideas on where they're headed?"

"No sir, not without more information."

"Want me to follow them?" the helmsman asked.

"If we don't begin pursuit immediately," Steropes said, "we will have a hard time catching up with them. They are continuing to accelerate at a significant rate."

"Is there anything significant in the direction they're heading?" Captain Sheppard asked.

"No sir," Steropes replied. "There are no planets, mapped stargates or anything else significant on that bearing."

"So they're probably heading for a stargate we don't know about?"

"That is the likeliest option. The ephemeris information we have from the Ssselipsssiss is extremely deficient. The only stargates listed are the ones they wanted us to follow to the Dark Star. They provided nothing more than the minimum necessary for us to accomplish their task."

"Well, keep an eye on them, then. We know next to nothing about this system; it would be helpful to know where the exits are, if nothing else."

"So we're not going to follow them?" the helmsman asked.

"No. Not with troops on the planet in the other universe. In fact, once we get a good idea which direction they're headed, we need to jump back and pick them up. Who knows what kind of trouble our folks will get into if we leave them there too long?"

Outside the Shaitan Shuttle, Anti-Kepler-186 'e', December 18, 2021

"Should we shoot it?" Sergeant Anne 'Fox' Stasik commed. *"It looks like it's about to lift."* Like the rest of the squad, she had her rifle aimed at the shuttle but wasn't sure if she should pull the trigger.

"Hell, yes!" Night replied. *"Shoot its damn motors! Don't let it take off!"*

"I don't see any motors!" several troopers commed at once.

"Switch to thermal and shoot at anything hot! If that doesn't work, shoot the damn canopy!"

The troops began firing, but Night could see they were having little effect. The ship was obviously a combat shuttle, and its armor shrugged off most of the platoon's lighter weapons. Similarly, the canopy was built to withstand micro-meteoroid strikes; it was also impervious to the Terran's lasers.

"*Fire in the hole!*" Sergeant Ken 'Boom' Weinert warned as the shuttle lifted from the ground. He fired, and the round left a phosphorescent trail as it streaked toward the alien shuttle. The round detonated spectacularly on the side of the ship with a flash of gold and silver that left afterimages on the troops' retinas. Pieces of shell made a starburst pattern like an enormous firework exploding as they flew off with a brilliant golden iridescent glare. The round left a burning hole in the side of the shuttle, with a spider web of molten lines extending out from it. The engine noise diminished, and the shuttle crashed down onto its skids.

"*Nice shot, Weinert,*" Night commed. "*What the hell was that?*"

"*High-velocity discarding sabot round, sir,*" the trooper replied. "*The core of the projectile was filled with silver.*"

That explained why the metal was still burning down the side of the shuttle, Night thought. Silver, and the other metals in that period of the periodic table, were unstable in this universe and reacted explosively when they were introduced.

Motion caught Night's eyes. Two tubes extended on a metal framework from the top of the shuttle. One spun in the direction of the cyborg; the other toward the largest concentration of troops. "*Look out!*" he yelled.

Shaitan Shuttle, Anti-Kepler-186 'e', December 18, 2021

"Come on, mon," Witch said. The roar of the shuttle's engines got louder as the second motor came to life. "We got to find the cockpit."

"Which way is that?" Valkyrie asked.

"No idea. Forward some place. Let's go." She turned and sprinted up the passageway, Good Twin and Valkyrie close behind. The passage ran toward the front of the shuttle without any more turns, ending suddenly in a blank wall.

"Shit! Where be the door, mon?"

"Looks like the whole panel slides," Good Twin said, looking at the left side of the door. "You can see where it goes into the frame here."

"Well, try to figure out how to open it!" The shuttle tilted slightly as it lifted. "Now!"

"There's nothing on the door or on the wall near it," Good Twin replied.

"Got it!" exclaimed Valkyrie. She pointed to a small square cut into the bulkhead about five feet from the door. "Doesn't that look like a pressure plate?"

"I don't care what it be looking like, mon," Witch said; "just push the damn thing!"

"Okay," Valkyrie said with a shrug. "Here goes." She reached for the plate but was knocked to the deck as the shuttle crashed to the ground.

She climbed back to her knees. "Now!" she added as she slapped the plate.

Without a sound, the door retracted into the starboard bulkhead, allowing access into what was obviously the cockpit. Although the space was a 15-foot square, it seemed cramped with two of the Shaitans manning it, especially since each was wearing a six-point harness to hold it in place. At the front of the cockpit one of the cowtaurs stood furiously working what appeared to be the flight controls while looking out the cockpit window. All four hands were in motion, with its upper hands on a pair of flight controls and the other two pushing a variety of strange-looking buttons and switches on a slightly lower console.

The other Shaitan stood to the right. A dual monitor display was mounted on the bulkhead with the one on the left slightly higher than the one on the right. Its upper hands worked a set of controls beneath the left monitor while its lower pair operated a set of controls under the right monitor.

Both monitors showed pictures of the Terran forces surrounding the shuttle with a series of concentric circles around them; a group of three soldiers appeared on the left monitor, and a close-up view of Sergeant Weinert dominated the one on the right.

As Witch ran into the cockpit, the Shaitan threw a lever, and several plasma bursts walked up the cyborg's chest. The final one struck him in the face. Sergeant Weinert fell backward missing most of his head. The Shaitan threw a similar lever on the left side, and plasma bolts began exploding in the Terrans' midst. At least one plasma bolt hit a Kuji trooper, removing an arm and about half of its chest.

"*Bastard!*" Witch yelled as she leveled her rifle and began firing into the creature. Good Twin and Valkyrie joined in, moving to the left and right to get clear fields of fire into the creature.

The Shaitan screamed as the bolts hit, and all four eyes turned toward the Terrans. It kicked out behind it, and Good Twin was launched backward into the passageway.

Witch fired several more times into the creature's head, and the screaming stopped as the Shaitan collapsed to hang within its harness. The straps coming from the ceiling kept it from falling to the deck, and it blocked access to the other Shaitan.

Valkyrie dropped her rifle to hang from its sling and reached out to grab the Shaitan. Finding the creature had no tail, she grabbed its leg and pulled as hard as she could, and the corpse spun fractionally on its tether. It wasn't much, but it was enough to allow her passage, and she squeezed by the corpse to find the pilot still working the controls.

One of the eyestalks turned to look at her while it continued to work the shuttle's controls. Through the cockpit glass, Valkyrie could see the shuttle start to rise again.

Grabbing her rifle, she lifted it to within inches of the Shaitan's eye that had turned toward her.

"Set us down!" Valkyrie ordered.

The creature's four hands lifted from the controls, and Valkyrie was thrown from her feet again as the shuttle crashed to the ground again. She hit her head on the bulkhead behind her and was knocked unconscious, falling motionless to the deck.

The Shaitan unsnapped several of its tethers and stooped to pick up Valkyrie's rifle from where it had fallen.

"Don't even be tinkin' about it, mon," Witch said from the other side of the cockpit.

The creature's eyestalks whipped around toward Witch. Seeing the laser rifle leveled at it, the creature lifted its hands and held them away from the console.

Witch smiled. "Good beastie. I might not have to kill you after all."

Task Force O'Leary, Anti-Kepler-186 'e', December 18, 2021

O'Leary realized he had been wrong. Although the Sila didn't appear scared or nervous, they obviously were; several of the locals fired before the majority of the Shaitans entered the killing ground, prematurely alerting their enemies.

What could have been a nice little ambush blossomed into a massive free-for-all as cowtaurs dodged off the path on both sides, and a knot of eight Shaitans charged head-on at their attackers.

"*Fire!*" O'Leary ordered. At least his troops were still behind the locals so they didn't have to worry about getting a poisoned arrow in the back. All they had to worry about were the Shaitans' damn plasma weapons.

It seemed like the Shaitans were everywhere in the confining forest, and the streaks of plasma bolts flickered through the trees like thousands of tiny rainbows of death. Until they hit flesh, at which point they looked less like rainbows and more like hollow-point ammunition hitting home. The charged gas deposited its heat energy like a laser cutter, and the water in the Silas' flesh flash-boiled.

Blood exploded from the front rank of the locals in a spray of yellow as the Shaitans burst through their meager defenses, and the smell of charred flesh filled the air. Those Sila that didn't throw themselves to the side were ridden down, turned into paste under the claws of the cowtaurs.

As the lead group of Shaitans slowed to turn around for another attack, the Terrans' laser rifles joined in, blasting chunks from the Shaitans' bovine bodies in sprays of purple. Several of the Shaitans began their high-pitched keening as the lasers struck home, but most of them fought on, even after being wounded a number of times.

O'Leary did a quick scan. At least a third of the local forces were killed in the initial assault, and the Shaitans that had originally turned away from the ambush were turning back toward him. This was going south fast.

A Shaitan wearing a green sash charged at him, and he killed it with an extended blast through the head. The amount of energy required would have killed three Terrans. *"Aim for their heads!"* O'Leary commed. *"Wolf, hit 'em with everything you've got!"*

The Shaitans on the other side of the path paused as the force behind them began firing, raking them with focused blasts of laser fire and oversized antimatter grenades.

Lieutenant O'Leary killed a second Shaitan, then had to dive to the side as one of the others tried to run over the source of laser fire.

The Shaitan wheeled and turned back toward where O'Leary had landed. As the creature gathered itself to charge, one of its front legs suddenly separated at the knee joint, and the creature collapsed to the ground. The cowtaur struggled to rise, but a katana materialized in the side of the Shaitan's neck. The katana didn't completely sever the creature's neck, but it cut through far enough; the Shaitan dropped to the ground.

The threat neutralized, O'Leary jumped back up and spun to look for targets.

The Shaitans were gone.

"Did we get them all?" he asked.

"No, damn it. There are too many trees," Wolf replied. *"Some of them got away."*

"Any idea how many?"

"At least five...no more than ten."

Damn. That was worse than he had hoped for. He surveyed the ambush site. At least half the locals were down. The life signs were zero for several of his troops, too. Stupid locals. He shouldn't have tried to help them after all. He shook his head. Too late now.

"Night, O'Leary. Stand by for incoming. Between five and ten got past us."

"We'll be ready for them."

Sergeant Hattori 'Yokaze' Hanzo materialized and began working the katana out of the cowtaur's neck.

"Thanks for the help," O'Leary said. He looked down at the body of the Shaitan. "Did someone order steak?"

Ducting, Jotunn Ship *Falcon*, Kepler-186, December 18, 2021

"Being a rabbit is *not* exciting," Farhome stated. His whiskers twitched. "It's gross. This is what thousands of years of practice with life 'bots gets me? Turned into a giant rabbit? Bah. *All* of us don't like it."

"Oh, cheer up," Calvin replied, petting the four-foot tall furry creature, who really did look like an over-sized rabbit. "Don't get your fur in a bunch. Besides, you won't have to look like this for long."

"Couldn't you just have one of the bugs do this? I've discussed it with Max, and we don't like being vermin."

"No, we can't have the bugs do it," Calvin said with a sigh. Calvin had been through this three times now, with a couple of Farhome's selves, but he seemed to have pulled himself together again. Which didn't mean he liked the idea any better.

"We can't let the bugs get caught by the Jotunn," Calvin continued, "or the giants will come after them. In fact, we want you to do this so the giants think there's something else *beside* the bugs chewing up their wiring. We may want to leave, but this is their home, remember?"

"I thought they wanted to leave too."

"They do, but until we can take them off this ship, it remains their home, and I don't want Jotunn exterminators coming up here to kill off everything in the ducting. That also includes us at the moment, remember?"

Farhome's whiskers drooped. "Okay, we'll do it."

"Awesome. You remember what to do?"

"Just because I'm a rodent doesn't mean I'm stupid," Farhome replied. "After you cut the wire, the Jotunn will send a robot. I let it see me and lead it on a chase away from you."

"That's it," Calvin said. "After a couple of minutes, you can lose it or destroy it, and one of the bugs will lead you back here. Nothing could be easier."

"Wait a minute," Farhome said, his head snapping up. "The last robot that came up here was armed. What about that?"

That was one of the nice things about Farhome's hyper-focus on being a rabbit; he hadn't thought the implications of his task all the way through. Until now.

"Well, maybe this one won't be," Calvin said with a shrug. "If it is, my advice would be to run. Fast. And maybe dodge once in a while. I doubt the Jotunn will have loaded it with a combat program that can actually lead you. They won't be expecting you to be intelligent. Just don't get shot. If you can get behind it, you can shoot it…just don't let it see you with a gun."

Calvin smiled. "See, I told you it would be exciting. What could be more exciting than having a robot chase you through the ducts of a Jotunn ship in a live game of 'Cat and Mouse?'"

"Sitting by a fire while listening to Gray Rinehart play the harp?"

"We don't have time for this. Are you going to do it or not? I'm sure one of the Ssselipsssiss will do it if you you're too afraid to."

"I will," Karver stated.

"Of course, once the Jotunn see him, they're going to start wondering where he came from and will probably be up here in the ducts looking for more of them."

"Now who has his fur ruffled?" Farhome asked. "No, I'll do it." A lopsided smile flickered across his face. "Hehe, it may even be fun. Who knows? Besides, I'm also the only one who can take a laser hit or two without dying."

"Finally," Burkuri muttered. Louder, she asked, "Can we get on with it now?"

"Yes," Calvin replied. "Hopefully, the *Gulf* hasn't jumped back to the other universe yet." He turned to Paxton who was holding a wire and a pair of molecular cutters. "Go ahead."

Without a word, the lizard cut the wire and used one of the blades to trim the insulation from both of the resulting wires. He had obviously done it before, and he was finished in under a minute. "Here you go," he said, handing the two wire ends to Calvin.

"Thanks," Calvin replied. He started tapping the metal ends together.

* * * *

Chapter Eighteen

"Huh…" the DSO said. "That's odd,"

"Didn't we already have this discussion?" Captain Sheppard asked.

"The Jotunn ship's got a problem with its forward shields. They went out for a few seconds, now they are flickering on and off. If we wanted to chase them down, we might be able to time it where we could get some shots in on them."

"Do we know what's causing it?" the CO asked. "Better yet, is there anything we might be able to take advantage of? They've got to be pretty far away, though, don't they?"

"Well, yes sir, they are."

"I don't see any additional issues with the ship," Steropes said. "Their engines seem to be producing the same amount of thrust, and I am unable to detect any other abnormalities."

"Just the shield failure," the CO said.

"Yes, just the shield failure," Steropes agreed. "It's odd, though. There must be something wrong with the Jotunn's power supply after all; the failure seems to be cyclic."

"Cyclic?" Captain Sheppard asked. "What do you mean?"

"The shields come on briefly three times, then three times a little longer, then three times briefly again," Steropes replied. "After a short pause, the pattern repeats. There must be some difficulty in the power supply where it keeps cycling."

"Three shorts, three longs, and three shorts?" Captain Sheppard asked. "Repeated over and over?"

"Yes sir," Steropes said with a nod. "That is what my system is telling me, anyway."

"That's Morse code!" the CO exclaimed. "Someone is sending us an S.O.S.!"

"Why would the Jotunn do that?" the helmsman asked. "Better yet, how do they know Morse code?"

"It's easy," Captain Sheppard replied. "They wouldn't. And there's only one person who would. Calvin. I've got no idea how he did it, but he's on that ship, and he's trying to communicate with us."

"You think so sir?" Steropes asked.

"It's the only possibility. We transmitted to him, and shortly thereafter the Jotunn's shields start flashing an S.O.S.? It's got to be him."

"Why wouldn't he just transmit back to us?"

"I don't know," the CO replied. "Maybe he doesn't want the Jotunn to know he received the transmission. Maybe he took a blow to the head and doesn't have the ability to transmit. Who knows?"

"Maybe he doesn't want the Jotunn to know he's there," Lieutenant Commander Sarah 'Lights' Brighton said.

"Doesn't want them to know he's there?" the CO asked. "How could they *not* know he's there?"

"Well, look at the evidence," Lights said. "If Lieutenant Commander Hobbs is onboard that ship, it's unlikely he's there as an honored guest. If he's there, it's because he got captured and is a prisoner. In that case, he wouldn't have free reign of the ship."

"Maybe they do know," Steropes said. "That would explain why the ship was leaving so fast. They may be taking him back to their home world for interrogation."

"If he were their prisoner, though, how would he have access to the shields? Wouldn't he be in some sort of confinement facility? The Jotunn must have some kind of brig, wouldn't you think?"

"Well, yes, I doubt he'd be given access to the ship if he were a prisoner."

"Also, the Jotunn have to know their shields are malfunctioning, right?" Lights looked at Steropes.

"It does stand to reason the Jotunn would know that," the Psiclops agreed.

"Okay, so if Calvin is the person causing the shields to malfunction, he isn't under Jotunn control because they would stop him immediately."

"That makes sense," the CO said.

"So, if the Jotunn knew he was there, and he wasn't under their control, why wouldn't he just transmit back to us that he's aboard?"

"Maybe they removed his implants or disabled them," the CO replied.

"If they did that, though, he wouldn't have heard our transmission in the first place, and he wouldn't know to try to communicate with us."

"Maybe he just got lucky with the timing."

"I guess that's possible, but it seems pretty unlikely that he started transmitting right after we tried to reach him."

"So why do you think the Jotunn don't know he's aboard?"

"Well, just assume he snuck aboard the ship somehow and is in hiding. All of a sudden, he picks up the transmission we sent. He knows we're here and looking for him, and he knows he has to reply to us, or we'll leave and never know where to look for him. Still...the Jotunn don't know he's there, and he doesn't want to alert them to his presence, so he can't reply to our transmission directly. If he does, the giants will find him and capture him, and then he's screwed. So he uses the only means of communication available to him—he cuts a wire to the shield and starts tapping out Morse code on it. Voila! Problem solved. He can communicate with us without the Jotunn realizing he's doing it. Maybe they won't even know he's sending a message; maybe they'll just think they have some weird sort of failure." She sat back in her seat. "It's the only thing that makes sense."

"There are numerous flaws in that hypothesis," Steropes countered. "If he has done as you suggest, the Jotunn will know they have a problem and will immediately begin tracking down the nature of their shield malfunction. He would have to know that, too."

Lights shrugged. "I don't know how he thinks he can get away with it, but you're right, he would have to know that too. Either he thought the risk worth taking or he has some other plan. I don't know which it is, but I stand by my opinion."

"If you are right," the CO said, "he won't have much time before the Jotunn come looking for their malfunction and find him. We've got to contact him now. Communications officer, send out a burst message to him. Tell him to send out five long transmissions if he is aboard the Jotunn vessel."

"Sending, sir."

Steropes looked up from his sensor. "I believe Lieutenant Commander Brighton is correct. I just received five of the longer transmissions. The shield has gone back out now."

"I saw it too," the DSO confirmed. "There were definitely five pulses."

"Holy shit…" the helmsman muttered. "How the hell did he *do* that?"

"I don't know," the CO answered, "but it looks like he did. Comms, tell him we know he's there and we're coming for him. Ask for three long pulses if he receives us."

"Transmitting…"

"Sir! The Shaitans are firing!" the DSO exclaimed.

"Where?" the CO asked. "At us?"

"All over the place," the DSO replied. "Generally in our direction, but all over the place. They must have picked up our transmission. It looks like they have a general idea where we are."

"Understood," the CO said. "Duty engineer, stand by to jump to the other universe. We need to go pick up our troops so we can pursue the Jotunn ship. Steropes, did we get confirmation that Lieutenant Commander Hobbs received our transmission?"

"No sir, the Jotunn ship's shields have remained down since they went out."

Captain Sheppard turned to Lights. "What do you suppose that means?"

"No idea sir," she replied. "Hopefully, he hasn't been bagged…"

Shaitan Shuttle, Anti-Kepler-186 'e', December 18, 2021

The ramp to the Shaitan shuttle came back down. It almost reached the ground, but the shuttle's left skid had crumpled in the second crash, and the craft leaned heavily to port, leaving a gap of about two feet.

Valkyrie marched a Shaitan down the ramp, followed by Witch and Good Twin. The Jamaican helped the bigger soldier down the ramp.

"What happened?" Night asked as they reached the end of the ramp and jumped down.

"The shuttle's gunner kicked Good Twin in the chest," Witch replied. "He be havin' some broken ribs."

"And this is the shuttle's pilot," Valkyrie added with a touch of pride in her voice. "After we killed the gunner, it decided to play nicely with us."

"Does it understand us?" Night asked.

"No, sir," Valkyrie replied. "It speaks Jotunn, but not any other language we tried. The Shaitans must have some sort of implant system because it speaks Jotunn fluently."

"What has it said?"

"Nothing much," Witch replied, handing Good Twin off to the squad's medic, Corporal Anaru 'Spuds' Ngata. "He just asked for us not to be killin' him. I told him I wouldn't if he came along nice and quiet, and he did."

"Lieutenant Contreras, I want you, Valkyrie and Skank to take our prisoner back to the shuttle and see if you can start learning its language. The more we know about them, the better we'll be able to kick their asses."

"Yes sir!"

"Gunny Dantone!" Night called.

"Yes sir?" asked the cyborg as he jogged over.

"Take everyone who's left and start going through the shuttle's cargo and—" he paused as a transmission came in. "Disregard my last. Set up a perimeter along the path that leads to the town. We'll have five to ten more Shaitans here momentarily. They've already been hit once, so they may be expecting us. Capture them if you can, kill them if you can't." He looked pointedly at the remains of the Kuji known as Bill. "I don't want any more casualties."

"Yes sir!"

Ducting, Jotunn Ship *Falcon*, Kepler-186, December 18, 2021

Calvin finished tapping out the five long pulses, his hands shaking so badly he had to concentrate with all his might to make sure the metal ends came in contact correctly. He dropped the wires when he nearly sent a sixth pulse by mistake.

The plan had worked beyond his wildest dreams. The bugs had reported that the robot the Jotunn sent had followed Farhome, who was leading it on a chase toward engineering, somewhere about a mile aft of where he was. It would take a long time for the robot to return.

"We've got to go!" Paxton exclaimed as he ran up.

"Why?" Calvin asked.

"The bugs just said there are several robots headed toward us. At least the first two are armed!"

"Just a second," Calvin replied. "I'm in contact with my ship. It will only take another minute or two…"

"We have to leave *now!* The robots are only a couple of turns away." In confirmation, all of the bugs left, scurrying off down one of the passages. Only the Ssselipsssiss remained…and they were edging away.

"We've got to go!" Burkuri agreed. "You said we can't get caught here, remember? They're going to catch us!"

"I can shoot them if you want," Karver said.

Calvin sighed. "No, you're right, damn it. Let's go." He took one last look at the wires and then began crawling as fast as he could on his hands and knees in the direction the bugs had fled.

"Lieutenant Commander Hobbs, Vella Gulf. *We received your reply and understand you are aboard the Jotunn vessel. The CO says to tell you we'll be coming for you. Please transmit three long pulses if you copy my transmission."*

Damn it, Calvin thought. No way to reply. They'll come anyway…I hope.

Cargo Bay, *Shuttle 01*, Anti-Kepler-186 System, December 18, 2021

Valkyrie led the captive up the shuttle's loading ramp. While the shuttle was primarily configured for troop seating, the Terrans had left some room for the cargo they were hoping to acquire on the mission.

"That's far enough," Valkyrie said in Jotunn as the creature stepped off the ramp and fully into the cargo bay.

Lieutenant Contreras looked the Shaitan over slowly. Although the creature's body resembled a Terran cow, up close he could see it was actually covered in fine scales that overlapped each other like mail armor. The two sets of hands were generally human-shaped, but the fingers were more spread out around the periphery; not only were the thumb-like appendages opposable, the digits corresponding to the Terran's pinkie fingers were opposable as well, with four fingers in between. The creature looked at Contreras, slowly opening and closing its upper hands; they closed more like a bird's claws than human hands.

The similarity to Terran evolution ended at the creature's head. The two eyes on stalks were unlike anything he had ever seen, destroying any resemblance to a lizard the scales might have given. While the two lower eyes stared back at Contreras, the ones on stalks never ceased moving; they scanned the shuttle from front to back. Up close, the Terran could see two holes under the stalk eyes, which matched a similar set of perforations under each of its lower eyes.

Its mouth was directly under its eyes and seemed larger than normal. It hung open, exposing a mouthful of pointed teeth meant for tearing food to shreds, not chewing a cud, and it appeared to serve double duty as part of the creature's respiratory system; the Shaitan's breath went in and out through it. A slight odor of citrus permeated the cargo bay with every exhalation.

Aside from the fist clenching, the alien gave no other visible indication of being tense, if that was indeed what the hand motions meant. It stood still and silent as if patiently waiting for the Terrans to determine its fate.

"So let us talk," Lieutenant Contreras said in Jotunn as explosions began sounding outside. "I am Second Lieutenant Cristobal Manuel Contreras," he added when the Shaitan remained silent. Aside from one of the eye stalks turning toward the source of the explosions, the creature neither moved nor flinched. "To whom do I have the pleasure of speaking?"

"Come, come," he added after another few moments of silence. "My men tell me you speak the language of the Jotunn, so you understand me, yes?"

"He definitely speaks Jotunn," Valkyrie interjected. "He understood what we were saying to him and obeyed us; he couldn't have followed our instructions if he didn't understand."

"So you do speak Jotunn," Lieutenant Contreras said. "Then one of two things is keeping you from talking. Either you can't talk, or I haven't given you a sufficient reason to. I suspect that if you can understand the language, you can also speak it; therefore, I am left to believe that it is a matter of you choosing not to speak with me."

He noticed the eye stalk continued to face the open cargo bay door. The sounds of fighting had slackened noticeably.

"If you are hoping your comrades will save you, I am afraid it isn't going to happen. Our forces have already met yours in battle once and defeated them; they are not going to rescue you."

"They *will* come," the Shaitan said. Its voice was high; far higher than Contreras would have expected from something so large. "They will never surrender, especially to you."

"What do you mean, 'they won't surrender?'" Lieutenant Contreras asked. "You surrendered."

"Yes, but I am not one of the—" His sentence ended in a harsh squeal. "I only surrendered because I knew they would come for me. They will come. They can't leave this planet without me."

"They won't come," Lieutenant Contreras stated. "If they won't surrender, then they will be destroyed."

"It is not possible. They cannot be defeated, especially by you—"

"I'm sorry, your last word didn't translate."

"They will not be defeated by beings from your universe. It is neither permitted nor possible."

"Permitted by whom?"

"I have said all I am going to."

"Ah, but I still have questions," Lieutenant Contreras said. "You still haven't said how you learned to speak the Jotunn language."

The Shaitan didn't respond.

"Well, either your kind is incredibly intelligent and has an excellent language training program," Contreras continued, "or you have some sort of implant system in your brain to help you learn. As I have not seen anything to indicate superior intelligence, you must have some sort of implant."

The creature neither moved nor spoke.

"If you won't tell us, perhaps we will need to kill you and remove it to find out how it works."

All of the creature's eyes turned to the Terran. "No," it squeaked, "you do not need to kill me. I will tell you what I know."

"Good," Lieutenant Contreras said. "I rather hoped you would."

Outside the Shaitan Shuttle, Anti-Kepler-186 'e', December 18, 2021

"The Shaitans are all down," Gunnery Sergeant Dantone reported. "All are dead except for one that appears unconscious."

"How bad off is it?" Night asked.

"Hard to tell," Dantone replied. "It doesn't appear to be very badly wounded. There are some superficial cuts but nothing major. It looks like something hit it on the head, though; it may have gotten knocked out. Assuming they get knocked out, that is. It's down, but it still appears to be breathing."

"Well, get it tied up and have Spuds take a look at it. We'll take it back with us and see if we can interrogate it."

"That's going to be a problem, sir," Staff Sergeant Collyn 'Canary' Loftis said. "I was moving the unobtanium to our shuttle, and there isn't going to be a lot of room. We've already got the one damn alien in our shuttle, and it's taking up an ass-load of room. If we bring back another one of these bastards, we're going have even less."

"Well, we need to bring back everything we can," Night said. "We need it for our weapons and to make more transporters. How much are we going to have to leave behind?"

"A lot, sir," Canary replied. "There's tons of it in the back of the shuttle. Tons. If we take both the damn cowtaurs, we're going to have to leave most of it behind."

"Well, that ain't gonna work," Night said.

"We don't have to bring back the second one," Dantone said. "I can put it down for good if you'd like."

"Hell, if you're going to do that, just give it to the locals," Lieutenant O'Leary said as he jogged up. "I'm sure they'd love to have one of the Shaitans to play with. The ones I talked to were pretty pissed."

"No, the damn thing is a prisoner of war, even if it *is* an alien. We're not going to kill it, nor are we going to give it to the locals so they can kill it." Night shook his head. "No, we're going to have to take it home with us."

"But what about the unobtanium?" Dantone asked.

Night's face was grim as he looked around, searching for answers. Finally his eyes stopped moving, and the beginnings of a smile touched the sides of his lips. "Maybe we don't have to decide which one we're going to take."

Lieutenant O'Leary turned to see where he was looking. "Sir, I think you've been around Lieutenant Commander Hobbs too long."

Chapter Nineteen

Bridge, TSS *Vella Gulf,* Kepler-186 System, December 18, 2021

"Stand by to make the jump," Captain Sheppard ordered as he scanned the bridge.

"Standing by," the helmsman replied.

"All defensive and offensive systems operational?" Captain Sheppard asked. They looked ready, but it didn't hurt to make sure.

"Yes sir," the officers chorused.

"Make the jump!"

"Jumping now," the helmsman replied.

Everything flashed, and there was a brief period of nausea, but like the rest of the crew, Captain Sheppard had done it so many times he barely noticed.

"All systems operational," the duty engineer advised. "Stealth holding."

"We are established in the anti-Kepler-186 system," Steropes noted.

"Comms, get ahold of the shuttle and see if they're ready for pickup," Captain Sheppard ordered. "We need to get them back aboard before one of the Shaitan ships jumps back in here. We won't have our normal advantages with the stealth modules blocking our weapons ports. If a couple come back at the same time, it'll get interesting, and I *hate* interesting even more than I hate 'odd.'"

"I've got them on my system," the DSO announced. "They're close to the rendezvous point, but…" She stared at her monitor.

"But what, DSO?"

"Their signature is all messed up, sir. The shape doesn't look quite right and the engine harmonics are off…clearing…Sir! I'm getting indications of a Shaitan engine! There's a Shaitan ship on that bearing! It's a trap!"

"Keep the stealth up," Captain Sheppard ordered. "Steropes, what have you got?"

"There is definitely a Shaitan vessel nearby," the Psiclops replied.

"It's okay sir," the communications officer interrupted. "I just spoke with the shuttle crew, and they captured the Shaitan shuttle. It was damaged in the fight, so they had to attach our shuttle to it to get it into orbit. The shuttle crew says the Shaitan ship is full of unobtanium; they are recommending bringing it aboard."

"Sir, I don't know if that's a good idea," the duty engineer said. "Keeping that much unprocessed unobtanium next to the ship is a recipe for disaster when we jump back into our universe. If it detonates…"

"Yeah, if it goes high order, we'd be destroyed," the CO agreed. "Still…having a shuttle load would give us a lot of capability we currently don't have." He thought for a couple of seconds, weighing the options.

"Get us to the rendezvous," he finally decided. "We'll take both shuttles aboard and begin processing the unobtanium through the replicator while we chase the Jotunn. We will stay in this universe as much as possible to keep it stable."

"How will we know where the stargate is?" the helmsman asked. "I don't have any data on how to get to the Jotunn home world. If we can't see where they jump, we run the risk of losing them while we look for the stargate."

"I'm aware of that," Captain Sheppard said. "We'll jump back and forth periodically so we can keep track of the Jotunn. If we don't stay in our universe long, we shouldn't have any problems with the unobtanium."

At least I hope not, he added to himself.

CO's Conference Room, TSS *Vella Gulf*, Anti-Kepler-186 System, December 19, 2021

"After we killed the Shaitans," Night reported, "we realized we didn't have enough room to bring back all of the metal they had stolen plus the two captives. The only way we could get everything back was to use the Shaitan's shuttle, but it had been damaged in the fighting, and one of its motors was destroyed. Lieutenant Walsh jury-rigged a way of attaching our shuttle to theirs, and with ours helping we had just enough boost to get both the ships into orbit. It was close, but Harv pulled it off."

"You trusted their pilot to fly their shuttle for us?" Captain Sheppard asked. "That seems pretty risky."

"Trusted him?" Night asked. "No sir. I wouldn't have trusted the Shaitan to do it alone. Lieutenant Walker, our shuttle's WSO, rode up with it to watch what the pilot was doing, as well as Lieutenant O'Leary and several of our troops. The Shaitan pilot really doesn't want to die, and Lieutenant O'Leary is really good at threatening bodily harm; it all worked out fine."

"I didn't even have to threaten it that much," Lieutenant O'Leary added. "As long as we kept a couple of weapons on it, the thing pretty much did what it was told."

"What about the other Shaitan?" the *Vella Gulf's* executive officer, Commander Russ Clayton, asked. "That one was one of their soldiers, right?"

"Yes sir," Night replied. "That one was a lot less tractable. He got knocked out in the fighting, and we hand-cuffed and hoof-cuffed the bastard before he woke up. Good thing we did, too; he did everything he could to break out and attack us even though he was greatly outnumbered. We've got to watch that son of a bitch. I don't trust him as far as I can throw him, and he's too big for me to even lift. He has no sense of self-preservation—he just wants to kill us."

"Interesting," Captain Sheppard replied. "The two sound completely different. Is there any indication whether that is just their individual personalities, or if they are two different races or nationalities or something?"

"I don't know," Night replied, "but we better watch the second one at all times. I told Solomon to keep an eye on him in the brig, but I almost think we ought to have killed him rather than bringing him back onboard."

"Well, I'm glad you didn't," Captain Sheppard said. "We're not going to start killing them for no reason. We'll play by the rules of war until we're told otherwise."

"Even if they don't?" Lieutenant O'Leary asked.

"Even if they don't," the CO confirmed. "Have we made any progress translating their language?"

"I have been overseeing the effort with the Shaitan pilot," Lieutenant Contreras said. "The Shaitan soldier refuses to cooperate. I was unable to make much progress until we returned here, and then it was Solomon who made the breakthrough. We are now making great headway."

"What changed?"

"Solomon realized that part of the Shaitans' communications are at a higher frequency than we can hear. They use ultrasound to see and communicate with each other, in a technique similar to what dolphins use back home. We couldn't hear that and were missing out on a lot of the cueing. Just like a lot of Terran speech involves facial movements, tone and gestures, without being able to hear the ultrasound, we were unable to understand the nuances. Once Solomon recognized it, we began to understand their speech. Somewhat, anyway."

Captain Sheppard turned to Steropes. "Were you aware of this?"

"Yes sir, they told me."

"What do you make of it?"

"Well, we know the Ssselipsssiss call the Shaitans' system the "Dark Star" and the "Dark Planet." Sonar may have been necessary for them to evolve in an environment with reduced lighting. It is also possible they initially evolved underground in caves where it might have been warmer, which may have resulted in the necessity for an ultrasound navigation and communications system."

"But you don't know."

"No sir, I cannot say for sure without additional information."

"Solomon, how confident are you that you can understand their language?" Captain Sheppard asked.

"I can understand a number of their words, but without access to actual conversations, it is impossible to determine how those words go together to make up Shaitan speech."

"Have the two prisoners been in contact with each other?"

"No sir, they have not."

"Let's allow them to talk with each other, but keep them separate," Captain Sheppard said. "I'd like to see what they have to talk about, and that will give you the opportunity to hear their conversation."

"I'll take care of it," the operations officer, Commander Dan Dacy, replied.

Captain Sheppard nodded. "What's the status of the Shaitan shuttle offload?"

The operations officer pushed a button and an exterior view of the ship appeared on the conference room's video screens. A variety of ship's crewmen and the platoon's soldiers, distinct in their different suits, covered the shuttle and formed a trail into the interior of the *Vella Gulf*. "Everyone from off duty pilots and WSOs to crew coming off watch are working to get the material in and processed," he explained. "They're all aware that we can't follow the Jotunn until we either get the material processed or jettison it."

His tone indicated which way he thought they should go. The fact that no one else had mentioned jettisoning the metal also gave a good indication.

"Have we found the stargate?" Captain Sheppard asked. The Jotunn ship had jumped while the *Vella Gulf* was in the Jinn Universe, and the Terrans had been forced to search for it. At least they knew the Jotunn's line of travel, which narrowed it significantly. They had jumped back into their universe three times to take scans.

"The sensor sweeps from the last survey are still being analyzed," Commander Dacy said. "We should know something—"

The screen changed to the face of the helmsman. "Captain Sheppard!" he interrupted. "We've got the location of the stargate!"

"Very well," the CO replied. "Full speed ahead to the stargate." He turned back to Commander Dacy. "We'll settle with what we've unloaded so far. Jettison the Shaitan shuttle and get everyone back inside. We've got a ship to catch."

Bridge, TSS *Vella Gulf*, Kepler-186 System, December 19, 2021

"Five minutes to stargate," the helmsman noted.

"Understood," Captain Sheppard replied. "Sound General Quarters."

"Sound General Quarters, aye!" the duty engineer replied. Within moments, the horn began sounding and the warning lights flashing.

"I'm sorry we weren't able to go back and advise your country-men," Captain Sheppard said to Lieutenant Rrower.

"I understand," the Mrowry officer replied, "just as they, too, will understand. I'm sure my father would have done the same to rescue one of his cubs."

"How long will they wait?"

"As long as is needed. We can be very patient hunters. You do not need to worry about them. They will prepare our defenses and will be ready to attack when we return."

"Captain Sheppard," Steropes said, "I'm sorry, but I fear I must apologize too."

"For what?"

"I have failed to advise you appropriately. When we go through the stargate, the Jotunn will know we are following them. The stargate pulse will give us away. We should have slowed to minimize it."

"I am aware of the consequences of what we're about to do," Captain Sheppard replied. "You assume I don't want the Jotunn to know we're following them, but you're wrong. I *want* them to know."

"Are you hoping to frighten them? They do not scare easily," Steropes warned.

"I'd love it if they were afraid of us, or at least afraid of our capabilities. Based on what I know about the Jotunn though, I doubt that is going to happen. My goal is to get inside their heads and make them wonder *why* we're chasing them, and what we intend to do once they get to their destination. If I can do that, I'll be happy."

Bridge, Jotunn Ship *Falcon*, Unknown System, December 20, 2021

"Sir! I just received a pulse from the stargate behind us. We are being followed."

"And? Who is it following us?" Captain Magnusson asked.

"I only captured a few seconds of video before the ship disappeared. I'm trying to identify it now."

"What do you mean, 'disappeared?'" the captain asked. Not known for his patience at the best of times, it was in even shorter supply after his recent dealings with the Shaitans. "Did it jump to the other universe like the Shaitans, or did it go into stealth like those drinkers of sheep's piss, the Terrans?"

"I can't tell which it did, sir; it just vanished. I can, however, tell you it was the Terrans. It was their ship with the smaller craft mounted on both ends."

Captain Magnusson sat back in his command chair and stroked his beard. "The Terrans, eh? They probably saw our shields flickering and hoped to get close enough to use some of their weapons on us while our shields were down. How close are they?"

"They are almost a full day's travel behind us, and I don't believe they will catch up with us before we reach Jotunheimr."

"Good. Continue at full speed. We'll have a reception waiting for them when they get there."

Ducting, Jotunn Ship *Falcon*, Kepler-186, December 20, 2021

"Your friends are here in this system and are still following us," Burkuri said to Calvin and the assembled group of bipeds and bugs.

"Good," Paxton said. "Hopefully they will catch up with us shortly, although I have no idea how they are going to get us off this ship."

"I don't know that yet, either," Calvin replied, "but we will work something out. How far back are they?"

"Almost a day's travel, according to the bridge crew," Burkuri said. "There's a problem though. It doesn't sound like your friends will catch up with us before we reach the Jotunn home system, and the captain referenced a 'reception' they would have waiting for them."

"We have to warn them," Calvin said. He rubbed his chin while he thought. "I'd even risk trying to comm them, but if they are as far back as you said, they'll be out of range. We may have to try to communicate with them using the shields again…"

"Well, you can find someone else to be the rabbit next time, because I'm not doing it," Farhome stated. "Besides, I'm almost out of nanobots and won't be able to get any more until we get back to the *Vella Gulf.*"

"We need to come up with another plan then," Calvin said; "we've *got* to warn the *Gulf.*"

Everything flashed as the ship jumped through a stargate.

"Too late now," Burkuri said.

Bridge, TSS *Vella Gulf*, Kepler-11 System, December 20, 2021

"There they go," the OSO said. "The Jotunn just hit the stargate out."

"Well, at least we know where the gate is," Captain Sheppard replied. "Steropes, have you figured out what system we're in yet?"

"Yes sir. We are in the Kepler-11 system. Kepler-11 is a G-type star that is very much like your sun, with about 96% of its mass. It is about twice as old as the sun and slightly cooler. The system has six planets that orbit close to the star; all six lie inside Venus' orbit around the sun. None are habitable."

"Captain Sheppard?" the AI asked.

"Yes, Solomon, what is it?"

"I have been listening to the Shaitans talk with each other, and I believe I have deciphered most of their language."

"And? What are they talking about?"

"Most of their discussion revolves around being on the devils' ship, and what they can do to destroy us. The soldier continues to urge the pilot to attack us, and if he won't do that, then the soldier says the pilot should kill himself. I would recommend caution when dealing with the soldier; I believe he will attack without provocation or advance warning."

"Understood," Captain Sheppard said. "I believe it's also time to cut off communications between them again. It's not in our best interest to have the pilot subjected to that kind of influence."

Bridge, TSS *Vella Gulf,* Kepler-11 System, December 21, 2021

"Five minutes to stargate."

"Understood," Captain Sheppard said. "Sound General Quarters." He turned in his chair. "What do you think, Steropes? Is this going to be the one?"

"There is no way to know, sir. With each passing stargate we cross, the odds increase that the next system will be their final destination."

"And where do you think that will be?"

"That is also unknown," Steropes said, "although it stands to reason the Jotunn have a destination in mind and are not randomly leading us on a chase to nowhere."

"Why is that?"

"Well, the Jotunn left the front lines of the war, but we have no idea why. Regardless of their reasons for leaving, they are probably headed to a repair facility or fleet base somewhere, both of which are probably in occupied systems. Wherever they're going, that place probably has more Jotunn; likely a lot more. Also, they know we are following them and have the advantage of being 19.3 hours ahead of us."

"What are you saying?" Captain Sheppard asked.

"When we get to the Jotunn's destination, they will have some time before our arrival to prepare for us, and there will probably be other Jotunn there to help."

The DSO stiffened at his console as he realized what Steropes meant. "Just like Rikki-Tikki-Tavi going down the cobra's hole," he muttered as he adjusted his console's setting.

"Who is Rikki-Tikki-Tavi?" Steropes asked.

"It was a fictional mongoose," the DSO replied. "The story goes that you're not supposed to chase a cobra into its hole because, at some point, the tunnel is going to widen enough that the snake can turn around. Then you get the fangs, not the tail."

"I'm not familiar with the story," Captain Sheppard replied, "but I fully understand the warning, and that we are eventually going to run into the Jotunn defenses. Solomon, when we do, I want you to immediately jump us into the Jinn Universe and to activate our stealth. Do not wait for orders; if you see us about to be overwhelmed, just do it. Am I clear?"

"Yes, Captain Sheppard," the AI confirmed. "Upon sighting Jotunn defenses, I will immediately initiate a jump into the Jinn Universe."

"Thank you," the CO replied.

"Here we go," the helmsman advised. "Stargate in 3…2…1…"

* * * * *

Chapter Twenty

Bridge, TSS *Vella Gulf*, Kepler-20 System, December 21, 2021

"System entry, unknown system," Steropes noted. "Scanning…"

"We're still here," Captain Sheppard said, scanning the bridge, "so I'm guessing there aren't any Jotunn defenses, eh Solomon?"

"No sir," the AI replied, "my scanners are not detecting any defenses. In fact, they are not showing anything at all."

"Solomon's right," Steropes confirmed; "the Jotunn ship has vanished."

Overhead the Bridge, Jotunn Ship *Falcon*, Jotunheimr System, December 22, 2021

Calvin made it to his watch station above the bridge as the front view screen lit up to show an impressive Jotnar. Not only was it one of the biggest giants he had ever seen, it was also the first Calvin had seen dressed in any sort of uniform, and the overuse of gold braid, silver piping and medals on both sides of the giant's chest made him look somewhat pretentious.

"Good day, admiral," Captain Magnusson said.

"Welcome back, captain," the admiral replied. "How goes the war?"

"It goes well; we are well on the way to eradicating the Ssselipssssiss. We have only returned briefly for some necessary maintenance at the shipyard. We have some vermin in our ducting that needs eradicating. I don't expect to stay more than a day or two."

"While you are here, you will have to contact your uncle; he has quite the surprise for you."

"Oh? What has he been up to now? He hasn't brought me home another wife from one of his raids, has he?"

"He may have; you never know with him. That isn't what I was talking about, though. His surprise will be of great assistance in our war."

"Now you have me curious," Captain Magnusson replied. "Perhaps you'd like to give me a clue?"

"You'll see," the Jotnar admiral said with a twinkle in his eye. "Once again, he has lived up to his nickname."

"He is always full of surprises." Captain Magnusson shook his head, then his smile faded. "Be on the lookout," he warned. "There is a ship following me. It will be here in 20 hours or so, depending on how long it takes the ship's crew to find the stargate. The ship is only as big as one of our frigates, but it must be destroyed immediately upon its entry into the system. Don't try to talk to them, just destroy them."

"Ho, ho, ho," the admiral guffawed. "Please tell me the mighty Captain Magnusson isn't running from a ship less than half his size."

"Not hardly. The ship has the same ability as our Shaitan allies and can jump out of our universe at a moment's notice. That is why you must destroy it quickly, lest its crew transit to the other universe and escape."

"If it is only the size of a frigate, it should not be much of a challenge," the admiral said; "I will make sure we are ready."

"Any news from the other front?"

"I am sorry to be the bearer of bad news, but we had some setbacks in the war against the Aesir. The plan to initiate Ragnarok had to be delayed due to contact with a race called the Terrans. Your father, the Odin, was killed in battle."

"Terrans? The ship following us is also Terran in origin."

"Indeed, they have the secret for transiting between universes. The forces that killed your father were led by one such ship called the *Vella Gulf*."

"*The* Vella Gulf*!*" Captain Magnusson exploded. "*That is the ship following us! I will stay here and kill them myself!*"

"As much as I would love to allow your revenge, our honor demands that you get back to assist our Shaitan allies as soon as possible. We don't want them to come looking for you here. There are things in this system we do not want them to see."

"What things?" the captain growled.

"Things you will see in due time," the admiral replied. "Although your desire for revenge is just, you must honor your father by meeting his commitment to the Shaitans. You can count on me to carry out your revenge."

"I am forced to drink a bitter tea, but I will do as honor demands. Just make sure you kill the Terrans…" His sentence trailed off, leaving the threat unvoiced, but it hung there nevertheless.

Calvin shivered. They had made an implacable enemy of someone who wasn't afraid to threaten a senior officer. The ship somehow seemed a lot smaller.

Bridge, TSS *Vella Gulf,* Kepler-20 System, December 22, 2021

Captain Sheppard stared at the stargate on the front screen. So close, and yet the damn thing had been so hard to find. He shook his head. "How far behind them are we now?" he asked.

"We are 26 hours and 17 minutes behind the Jotunn ship," Steropes replied. "We lost over four hours looking for the stargate and a little over an hour getting aligned to enter it. We are lucky we knew the Jotunn's original vector on entering the system; it greatly narrowed our search."

"Yeah, lucky," the captain said with a snort. "26 hours is a long time for them to prepare for us, or get to where they're going and flush out Calvin."

Steropes didn't reply. There was nothing to say. The awkward silence stretched for another minute, until broken by the helmsman.

"Here we go," he said. "Stargate in 3...2...1..."

The stars in the viewer expanded into infinity, and everything went black...then sideways...then blue...then sweet...

"System entry—" Steropes said.

"Dreadnought!" the DSO shouted, overriding him. The ship rocked as it was hit. "Fuck! Plus two battleships and a butt-ton of other targets! *Missiles inbound!*" His fingers flashed across his keys, although he knew the end was a foregone conclusion.

"Firing all tubes at the dread—" the OSO said.

Everything flashed as the ship jumped.

"Holy *fuck!*" the DSO said, slumping back into his seat. "I've never seen so much shit lined up to kill me. I recommend we do *not* go back there any time soon!"

"Nice job, Solomon," Captain Sheppard said, trying to control his breathing. "Get me a damage report, ASAP."

"Minor damage in several areas," the duty engineer responded. "Damage control crews are responding; I will have a more thorough report momentarily once they're on-station."

"We got lucky," the DSO said. "We only took a couple of laser strikes, but they were from the dreadnought, or whatever the hell that big-ass ship was. The second hit collapsed our shields. If any of the near misses had hit us…" he shook his head. "We're lucky to be alive. Happily, it looks like they can't make the jump."

"Why's that?" the helmsman asked.

"You're still breathing, aren't you?"

"Focus," Captain Sheppard said. "In addition to damage control, let's get a scan going and see what we've got here. Steropes, did you get a scan of the area before we jumped?"

"No sir. There were too many ships, too close, to perform an effective scan."

"You got that right," the DSO muttered.

"Contact!" the OSO exclaimed. "I've got a bogey in the vicinity of the nearest planet. It's turning toward us…cruiser-sized…the engine signatures are…*Shaitan!*"

Overhead the Bridge, Jotunn Ship *Falcon*, Jotunheimr System, December 22, 2021

Greetings, uncle," Captain Magnusson said to the giant on the view screen.

"Welcome home, nephew," the Jotnar replied. "It is good to see you, although I hadn't expected you quite so soon. Have the Ssselipsssiss been eradicated?"

"I believe they are almost extinct. They cannot have more than a planet or two left, and their fleet has been all but eliminated."

"If the war continues still, why have you returned?"

"Our ducts have been infested with some sort of creature that finds the wiring for our shields tasty. They keep chewing through the wires faster than we can replace them. We have returned to get the ducting swept and the vermin exterminated."

"The bugs are eating your wiring?"

"No, it is a different type of creature. Something furry."

"I'm sure the shipyard can clean them out quickly enough," the giant said. "There is a bigger war coming, and you will need your shields."

"That is certainly true, uncle. How are things with you?"

"Ho, ho, ho," the elder Jotnar laughed. "They go very well." He laughed again. "I captured a Shaitan ship, and now we have the secret of how they are able to travel between universes."

"And how is it done?"

"There is a piece of machinery they use to make the transit. We swapped the engines from the ship I captured to one of our frigates, and now we can go to the Shaitans' universe, too."

"How were you able to take one of their ships?"

"I tricked them, of course."

"That has always been your style, uncle." Both Jotunn laughed.

"Sir!" one of the bridge watch called. Calvin knew from experience it was the Jotunn communications officer. "We just received word from the stargate. The Terran frigate is here."

"And they killed it, I assume," Captain Magnusson replied.

"No sir, the Terrans got away. Apparently the *Long Serpent* hit it several times but was not successful in keeping it from transiting to the other universe."

"Those sheep-fucking *oskilgettin*! I will sew their testicles to my shield and let every enemy I know beat on them at will!"

"The Terrans?"

"No, our worthless sacks of rotten flesh guarding the stargate. How could they let one tiny frigate escape? They must have been too busy pouring salt water down their pants to keep their crabs fresh, those worthless, fatherless *bacrauts*."

"Fear not, nephew; I will get your revenge."

"Did you not hear my communications officer, uncle? The *modur helviti* Terrans have transited to the universe of the Shaitans. They are beyond our reach until they choose to come back, and they will not come back to fight. Even *they* are not that stupid."

"You forget about my new ship. I will cross over and put an end to their meddling in our affairs. They cannot escape me. Consider your revenge…fulfilled."

Bridge, TSS *Vella Gulf,* Anti-Jotunheimr System, December 23, 2021

"Captain, the Jotunn vessel, the *Huggorm*, is calling us," the communications officer said.

"On screen," Captain Sheppard replied.

The screen lit up with the visage of a giant who was unlike any Jotnar the CO had seen previously; the giant's skin, while bluish-tinged, was closer to the hue of a Caucasian Terran than any Captain Sheppard had seen before. The Jotnar could have passed as a human who had been out in the cold too long...if he hadn't been about 14 feet tall. He wore a long woolen tunic and trousers, held up by a belt with a large golden buckle. A cape flowed from his shoulders, held together in the front with a golden brooch. Although his hair and beard were long like the rest of the Jotunn that Captain Sheppard had seen, the giant was well-groomed. He exuded charm and charisma, and Captain Sheppard instantly took a liking to him.

"Welcome to Jotunheimr," the Jotnar said. "Or, what would be Jotunheimr if we weren't in this other...place. I am Loki of the Saekonungar, the rulers of the seas between the stars. Unfortunately, I am not able to offer you the hospitality due someone who has journeyed as far as you have. Your race has proven to be a thorn in our side, and I am afraid it is my duty to remove that thorn. You killed our previous Odin, my brother, and I am honor-bound to return the favor. Defend yourselves, strangers; Loki is coming for you."

With that, the screen went dead.

"How long until they are in missile range?" Captain Sheppard asked.

"About four hours," the OSO replied.

"Good," Captain Sheppard said. "We have time to prepare."

"We're going to fight him?" the DSO asked.

"I don't see any other possibility. We can't go back through the stargate we came through; they'll be waiting for us. We didn't have time to survey the system before we jumped into this universe, so we don't know where the other stargates are. Even if we did, the Jotunn are probably blocking them to keep us from leaving. We could move around in this universe and jump back to find out that information, but our movements are currently impeded by the Jotunn ship headed toward us. Our choices are to either fight or run. If we run, they will chase us, and we'll have to fight them on their terms. If, however, we attack them now and defeat them, we gain a flexibility and mobility advantage over the rest of the Jotunn. If they don't have any other ships that can jump to this universe, once we kick their asses, we can move around here however we want."

"What if they do have other ships that can jump into this universe?" the OSO asked.

"Then we'll kick their asses too. It's the only way we're going to get out of here."

No one said anything else, but Captain Sheppard could see the crew looking around nervously. The situation was bad, but not unrecoverable. Captain Sheppard stared at the screen, picturing Loki's face on it. He might have to rethink liking Loki after all.

CO's Conference Room, TSS *Vella Gulf*, Anti-Jotunheimr System, December 23, 2021

"All right, we'll start with Steropes," the CO said. "What can you tell us about where we are?"

"This system is the Keppler-20 system. Kepler-20 is a yellow star just slightly smaller and cooler than the Sun. The system has six planets, of which five are inside the habitable zone. The sixth planet is on the outside edge of the habitable zone. Although too cold for us, based on what we know about the Jotunn, it would not be too cold for them. The sixth planet in this universe is uninhabited, but I believe it to be the planet Jotunheimr in our universe. It is on almost the opposite side of the star from our current position."

"Anything interesting we can use to our advantage here?"

"No sir; there is nothing out of the ordinary in this system."

Captain Sheppard turned to the operations officer. "What's the latest on Loki and friends?"

"They continue to head straight for us. They will be in missile range in about 2.5 hours. They continue to ignore all communications."

"Well, it appears they are determined to fight, and we're going to give them everything we've got. Yes, I know we could stealth up and try to hide from them, but I don't want to have to try to outmaneuver them the whole time we're trying to get Calvin back. I want to take care of them now and be done with it."

"What about the stealth modules?" the OSO asked. "Are we going to keep them on?"

"No," the CO said. "We're not going to fight handicapped. Blow them now and get everything ready for full broadsides. I want a fighter strike to precede us, then we will close to missile range. They have probably seen the Shaitan's missiles before, but I'll bet the Jotunn haven't had the missiles used on them yet. I want to stay just inside missile range, and we'll see what their capabilities are. If we need to rearm the fighters and send them back in, we will. I do not want to get in close with the Jotunn ship until we know more about their capabilities."

"We are working to replicate more of the jump units for our missiles," the operations officer said, "but we will only have about two broadsides worth of them, as well as enough to give the capability to about half of the fighters' missiles. Do you want us to use all of the ones we have?"

"I do," Captain Sheppard said with a nod. "My goal is not to give them a fair fight, but to smash them to wreckage as quickly as possible so we can go after Lieutenant Commander Hobbs. Loki has already delayed us too long. Any questions?"

Cockpit, *Viper 01*, Anti-Jotunheimr System, December 23, 2021

 ll *Vipers, launch on my mark,*" Lights transmitted. "*Stand by, stand by, mark!*"

She jabbed the button that released *Viper 01's* missiles and received five good launch indications. Her system showed all but one of the squadron's missiles had launched; 59 missiles raced toward the Jotunn ship.

"You play with fire, you're going to get burned," she muttered as she changed the navigation system to the holding point where the fighters would wait until they were needed. She hoped the Jotunn liked it hot because there was a hellstorm headed for them.

Bridge, TSS Vella Gulf, Anti-Jotunheimr System, December 23, 2021

"Sir, the fighters have launched," the OSO said. "59 missiles tracking outbound toward the *Huggorm*. 10 minutes until we're in range."

"Have they turned broadside yet?" Captain Sheppard asked.

"No sir. They are still heading toward us. I'm not sure what they're doing. They're launching anti-missile missiles (AMMs), but only from their chase armament; they haven't turned to use their broadside defenses." He watched as two of the fighters' missiles jumped out of the universe and came back, avoiding the AMMs targeted on them. "They're going to eat a bunch of these. It doesn't make a lot of sense."

"It might if they didn't have a lot of anti-missile defense," the CO commented. "Maybe they knew there were going to be a bunch of leakers, and Loki decided to sacrifice the bow of his ship to get past the fighters. They're going to take a lot of hits, but their engines and most of the back end of the ship is protected. It's pretty smart, actually. They get a look at our missile capabilities, without our special missiles being able to do a lot of damage to them. They'll have to rotate to fire at us, though, and then they're ours."

"You're right sir; they're rotating," the DSO said. "And they're firing!" His voice was a little higher this time.

"Defend the ship," the CO ordered. "Missiles free."

"What the hell…" the DSO muttered, staring at his system.

"What's wrong, DSO?"

"Uh sir, they only launched five missiles. That's it? Five missiles?" Incredulity tinged his voice.

"We're in range," the OSO noted. "Firing." The ship jolted at the anti-ship missiles (ASMs) launched.

"AMMs launching," the DSO noted. "Three missiles killed...second round launching...all incoming missiles destroyed."

"Missiles running true," the OSO commented. "The Jotunn are launching AMMs against them...not very many...*BAM!* At least seven hits on the enemy ship!"

"Oh, I get it!" the DSO exclaimed.

"What's that, DSO?" the CO asked.

"Their ship is the same size as us, and I automatically figured it would have about the same capabilities, but it doesn't. Even though the ship is the same size as the *Gulf,* it's a Jotunn frigate, not a cruiser. The Jotunn are a lot bigger than us, so the living spaces on board have to be a lot bigger too. By the time you upsize everything, the ship is only going to have the same weapons capability as a much smaller ship. The Jotunn's missiles are going to be a lot bigger than ours, but there aren't going to be as many as there would be on a Terran cruiser. That's what we're seeing. We can fire a lot more missiles than they can."

"Good," Captain Sheppard said. "Kill them, please."

"My pleasure," the OSO said. "ASMs launching."

Bridge, TSS *Vella Gulf*, Anti-Jotunheimr System, December 23, 2021

"Sir, the Jotunn are calling."

"On screen."

Loki's face appeared on the screen. A thin haze of smoke partially obscured his face, but Captain Sheppard could see he was smiling. "You have gotten the better of us," the Jotnar said. "We cannot defend against your missiles. I believe it is time to discuss a truce."

"A truce?" Captain Sheppard asked.

"Yes, a truce. Unfortunately, your last volley destroyed one of our engines and the machinery we need to make the transit back to our world. The transit technology isn't ours, and my engineering section doesn't believe they can fix it, which means we will be trapped here with no hope of rescue; this is the only ship we have that can make the transit here."

"So what do you propose?"

"We need your assistance to return home, and I am requesting you send over some technicians to help us repair our transit capability so we can return home. If you will fix our ship, we promise to transit back with you to our world, where we will give you free passage out of our system."

"You can guarantee free passage for us?"

"I cannot *guarantee* free passage, but I give you my word that if you help us return to our world, I will do everything in my power once we are there to get you safe passage out of our system."

"I would want to have safe passage for all Terrans and all of our allies that are currently in-system."

"Of course," Loki said. "All of your forces."

"Do I also have your word that you won't fire on us, and that you will return any of my men and women who come over to restore your jump capability?"

"Yes, any Terrans who come over will be allowed to return to your ship any time they would like to leave. On my honor, I so swear. I also give you my word that my ship will not fire on you; in fact, I will take all of my weapons systems offline, and if you do not fire on us, I will not bring them back online while we are in this system."

"But once we make it back to your home world, you will use them on us?" Captain Sheppard asked.

Loki grinned. "I did leave out that possibility, didn't I? But I am not trying to trick you. I have already given my word that you will have free passage out of our system if you help get us back to our world. We can't get there without your assistance, and if it makes you feel better, I will promise not to use any of my ship's weapons against you in that system too."

"Ever?"

"Well, I don't know that I can promise not to use them forever, since the gods only know what will happen in the fullness of time, but I will promise not to use them against you until after you have been allowed to leave the system of our home world."

"I think that will be sufficient. Remember, you're going to help get *all* of our people the ability to leave."

"I give you my word," Loki said. He smiled and added, "Trust me."

"I don't know that I can do that," Captain Sheppard replied; "however, I know I can't leave you here without the ability to return to our universe. I will trust your word is good, and we will close on your position and send over a party to help repair your motor."

"We appreciate your assistance. Getting stuck here, wherever here is, is not where I hope to meet my end."

Captain Sheppard broke the transmission.

"Do you trust him?" Steropes asked.

"Not as far as I can throw him," the CO replied. "However, stranding them here is a death sentence to them, and if we can help him get his crew back, he will be honor-bound to not only give us free passage out of the system, but to help us get Calvin back, as well. I wasn't sure how we were going to accomplish that."

"It's a dangerous game you're playing."

"It is…but it's the only way we get everything we need." He turned to the OSO. "I want you to keep a close eye on the Jotunn. If you see any of their weapons start to power up, blast 'em. If they even flinch, I want to know about it. But only after you blast them, first."

Ducting, Jotunn Ship *Falcon*, Jotunheimr System, December 23, 2021

"I hope we hear something soon," Calvin said. "I'm beginning to get worried."

"Do you suppose your friends won?" Burkuri asked.

"I don't know," Calvin replied. "I certainly *hope* they did."

"I don't know whether your friends won, or if the battle continues," Farhome said, "but I doubt the Jotunn have won. If Loki had been victorious, he would have come back by now to gloat. It's what Jotunn do."

"Well, perhaps the battle is still going on then," Karver said. "Or maybe the Jotunn won and are staying in the other universe to gloat over your fr—oof!" Burkuri's elbow to his chest cut him off.

"My brother didn't mean that like it sounded," Burkuri said.

"It's not something I haven't already thought about," Calvin replied. "I just wish I was there to help."

"Bad news!" Paxton exclaimed as he came running up. "We are less than a day from the shipyard. The bridge crew said that everyone is going to have to leave the ship on arrival so they can fumigate it. There is supposed to be enough gas to kill a punton, whatever that is."

"It's a four-legged animal almost as tall as the Jotunn," Farhome answered. "If it will kill one of those things, our odds of surviving the gas are...considerably worse."

"What's worse than dead?" Karver asked.

"I don't know," Farhome replied. He paused, and Calvin could tell from the way he cocked his head that he was discussing it with himself. "The best we can come up with is being dead faster. Or maybe dying more slowly and in great pain. Either way, we're going to die."

"Maybe your friends already won," Syrusss said, "and they are in stealth next to us right now, just waiting for the right opportunity to spring their assault and rescue us."

"That's possible," Calvin replied.

"Do you think they are?"

"No, I don't," Calvin said with a shake of his head. "If they were, I think they would have tried to contact me. I think we're going to have to come up with something on our own to get us out of this."

"Do you have an idea?" Farhome asked.

"At the moment? No. But we still have a little time…"

Bridge, TSS *Vella Gulf*, Anti-Jotunheimr System, December 23, 2021

"Uh, sir, you asked to know if the Jotunn did anything strange…" the OSO said.

"Are they arming their weapons?" Captain Sheppard asked.

"No sir. I'm not getting any indications of weapons employment; however, their remaining engine just went to full power, and I'm not seeing an increase in thrust or anything else that correlates with a need for more power. It's weird."

"Steropes, what have you got?"

"Something onboard the Jotunn vessel is definitely using a lot of power," Steropes replied, "but I agree it is not their weapons systems nor are they generating additional thrust."

"Are they testing out their jump systems? Have we received any communications from the engineering personnel we sent over?"

"No sir," the communications officer said. "We haven't heard anything since they reported that the engine room was slagged pretty badly, and they were working on repairs. They have checked in a couple of times since then, as scheduled, but haven't given us any other information. I will contact them and ask."

"There's a second burst of power usage!" the OSO exclaimed.

"Get Loki for me," the CO ordered. "We'll see what he has to say."

"Sir, I just talked to the engineers. They don't have any idea what's using the extra power; it isn't them. Also, I spoke to the *Huggorm,* and the bridge watch says Loki isn't available right now but will talk to you in a few minutes."

"That's it," the CO said. "Call the away team and get them back here ASAP. Engines to full; get us out of here, helm."

"Engines to full, aye," the helmsman replied. "Turning away from the Jotunn vessel."

"It is too late," Solomon announced. "A large number of Jotunn are on the exterior of the hull and are cutting their way in."

"*What?*" Captain Sheppard asked. "How many? How'd they get there?"

"I am unable to determine their exact number as they are employing scramblers and are destroying my sensors. I estimate approximately 30 Jotunn are now aboard. As for how they arrived, they appear to have beamed close aboard and maneuvered to make contact with the ship. My sensors show several other Jotunn in the vicinity were left behind when we accelerated to full power."

"Confirm General Quarters is still set about the ship," the CO ordered. "Get the platoon armed and send them to where the Jotunn are cutting their way in."

"Reconfirming GQ," the duty engineer replied.

"Sending the platoon to repel boarders," Lieutenant Contreras added. "Request permission to rejoin the platoon. We are already short-handed, as several of our troops are onboard the Jotunn ship."

"Granted; go!" the CO ordered. "Solomon, what are our options? Can we electrify the hull or anything like that?"

"No sir," the AI replied. "I do not have a method to remove them. Ships normally do not stop in combat, so beaming onto a ship in combat isn't something I have defenses for. I recommend arming the crew as quickly as possible, especially the bridge crew as one of the groups of Jotunn is cutting through nearby."

Arm them, the CO asked silently. With what? This wasn't the 1700s. They had never practiced repelling boarders, nor were there weapons readily available with which to do so. They were screwed.

The CO activated the ship-wide communications system. "All hands, this is the Captain. We are being boarded by several parties of Jotunn. Our platoon is responding, but it will take some time to counter them. Everyone needs to be in suits with helmets on, as pressurization will likely be failing shortly in a number of places. Avoid the Jotunn where possible and let the soldiers do their jobs, but under no circumstances can we let engineering fall to them. Officers and chiefs, exercise local control; do what you must to defend the ship. That is all. Captain Sheppard, out."

The CO scanned the bridge. "That goes for you too," he added, snapping his helmet into place. "*Helmets on. Solomon, if the bridge falls, deactivate all consoles and transfer the helm to aft control in engineering.*"

"*That will happen shortly,*" the AI replied. "*The closest party of invaders is inside the ship and working its way toward the bridge.*"

"*All right, what else can we do?*" the CO asked.

"*I have called in the fighters,*" the OSO said. "*They have their lasers set at one-quarter power and will strafe the ship. At that setting, they shouldn't damage the ship, but will clear off any of the Jotunn still outside.*"

"*Good idea,*" the CO approved. "*What else have we got?*"

Silence rang throughout the bridge...until it was broken by the sounds of the cutting torch breaching the door.

Armory, TSS *Vella Gulf,* Anti-Jotunheimr System, December 23, 2021

"**M**other *fucker!*" Lieutenant Ryan O'Leary snarled. Captain Train was onboard the enemy vessel, so O'Leary was responsible for…repelling Jotunn boarders? Really? What the *fuck*?

"All right, damn it," he said to the remaining troops as they hurriedly strapped on weapons and implements of destruction. "The bastards are breaking into the ship in at least three places, and we're the only hope the swabbies have of ever seeing their families again. With Captain Train and his group still over on the Jotunn ship, we're already short-handed, and we've got more damned enemies than we have people to kill them. What does that mean? *It means you don't do anything stupid, heroic or foolish.* For the first time in most of your miserable lives, your life is actually worth something. If you find yourself in a position where you have to give that life, make sure you take at least several of the mother fuckers with you. *Got that?*"

"Yes Lieutenant!" the assembled troops roared.

"Good. Lieutenant Contreras, I want you to take the remaining two fire teams from the Ground Force and go see if you can save the ship's CO and bridge crew from the Jotunn breaking in there. Gunny Dantone, I want you to take the second fire team from the space force and go hunt down the group of Jotunn in the center of the ship. They're probably headed for our weapons spaces. Find them and kill them. I'll take the rest of the Space Force and head back to engineering to stop that group. Once you deal with your group of Jotunn, help one of the others."

Lieutenant O'Leary looked around the crowded room. Everyone seemed ready. "All right," he said, liking the focused looks he saw, "they say 'the bigger they are, the harder they fall,' so don't be underneath any of these bastards when you kill them because I don't want anyone getting squashed. Let's go."

Lieutenant O'Leary heard a polite cough behind him and turned to find Father John Zuhlsdorf and Lieutenant Rrower.

"You said you were short-handed," the cleric said; "we would like to offer our services."

"We could definitely use them," O'Leary replied. "I've got more giants than I do troops to fight them. Father Z, you're with my group. Lieutenant Rrower, you're with Lieutenant Contreras. Thanks for volunteering."

"Sometimes you have to go on crusades," Father Z said with a smile; "other times, they come to you."

Engineering, Jotunn Ship *Huggorm*, Anti-Jotunheimr System, December 23, 2021

 *ou've got to be shitting me!"* Night exclaimed. Before anyone could move, he brought his laser rifle up and fired several times into the face of the Jotnar who was watching the engineers work. The giant slumped to the deck without a sound.

"What'd you do that for?" Staff Sergeant Hirt asked.

"The Jotunn just sent a boarding party over to the *Vella Gulf*," Night replied. "The fight's back on, and it sounds like it's going badly for our guys. The bridge crew is evacuating."

"What are we going to do?" Corporal 'Bob' Bobellisssissolliss asked.

"We're going to head back and kick their asses, assuming they let us leave like they said they would. Before we go, though, we're going to leave them a little present for their treachery. I wish Lieutenant O'Leary were here. Bomb-making is his specialty, but I think I can make up something that will work well enough. Watch the doors while I put this together." He looked up and saw the engineers staring open-mouthed at him. "As for you guys," he added, "whatever you've fixed, go ahead and break it again, just in case. You've got three minutes. Go!"

* * * * *

Chapter Twenty-One

Cockpit, *Viper 01*, Anti-Jotunheimr System, December 23, 2021

"*I copy,* Vella Gulf," Lights transmitted. "Viper 01 *and flight inbound for strafing runs.*" She shook her head. "You're never going to believe this, but we just got called in to strike the *Gulf.*"

"Wait...what?" her pilot, Lieutenant Denise 'Frenchie' Michel, asked.

"Apparently, the Jotunn sent some boarders, and they're cutting their way in."

"What are we supposed to do about it?"

"We're going to strafe the ship with our lasers at one-quarter power and shoot the bloody bastards off."

"That is just...merde."

Cockpit, *Viper 09*, Anti-Jotunheimr System, December 23, 2021

"You've got to be freaking kidding me!" Lieutenant Daniel 'Money' Wages exclaimed as he yanked the space fighter around in a tight turn. "We're going to go shoot the *Vella Gulf?*"

"Yep," replied his WSO, Lieutenant Mike 'Retro' Burke. "Mom's got Jotunn on her hull that are trying to break in and steal our stereos." He pushed a button and added, "Nav's good."

"Not on my watch," the pilot muttered, turning to follow the updated navigation instructions. Sure enough, the *Vella Gulf* was on the nose.

Engineering, TSS *Vella Gulf,* Anti-Jotunheimr System, December 23, 2021

"**G**et in here!" Master Chief Michael Agejew shouted to the sailor standing in the middle of the passageway. "Quickly, and bar the hatch!" Conditioned to obey master chiefs like their words were sent straight from God, the sailor immediately did as told.

"What the hell are you doing standing in the passageway?" Master Chief Agejew asked. "Didn't you hear the CO? The Jotunn have invaded the ship. Who the hell are you, anyway? I don't think I've ever seen you before."

"I'm Culinary Specialist Seaman John Matthews," the sailor replied. "I serve meals in the wardroom. I was going up there, but there was a lot of fighting so I came around this way, but I've never been in this part of the ship, and I got lost, and I don't really know where to go with the giants in the way, and I don't know any other way to get back to the wardroom…" His voice finally trailed off.

"Huh, well that's why I don't know you, since I don't eat with the officers." He stared. "A mess crank, eh? Well, you look about as confused as a bunch of short bus riders in a fucking house of mirrors. You'd better unfuck yourself because you're now a front line defender of the good ship *Vella Gulf*. You may not know where you are, but you're in After Steering. This is where you control the ship if the bridge gets hit in combat. Or captured by wandering Jotunn boarders." His arm swept around, indicating the consoles behind him. "You can do almost anything from these consoles that you can do from the bridge."

"Uh…okay…"

"You don't get what I'm talking about, do you?"

"Uh, no Master Chief, I don't understand what you're talking about."

"Whoever controls those consoles can control the ship," Master Chief said. "If the giants make it in here…"

"They can control the ship!" Matthews exclaimed, looking scared.

"Exactly. The Skipper said we can't let Engineering fall into the enemy's hands, and this is what he meant. Right now, it's just you and me defending it; we have to keep the giants out until the soldiers can get here and take over."

"How are we going to do that?"

"Well, first we're going to pray a lot that they don't find it."

The dogging handle to the hatch rattled as someone on the other side tried to open it, then shook harder as more force was put into opening it. Whoever was outside the hatch was strong…very strong…and he spoke in a language the Master Chief had never heard before.

"And when praying doesn't work?" Matthews asked, now looking *very* scared.

"Then we'll have to get a little more creative."

Master Chief Agejew bent over, opened his tool chest and pulled out a pair of heavy rubber gloves. Grabbing one of the electrical lines that entered the junction box near the door, he yanked with all of his might and pulled it out as the Jotunn on the other side of the door began slamming into the hatch.

"We'll see how he likes 450 volts," Master Chief said, applying the live end of the wire to the hatch. Sparks flew, and the Jotunn on the other side of the door bellowed.

"That'll hold them for a minute or two," Master Chief said. He surveyed the space before looking back to the younger sailor. "Seaman Matthews, what do you know about steam?"

"Well, I can steam some vegetables pretty good, but that's about it."

"Close enough. See this line here?" He pointed to a set of pipes that ran along the wall.

"Yes, Master Chief. What about it?"

"This is a steam line. I need you to follow it into the next room and find the shutoff valve. It's a little thing that looks like a handle on the pipe." He bent down and began rummaging through his tool box. The hatch boomed as it sustained another blow; although the pins holding the dogging latch shut held, Master Chief could see that one of them had bent a little under the pressure.

"Now, Master Chief?"

Master Chief Agejew looked up. Rather than leave to carry out his tasking, the younger sailor had actually edged closer to him, and his eyes were darting back and forth across the room. The cook was in danger of losing it.

"Yes, right now, you dumbass!" Agejew yelled, focusing the sailor on the task at hand. "Get yer friggin' ass in gear and go find that damn handle!"

Grabbing a pipe wrench, he set to loosening the bolts holding the pipe to the bulkhead.

Cockpit, *Viper 08*, Anti-Jotunheimr System, December 23, 2021

"Take that, bitch!" yelled Lieutenant Sharon 'Stripes' Green as the fighter screamed past the *Vella Gulf*. "I got one of them!"

"Shit," replied her pilot, Lieutenant Simon 'Straw' Berry, as red lights began flashing on the port wing of the ship on his in-head display. "Looks like one of them got us too."

Straw craned his neck to look out the canopy. "Apparently the Jotunn aren't under the same restrictions we are to use low-power lasers," he noted.

"What do you mean?"

"There's a freaking *hole* through our wing!" He began running through the procedures to shut down the affected equipment.

"*All Vipers*, Viper 08," Stripes transmitted, "*watch for laser fire in the vicinity of the* Vella Gulf! *Targets are returning fire!*"

Cockpit, *Viper 09*, Anti-Jotunheimr System, December 23, 2021

"Oh, I see the little bastards," Retro said, looking through his targeting scope. "There's some sort of crew-served laser. This will just take a sec…"

Retro pushed the "Enable" button on his system, and laser bolts speared through the Jotunn force manning the weapon.

"That'll teach you to try and take my stereo, bitch!"

Neither aviator saw the missile lift off behind them.

Cockpit, *Viper 10*, Anti-Jotunheimr System, December 23, 2021

"*Look out,* Viper 09, *there's a missile on your——*" Lieutenant Dan 'Admiral' Walker called, ceasing when the icon for *09* disappeared from the plot. "Tail," he added under his breath.

"Did you see where it came from?" his pilot, Lieutenant Tom 'Harv' Walsh, asked.

"Yeah, I got 'em," Admiral replied. "There's a big junction box or something; the missile came from behind it, so there must be a giant hiding there."

"Well, blast him, would ya?"

"I'm trying…Come around to starboard a little more so I can see him…got him." Admiral winced; even at one-quarter power, the laser was more than powerful enough to explosively destroy its target.

"Vella Gulf, Viper 10, *all targets outside have been eliminated.*"

There was no reply.

Bridge, TSS *Vella Gulf,* Anti-Jotunheimr System, December 23, 2021

Captain Sheppard secured the escape hatch from the bridge and turned to follow the rest of the crew away from the bridge. "*Sir,*" Solomon commed. "*Loki would like to communicate with you. I can facilitate this if you would like.*"

"*Go ahead.*"

Loki's face appeared in his mind. "*It is over,*" he said. "*We control your bridge and will soon control your engineering and weapons control spaces as well. If you surrender now, I will give you my word that we will not harm your people.*"

"*Like you gave me your word you wouldn't attack us? No thanks. I think I'm starting to understand how you acquired the Shaitan jump modules.*"

"*You wound me,*" Loki said, "*but my honor is pure. I said I wouldn't use my ship's weapons against you, and I haven't. They have been offline the entire time.*"

"*When we get the ship back under our control, I'm coming for you, Loki.*"

"*Why wait? I'm on your bridge, sitting on your chair. Unfortunately, it is not big enough for me to sit in as it looks like it would be comfortable.*"

"*Enjoy the view. Too bad nothing's working for you.*"

"*But it will,*" Loki said. "*Once we get into engineering, it will.*"

Chapter Twenty-Two

Lieutenant O'Leary peeked around the corner in time to see a pair of enormous horizontal legs go around the next corner. "_Contact_," he commed. "_The Jotunn have some kind of anti-gravity sled they are sitting on; that's how they're moving around the ship._" He hadn't thought about it before, but the ceilings weren't tall enough for the giants to stand. They would have had to crawl on their hands and knees...or ride anti-gravity sleds. Maybe the Jotunn were smarter than he had given them credit for.

He ran to the next corner and peered around. "Fuck!" he yelled as he dove back from the next passageway.

"_Okay, this sucks,_" O'Leary commed. "_There are two Jotunn sitting side-by-side on anti-gravity sleds. They're each holding big-ass shields and some sort of shotgun-like weapon. Behind them are two other giants armed with the same shotgun-like weapons, who are firing over the shields of the first rank. There are more giants on the other side of them, breaking into Aft Steering. At least four or five of them. Aside from an awful lot of high explosives, I don't see any way we're going to stop them._"

There had to be a better way; taking on the Jotunn in a frontal-assault was going to get a lot of people killed, including himself, and even then, there was no guarantee they could breach the Jotunn's defenses. He called up the _Vella Gulf's_ schematics on his in-head display, but he didn't see any way over, under or around the Jotunn.

"*Solomon, Lieutenant O'Leary,*" he commed; "*is there any way to get to Aft Steering without going down the next passageway?*"

"*There is a shaft in the overhead that my maintenance robots use to repair the cable runs,*" the AI replied; "*however, it is extremely narrow and nearly all of your platoon won't be able to fit through it.*"

"*How many of my troops can make it?*"

"*Just one; if Staff Sergeant Loftis removes most of her gear, she may fit through the access shaft. In addition to the shaft being narrow, there is also a blind switchback she will have to negotiate. It will be most difficult for her to complete the maneuver. I believe it will be impossible for anyone else.*"

"*Did you hear that, Loftis?*"

"*Yes, Lieutenant, I did,*" Canary replied. "*I hate narrow places, especially in the dark, but I'm willing to try it rather than going into the maws of the Jotunn's shotguns.*" The entry port for the access shaft appeared about 15 feet away on the map in her head.

Staff Sergeant Loftis sat down underneath the hatch and took off her gear, then she threw some of her equipment into a small bag and stood up. "Ready," she said.

A couple of the troops gave her a boost up to the hatchway. She took off the cover and handed it down. "Damn, it's dark," Canary said, sticking her head up through the port. She looked around inside.

"I'm going to need a light source," she added. "Can someone hand me up my cell phone?"

"*A cell phone?*" Lieutenant O'Leary asked. "Why the fuck do you have a cell phone in outer space?"

"Some of the apps are really helpful," Canary replied with a shrug. "Like now."

Valkyrie handed her the phone, and Canary turned on the flash-light app and pushed the phone down the narrow shaft in front of her. Valkyrie handed Canary her gear bag and her rifle, and she slid them down the duct after the phone. Just those few items made the shaft seem even smaller than it had before.

Canary slid the pile forward again and climbed into the shaft. Damn, it was narrow. She hated confined areas, and this wasn't even as wide as her shoulders, which touched both sides of the passage-way at the same time. The walls became even narrower in front of her, and it looked like she would have to go through sideways. Damn!

She had no idea what kind of robot could negotiate the twists and turns, but they had to be pretty darn flexible. Trying not to think any more about the size of the ducting or the need for speed, Canary began sliding down shaft, the walls pressing in on her from both sides. She tried to slow her breath. It was narrow, but she thought she could make it.

Until she reached the 'S' turn.

"Solomon, I don't think I can fit through the next section," she commed, *"and I know my rifle can't. Is there another way around?"*

"No, there is not," the AI replied. She could hear banging beneath her. *"It is not much further, but you have to make it through that section."*

Fuck. Tears brimmed in her eyes. There was no *way* she could make it through. The banging beneath her grew louder. She struggled forward to make the attempt, forcing herself through the corner until she was totally wedged into the center of the turn. She was almost through the narrowest part, but due to the angle, her boot couldn't get enough purchase to push her the rest of the way through. She couldn't go any further forward…and in a moment of panic, she realized she couldn't get back out either.

She squeezed her eyes shut to keep from screaming and realized it had grown quiet. The banging below her had ceased, which was even more ominous. The boost of adrenaline helped her wriggle three fingers free. Blowing out all of her breath to become as small as possible she used the three fingers to push herself back out of the narrows.

Still quiet. Canary frantically removed her boots with the one hand that was in a position to reach the lower part of her body. Her numb fingers struggled with the laces, but worked them free. Her traction improved, she was able to work her way through the turn, and she made it to the access hatch into engineering without further difficulty.

Her breath roared in her ears, and she struggled to control it as she lifted up the cover. She set the lid aside, dreading what she would see, but was energized to see the space was Jotunn-free. Instead, a burly chief worked on some piping while a junior seaman stood idly by, awkwardly shifting from one foot to another. She let her legs swing into the opening, then slid through on her stomach, both hands tightly gripping the bag and her phone as she dropped the rest of the way to the floor.

"Ow!" she exclaimed, landing awkwardly on the steel deck.

At the sound of her cry, the chief spun around, holding his wrench like a club, and she could see the stars on his anchor insignia.

"Uh, hi, Master Chief," she said. "I'm here to help."

Seeing the short, barefoot girl clutching a camouflage bag and cell phone, the master chief lowered his wrench and barked a short laugh.

"I'd love a little assistance," he said, nodding at the other sailor; "Matthews here isn't worth half a cup of warm spit. I'm not sure how you're going to help, though. What are you going to do, call 9-1-1 for me?"

Canary saw where he was looking and held up her phone. "Oh, this was just to help get me here," she said, opening her bag; "this is what I brought to help."

Master Chief gave a low whistle of appreciation as she pulled a number of grenades and two pistols from the bag.

"I've found that most extraterrestrial problems can be solved with the proper application of high explosives," Canary noted.

"I'm sure you have," the master chief murmured. Even lower, he added, "And I'm glad I'm not one of your problems."

Canary surveyed the area, frowning. "So…what else do you have to defend the space?"

"Well, I was going to hit them with some steam," he said, pointing to the pipe he had shifted. "But it's not something I want to do unless I absolutely have to, and it's not something I can do for very long."

"Why's that?"

"The steam in that pipe is 700 degrees and it's pressurized to 3,000 PSI. If we start dumping it in here, it's going to get hot, fast. It'll be worse if you're actually hit with the steam blast, like I hope the Jotunn will be, but it will start to suck in here pretty fast, even if you're not."

"Okay, so the steam option's the last resort," Canary said. She turned to Matthews. "And what have you got?" she demanded.

"Me?" the sailor asked in a squeaky voice. "I'm just waiting to see what Master Chief wants me to do."

"Boys," Canary said with a sigh and a shake of her head. "It's so hard to get them to do anything that involves thinking." She turned back to the senior sailor. "Okay, so the grenades are our best bet, but I don't want them going off next to me. I've got strict orders to kill several of the Jotunn before I'm allowed to die."

She inspected the hatch critically as it boomed with repeated contacts from outside. It wasn't going to last much longer; there was already a small gap at the top where the seal had been broken.

"Think you could open that long enough for me to throw a couple of grenades through, then get it shut again quickly?"

"If it means the difference between the grenades going off out there rather than in here, you're damn well right I can," he said.

"We need something to get them off the door first. I don't want them grabbing the door and holding it when you open it. Hmmm…maybe I can have the squad create a diversion."

"I've got just the thing," Master Chief Agejew said, pulling on a rubber glove. "Just let me know when you're ready."

Taking a grenade in both hands, she checked the settings and pulled out the pins with her teeth. She spat them out and gave him a predator's grin. "Ready."

Task Force Contreras, TSS *Vella Gulf,* Anti-Jotunheimr System, December 23, 2021

Second Lieutenant Cristobal Contreras checked his in-head display as the group jogged toward the bridge. All nine members of his force were operational.

"*Solomon,*" he commed, "*can I get a status update on the Jotunn force assaulting the bridge?*"

"*There are 10 Jotunn in the vicinity of the bridge,*" the AI replied. "*I believe six are on the bridge and four are in the passageways, with two guarding each entrance.*"

"*You believe?*"

"*The Jotunn continue to destroy my sensors, so my analysis has an inherent margin of error included in it, currently estimated at 7.2%. I am 89.6% confident there are 10 Jotunn in the vicinity of the bridge. Based on the size of the bridge, I do not estimate more than six Jotunn would fit comfortably in the space with the vehicles they are using to move about the ship. That estimate is based on the amount of space the median Terran is comfortable with, extrapolated upwards to the size of the Jotunn and the number of voices and the sounds of breathing currently audible. I am fairly confident in that estimate, but it could be plus or minus two.*"

"*Is the CO safe?*"

"*Yes, the entire bridge crew escaped before the bridge was captured. The bridge crew is currently waiting in the escape pods, but have not yet jettisoned.*"

"*Can you tell what the Jotunn are doing?*" Contreras asked. "*Can they operate the ship?*"

"*Before the CO left, he transferred ship's control to Aft Steering and deactivated the bridge, so the Jotunn on the bridge are unable to operate any of the bridge consoles. They are waiting for Engineering to fall; when the Jotunn capture Aft Steering, they will be able to control the ship.*"

"*Are they likely to capture Aft Steering?*"

"*The Jotunn force is far larger than the defending force. It is likely they will succeed in capturing it.*"

"*We need to hurry then.*"

"*That is a logical conclusion.*"

Task Force Dantone, TSS *Vella Gulf,* Anti-Jotunheimr System, December 23, 2021

Gunnery Sergeant Patrick "The Wall" Dantone led the way to the ship's Weapons Control facility at a jog. It was simply more practical for the cyborg to lead; despite the CO's instructions, a large number of the ship's crew were milling in the passageways. Worse, they didn't always move out of the way, despite an amplified call to "make a hole." When they were too slow clearing his path, he simply smashed his way through without slowing, leaving a trail of injured sailors in his wake. Medical would be busy tomorrow...if there was a tomorrow.

The Wall checked the vital signs of his fire team as he scanned ahead for enemies. He had been multitasking a lot more recently. Whether that was because his "body" required a great deal less thought, both conscious and unconscious, to operate, he didn't know. Perhaps, freed from these tasks, his brain was reprogramming itself to utilize the additional processing power. While the ability to complete a number of tasks simultaneously was cool, the thought that his brain was becoming more...robotic...and that he might be losing some of his humanity was troubling.

If they survived, he would have to talk to someone about it, although he wasn't sure who. Anyone in the military was probably out; he didn't want to risk being thought crazy. He wasn't crazy. If anything, he was operating more efficiently than the biologicals. Talking to Medical was *definitely* out. While having a machine-to-almost-machine conversation with the medibot would be instructional, it was even more dangerous than talking with someone in the military. Not only was there the risk of a "crazy" diagnosis, the eccentric medibot might decide his condition was worthy of study and give him a medical discharge or put him on a limited duty status.

Neither of these options bore further consideration. He wasn't going to do anything that would get him kicked out of the platoon while the war was on, especially if it turned him into a lab rat. Not. Going. To. Happen. He had neither asked for nor wanted his undead status, but if he could use it to ensure it didn't happen to anyone else, he would.

Sergeant Jamal 'Bad Twin' Gordon was falling behind. Extra PT would be required to bring him up to standards. He added the thought to his mental "To Do" list.

The scent of Jotunn pheromones was growing stronger as he approached Weapons Control. Based on the rate of change, they would already be in the facility by the time the Terrans arrived. Caution was indicated. The Wall slowed, which had the secondary benefit of allowing Sergeant Gordon to catch up.

"*The Jotunn have reached the facility,*" he commed. "*We will need to exercise caution. For those of you who have never been here, this is where the ship's weapons are assembled. Mark your targets and do not shoot anything that looks like it might be an anti-ship warhead. If you do, well, it won't matter to you, since you'll be dead…as will the rest of us.*"

"*What do the warheads look like?*" Sergeant Anne 'Fox' Stasik asked.

"*No idea,*" The Wall replied. "*They don't look like Jotunn though; that much I know. If it is big and looks like a giant, kill it; otherwise, don't. Got it?*"

"*Yes, Gunny!*" the group agreed.

"*Good,*" The Wall replied. "*There's probably going to be as many of them as there are of us, so don't do anything stupid that's going to leave the rest of us more shorthanded than we already are.*"

Dantone slowed to a human's walking pace then stopped at the next corner. Motioning the group to hold their position, he eased out into the passageway then jumped back.

"*All right, boys and girls,*" he said, "*we're in some serious shit here.*"

Engineering, TSS *Vella Gulf*, Anti-Jotunheimr System, December 23, 2021

"*H*ow's it coming, Staff Sergeant?" Lieutenant O'Leary commed.

Damn, Canary thought, I forgot to check in. She held up a finger to Master Chief indicating he should wait a minute.

"*Good, sir. I made it to Aft Steering without too much difficulty although I had to leave my rifle in the overhead. There are two other people here. We're about to hit the Jotunn with grenades; you may be able to hit them while they're distracted.*"

"*We'll be ready.*"

Canary met Master Chief Agejew's eyes. "Sorry, the boss called. They're going to hit the Jotunn from behind when we get their attention. Hopefully, they can break through to us." She nodded. "Okay, I'm ready."

"What about me?" Seaman Matthews asked.

"What do you mean, 'what about you?'" Canary asked.

"What do you want me to do?"

"Do you know how to use a laser pistol?"

"Umm…no. Is it hard?"

One of the pins on the hatch snapped in half and went flying. The hatch now hung askew, leaving a big enough gap that Canary could see the pale blue eyes of a giant as it peered through.

"No time!" Master Chief yelled. "Get to the steam line and be ready to pull the handle if I tell you!"

The giant hit the hatch again, and the remaining pin bent. The gap in the hatch was now at least six inches wide and one of the giants stuck the barrel of his gun through it.

"It's now or never!" Master Chief shouted.

"Go!" Canary yelled.

Master Chief applied the end of the wire to the gun barrel, and the giant holding it screamed. Without pause, Agejew grabbed the latching mechanism and pulled, but the handle was bent and didn't move.

He released the wire in his other hand and grabbed the handle with both hands. This time the mechanism moved, slowly as he forced it open. With a screech, it opened the rest of the way, and the hatch sagged even further. Agejew jumped out of the way and threw the door open, just as a giant reached forward to push on it.

On its hands and knees, the Jotunn fell forward when the door opened, and Canary threw both grenades over the giant as it tried to get back up.

The giant had one hand in the space with them, and Master Chief knew the giant's arm would prevent him from shutting the hatch. He grabbed the wire from where it hung next to him and jammed it into the giant's face.

The Jotnar went rigid as the electricity coursed through its body, and steam began to pour from the giant's closest eye. Master Chief withdrew the wire, and the creature slumped, falling to the deck outside the hatch although one arm remained across the hatch coaming. Master Chief kicked the offending hand out of the way and tried to slam the hatch, but the giant's gun had fallen into the corner of the opening, and the hatch wouldn't shut.

Agejew saw the problem, bent down and yanked the massive weapon into Engineering. He stood up, his burly form blocking the hatchway, as the grenades exploded.

Task Force O'Leary, TSS *Vella Gulf*, Anti-Jotunheimr System, December 23, 2021

"*Now!*" Lieutenant O'Leary commed as two explosions rocked the passageway. He rolled into the passageway and fired his rifle at the mass of Jotunn outside of Engineering. Several were already down, and the rest had turned away from him. The volume of fire picked up as Valkyrie and Skank came around the corner.

O'Leary immediately saw a problem; the giants weren't dying fast enough.

Body shots didn't cut it. He didn't know whether it was because the Jotunn suits and armor could absorb more of the Terrans' laser fire or because it took more damage to put one of the giants down, but he knew his force was in trouble as the rear ranks of the Jotunn spun around and aimed their weapons.

"Back!" he yelled as he shot the one in front of him in the helmet. The long laser blast burned through the facemask and into the giant's head.

O'Leary risked a glance and saw that Skank and Valkyrie were still standing next to him, firing calmly down the passage. Dropping his rifle, he pushed off the bulkhead and crashed into the two troopers, tackling them out of the corridor as the giant's weapon roared.

Fire ignited in his leg, and he looked down and saw a two-foot-long flechette through his right thigh. It missed the bone, but protruded from both the front and back of his leg.

"Damn it," O'Leary said, rolling off the troopers and coming awkwardly to his feet. "I told you to move."

Both troopers looked like pin cushions. They had caught the brunt of the flechette cannon blast and were covered in the slivers of metal from head to toe. Neither was moving, and he brought up their vital signs in his display. They were both low and fading fast.

"*Medic!*" he commed.

"*Already on it,*" the squad's medic, Corporal Anaru Ngata, said as he pushed Lieutenant O'Leary out of the way. "*Move, please.*"

O'Leary moved and turned back to the cross passage. "*Wraith, we're going to need some anti-matter down the hall; the lasers aren't enough.*"

"*On it, sir,*" she said, setting her rifle to the side and pulling the trident from where it was strapped across her back.

"*Don't go long,*" O'Leary added, wincing as he drew the flechette through the back of his leg; "*there are friendlies on the other side of them.*"

Task Force Contreras, TSS *Vella Gulf*, Anti-Jotunheimr System, December 23, 2021

"Fuck!" Gunnery Sergeant Jerry 'Wolf' Stasik yelled as he jumped back from the cross-passage leading to the bridge. A storm of laser bolts raged down the corridor behind him, followed by a massive explosion.

"*Sir, we're pretty screwed,*" Wolf said. "*There's a long stretch of passageway and two giants at the end. They are sitting on some sort of vehicles that have mounted lasers, and at least one has a grenade launcher or some sort of explosives projector. They will be difficult to assault.*"

"*Solomon, is there any other way to get to the bridge?*" Contreras asked.

"*No, there is not. If one of the escape pods launch, then you could go outside the ship and re-enter from where the pod launched to assault the other side of the bridge; however, there is another pair of Jotunn waiting there. That pair is probably armed similarly to the ones currently facing you.*"

"*Sir, my fire team will take the hatch for you,*" Staff Sergeant Brian 'Huge' Mchugh offered. "*There are four of us and only two of them, and I have my trident to even the score.*"

"*They've got their own grenade launcher,*" Contreras noted, "*and that will make the odds very much against you. Not only that, it will leave us shorthanded against the ones on the bridge. No, I forbid it.*" He paused for a moment, and a big smile came over his face.

"*I have an idea,*" Contreras said. "*Huge, if you really want to assault the bridge, I think I have a way for you to do it, and hopefully, some of us will still be alive afterward. Zoromski, you and Phil stay here and guard the passageway. Everyone else, come with me. We have to go aft to go forward.*"

Task Force Dantone, TSS *Vella Gulf,* Anti-Jotunheimr System, December 23, 2021

"W*hat's wrong, Gunny?*" Fox asked.

"*There are two Jotunn at the hatch into Weapons Control. Both are alert and both have weapons that look like cannons.*"

"*Yeah, that's some serious shit, all right,*" Bad Twin agreed. "*So what are we going to do about it?*"

"*Stand by.*" The Wall pulled up the ship's schematics. If he could have frowned, he would have. The facility was constructed to be defensible—there was only one way in and out. Unless...

"*Stay here,*" he ordered, "*and do* not *let them get past you. Keep them occupied with your lasers until I'm ready.*" He removed his trident and handed it to Bad Twin. "*When I tell you, hit the ones in the hatch with this. Whatever else happens, though, you cannot let them get past you and out of here with any of the weapon jump modules. Use the trident if you have to, but stop them at all costs. Got it?*"

"*Sure thing, Gunny,*" Bad Twin replied, "*but I thought you said the indiscriminate use of high explosives was a* bad *thing.*"

"*Yeah, it is,*" The Wall agreed. "*That's why I only want you to do it when I say to.*"

Engineering, TSS *Vella Gulf,* Anti-Jotunheimr System, December 23, 2021

Master Chief Agejew fell backward in slow motion. Although the Jotunn absorbed most of the explosions, Staff Sergeant Loftis had seen a piece of shrapnel blow out the back of Agejew's head; the senior enlisted man was dead before he hit the floor.

Which left everything up to her.

Shaking off the overpressure of the grenade blasts, she struggled to her feet and staggered to the door. Grabbing her last grenade, she pulled the pin and tossed it out the hatch—right into the face of an oncoming giant. The Jotnar was riding some kind of sled, and it couldn't catch the grenade, which fell to the deck. As the giant bent down to pick it up, she slammed the hatch shut and pulled down on the dogging lever.

Canary felt the concussion of the grenade through the mangled door as the weapon exploded. Several pieces of shrapnel pinged off the other side.

She slumped against the hatch but was flung to the side as one of the giants crashed into it, shattering the last pin and launching the hatch through the air. Stunned, she hit the floor and rolled to a stop as the hatch flew past her. She lifted herself enough to look back toward the hatchway, just in time to see the first of the giants stick his head through. Her hands reached for her pistols, but both had been separated from her when she hit the deck. All she had was her knife, which wasn't going to do much more than annoy the giant. She knew she was doomed.

Drawing her knife, she climbed to her feet as the giant entered the space, passing the pipe next to the hatchway. The pipe!

"*Steam on!*" she yelled, hoping Matthews was still manning the valve.

3,000 PSI steam jetted from the pipe, cutting into the Jotnar like an invisible giant sword. His left arm was severed; the stump flash-fried in the 700 degree steam, but not enough to cauterize the wound. Green blood sprayed from the severed artery as the giant spun away from the pipe and fell to the floor.

Within seconds, the temperature in the space went from 'pleasant' to 'hot' to 'stifling,' and Canary found it hard to breathe in the steamy air.

"*Steam off!*" she cried, gasping for breath.

The steam ceased, and Canary realized the master chief had been right; another few seconds and she would have started cooking. The way the steam displaced the air also made it hard to breathe. Turning the steam back on immediately would be suicide.

It was enough, though. The giant was down in a small lake of blood and had stilled. The sounds of battle drew her eyes to the passageway through the hatch. Although a number of the Jotunn were down, at least four more were still firing down the passageway in the opposite direction. One looked back and saw her staring at him through the open hatch; he immediately turned his anti-gravity vehicle around and sped toward her.

She spun around frantically, looking for her pistols, as explosives detonated in the passageway. She saw one of the weapons as she dove away from the blast. The pistol was up against the opposite wall in two pieces. The hatch must have hit her where the pistol was holstered when it separated from the frame; that would explain the blinding pain in her hip as she limped to fetch the other pistol that was still near the hatch.

With a roar, the giant entered the space on his hands and knees. The visual image might have been amusing, were it not for the hatchet he carried. Green blood speckled his light blue combat suit in a number of places. Giant-sized, the hatchet he carried was as big as a Terran axe, and Canary had to jump back as the giant took a wild swing at her.

She looked longingly at the pistol, out of reach beyond the arc of the hatchet. Without the pistol, she was down to her knife and the last grenade. She dove back and right to avoid another swing of the hatchet as she looked for an opportunity.

There wasn't one.

Weapons Control Facility, TSS *Vella Gulf*, Anti-Jotunheimr System, December 23, 2021

"*E*verything still okay?" The Wall asked.

"*Sure is, Gunny...now,*" Fox replied. "*We were starting to get worried about you.*"

"*When this is over, we'll see how long it takes you to go outside, climb back in through an anti-ship missile tube and then squeeze yourself through the loading tube to get back to Weapons Control.*"

"*Holy shit, Gunny,*" Bad Twin said. "*You did all that?*"

"*Yeah, I did, and I'm ready to hit the bastards from behind. I'm on the other side of an access hatch from the facility, and I can hear the Jotunn on the other side. It sounds like they're disassembling missiles to find jump modules they can steal. When I give you the word, light them up with everything you've got, including a couple of grenades from the trident. Got it?*"

"*Yes, Gunny, we're ready.*"

"*Solomon, do you have any idea what I'm going to find on the other side of the access hatch?*"

"*They have destroyed the cameras I had in that space, but by using the room's heat sensors, I can predict with a good deal of certainty there are nine Jotunn inside. Two are near the door, and seven are scattered throughout the room. It is likely they have acquired at least one jump module at this point.*"

Damn. *Seven* by himself? That was more than he really wanted to bite off. Especially with the possibility of it becoming all nine if the two Jotunn at the door turned around. What the hell, Medical could always rebuild him, assuming he didn't take one to the head. Of course, if he did, he wouldn't have to worry about it anymore. Being a cyborg came with a certain sense of fatalism.

"*Well, we can't have them getting their hands on any of the jump modules,*" Dantone replied. "*Can you remotely open the access hatch in front of me when my troops begin firing?*"

"*Yes, I can. Shall I do so?*"

"*I would like you to open it after the second grenade detonates.*" No sense getting fragged by your own troops. "*All right, everyone, here we go. 3…2…1…attack!*"

* * * * *

Chapter Twenty-Three

"That's your good idea?" Wolf asked as Lieutenant Contreras walked onto the transporter platform. "I didn't think we were allowed to use the transporter since we haven't been scanned yet."

"This is the perfect way to get onto the bridge without having to battle the Jotunn to do so," Contreras replied. "And, as I understand it, the danger of using it internal to the ship will be minimal since Solomon has the ship mapped out to the micrometer level. Can you confirm that, Solomon?"

"That is only partially true," Solomon replied. "I have an excellent scan of the ship, and normally I would be able to transport anyone to anywhere within the ship. If you desire it, I am currently able to do so with you. The danger will be more than minimal, however, as I do not have firm positions for where the Jotunn are on the bridge. Without my sensors, there is a very real chance you could reappear on the bridge in the same space as one of the giants. If that happens, it will likely cause a very painful death for both of you."

"When you say, 'small,' what do you mean?" Contreras asked.

"I mean there is a 3.2% chance for each of you. Cumulatively, there is a 28.8% chance for the group that at least one of you will be transposed."

"That's good enough for me," Huge said. "I'm in."

"Us, too," added the other members of his fire team, Corporals Sam Ward and Joshua King.

"The Jotunn attack is not honorable," Yokaze said; "if this will put me in contact with them, I am in." He slung his rifle and drew his katana and wakizashi. "Hai! I am ready."

"Always loved big game huntin' back home," Staff Sergeant Chris Upton said. "Don't get much bigger than this. I'm in."

Lieutenant Rrower nodded. "It will be the biggest prey I have hunted too," he said. "I'm with you."

"Well, if all of you idiots are in, I am, too," the Ground Force medic, Sergeant Brandi 'Doc' Walker, added.

Wolf sighed and stepped onto the transporter platform. "This is the dumbest thing I've ever done in my life, but you're not going without me," he said. "Before we go, though, I've got some words of advice. I'm less worried we'll have problems transporting than I am about what we'll find once we get there. There are six Jotunn on the bridge. If you haven't seen one, they're big, really big. Enormous. I've studied all the info we have on them, and I'm here to tell you they take a *lot* of killing to bring down, and we only have eight folks to do it. There are more of us numerically, but really, we're the ones who are outnumbered."

He paused to scan the faces of his troops then added, "If you're not scared, you should be. They're bigger and tougher than we are, even with our suits. Don't try to meet them strength for strength. If they swing at you, don't try to block; they will cut you in half. You're smaller and faster. Use your mobility to evade and kill them as fast as you can. Violently. And don't stop killing until they are all down and unmoving. Kill them *dead*. As soon as the one you're fighting is down, help someone else and be ready for the ones at the door to come in. It's going to get crowded. Mark your targets and don't frag each other."

His voice got louder. "The winners of this fight are going to be the ones who are the fastest and the meanest. If you're not the meanest mother fuckers in this system, you better get that way right now. *Do you get me?*"

"*Yes Gunnery Sergeant!*"

"Good." He turned to Lieutenant Contreras and assumed a combat pose with his rifle at the ready. "Enough talking. Let's go take back our bridge."

Contreras nodded once, then drew his saber and laser pistol. "Solomon, please beam us to the bridge. On my mark. 3…2…1…*Mark!*"

Weapons Control, TSS *Vella Gulf,* Anti-Jotunheimr System, December 23, 2021

The access hatch slid open and The Wall got his first look into Weapons Control. The space was one of the largest on the ship—a square nearly 80 feet to a side. Eight of the Jotunn remained; the grenade barrage had killed one of the giants at the hatch. The other was on his knees with green blood running in torrents from a number of wounds. As The Wall pulled himself from the tube, the remaining door guard was hit by at least three laser bolts from his fire team and sprawled on the floor.

Seven remained. Six were in the center of the room, with one in the corner to the right.

"Godfried and Jorn, cover the door," one of the Jotunn in the center of the room said, nodding to the door. "We will leave momentarily; go down the hall and kill them."

"Aye, Jarl, we'll teach them to be good slaves," one of the Jotunn said as two of them went to the hatch.

Dantone dropped to the floor, his knees bent to absorb the impact and land as silently as was possible for a cyborg. He had neglected to take into account all of the junk the Jotunn had disassembled and strewn around the space, though, and he landed on a circuit board. The delicate electronics shattered under the impact, and the sound echoed throughout the space.

"What?" the Jarl asked, looking up. "Kill the Terran!"

Unlike the other Terran soldiers, The Wall was equipped to deal with the Jotunn, and his Hooolong pulse rifles began firing, starting with the four Jotunn in the center of the space. The pulse rifles were devastating to smaller targets as they fired the Mrowry equivalent of explosive 20mm shells; the rifles were nearly as effective against the massive Jotunn. Even better, his cyborg frame was strong enough to hold a rifle in each hand. He had practiced doing it with a rifle in one hand and a trident in the other…but setting off antimatter grenades in the middle of this many anti-ship warheads was contraindicated, so he had settled on two pulse rifles. One eye provided targeting for each, and he fired bursts of five shells into each of the giant's chests, then three-round bursts into each of their heads. Distance vision was slightly off with only one eye on each of the targets, but it didn't really matter at this range.

Two of the Jotunn by the Jarl were killed before they could move, and the other one moments later. The Jarl had enough time to draw his weapon before being hit by 10 of the projectiles. The Wall's aft infrared sensor showed the giant from the corner approaching, and he reached back to fire several bursts into the enemy, while evaluating the giants in the center of the room. All dead.

He turned to find the doorway empty; the other two giants had gone down the passageway. The giant behind him was dead, with three shots through his facemask. Although he had practiced firing behind him without looking in the combat simulator, he'd never had the opportunity to use the rear sensor in combat before. While its success didn't make Dantone a fan of being a cyborg, he did have to admit that having eyes in the back of his head *was* something of a perk for a soldier.

Screams and laser fire echoed down the passageway.

He turned and ran out the hatch. The other two giants had made it to where he had left the remaining members of the fire team. One went around the corner, while the other chopped down with its sword, splitting Staff Sergeant 'Mr.' Jones nearly in half. The Wall's rifles came up as he ran, and he put five rounds into the giant's head before he could pull the sword out of the former CIA agent's body.

As The Wall rounded the corner, the other giant was already going down, hit countless times by the fire team's laser rifles. The Jotnar collapsed, falling forward to bury his knife in Sergeant Anne Stasik's chest. As big as a broadsword, it burst explosively from her back as she was driven to the deck by the giant's collapse. The sword pinned her to the deck like a butterfly in a collector's case.

Dantone fired a three-round burst into the Jotnar's head, just to be sure, and went to check on Stasik. There was no hope for Jones; the long-time member of the platoon had no chance of surviving his injury. The Wall knelt down next to Sergeant Stasik and could see she wasn't dead yet. The knife had missed her heart, and she lay there gasping, blood running out of the corner of her mouth.

"*Solomon, we need medical assistance,*" Dantone commed. Medical was only a short way down the passage. If help arrived soon, she might still be saved.

Engineering, TSS *Vella Gulf,* Anti-Jotunheimr System, December 23, 2021

Staff Sergeant Loftis flung herself back from the giant. The axe passed through the space where she had been, narrowly missing her, but she was brought up short as she slammed into the bulkhead behind her. With nowhere to go, she dropped into a defensive pose, holding up her knife as if to ward off her massive opponent.

"Ho, ho, ho," the giant guffawed. "Ooh, I am so scared. Perhaps I should run away." He chuckled again then asked, "How many times do you think you would have to stab me with that in order to kill me? Quit fooling around and come over here so I can end your suffering for you."

The Terran risked a glance over both her shoulders. She could lead the giant to the right into the interior of Engineering, where there was more space for her to maneuver, or she could go left into the dead end where she would be trapped and unable to run. There was only one way to go.

The axe descended again, and she dove to the left. Matthews was hiding to the right; she couldn't risk exposing him.

The giant was unprepared for her choice and missed to her right, overextending himself in the wrong direction. Canary turned the dive into a roll and came up running down the side of the giant. Reaching out, she grabbed a handful of his suit and used her momentum to vault up onto the Jotnar's back.

The giant reached behind himself, but only grabbed a handful of air as she scrambled to the center of his back and drove the knife into it. The giant bellowed in pain as she pulled back on the knife, cutting a six-inch gash in his suit. Unclipping her last grenade from her belt, she pulled the pin and dropped it into his suit, diving out of the way as he reached back over his shoulder to grab her.

This time she dove toward the main engineering spaces and ran several steps into it before turning to confront the giant.

"How many times do I have to cut you?" she asked. "Just once."

The grenade detonated. Dialed up to its highest setting, it shredded the Jotnar from behind, but Canary was shielded from the blast by the giant's massive body. His eyes rolled back into his head, and the giant fell forward; the deck shook with the impact as the Jotnar's enormous body hit.

"That was *awesome!*" Seaman Matthews said, coming out from hiding to stand next to her. "How did you learn to do all that?"

"You killed Sven!" a voice boomed from the hatchway behind Canary. "Now I kill you!"

Canary turned to find an even bigger giant coming through the hatch with a gleaming silver sword that was almost twice as long as she was tall.

"Run!" she ordered over her shoulder to Matthews.

"You can't fight it with just your knife," the sailor said. "You'll be killed!"

"We were told not to let any of these bastards into Engineering," Canary replied. "And I'm not going to." She turned and advanced on her new adversary, knife in hand.

The new Jotnar neither laughed at her knife nor taunted her; instead, he swung the sword in a massive stroke that would have decapitated her had she stood her ground. Diving to the left, the sword passed over her; the breeze from its passage would have been enough to knock her over if she hadn't already been in motion. Canary rolled to her feet, happy to be alive, but the giant backhanded her, and she went flying backwards to crash into the bulkhead 10 feet behind her. She slid to the ground, stunned.

The giant advanced on her and picked her up around the waist. Canary found she had somehow held onto the knife, and she stabbed it into the giant's thumb.

"That tickles," the creature said. He looked down at her, then he threw her into the wall again. She blacked out.

Task Force O'Leary, TSS *Vella Gulf*, Anti-Jotunheimr System, December 23, 2021

"*Solomon, can you see how it's going in Engineering?*" Lieutenant O'Leary asked.

"*Staff Sergeant Loftis has been rendered unconscious,*" the AI replied. "*The capture of the facility by the Jotunn is imminent.*"

"Fuck."

Lieutenant O'Leary looked into the faces surrounding him. Wraith, Witch, Father Z, Good Twin and the squad's medic, 'Spuds' Ngata. Six Terrans versus two of the Jotunn down the passage. As he looked into their eyes, he knew it would be the last time he saw some of them…if he survived to see any of them at all.

"Okay," he said. "Here's the deal. Loftis is down and Engineering is about to fall. You heard the Skipper; we can't let that happen. When I say so, Good Twin, I want you to lay down a suppressing fire with the trident while we attack the remaining Jotunn in the passageway. We have to kill them and get into Engineering. Don't stop until they're all dead. Any questions?"

The remaining members of the squad shook their heads inside their helmets. Veterans, they knew what he left unsaid.

"Good Twin, make sure you aim over us; I don't want a grenade in the back of my head. Got it?"

"Yes, Lieutenant!" the trooper replied.

"Good. Here we go. Ready. Set. Go!"

O'Leary turned the corner, accelerating to full speed, firing from the hip as he ran. As he thought, there were still two Jotunn in the passageway although one of them had been hit numerous times; the Jotnar's white suit was polka-dotted with green.

The other giant brought up its flechette cannon and fired, and O'Leary dove to the side of the passageway. With a flash, a grenade exploded as it hit the Jotnar's chest, blowing the giant backward and ripping apart its torso. As it toppled over, the remaining squad members' lasers converged on the wounded giant, striking it over and over again as it knelt in the passageway, stunned. After a few moments and 15 laser strikes, it toppled over.

"*Let's go!*" Lieutenant O'Leary commed. He looked back over his shoulder as he started forward and slammed to a stop. Father Z was down and looked like a pin cushion. Witch stood over him, looking for a place to administer first aid without shredding her hands on the flechettes.

"He dove in front of me," she said softly, looking down at the fallen priest.

Wraith lay on the deck behind Witch. She had only been hit by one flechette, but it had gone through her facemask and straight through her brain. Her life signs had already zeroed. Damn, Night was going to be *pissed*.

"We'll come back for them," O'Leary said. "Let's go; we've got to get to Engineering."

Without another look, he sped down the passage.

Task Force Contreras, TSS *Vella Gulf*, Anti-Jotunheimr System, December 23, 2021

Lieutenant Contreras stabilized on the bridge next to a giant sitting on what looked like an oversized motorcycle. Although he thought he was prepared for the enormity of the creature's size, he froze in shock looking up at the monster. All the way up. The bridge ceiling was almost 20 feet high, allowing the giants to stand, rather than crawl or be hunched over, and they were simply enormous. And nothing could have prepared him for the smell. The Jotnar stank of rotten food and body odor.

Staff Sergeant Upton materialized on the other side of the Jotnar and fired into the creature's side. The giant roared and backhanded the soldier. Upton flew backward, his rifle flying off in another direction.

The giant turned to follow the flight of the soldier and drew a knife from his belt as big as a Terran long sword. Compelled to action to save his trooper, Contreras stepped forward and drove his saber into the giant's stomach and up under his ribs, then pulled back down, gutting him. The stench of the giant increased as his entrails fell out, and the giant fell off the motorcycle on the side away from Contreras.

Contreras ran to the other side of the motorcycle, and stabbed the giant through the chest. Pulling his saber out, he looked for Upton and saw him lying next to one of the side consoles. The soldier had landed in front of one of the other giants, who bent over and ran a sword through his chest twice. Upton's vital signs went red on Contreras' display, and Contreras turned away, disgusted, to find Staff Sergeant Mchugh trading blows with another of the giants.

'Trading blows' in the sense that Mchugh would fire his laser rifle at the giant and then dive out of the way as the Jotnar swung his battle axe at the trooper. It wasn't a fair fight, and there was really only one way it could end—with Mchugh in two pieces.

Contreras fired his laser pistol into the giant's face. Although it didn't penetrate the facemask, it distracted the giant, who turned to see his new opponent.

"Fight me!" Contreras yelled, waving his arms over his head. The giant turned and took a colossal stride toward Contreras, raising his axe along the way. Contreras had just enough time to rue the decision to distract the giant when it fell face forward, crashing down at his feet. A wisp of smoke curled up from the laser hole through the back of the giant's helmet.

"Thanks," Mchugh called.

"Look out!" Contreras shouted, pointing behind him.

Mchugh turned to find a giant had come in behind him from the back hatch of the bridge. He wasn't fast enough to evade the massive war hammer the Jotnar swung, and the gigantic maul smashed him to the floor. Mchugh's vital signs went red in Contreras's display, his body broken in more places than he could count.

"*Bitch!*" Corporal Sam 'Mental' Ward yelled, firing off several long blasts at the chest of the giant. The Jotnar staggered, but then took two steps toward the soldier, raising the hammer. Mental fired one more burst, then raised his rifle in both hands to block the giant's stroke.

The rifle snapped in half like a twig, and the hammer squashed Mental into a red paste on the deck.

Several rifle blasts from Corporal King and Wolf felled the giant, allowing the one behind it to step forward and level his rifle at the troopers.

"Move!" Wolf yelled. He pushed Corporal King away from him as the Jotnar fired the flechette rifle, sending hundreds of metal slivers across the bridge. Both troopers went down with a number of flechettes through their legs.

The giant cocked the rifle, loading the next round, but Contreras shot him in the face before he could fire. Once again, the pistol didn't have enough power to penetrate the Jotunn helmet, but it distracted the Jotnar long enough that Wolf could roll over and shoot the creature through the facemask, killing it.

Wolf rolled back the other way, looking for the next target, but was pinned to the deck as Loki drove his dagger through his chest and into the metal deck.

"Don't go anywhere," said the giant as he raised his battle axe in his other hand. Before the stroke could fall, Yokaze dashed in and cut his right Achilles tendon, and the giant lost his balance, staggering off to the side.

"Fight me instead," Yokaze said as Loki recovered and turned around. "I've already killed two of your troops; it's your turn now."

"It is your death you are asking for," Loki replied. "I will be happy to grant your wish."

He stepped toward Yokaze, dragging his right foot behind him.

Loki swung his axe in a circle several times, back and forth, hoping to distract the smaller warrior. As Loki approached, Yokaze held up both of his swords in a high block position. Sensing an advantage, Loki lunged forward with his good foot and swung his battle axe in an overhead blow meant to shatter Yokaze's guard and split the Japanese man in half. It would have, if Yokaze had tried to block it.

He didn't; instead, he dove forward, slicing out with his wakizashi and severing the Jotnar's other Achilles tendon.

Loki screamed in impotent rage, and he hobbled to turn around before Yokaze could reattack.

"No," Yokaze yelled to Lieutenant Rrower, who had been lining up a shot; "he is mine."

Engineering, TSS *Vella Gulf,* Anti-Jotunheimr System, December 23, 2021

Pain blinded Staff Sergeant Loftis as she came to. The upper half of her body hurt everywhere. The lower half didn't…and then she realized she couldn't feel anything from her waist down. Her back was broken. At least that part of her didn't hurt. She screamed. Her head throbbed, waves of pain radiating from her scalp as she swung…

Swung? She opened her eyes and saw that the giant was holding her in the air by her hair; her limp feet dangling a meter above the ground as she slowly spun around.

"Now I kill you," the giant said.

She spit into his face as she rotated past. "You can kill me, but you'll never escape this ship. Lieutenant O'Leary will come and kick your scrawny ass!"

"Ha, ha, ha," the giant replied. "You got one thing right. I *am* going to kill you, and I'm going to do that right now." His other hand drew back the gleaming sword; the tip pointed at her right eye as if accusing her of failing to defend Engineering.

She couldn't think about that anymore. She hurt so badly. The light shining off the sword seemed to be dimming...perhaps it would go out before the blow arrived. That would be nice. She closed her eyes so she didn't have to watch.

"Get down!" a voice whispered. "Move! Get away! Do something!"

She opened one eye a crack. It was all she had left. A three-armed creature pointed at her. No, it wasn't a three-armed creature, it was Seaman Matthews, who had the Jotunn rifle braced on a piece of machinery and was aiming it at her. Why would he want to kill her after all she had tried to do for him? She didn't understand.

She hurt so badly.

She wished he'd pull the trigger and be done with it. His lips kept moving, but she couldn't understand what he was saying.

"*MOVE!*" an augmented voice shouted in her brain, shocking her with a dose of adrenaline.

Oh, he wasn't trying to shoot her, but the giant behind her. She was in the way. She pulled her dagger out of her sleeve and sliced through the majority of her hair with one sweep. The rest pulled out on its own, and the agony blinded her again until she hit the ground and new waves of misery coursed through her body.

She heard the crack of the rifle through a thickening fog, and then more pain seared through her body as the ground bucked underneath her.

She opened an eye to see the giant lying next to her, its face riddled with steel slivers. Fuck you, she thought, too tired to speak. Things began graying, but movement caught her eye, and she tried to focus again.

Matthews. Sort of Matthews. His shoulder looked odd. Wasn't where it was supposed to be.

"I killed him! I did it!" the sailor rejoiced.

"Good...job."

"Move kid," another voice said, and Matthews was pushed out of her line of sight.

Another face took his spot.

She struggled to focus. O'Leary. Cool.

"I...did it," she breathed. "What you...said. Killed...four...to my one." She coughed and blood ran from the corner of her mouth. "Need...tell you...'thing," she added, her voice not much more than a whisper. "Lean. Over."

Lieutenant O'Leary leaned closer.

"Always liked...you." Her head moved up, and her lips brushed his cheek; then her head fell back to the deck.

She was gone.

Task Force Contreras, TSS *Vella Gulf,* Anti-Jotunheimr System, December 23, 2021

Yokaze knew it was extremely dangerous to battle the Jotnar singlehanded, but honor demanded it. Not the honor of the giant; he had none. No, Yokaze's own honor required it. Having engaged the giant in single combat, he couldn't allow his squad mates to shoot Loki down like the honorless dog he was.

Which left him with the problem of how to kill the giant. None of his weapons' instructors had taught him how to kill a being almost three times his size. None of his weapons' forms were designed to stop a battle axe strike with the force Loki could put behind it. *Nothing* any of the Terrans had, even Gunnery Sergeant Dantone, could stop one. Yokaze would have to make the giant miss to get under his guard.

Unfortunately, he had been too effective in laming the giant. With both Achilles' tendons cut, Loki neither advanced nor retreated; there were no mobility errors for Yokaze to exploit. Unable to move quickly, he waited patiently for Yokaze to come within reach, knowing he could get in at least one, if not two, strikes before Yokaze could reach him.

Yokaze circled the giant, feigning attacks, looking for an opening. As he maneuvered, he noticed that certain attacks caused Loki to back up. Not much, but enough. Yokaze altered his attack pattern to guide Loki backward toward the bulkhead near the Science station.

"Surrender, Loki," Captain Sheppard said from behind Yokaze.

"I would not give him the honor," Yokaze growled.

"I'm going to kill this insignificant pipsqueak first," Loki replied. "We can discuss the terms of my parole once he's dead."

"Are you sure about that, Sergeant?" the CO asked.

"Hai!" Yokaze exclaimed, sheathing his wakizashi. "He has no honor and must die."

"Any other time, I would say to capture him," the CO replied, "but in this case, I'm willing to make an exception. If he won't surrender, kill him so we can get his stinking body off my bridge."

"With pleasure."

Without warning, Yokaze sprang forward to the side of the giant. Loki was unprepared for the sudden attack and slow to respond. Expecting a feint, the giant held the battle axe across his chest to block and counterattack.

But no feint or attack occurred. Yokaze dodged past the giant, jumped onto the Science console and then took another two running steps up the wall behind it. Reaching the height he needed, Yokaze pushed off the wall, doing a backwards somersault with a twist. The giant was slow to turn due to his injuries, and Yokaze landed on Loki's back, driving his katana between the giant's shoulder blades, all the way to the hilt.

Grabbing a handful of the giant's suit, Yokaze pulled himself up to stand on the sword's hilt. A hand reached back, but before it could grab him, Yokaze drew his wakizashi and stabbed it down through the gap in the giant's collarbone, again burying it to the hilt.

With the hilt as a handhold, he drew his tanto and cut Loki's throat. A geyser of green erupted, which Yokaze only partially avoided as he flipped off the giant, somersaulting to land on his feet next to Loki's side.

Yokaze strode over to the CO and saluted. "It is done, as ordered," Yokaze said.

The deck shook as Loki collapsed behind him.

Engineering, TSS *Vella Gulf*, Anti-Jotunheimr System, December 23, 2021

Staff Sergeant Loftis' icon went red in Lieutenant O'Leary's in-head display. "Spuds, is there anything you can do for her?" He waved a hand to indicate the interior of the anteroom that led to Engineering proper. It was a mess. Giants and pieces of giants were everywhere, and the entire area was whitewashed in green blood. It looked like the fevered splatter painting of a crazy man. "She deserves to be saved."

"I'm sorry, sir, but she was too far gone when we got here," the medic explained. "How she held on as long as she did is amazing. She must have had a tremendous will to live."

"She just wanted to do her job," the sailor standing nearby said. "She said she was told not to let the giants into Engineering, and she didn't."

"Who the hell are you?" Lieutenant O'Leary asked. "Wait, you look familiar…"

"I'm Culinary Specialist Seaman Matthews, sir," the sailor said. "I'm one of the stewards in the wardroom. The master chief here…that's his body by the hatch…grabbed me to help defend the space. I really didn't know much about anything so I wasn't very helpful. I did kill the last giant, but it was too late to save her."

Lieutenant O'Leary looked the sailor up and down in disbelief. The cook's shoulder stuck out from his body at an unnatural angle. "You killed one of the Jotunn?" he asked. "By yourself?"

"Yes sir," the cook said. "I finally figured out how to use one of their guns," he said, nodding to the Jotunn flechette rifle lying nearby. "I killed the giant who was going to kill her, but by then he had already beat her up pretty bad."

"You fired that rifle?" O'Leary asked, disbelieving. "All by yourself?"

"Yes sir," Matthews said. "It had a pretty good kick, which is probably why my shoulder doesn't seem to be working quite right at the moment."

"He's in shock, sir," the medic, Corporal Anaru Ngata, interjected. "It looks like his shoulder is separated pretty badly. Probably a couple broken bones in there as well. When the adrenaline runs out, he's going to hurt a bunch."

"Well, do what you can for him," O'Leary said. "For a cook, he's had an awfully busy day."

"Yes sir," the medic replied.

"Hey, Lieutenant?" Matthews called as O'Leary turned to leave.

"Yeah?"

"What do you have to do to join your unit?" the sailor asked. He nodded toward Loftis' body. "I want to be tough, just like her."

"Send me a request, and I'll forward it," O'Leary replied. "We can use people who aren't afraid to do what needs to be done."

Sergeant 'Good Twin' Austin jogged up. "All of the giants here are dead, sir. None made it past this one right here."

O'Leary nodded. "Thanks." He switched to his comm. "*How's it going up there, Contreras?*"

"*Lieutenant O'Leary, it comes at great cost, but I am able to tell you that Loki is dead, and the bridge is once again ours.*"

"*Copy,*" O'Leary replied. "*Gunny Dantone, what's your status?*"

"*About the same as Lieutenant Contreras,' sir. We killed a bunch of the damn giants, but have a number of our own casualties. If you're taking suggestions, I vote we pop back over to our universe and nuke the shit out of the bastards' planet, sir.*"

"*I don't know what say I'll have in it,*" O'Leary commed, "*but I'm all for it too. You know what you call 10 million dead Jotunn?*"

"No sir. What do you call them?"

"*A good start. Get the wounded checked out at Medical, clean up what you can and we'll meet back at the Armory afterward.*"

"*If I send everyone to Medical that is wounded,*" Contreras replied, "*our meeting will be somewhat delayed. I don't have anyone, myself included, who isn't wounded in some manner. The fight to reclaim the bridge was...intense.*"

"*Understood. Go get checked out; I'll see you when you're done.*"

There was a commotion at the hatch as Night and four troopers entered the space. Unlike the rest of the troops already there, they were easy to spot as their suits were spotless; everyone else's suits looked like a weird Christmas design of red and green.

Night strode up to O'Leary, who saluted. "Welcome back sir," O'Leary said.

"Thanks," Night replied. "What'd I miss?"

"A lot of killing and the deaths of about half the platoon," O'Leary said, anger heavy in his voice. "The bastards were in here before we knew it and stopping them was difficult. I'm looking forward to killing a whole fucking bunch of them, as soon as possible."

"You've got blood on your face," Night noted. "Are you hit?"

"Nope."

"Are you going to wash it off?"

"Some time. Just not yet. This damn war just got personal."

Chapter Twenty-Four

"Ladies and Gentlemen, I would like to thank you for dropping what you were doing to come here, as well as for all of your efforts over the last 24 hours. Cleaning up after the attack will take some time, and we may never fully recover from it."

"You got *that* damn right," Lieutenant O'Leary muttered.

"Even though the cleanup continues, we need to move forward if we are going to recover Lieutenant Commander Hobbs before the Jotunn find and kill him. To that end, the ship is enroute to Jotunheimr as we speak. For those of you wondering what we're going to do with the remaining Jotunn in this universe, the answer is nothing because they don't exist. All the giants on the *Vella Gulf* are dead, and their ship has been destroyed. I was worried they had jumped back to our universe when we couldn't find it on the scanners, but Solomon tells me the ship detonated catastrophically shortly after the away party left it."

The CO turned to Night. "I assume your men had something to do with that?"

"Damn straight, sir," the soldier replied. "I built a bomb, and our engineers showed me where their fuel lines were and how to breach them. They expected at least the last quarter of the ship to be completely destroyed in the ensuing explosion."

"They were wrong," Captain Sheppard said. Night's eyebrows rose.

"Actually, more than 1/3 of the ship was vaporized, and the rest was so thoroughly shattered that it was hard to find on the scanners. Well done."

Night nodded, not in acclamation for destroying the ship, but in acknowledgement of having done what needed to be done. There was no joy or satisfaction in the successful completion of such a task.

"The bottom line is that we're probably safe while we're in this universe," the CO said, "but we need to work out our plan for what we do once we jump back to our universe."

"I don't get it, sir," Lieutenant O'Leary said. "Why don't we negotiate from a position of strength? Can't we just jump back into our universe and say, 'Give us our guy or we'll toss your crappy-ass planet into a black hole?' Then, once we get Lieutenant Commander Hobbs back, we go ahead and do it anyway? That would teach them."

"It might work to get him back," the CO agreed, "however, it probably wouldn't be great for long-term relations with the Jotunn."

"And that should bother me, why?"

"Because we need to think more long-term for the…" Captain Sheppard's voice trailed off, and he stared at O'Leary for a moment. "I think you've got…some dried blood or something on your cheek."

"I know," Lieutenant O'Leary replied. "I like it there. It's a reminder to never trust the Jotunn."

"You're forgetting that what they did is totally within their code of honor. They never actually declared a truce with us; all they said was that they wouldn't shoot their ship's weapons at us, which they didn't."

"With all due respect, sir, I don't give a shit. They intentionally tricked us and lured us in so that they could attack us. I lost about half my men and women in that attack, and I'm damned sure I won't trust them ever again. On second thought, hitting their planet with a black hole is probably too nice. Maybe we can firebomb the shit out of it or hit them with some disintegrators from orbit. I hear they hurt a lot."

"Okay, Lieutenant O'Leary, I understand where you're coming from. In fact, I feel the same way as you toward them. I'm the dummy that allowed it to happen and almost lost his ship because of it. When I say I understand, *I understand!* Now, we have to get past this if we're going to get Lieutenant Commander Hobbs back and have any hope of completing our mission."

"*Our mission?*" the *Vella Gulf's* executive officer, Commander Russ Clayton, asked. "You mean the mission to go to the Dark Star? You can't be serious about continuing on. With all the people we've lost, and the damage the ship has sustained?"

"Yes, we've had losses, and the platoon has been particularly hard hit. However, we are further into enemy territory than any Terran ship has ever been. To go all the way home and send another ship in our place would take months and would give the Shaitans time to finish off the Ssselipssssiss and start on the Mrowry. Or maybe they head for us and wipe out the Kuji. Either way, if we go back now, we will be allowing the Shaitans to get an even bigger head start than they already have."

"I'm sorry, Skipper, but I just don't see how we have enough capability to take on both the Shaitans and the Jotunn. If we continue toward the Dark Star, we will have to fight both of them along the way. Sure, we've had some pretty good success against the Shaitans, at least recently, but if we have to go head-to-head with another Jotunn vessel, we're going to be hard-pressed to win, even against something our size or smaller. With our losses, we don't have the manning or resources for another long battle."

"I understand that," Captain Sheppard replied. "Not only do I understand your position, I agree with it, too."

"So we're not going to continue on toward the Dark Star?"

"Yes, I fully intend to press on," Captain Sheppard said.

"But—,"

"I said I agreed with you that we couldn't continue against an alliance of Shaitan and Jotunn vessels," Captain Sheppard replied, interrupting his XO. "It isn't my intention to do so, either, at least, not if we don't have to. But I'm not sure we do."

"What do you mean?"

"I think there are cracks in the alliance between the Jotunn and the Shaitans," the CO said. "We've seen instances of it everywhere we've gone. The Shaitans don't trust the Jotunn enough to give them jump modules, but here, in this system, we fought a Jotunn vessel with jump modules. Where do you suppose the Jotunn got them? I'm willing to bet that Loki pulled the same stunt on one of the Shaitan vessels he did with us. He probably got the technology he needed and then dumped their ship into a star somewhere to hide the evidence. If the Jotunn are willing to risk that, then their alliance is on shaky ground."

He looked around the table, meeting each officer's eyes in turn. "I'm hoping to talk with the Jotunn rulers and get them to dissolve their alliance with the Shaitans. If I can do that, we won't have to worry about fighting the Jotunn on the way to the Dark Star…at least I hope not, anyway."

"That is a great plan," the XO said, "but only if it works. What's in it for the Jotunn if they break their alliance with the Shaitan? As honor-bound as they are, they won't want to go back on their word. We would have to be able to give them an awful lot to turn their backs on the Shaitans. What do we have to give?"

"I'm not sure yet, but I can't imagine they are happy with the genocide they've been performing on the Ssselipsssiss planets. Maybe if I can convince them they're next, they'll see the Shaitan as betrayers and will be willing to betray them first."

"That's pretty thin," Night said. "If things go badly, I don't have a whole lot of force to back you up. I would recommend keeping our forces as far from their ships as possible. If they get people onto the *Gulf* again, I'm not sure we can turn them away."

"Understood," Captain Sheppard said, "and I'm going to try my damnedest never to put you in that position again."

"This is what we have to do to accomplish our mission," Captain Sheppard continued, his voice strong; "if we fail, we will have to go back to Terra, and someone else will have to come all the way back here in our place. No matter who they send, the crew won't be as experienced as we are, and they are more likely to fail. If not us, then who? If not now, then when? We are here now, and we need to give it try. No, we need to succeed. If we don't, the Shaitans are likely to pour into our sector of our universe, and you saw what they do to the planets they conquer. Genocide. I don't want that to happen to Terra. We need to stop it here, and we need to stop it *right now*. Are there any additional questions?"

"No, sir," the XO said. "When you put it like that, it's obvious we need to try."

"Not try, XO. We need to succeed."

Outside the CO's Conference Room, TSS *Vella Gulf*, Anti-Jotunheimr System, December 24, 2021

"Can I talk with you a second?" Night asked Lieutenant Bradford as they left the meeting.

"Sure. What can I do for you?"

"Something O'Leary said in the meeting reminded me of an idea I had a little while ago. I was wondering…you may have read the report about the disintegrator round that Arges fired at me during the assault on his castle. I wondered if it would be possible to put something similar on the end of a missile to spray it around on a Shaitan vessel. Something that if it missed, we could turn back off again so we don't end up with disassemblers tearing up our ships or people."

"I'll take a look," Lieutenant Bradford replied, "although I don't remember ever seeing a disintegrator in the replicator database."

"It may not be in there," Night replied, "as the disintegrator was outlawed. Even if you do find it in there, it's probably password protected or however they do that shit. If it's not in the replicator database, I'm not sure where you would look, but Arges had one, so the technology still exists."

**Ducting, Jotunn Ship *Falcon*, Jotunheimr System,
December 24, 2021**

"Okay," Farhome said, "time's up. What's your brilliant idea for getting us out of here?"

"Brilliant idea?" Calvin asked. "I don't have one. The only idea I have is a totally shitty one."

"Totally shitty is better than nothing, which is the sum total for everything else we have. What's your idea?"

"Steal a shuttle and fly out of here."

"How are we going to get out of their weapons range without being destroyed?"

"I don't know," Calvin replied. "That's why it's such a shitty idea."

"What about the fact that we can't go through a stargate in a shuttle?" Burkuri asked. "We can't even jump into the other universe in one of their shuttles. How are we going to escape?"

"No idea," Calvin replied. "I'm still trying to figure that out. Hopefully, the *Vella Gulf* will show up and rescue us before we're destroyed. Stealing a shuttle is only a means of buying more time."

"That's a shitty plan," Burkuri noted.

"I know. If you've got any ideas, I'd be happy to consider them."

"Maybe we could capture their captain," Paxton said. "Based on what I've seen, he's the only Jotnar worth capturing. If we took anyone else, Captain Magnusson would most likely just destroy the shuttle and not worry about the collateral damage to his crewman. The crew, though, *probably* wouldn't destroy a shuttle with Magnusson in it. We'll have to capture him if we're going to get away."

"Any ideas on how to do that?" Calvin asked.

"None," Paxton said. "He would probably fight to the death rather than allow himself to be captured...especially by us."

Calvin sighed. "Yeah, probably."

Paxton looked at his chronometer. "We're about 15 minutes from docking," Paxton said. "Give them another 15 minutes to get us tied up and 30 minutes to shut everything down...We don't have much more than an hour before the gas starts flowing. Think you'll have a better plan by then?"

"I hope so..." Calvin said. He only thought the rest of the sentence, "but I doubt it."

Bridge, TSS *Vella Gulf*, Anti-Jotunheimr System, December 24, 2021

The cleanup crew had been thorough, Captain Sheppard noted as he strode onto the bridge. Not only had the Jotunn bodies been cut up and removed, the flashing General Quarters lights showed no signs of the gallons of green blood they left behind. He spied a spray pattern on the overhead, 20 feet up, but knew it wouldn't show on the view screen when they spoke with the giants. He thought about telling someone so that it would get cleaned, eventually, but decided to keep it for now as a memento of what they'd been through. The rest of the bridge was spotless, which was quite an effort considering a significant portion of the crew had been killed by the Jotunn as they rampaged through the ship. It would not do to let the Jotunn know that Loki had been able to get his men aboard.

The *Gulf's* bridge crew had been counseled on their duties— mostly, to look bored and as if nothing had happened; basically, to look like they didn't have a care in the world.

Nothing could have been further from the truth.

"Status check," Captain Sheppard said.

"Proceeding toward Jotunheimr," the helmsman said. "Standing by to jump to our universe with an immediate jump back if there is a Jotunn ship nearby."

"All systems normal," the duty engineer noted; "General Quarters is set throughout the ship. Stealth is unavailable until we go back and recover the stealth modules."

"Offensive systems operational," the OSO said.

"Defensive systems manned and ready," the DSO added.

"Science manned and ready," Steropes said.

"All right," the CO said, "here we go. Make the jump, helm."

"Jumping in three...two...one..."

Everything flashed.

"Stable back in our universe," the helmsman noted.

"All systems normal," the duty engineer reported.

"No targets within weapons range," the OSO added.

"While it is true there are no ships within weapons range," Steropes said, "I have a large number of ships on the long range scanner around Jotunheimr. There appears to be a shipyard there as well."

"Understood," the CO said.

"Sir, we are being hailed by the Jotunn ship *Falcon.*"

"On screen."

The front viewer lit up with the image of a giant on the bridge of his ship. Other Jotunn could be seen behind him going about their tasks. "I will say this about you," the Jotnar said in welcome, "you are persistent. How you evaded Loki is beyond me."

"I am Captain Sheppard of the Terran ship *Vella Gulf*," the CO replied. "Whom do I have the pleasure of addressing?"

"I am Captain Oleif Magnusson," the giant replied. "I am the commanding officer of the ship you have been chasing for several systems now."

"I am glad we finally caught up with you. We have a number of matters of great importance that I would like to speak with you and your leaders about."

"Oh you do, do you? How are your little matters of any importance to us?"

"One of the matters is the side you're on in the ongoing war. It is our opinion you have chosen the wrong allies, and they are stripping you of your honor the longer you support them."

"Anything like that must be brought before the Council of Jarls," the Jotnar said. "Sadly, I do not believe you have ever been recognized as a civilization worthy enough to attend the Council of Jarls, so I'm afraid you must wait where you are for my uncle to come and kill you. At least when you are dead, you will no longer be troubled by your 'matters of great importance.'"

"If your uncle is Loki, I am afraid we will be waiting here for quite some time. His ship was destroyed in the other universe with a loss of all hands."

"How am I to believe this? What proof do you have?"

"Well, we can sit here and wait for a week, and when he doesn't show up, maybe you'll believe me. I can also provide video of his ship's destruction if that would be helpful."

"Yes," Captain Magnusson said; "I would like that."

"Solomon, please send the video we have of Loki's ship exploding."

"Transmitting."

The conversation paused as Captain Magnusson watched something off-screen.

"That appears to be his new ship," the giant said when he looked back, "and if the video is authentic, it does appear his ship was destroyed. On your honor, is this the real video of Loki's ship, free from any editing?"

"Yes," Captain Sheppard replied.

"How was his ship destroyed? Although there is evidence of previous damage, the final explosion does not seem to be caused by the impact of any missiles or energy weapons."

"Unfortunately, I am not at liberty to say although I can tell you that the weapon we used to destroy Loki's ship was unlike any you have previously seen used in ship-to-ship combat. I wouldn't want to have to use it against the *Falcon*, but if I am forced to in order to gain an audience with the Council of Jarls, then that is what I will do."

"Ho, ho, ho," Captain Magnusson laughed. "I wouldn't want you to have to do that to my ship either; however, I have no say in getting you a voice at the Council. That is something you must do on your own."

"And how exactly do we do that?"

"You have to prove your worth as a civilization if you want the Council of Jarls to listen to you."

Captain Sheppard sighed. This was about as informative as talking to a wall. Or asking questions of a Psiclops. "And how do we do that?"

"Stand by," Captain Magnusson said. He turned and looked at something off screen. A brief conversation followed, with Magnusson mostly nodding and replying in the affirmative. Eventually, his attention returned to the Terrans.

"You are in luck," the giant said. "Our council has offered you a chance to speak to them. There is, however, one small task you must accomplish first."

"And that is…"

"Your champion must beat our champion in battle. If your champion can do that, the Council of Jarls will grant you a brief audience."

"So, let me guess. This battle our champion must beat yours in…is it to be hand-to-hand combat, or with weapons?"

"Why, hand-to-hand, of course, with only unpowered weapons allowed. Is there any other type of combat to settle issues among men?"

"Well, our society used to use pistols and rifles to duel."

"Not acceptable. Your champion can use swords and axes and weapons like that; no rifles or pistols are allowed in Odin's Longhouse."

"Okay, so unpowered, hand-to-hand weapons only. Does it in any way matter that you are three times our size? How do you consider that to be a fair fight?"

"It is one of your men versus one of ours. What could be more fair than two champions meeting in battle?"

"Sitting down to discuss our issues without any of this unnecessary foreplay."

"Ah, but that is where you are wrong. This is very necessary to judge the worthiness of your civilization to come before our Council."

"That's okay," Night interjected, speaking for the first time. "I owe the Jotunn. I'll be your champion, and I will kick the living shit out of whoever they want to put up as theirs."

"And you are?" Captain Magnusson asked.

"I am Paul Train, Captain, Terran Space Marines."

"Captain Train, eh? I'm sure our champion will be very happy to meet you."

"Before I agree to anything," Captain Sheppard said, "we need to discuss the matter of safe passage for my ship and those under my command. Will you promise safe passage to the planet and back for all Terrans?"

"Yes, we promise safe passage to the planet and back for all Terrans," the Jotnar replied.

"Are you able to make that promise for all of your civilization? No Jotunn or any nation allied with you will hinder our passage to and from your planet? Do you offer that protection free from all types of subterfuge or trying to trick us with words?"

"Yes, I give you my word that you will be granted safe passage by us or any of our allies. You have my personal word I will do everything in my power to protect you while you are in this system."

"Sir, the Aesir Farhome was with Calvin," Night advised in a whisper. "You need to open up his offer of protection a bit more."

"You're right," Captain Sheppard said. He turned back to the view screen. "Will you promise safe passage to the planet and back for all Terrans and any members of other races who might be accompanying them?"

"Yes, yes, yes," the Jotnar said. "The members of the Council want to see the combat between our champions. You are to be granted free passage. I so promise and give you my word."

Noises could be heard from off-screen, and all of the Jotunn looked up as something fell past the camera.

The picture pulled back to show Calvin on the deck next to the Jotunn captain. Calvin stood and addressed the viewer. "Thanks, Skipper, that was well done," he said.

Calvin turned and looked up to face Captain Magnusson. "I would like to take you up on your offer of safe passage to the planet," he added. Additional forms fell from above and resolved themselves into Farhome and a number of Ssselipsssiss. "And I believe my allies are ready to go to the surface, as well."

Several creatures flew down into the pickup range of the screen. They looked like giant cockroaches. "Oh, and I believe the S'nark would like to come, too," Calvin said.

Bridge, Jotunn Ship *Falcon*, Jotunheimr System, December 24, 2021

Calvin patted the S'nark that came to stand next to him. He thought it might be Zeeelbit, but he wouldn't have bet too much money on it. "We don't have a lot of belongings, so we can go down to the planet whenever it's most convenient, but hopefully before you fumigate the ship."

Calvin had never in his brief contact with the Jotunn seen any of them look confused or bewildered. Angry? Yes. Plenty of times. But Captain Magnusson changed that as his eyes swept the bridge, and his mind tried to process where all the creatures had come from.

He finally shook his head and began laughing. Before long, the entire bridge crew was laughing along with him, and Calvin, Farhome and the Ssselipsssiss joined in.

"We will meet with you tomorrow at Odin's Longhouse for the challenge," Captain Magnusson said, looking back to the view screen as he began to wind down. "We will send you the coordinates." He terminated the transmission. "Well, bend me over and call me a sheep!" he exclaimed with another laugh. "I think we've found the problem with our shields." He looked down at Calvin. "My uncle Loki would be proud of you," he continued. "I have no idea how you tricked us to get aboard, but I am very much looking forward to finding out."

The Jotnar's eyes roamed across the collection of creatures. "Not only that, but you have assembled quite a menagerie here. The only species I recognize are the bugs, but I do not understand how you have gotten them to do your bidding. They are nothing more than roaches we allow to exist because they do the cleanup tasks we prefer not to."

"The ones you call 'bugs' refer to themselves as the S'nark," Calvin said, "and they are actually quite intelligent. In fact, I had one of them pull a gun on me when I came aboard."

"A gun?" Magnusson asked. He laughed again. "Where would they get a gun? How would they know how to use it?"

In the blink of an eye, Zeeelbit drew his pistols and fired one of them past Magnusson's ear. The laser bolt burned a hole in the bulkhead that hissed and steamed.

Magnusson laughed again, a full belly laugh that infected the crew. Soon all were laughing. Zeeelbit neither moved nor flinched.

As the laughter wore off, Magnusson looked down to see the pistols now aimed at his face.

"You are full of surprises," he said, still chuckling. "Put down your weapons. I have already given you safe passage to the council, and I have no desire to explain to my friends how I got shot by a bug." With a blur, the weapons disappeared again.

Magnusson's eyes searched the group, and his eyebrows knitted. "I don't see the furry creature our maintenance robots chased. Will we still need to have the ship fumigated to get rid of it or is that another of your pets?"

"No, that creature is actually Bob Jones," Calvin said nodding toward Farhome, who had transformed himself to look Terran. "He has the ability to manipulate his appearance somewhat through the use of very small robots."

"That almost sounds like something the Aesir are known for," Captain Magnusson said. Although not experienced in Jotunn, Calvin could hear the suspicion in his voice.

"Really?" Calvin asked. "I didn't know that. I guess I need to learn more about the Aesir, because I had no idea. I thought our society was the only one with that capability." He shrugged. "Regardless, it was actually the Ssselipsssiss who caused the problems with your shields."

"This is all more than I can handle with a dry tongue," Magnusson said. "At the moment, you are guests on this ship, so we can discuss how you came to be here tonight at our night-meal. Until then, I will have one of my men escort you to a room where you may rest and prepare for tonight's feast."

He motioned, and one of the bridge crew led the assembled group away.

Chapter Twenty-Five

Officer's Mess, Jotunn Ship *Falcon*, Jotunheimr System, December 24, 2021

The Officer's Mess was like the wardroom of any Terran ship Calvin had ever been on, in that it was where the officers ate, but that was where the similarities ended. First, everything was triple in size, and Calvin felt like Gulliver in the land of the Brobdingnagians. Calvin couldn't even reach the seat of his bench without help; he had to be lifted onto it by one of the stewards. The furniture in the mess consisted of a long table that ran the length of the space with benches on both sides. Magnusson sat at one end of the table; Calvin, Farhome and the Ssselipsssiss were relegated to the opposite end, with Zeeelbit given a place on the floor next to them.

"You know this is the position of least honor, right?" Farhome asked. "Although they honor us with a feast, they dishonor us by placing us at the opposite end of the table from Magnusson."

"Hey, I'm just happy they're honoring their promise not to kill us," Calvin replied. "I don't care where they have us stand, as long as it isn't a gallows someplace. Besides, the smell of unwashed Jotunn is a lot less aromatic down here at this end of the table. Can you imagine having to sit between them and eat? I'm not sure I could hold down any food."

"Well, when you put it that way, I guess it isn't so bad."

Captain Magnusson stood. "Wife!" he yelled. "Serve the drinks!"

A female Jotnar, the first Calvin had seen, came into the mess carrying a large tray of tankards. Magnusson's wife was as tall as the males and had long blond hair she wore in braids. The woman wore a loose, brown linen dress with a brooch over the right shoulder to fasten it. A red over-dress wrapped around the woman, held up by a shoulder strap that was fastened with another brooch. A series of spaceships were embroidered on the hem of the over-dress as decoration. Although the men didn't wear them, she also had dark blue cloth leggings and covered her head with a flowered-print scarf. She wore a variety of bracelets, armbands and rings in gold and silver. They were crafted in intricate patterns, but before Calvin could tell what they were, the Jotnar next to him elbowed him in the stomach, sending him crashing into Farhome.

"Don't stare at the Captain's wife," the giant said, "not unless you want to duel him, anyway."

Calvin stopped staring.

The woman served Magnusson and then the officers before finally working her way to the end of the table where Calvin was. She slammed a tankard down in front of him, and he was doused by the foam that slopped out.

"Oops!" she said to a chorus of laughter and catcalls.

"Thank Bryggjemann for the feast we have today and Terra for providing us our amusement for the evening," Captain Magnusson said. "Let us drink to the Odin and his success."

"To his success!" the assembled officers toasted. Everyone took a drink, accept for the non-Jotunn, who looked at their four-foot-tall tankards with some dismay. Calvin didn't see any way that trying to drink out of one wouldn't end in disaster.

"And to the *Falcon* and our success!"

"To our success!"

"Now, let us eat and drink!" Magnusson said, clapping his hands twice. He sat, and the rest of the officers followed suit. Stewards brought in platters of food and pitchers to refill the officers' tankards, many of which were empty after the two toasts. The last steward brought in a tray of cups and saucers. The Jotunn cups were as big as large fish tanks, but Calvin was able to lean over and drink from it unassisted so he took a cautious sip. The drink had the flavor of honey, but without the sweetness.

"This is pretty good," Calvin said licking his lips. "What is it?"

"Mead," Farhome replied, standing up from his cup with a sigh. Calvin could see a large portion missing. "It's been a long time since I had any this good." He smiled. "Drink up!"

Cargo Bay, Jotunn Shuttle, Jotunheimr System, December 25, 2021

Calvin hurt. All over. Not only was his head pounding, he felt like vomiting with every movement. The sensory overload he was experiencing was only making it worse.

Although the Jotunn shuttle's cargo bay was cavernous, the giants had loaded it beyond what Calvin would have thought safe. In addition to Calvin, Farhome and the Ssselipsssiss, as well as a large party of guards to watch them, the shuttle was full of the S'nark. Calvin had no idea how many the Jotunn ship had held; most of them looked the same to him. Trapped in his seat for the journey to the planet, he had the opportunity to look closely at several of them for the first time under full light, and he realized there were a variety of different colors and markings. Although the differences were subtle, he imagined the bugs could tell each other apart as easily as a Terran could any other human.

The shuttle ride was not something he wanted to *ever* do again. In addition to the stink of a large number of Jotunn, who obviously didn't believe in showers or anything approaching Terran hygiene, the bugs emitted a weird odor when they were excited, which all of them were as they made their first-ever journey to a planet. Their odor clashed with the reek of the Jotunn, producing a miasma of stench he figured would stay with him for days. It would probably be easier to requisition another combat suit than to try to clean the one he had. He spent most of the shuttle ride trying to fight off another round of vomiting. Not because it would have made the smell in the back of the shuttle worse, it wouldn't have, but because his throat was already raw from the episodes of the previous night. He swore he'd never drink mead again.

He looked at Farhome in disgust. The Aesir was sleeping soundly. He had grown extra filters for his nose that strained out the smell. Cheater. He had also probably used his nanobots to clean out his system so he wasn't hungover. Calvin couldn't remember ever hating someone so much.

The Ssselipsssiss were seated across the aisle from Calvin. They looked like infants sitting in an adult chair; all five were buckled into the same seat. Young enough not to worry about the consequences of their journey, they were excited and chatting happily with each other. Calvin hated them too.

The pilot of the shuttle never announced to the passengers their landing was imminent; Calvin's first indication they were getting close to the ground was when the shuttle slammed into it, throwing all of the unsecured non-Jotunn into the air.

Apparently, the pilot had advised the Jotunn in the cargo bay the 'landing' was coming; all of them were braced for the impact and laughed uproariously at the non-Jotunns' discomfort.

"Boy, that makes me miss landing on the aircraft carrier," Calvin noted. "Not." He stood up and slowly stretched, trying to undo the damage of the landing without upsetting his stomach.

The ramp came down, and they got their first view of Jotunheimr. The capital city of the Jotunn looked much like the capital cities on any of the other advanced civilization's planets Calvin had been to; massive metal and steelglass structures reached for the sky that would have dwarfed the tallest structure on Terra, the 3,300-foot-tall Jeddah Tower in Saudi Arabia.

As Calvin walked down the ramp, he saw they had come down in a park in the center of the city; they were in a canyon formed by the massive structures surrounding them on all sides. Only one building was different than the others. Although it seemed out of place with the rest of the buildings, it wasn't out of place for the culture; the city was built around a central structure that looked every bit the part of an ancient Viking longhouse…but one on the grandest scale imaginable.

Odin's Longhouse was a long, narrow, single-room building like the Terran Viking longhouses of old, but that was where the similarity ended. Where the Viking longhouse might have been 150 feet long by 15 feet wide, this building was as big as a medium-sized Terran arena. The structure incorporated a pseudo-concrete monolithic dome measuring almost 900 feet in length, with a width of 150 feet and a height of well over 250 feet.

The planet's star was overhead but did little to warm the group; although the Jotunn had said it was the height of summer, it felt like winter back on Terra. The cooler temperatures helped settle Calvin's stomach, as did being on solid ground once more.

With a blast of sand and small rocks, the Terran shuttle set down next to its Jotunn counterpart, looking like a child's toy next to the other shuttle's enormous bulk. Within seconds, the cargo bay ramp came down, and Calvin's group was joined by Captain Sheppard, Night and Lieutenant O'Leary.

"Good to see you," Calvin said in greeting; "thanks for coming after us." He introduced the Ssselipsssiss to the Terran officers. "These are my...um...kids. Captain Skrelleth left them in my care. They are also something of a Ssselipsssiss combat team, so they have some skills you might not expect in Terrans their age."

Lieutenant O'Leary raised an eyebrow. "Got tired of collecting spaceships and decided to start collecting kids?"

"No, he left them with me right before he sacrificed himself to get us off their planet, so I owe him. Captain Sheppard, can we find room for them when we return to the *Gulf*?"

"That won't be a problem," the CO replied, his voice sad. "We have all too many rooms open at the moment."

"Well, it seems like we all have stories to tell," Calvin said.

"Not only that," Night said, "but guess what else is here on this planet? One of the red mountains you were looking for." Calvin had been given a staff by an avatar of an ancient civilization and told that he needed to take it to a number of mountains on planets across the galaxy; all of them were similar to Ayer's Rock in Australia.

"Did you happen to bring down the Progenitor's Rod?" Calvin asked. "I think I only need one more to find out what it does."

"No, sorry; we didn't see the mountain until we were on our way down."

A nearby giant started tapping his foot, causing a series of minor earthquakes. "It is time for me to take you inside," the Jotnar said.

"I guess the rod will have to wait," Calvin said; "it looks like the Jotunn are ready."

Odin's Longhouse, Jotunheimr, Jotunheimr System, December 25, 2021

The doors on the end of the longhouse gaped open, and the Terrans followed their guide to the structure with the Ssselipsssiss and the horde of S'nark following close behind.

It was even cooler inside the shade of the longhouse, with a breeze blowing through the tunnel-like facility that made it hard to walk through the doorway. As the group entered the structure, Calvin was surprised by its lack of furnishings. He had expected the building to house an auditorium-like facility; instead, it was nothing more than a packed earth floor with three rows of tiered benches on both sides. Long poles shaped like tree trunks held up the ceiling. The floor was shaped like a Terran eye—narrow at the ends and wider in the middle.

The giant led them into the longhouse and pointed to a spot about 1/3 of the way to the other end. "Combatants wait there," he said. "All others wait on benches on the sides. Don't worry, the battle won't last long."

The Terrans moved to the indicated spot on the floor while the rest of the group took their seats on the benches. The Ssselipsssiss and Farhome helped each other onto a bench; the S'nark scrambled onto the one behind them.

"You seem pretty calm," Calvin said. "Do you know something I don't?"

"I know that I'd hate to be their champion in a few minutes," Night said, "whoever he is."

"It's probably one of them," Captain Sheppard said, nodding to the other end of the hall.

A group of four giants stood talking in the opposite doorway, their hair blowing in the breeze. The largest of the group was facing away from the Terrans and had a massive battle axe strapped to his back. Seeing the Terrans, one of the others nodded in their direction, and the group turned toward them. The biggest giant was...

Fenrir.

"Oh, shit," Calvin muttered. "Fenrir. Do you remember how he introduced himself? Fenrir, son of Loki. And who was the captain of the ship you guys destroyed?"

"Loki," Night said. He shrugged. "Doesn't matter; I'm pissed off, and he's going to die."

"Ha, ha, ha," the enormous Jotnar said to his comrades. "These creatures look smaller in real life. This will take even less time than I originally thought."

Fenrir strode toward them. Easily over 17 feet tall and 3,000 pounds, the giant was colossal; the ground tremored with each of his footsteps. Dressed in red-spotted pelts, the Jotunn had a chain-metal shirt over his torso, and light blue hair. He stopped 20 feet away from them; the Terrans still had to crane their necks to look up and see the Jotnar's red eyes glaring back at them.

"Ha, ha, ha," the giant said again. "I am surprised you had the courage to meet me in battle." He reached over his shoulder and drew his battle axe. "Gaze upon thy destiny, mini-mortal. This is Hel, given to my family ages past by the goddess of death, herself. With this axe I will cleave your maggot head from your swine body!"

The battle axe was enormous, with a 10-foot wooden shaft and large, curved iron blades nearly three feet long. The Jotnar swung the blade easily back and forth in his hands, spinning it faster and faster until it became nothing more than a blur.

"Wow," Night said. "That *is* his face. Stupid me; I just thought his neck threw up."

"Ha! You are funny, Terran," Fenrir said as the axe continued to whir. "But you are not very good at insults. Would you like to just give up now? I promise your end will be swift."

"No thanks, you drinker of spoiled sheep's piss," Night replied. "When I'm done with you, I'm going to make you my sansordinn."

Fenrir's face went purple, and a choking sound came from the depths of his throat. His rhythm faltered with the axe, and he missed a catch. The enormous axe spun off through the air toward the benches lining the wall to the right; the Jotunn there scattered. With a loud "thwack!" the axe embedded itself in one of the benches.

"You will die slowly and in great pain," Fenrir growled. "Take your position; it's time for you to die." He stalked over to the bench and yanked the axe out with a single tug, his gigantic muscles bulging with the effort.

The Terrans turned and began walking toward their end of the long hall.

"What the hell did you say to him?" Captain Sheppard asked.

"Sansordinn is the worst curse you can use in their language," Night replied. "It basically means 'to be used in the position of a female by another man.'"

"Well, if pissing him off was your goal, I think you succeeded."

Night cocked his head to listen to the swearing from the other end of the long hall. "It appears so," he agreed.

"More to the point," Calvin said, "what do you know about fighting 17-foot-tall giants with battle axes?"

"I did some research," Night admitted. "I figured he would fight with one of three weapons, and the battle axe was one of them."

"You're not worried?" Calvin asked. "He had it spinning pretty fast."

"Bah, that's easier than it looks, and it requires less swinging power than you might expect; gravity and momentum do most of the work to keep the blades spinning. What you don't see is the axe's blade tips have points that can also be used to thrust or hook an opponent. It's a pretty effective weapon."

"So what are you going to do to defeat him?"

"Try not to be where he swings it, for the most part."

"That's a good plan," Calvin agreed. "I was talking more about how you're planning on killing him. You can only avoid his blade for so long before you make a mistake. It doesn't even look like you're armed; I don't see a sword or even a long knife."

"No, but I have these," Night said as he reached into a leather pouch at his side and pulled out a handful of large, five-pointed shuriken in a variety of dark colors. Three other bags were strapped to his belt.

"You're going to beat him with throwing stars?" Captain Sheppard was incredulous; his mouth hung open as he shook his head.

"Even if you hit him with them, they're barely going to scratch him. Maybe you could put out an eye, but even that's going to be a damned near impossible."

Night smiled. "I've got a plan."

"Well I certainly hope so," the CO replied. "There is an awful lot riding on this."

"Don't worry, sir; I've got it. I owe them."

"Well, good luck then," Captain Sheppard said, turning to walk to the left-side bench.

"Thanks for coming," Calvin said. "No matter how this turns out."

"Heh, I'm the lucky one," Night replied. "If I lose, I'm dead; you, however, are still stuck here."

"So don't lose, okay?"

"That's the plan."

Calvin turned and walked over to where the CO waited.

"Are you ready to meet Hel?" Fenrir yelled from the other end of the long hall.

"Are you ready to bend over?" Night yelled back.

Fenrir roared something unintelligible and charged.

The ground shook as the giant approached with the finesse of a runaway steam locomotive, the battle axe held high in his right hand. Seeing the Terran appeared unarmed, he leaned forward and ran harder, as if he intended to stomp the Terran into the ground.

Night started moving and took up a loping pace toward the Jotnar, trying to time his steps so they didn't coincide with the giant's footfalls. At the last moment he feinted left and dove to the right. Having swerved for the feint, the giant missed his strike and roared past, screaming curses.

Night rolled several times and sprang to his feet, a shuriken held high. The giant stopped and turned, faster than anything his size had a right to.

Not wanting to be made to look like a fool a second time, Fenrir advanced on Night more slowly this time, his battle axe held in front of him in both hands. Night waved the shuriken a couple of times then threw the star toward the giant's face.

Fenrir turned the battle axe sideways, and the shuriken glanced off the face of the axe toward the crowd on the left.

"That is the best you have?" Fenrir roared. "Ho, ho, ho. That would scarcely even break my skin, much less injure me."

The giant swung the axe, trying to disembowel Night, but Night dove back out of the way and began circling back to his right. When he saw that Fenrir had recovered from the swing, he threw another of the stars at the giant's face. Like the first one, Fenrir blocked it with the axe head, and it went spinning off toward the crowd.

As the giant blocked the star, Night sprinted forward and dove through the giant's legs. He rolled once and then was up and on his feet again.

Fenrir spun, leading with his axe, but Night was already out of range. As he recovered from the stroke, a shuriken slammed into his upper left arm.

"Oh no!" Fenrir roared. "A little bug just stung me." He shifted the axe to his left hand and pulled out the star. With a flick of his wrist, he flipped it off to the side as if not worthy of his notice. Farhome dove out of the way as it whizzed past his head.

"Come now, mini-person, and let us end this," Fenrir said, stepping toward Night. "We both know that—"

Fenrir screamed and jumped up into the air on one foot, dropping his axe. Calvin saw a flash of light from the underside of the giant's boot; one of the throwing stars was buried in the Jotnar's boot. Calvin wondered how it got there, and he scanned the arena floor. It took a moment, but then Calvin saw them. There were a number of other stars sticking up…from everywhere Night had rolled. Calvin watched as Night feinted and dove to the side. As he stood up again, Calvin could see the faint outline of a star where he had rolled, but the color matched the hue of the dirt, making it difficult to see. It pointed straight up, sure to penetrate the footwear of anyone who stepped on it, especially if that person weighed almost two tons.

Night dove forward and rolled past the giant again, who tried to grab him but missed. Favoring his foot, Fenrir turned and hobbled over to his axe, using only the heel of his right foot. Seeing motion out of the corner of his eye, he turned as Night dove past him again, but was unable to seize the Terran, who once again rolled underneath his outstretched arm.

Picking up the axe, Fenrir turned to find Night cleaning dirt from a fingernail with one of the points of a throwing star. Night covered his mouth as he yawned. "This is the most boring fight I've ever been a part of," he said. "I had expected a lot more from you." He yawned again.

"*I will kill you!*" Fenrir bellowed. He took one more step, then he screamed again and dropped to his knees, another throwing star through the sole of his other foot.

As the giant fell forward onto his hands and knees, Night raced forward, drawing a 12-inch blade from a hidden scabbard in his sleeve. He ran down the right side of the giant and, wielding the knife like a sword, sliced across the back of the giant's arm, severing the tendons there.

The giant collapsed to the right, and Night dove under the falling form. Rolling once, he stood back up again and severed the muscles and tendons in Fenrir's left arm. The giant fell forward onto his face, and a whimper escaped his lips.

Night ran forward and plunged the slender knife into the back of Fenrir's neck, cutting his spinal cord. The giant collapsed. Reversing the knife, he drove it up as far as he could into the giant's brain. Fenrir shivered once then lay still.

"Merry Christmas, asshole," Night said as he turned away from the body. "That's for Wraith."

Odin's Longhouse, Jotunheimr, Jotunheimr System, December 26, 2021

Captain Sheppard, Calvin, Night and Lieutenant O'Leary stepped off the end of the shuttle's cargo ramp and marched in a line abreast to the longhouse.

"Well, that's different," Lieutenant O'Leary noted. "Guards."

Calvin shaded his eyes to get a better look. Where the doors to the structure had stood open the day before, today they were closed and two of the largest Jotunn Calvin had seen stood in front of them. The giants were clad in leather armor, except for spiked metal gauntlets and boots that shone in the wan sunlight. A punch or kick could easily skewer a couple Terrans at the same time. Even more threatening were the massive halberds they held at the ready. Both were grim-faced and alert. If the Jotunn were trying to intimidate them, Calvin thought, it was working.

"Yeah," Calvin said, "try not to piss them off, all right? They look like they're ready for war."

"I'll think about it," Lieutenant O'Leary replied.

"Do I need to make that an order?" Captain Sheppard asked.

"No sir," O'Leary muttered as they drew near to the structure and the massive door guards. "I'll be a good boy."

As the Terrans approached, both giants snapped to attention.

"I am Hraesveglur, Guardian of the Gates," bellowed the giant on the left. "State your names and purpose."

"My name is Captain James Sheppard," the CO replied. He tried to imitate the tone of the guard but couldn't approach it in contempt or volume. "I am the commanding officer of the Terran ship *Vella Gulf*. With me are Lieutenant Commander Shawn Hobbs, Captain Paul Train and First Lieutenant Ryan O'Leary. We have come to speak with the Council of Jarls."

"You are expected," Hraesveglur replied. "You may enter."

The Jotnar on the right spun around, threw open the door behind him and announced the Terrans.

The group continued into the longhouse to find the interior had changed as well. A large platform had been erected which ran down the left side of the longhouse floor. As the group approached, Calvin could see the platform held nine chairs, although only the five in the center were occupied. A man sat in the central chair, which was larger than the rest. Two men waited to his left, including Captain Oleif Magnusson; a man and a woman sat to his right. The 20-foot-high platform wasn't overly large by Jotunn standards, but by human standards it was immense; the humans had to look 30 feet above them to make eye contact with the Jotunn.

Like the door guards, none of the giants looked entirely pleased to see the Terrans.

"Welcome, emissaries of Terra," the giant in the center said as the group approached. "I am Mimir, Odin of the Jotunn." He motioned to the two men to his left. "With me on the Council of Jarls are Baugi and Oleif. On my right are Surt and Angrboda, wife of Loki. She is here in his place until a final determination is made about his fate. Normally we are nine, but two are away and two others have not survived contact with your race."

"Greetings, Odin. I am pleased to be able to speak with you and the council today. There are many things we have to discuss which I feel will be beneficial to both our nations."

"We have granted you permission to speak based on the contest of champions yesterday," the Odin said; "however, do not assume we have ears ready to listen to any proposals you intend to make. Everyone here has personally felt your coming in the loss of those we loved, no less than Angrboda, who has now lost both a son and a husband to you."

"Both of those are a tragedy, of course," Captain Shepard replied, "and we would have avoided them at all costs; however, in both of those cases, we were not to blame. They attacked us and were killed when we defended ourselves. We do not desire any further bloodshed between our two civilizations. We would rather have peace."

"It is easy for you to say you were wrongly attacked," Angrboda said, "but how are we to know if that is true? Perhaps you gave them offense, and they felt honor-bound to reply."

"That is not the case," Captain Sheppard replied. "In the case of your husband, we were by ourselves in the other universe, and his ship jumped in and attacked us."

"Well of course they did," Angrboda replied. "You were assaulting our home planet; how could they do otherwise?"

"All we were doing was trying to get some of our crew back from onboard the *Falcon*. We asked to talk, but instead they replied with missiles. We were forced to defend ourselves, and Loki and his ship were destroyed in the fighting."

"With no survivors?" Captain Magnusson asked. "Isn't it odd to have a battle where no one survives?"

"It is not unknown for that to happen," Captain Sheppard said. "Our weapons are powerful."

"Our allies have powerful weapons too," the Odin said. "They are powerful enough to affect time itself."

"I know," Captain Sheppard boasted. "We have fought them and defeated them on many occasions. Just like their ability to jump between the universes, we have also acquired their ability to use time-based weapons." He shrugged. "They must not be very good allies if they haven't given you the secrets to these things."

"That is a point of some contention," the Odin agreed. "We have asked on many occasions; however, I believe they are afraid of what we might do if we could get to their home world."

"Having been tricked by your countrymen on a couple of occasions," Captain Sheppard said, "I'm not sure I can blame them. Not having the ability to jump between universes probably keeps you from destroying their home world."

"Truth," Captain Magnusson said. "There are many times I have had to accept insults from them because I knew there was nothing I could do to them. When a nation can destroy your planet, and you can't stop them, there are times when insults must be borne."

"We also have this ability," Captain Sheppard said; "however, we have not insulted you or threatened to use it on you."

"That has not gone unnoticed," the Odin said, "which is one of the reasons we have allowed you to speak."

"I thought we were allowed to speak because I killed your champion." Night interjected.

"That is no more than anyone else who made contact with us has had to do to prove their worth," the Odin replied. "We gave you the opportunity because you hadn't threatened us, even though you had the power to do so. You chose not to dictate terms to us as a conqueror, but to approach us as equals. We were curious as to why this was."

Calvin saw O'Leary's face go red as Captain Sheppard replied, "We are interested in long-term relations with you, not war. The war you have with the Aesir is a drain on both of your societies, and it is one I think is past time to end. We would be willing to help negotiate a settlement for you."

"With the Aesir?" Surt asked. "The only good Aesir is a dead one."

"Let us stick to the matter at hand," the Odin said, "as that issue is greatly beyond our level of trust in you at the moment. We may never trust you to intervene in matters so grave, but that is a question for the future, and today is not that. Why are you here?"

"To be blunt, we are here today to ask you to reconsider your alliance with the Shaitans," Captain Sheppard said. "We believe it is in the best interests of both of our civilizations for you to do so."

"Just turn our backs on our friends?" the Odin asked. "You ask much and presume more."

Captain Sheppard shook his head. "No, Odin, I do not ask for much, other than a chance to help you see that the Shaitans are not your friends, as you would have us believe."

"I know they aren't your friends," Calvin said, "because I have listened to you talk. When I was onboard the *Falcon*, I heard Captain Magnusson speaking with the captain of the Shaitan ship. The discussion they had was not one held between allies, but between a ruler and the ruled. The Shaitans told your captain what he had to do, offering him insults throughout. I have worked with our allies on a number of occasions, and we have never spoken in such a manner."

"Truth." Captain Magnusson said. "There are many times where I have been close to open feud with them, and the taste it has left in my mouth is galling."

"Not only do the Shaitans treat you poorly," Captain Sheppard added, "they are also causing you to lose your honor. Since when has it ever been okay to wipe out entire races like they are having you do to the Ssselipsssiss? I have spoken with a couple of the Shaitans, and they do not honor life the way we do. I'll bet they've already spoken with you about what happens after the Ssselipsssiss are eliminated. What next? Eliminate the Mrowry? Terra? I'll bet their goal is to wipe out the next race, and the next and the next."

"It is to be Terra," Captain Magnusson said. "They hate your race more than any other."

"Not only do they hate us," Captain Sheppard said, "they *fear* us. Why do you suppose we're next? We're the only ones who have destroyed any of their ships! Not only that, we're the only ones who have shown an ability to get to their universe. I'm sure they are *very* afraid of us. They have no idea what we are capable of; I'm sure they are worried we might give you that secret too, and then they would lose their best ally. Of course we have to be destroyed next—we're their biggest threat."

"Truth," Captain Magnusson said; "however, the same can be said from our perspective. You are also *our* biggest threat. Just like the Shaitans, we cannot bring you to battle if you do not choose it; you simply jump to their universe and escape. While they are our allies, they present a balancing force to your nation. Without them, there is nothing we can do to stop *you*."

"That is certainly true," Captain Sheppard conceded; "however, you have to look at the motives involved. We are allies with a number of races like the Mrowry, the Aesir and the Archons. Never once have we taken any of their planets or tried to steal any of their technology. In fact, there are a number of technologies we have shared with the Mrowry, including the jump technology which you seek. What have the Shaitans shared with you? Of all of the planets you've conquered, how many have they given to you? If the answer to those questions is anything other than 'zero,' we will leave right now, as I have underestimated their value as an ally."

"You needn't leave," the Odin replied. "You are correct; they have neither shared any of their technology with us nor told us we could settle on any of the conquered planets."

"And why do you think that is?"

"Because they are afraid of us," Surt said, "as well they should be!"

"I see," Captain Sheppard said. He cocked his head and looked puzzled. "The question I have for you then is, what do the Shaitans do with races they are afraid of? For example, what do they want to do with Terra?"

"Eliminate you," Captain Magnusson said. "I believe they said every Terran must be killed and all of your planets burned."

"Uh huh," Captain Sheppard said, nodding his head. "And what do you think happens when there are no more Terrans for you to kill and your usefulness as an ally declines?"

"They will turn on us next," Baugi said. His voice was quiet...muted...thoughtful. "Once they no longer need us, they will turn on us too."

"I don't think I'm telling you something you don't already suspect," Captain Sheppard said; "otherwise, Loki wouldn't have taken one of their ships. I think you know what I'm saying is true, even if you aren't prepared to admit it to yourselves yet." He paused to let that sink in.

"Skipper, did you say you'd spoken to the Shaitan?" Calvin asked into the silence.

"Yes, we captured a couple of them. One is a pilot and the other is one of their ground forces."

"Have you translated their language?"

"I think so," Captain Sheppard replied. "Solomon said that he was pretty sure he had been able to break it. Why?"

"Because I recorded something that might shed some light on the Shaitans' motives." He looked up at the Odin. "Do you have a method of playing a recording?"

"Of course," the Odin said. "What do you take us for, rubes from the country?" He pushed a button on the arm of his chair and a screen sprang up behind them.

"*Solomon*," Calvin commed, "*please get in touch with the Ssselipsssiss Paxton and get his copy of the argument we recorded between the two Shaitan officers. Translate it and work out a method of sending it to whatever AI manages the technology here in the longhouse. Can you do that?*"

"*Yes I can. In fact, I already have the recording and have it translated. Negotiating access…done. Just let me know when you would like it to play.*"

"*Now, please.*"

"*Coming.*"

The screen lit up to show two Shaitan officers. "This is a conversation recorded onboard the *Falcon* between Captain Tectamus and Admiral Zeontes," Calvin narrated. "It occurred after Captain Magnusson stepped out of the room."

"I remember that," Captain Magnusson said. "That looks like them and my conference room where the meeting was held."

"The recording has been translated by our artificial intelligence, which has been studying the language of the Shaitan. Here we go." The recording began playing.

"*I will be glad when we no longer have to maintain the appearance of friendship with the Jotunn,*" Captain Tectamus said. "*It will be a happy day when we can kill them all.*"

"*Until that time, we must not antagonize them,*" Admiral Zeontes warned. "*I do not care to have to fight the Jotunn at the same time as the Ssselipsssiss and the Terrans. Especially the Terrans.*"

"*But we are going to kill them, right?*"

"*The high lord has decreed that everyone in this universe is an abomination and an affront to our gods. They must all be destroyed, and that includes the Jotunn. Now that the Terrans have shown an ability to come into our holy universe and pollute it with their presence, their destruction has to be the priori-*"

ty...and to do so, we need the Jotunn to assist us. They are better equipped to take on the bigger ships of the Terran navy."

"But then we're going to kill them?"

"Absolutely. Everyone in this universe must be destroyed."

* * * * *

Chapter Twenty-Six

"It appears the Shaitans leave something to be desired as allies," Captain Magnusson noted. "To say that on my ship with me just on the other side of the door..." He looked down the row to the Odin. "I will have some difficulty fighting alongside them ever again."

"I think it is apparent we have been betrayed," the Odin said, "assuming that is an honest translation of what was said?" He looked at Calvin with a raised eyebrow.

"Solomon, how sure are you about that translation?"

"I am not sure if the word 'holy' is correct, but it appeared to be the most accurate translation, based on the cultural norms of Terran linguistics," the AI replied. *"Aside from that, I am over 97% confident that is what the Shaitan officers said."*

"Thanks; that was a big help."

Calvin nodded. "Yes, Odin, my AI confirms that is an accurate translation, to the best of its considerable abilities. Honestly, though, their intentions are no different than what we already figured...although the reason behind them is new."

"So it comes down to a matter of the gods, then," the Odin said; "theirs against ours for who lives and who dies. As I am not quite ready to make the journey to Valhalla, I think it is time to betray the betrayers before they can do the same to us."

"Aren't you angry?" Calvin asked. "You don't seem at all disturbed by the fact that they were going to turn on you."

"Oh, we are indeed angry," the Odin replied; "however, my blood sings to me in preparation for battle. I have long hated this alliance; now we can break it with honor and destroy the betrayers from surprise. Yes, I am full of anger, but I am holding it close inside to use on my foe with my axe and my sword."

The Odin laughed. "The joy of battle is upon me, and we will bring down Hel on the traitorous bastards. *Cry havoc and let slip the hounds of war!*" He laughed again and was joined by the rest of the council.

Eventually, the laughter wound down, and the Odin wiped a tear from the corner of his eye. "You are not much of a warrior, though, if you came here to tell us this without having a plan," he said to Captain Sheppard. "What are your intentions?"

"We are going to find the home world of the Shaitans and convince them, by force if necessary, to give up this war. Failing that, we will do everything in our power to destroy them and ensure they no longer have the ability to wage war on our universe."

"You may be small, Terrans, but you are full of spirit," the Odin said. "You intend to do all of this with your one little ship?"

"With all due respect, that little ship has been the bane of your plans for some time now," Captain Sheppard said, "and has been successful in battle against a number of foes. The strength of the ship doesn't come from its size, but from the ingenuity of its crew and the many different approaches we bring to warfare. We are only standing here now because we have beaten *your* forces twice."

"So you think you can find their planet and convince them to quit fighting?" the Odin asked. "While you may be able to do the first, I believe you will find the second objective to be impossible. Although I haven't personally met their ruler, the emissary who survived speaking with him said High Lord Sarpedon is crazy. Worse, he has a huge number of loyal supporters who carry out his every whim. I do not believe you will convince him to change his ways, nor will you survive the effort. Anyone who displeases him is killed."

"In that case, I cannot tell you what we will do until we get there," Captain Sheppard said. "What I can tell you is our race values life, all life, and that it is not my intention to destroy their planet unless there is no other way to end this war."

"If you want to end the war, then you must be prepared to destroy their planet," the Odin replied. "There *is* no other way."

"If that is what we must do, then so be it," Captain Sheppard said.

"I fear that it will not be as easy as you make it sound," Captain Magnusson warned. "I have been there, and I can tell you their planet is well defended. There are stargate defenses in our universe and a variety of space-based defenses around the planet in theirs. You will need to be even more industrious than you make yourselves out to be; you may have a few seconds to make your plea to surrender before you are destroyed, but that will be about it."

"We have made it into a number of heavily guarded systems," Captain Sheppard said, "including this one. I'm sure it can be done if we put our heads together and work something out. That is, of course, if you'd like to join us in the effort."

The Odin looked at his council members and saw four nodding heads. "We are in agreement that we will put aside our present conflict with you and will join in your assault on the Dark Star."

"And after that?"

"We will see how the war against the Shaitans goes and make our determination."

"Speaking of our betrayers," Captain Magnusson said, "why don't we get together tomorrow on my ship to discuss our plans for how best to betray them in turn?"

Passageway, Jotunn Ship *Falcon*, Jotunheimr System, December 27, 2021

One of the giants waited for the Terrans as they came on board the Jotunn vessel. The planning group was led by Captain Sheppard and consisted of Calvin, Night and Lieutenant O'Leary. Captain Sheppard had decided to keep the group small and eliminate as many sources of contention as possible on the visit; despite his desire to attend the meeting for Calvin's safety, Farhome had been left on the *Gulf*.

"If you will follow me," the giant waiting for them said, "I will take you to Captain Magnusson's conference room where he is holding the planning session."

Without waiting for an answer, the Jotnar turned and began striding down the passageway. To Calvin, the enormity of the ship made the corridor seem to stretch into infinity, and the Terrans were quickly left behind.

"Hey!" Night yelled at the Jotnar's rapidly shrinking back, "Could you slow it down a bit?"

The giant retraced his steps. "What is the problem?" he asked.

"Uh, this," Night said, pointing at the coaming around the bottom of the hatch he was going through. About 12 inches high on a Terran vessel, the coamings on the *Falcon* were three-foot-high obstacles; to traverse them, the Terrans were forced to pause and belly-roll over each of them in turn.

"Want me to carry you?" the giant asked.

"No, that's all right," Captain Sheppard replied. "Just slow down."

The procession started off again, slightly slower this time. Lieutenant O'Leary led the group of Terrans, his eyes constantly in motion.

"They aren't going to attack us here," Calvin whispered after watching O'Leary slow down at the third intersection in a row as if expecting an ambush. "They gave us their word."

"You weren't onboard the *Gulf* when they attacked," Lieutenant O'Leary replied. "With all due respect, sir, you wouldn't understand the depths of their treachery."

"Well you didn't have to come if you're so worried about it."

"They invited us for a planning conference. I wouldn't have wanted to let them come aboard the *Gulf*, but that doesn't mean I have to like being here. Besides, I couldn't let you put together a plan without my input. You may have been in charge of the platoon for a couple of years now, but, no offense, you still think like an aviator, not a soldier. And, if I'm here, maybe I can help get you and the Skipper out when this situation turns to shit, which I'm sure it will."

The conversation ended as their guide stopped in front of a hatch. He knocked then held the hatch open for the Terrans to enter.

Calvin found himself in the same conference room where he had watched Captain Magnusson negotiate with the Shaitans. Although it was furnished much the same as it was when Calvin had viewed it from above, the new perspective posed several problems. If there was a map on the table, he couldn't see it as the table was seven feet high. The height of the table also precluded him from seeing the three Jotunn on the other side of the table—although he had a great view of their legs. At six feet high, the seats of the chairs were too high to climb into gracefully, and there were no bars across the legs to use as a ladder; he would need a boost to get up to the seat.

Before he could ask Night for a lift, one of the giants walked down the Terran side of the table and lifted the four humans into their chairs.

Captain Magnusson cleared his throat. "Thank you for coming," he said. "I know you said you want to see the home of the Shaitans before you decide on your course of action. I don't understand it, but I suppose it is due to your tiny stature that you are unable to make bigger plans than that. However, with that in mind, there are many issues you need to be aware of, or your mission will fail spectacularly."

"Ha!" Lieutenant O'Leary said, "You almost make it sound like you want us to succeed."

"Oh, but we do," the Jotnar said. "We want you to succeed in bringing them to heel. If you do not, then I will have to fight them. That is a problem as I can't get into their universe."

"But if we win," O'Leary said, "you still have to deal with us, and we can jump to the other universe too."

"That's true," Captain Magnusson said, "but there is a big difference between your nations, besides the fact they betrayed us." He smiled, but his face held no warmth. "You are a life form of this universe. You have to come back here periodically, or you will die. Your home planet is also in this universe, so you can only run for so long. If we threaten your world, you will have to come back and honor the threat. If nowhere else, we can draw you into battle there."

"That's pretty cold-blooded," Captain Sheppard noted.

The giant shrugged. "You have to look out for the future of your civilization," he said; "I have to look out for mine."

"Getting back to your original point," Captain Sheppard said, "what are the issues you said we need to know?"

"The first obstacle to your plan is that the Shaitans keep a large concentration of their ships at the stargate into the Dark Star system in our universe. You will have to fight to get past them."

"You're right," the CO said; "that's a problem. Even if we use stealth, there's still going to be some time where we're visible when we come through the stargate. They're going to know we're there."

"Second," the giant continued, "there are defenses around the planet in their universe once you jump to it. There are either three small moons or large asteroids which orbit the planet. The Shaitans use these bodies as defensive bases."

"Stealth would work against them," Calvin noted.

"Up to a point," Captain Magnusson replied. "The asteroids are also used to project a defensive energy shield around the planet. I do not know if it will cancel your stealth, but I suspect it will."

"I take it the projectors are defended," Night said.

"Yes. There are bases on each of the asteroids, which guard the projectors."

"Could we shoot a missile at one of the projectors?" Lieutenant O'Leary asked. "Maybe we could make it look like a piece of space junk or something?"

"Perhaps," the giant replied, "although I'm told they are well defended."

"Well, you've certainly given us a lot to think about," the CO said. "Can you tell us anything about the surface of the planet?"

"I don't know much about the planet as I haven't been to the surface, but I can tell you enough."

"What does that mean?" Lieutenant O'Leary asked.

"It means there isn't anything on the surface of the planet," Captain Magnusson replied. "The Shaitans evolved underground, and all of their cities, their civilization…everything… is underground."

"So how do you get to where their ruler is?"

"How do you get to where their high lord is?" Captain Magnusson asked. "It's easy. You don't."

CO's Conference Room, Jotunn Ship *Falcon*, Jotunheimr System, December 27, 2021

"You seem to know an awful lot about the Dark Star system," Captain Sheppard noted.

"I have been to the Dark Star system in this universe on two occasions," Captain Magnusson replied. "Since we do not have the ability to transit to the other universe, my knowledge of what the planet looks like there is based on what the ambassador who returned from the other universe told me."

"The ambassador? I would have thought you'd been allies for longer than the time it would take for one ambassador to go and return. Can you stay in the other universe for long periods of time without experiencing health problems?"

"No. We cannot stay there for more than about 50 days without our health degrading. And yes, we have been 'allies' with the Shaitans for much longer than that. Unfortunately, their high lord has a penchant for killing our ambassadors for slights he feels they have given him. Whether real or perceived, it does not matter; he kills anyone he feels has damaged his honor or not done as they have been told."

"And you put up with this?" Night asked.

"Sometimes the honor and safety of your race cause you to endure things you would otherwise not put up with. We needed them to help us defeat the Aesir. Their ability to jump back and forth to the other universe makes them very difficult to kill. Even our biggest ships were unable to defeat their ships when we first came upon them. If our battleships weren't as large as they are, or able to absorb as much damage as they can, we would never have survived first contact with the Shaitans. Once they saw they couldn't destroy our ships, they finally tried communicating with us. It took a long time to establish communications, but we ultimately prevailed."

Captain Magnusson shook his head. "I was a mid-grade officer on one of the battleships at the time, and trying to speak with them was the most frustrating thing I have ever done. We still don't understand their language very well; most times they use our language, which they can speak better than we can speak theirs."

"Their language *is* very difficult," Captain Sheppard said; "it uses frequencies higher than we can hear, in addition to ones we can."

"That would explain why we were never able to communicate with them very well in their language," the giant admitted. "Once we figured out how to communicate with them, we learned they were already at war with the Ssselipsssiss. The war had started out well for the Shaitans, but the Ssselipsssiss were adapting to their attacks, and the Shaitan high lord was furious. Our ship's captain talked with their high lord and worked out an alliance with them. Although our civilizations are very different, the alliance worked well for both of us, at least until your ship arrived. The addition of the Shaitan ships helped us surprise the Aesir, and the addition of our fleet units allowed the Shaitans to roll through the Ssselipsssiss with little resistance. They began to adapt toward the end, but by then there weren't enough of them left to make a difference."

"So you went to the Dark Star system at the start of the war," Captain Sheppard said. "You said you'd been there twice; when was the other time?"

"I was there about a year ago when I was chosen to take the new ambassador to the Shaitans and bring Uncle Loki home. He was just completing his time there and was our only ambassador to actually survive being stationed there. Apparently Loki got into trouble several times, but he was always able to talk his way out of it by tricking the high lord into believing it was someone else's fault."

"Did you cross into the Shaitan's universe?"

"No, but I spoke to my uncle several times about what he had seen and done there. Loki hated the Shaitans and wanted nothing more than to steal their technology so we could end the alliance with them and crush them. He found them to be disgusting creatures with no honor."

"That's what I don't get," Calvin said. "Your civilization is based on honor, yet you let the Shaitans do things that lack honor. How is genocide honorable?"

"It is not," Captain Magnusson stated; "however, the war was going well, and we had just announced the commencement of Ragnarok when we learned of their genocidal tendencies. It was easier to look the other way than it was to break the alliance when we needed them most."

"That answers the question of how you know so much about the Dark Star system," Captain Sheppard said. "Knowing what you know, what is the best way for us to get into the system?"

"By yourself? It can't be done; not without the Shaitans knowing you're there. If you are trying to spy on them stealthily…"

"We are."

"Then you are going to need help."

"We cannot go to the Dark Star system," Commander Sturl Halson, the *Falcon's* XO warned. "We left the Shaitan war against the lizards without the high lord's permission. He's probably already put out a death warrant on you. If the rest of us are lucky, it's only on you; however, it's far more likely he has condemned the entire ship and crew of the *Falcon* to death."

The giant CO shrugged. "It is not without some danger," he agreed. "Certainly for me and probably for you. Still, do you want to live forever? There is sure to be battle if we assist the Terrans; what could be better than betraying the betrayers? How many of us have died at the hands of the Shaitans? If I am going to die, I would rather do it in battle…and I would rather die killing the Shaitans."

"Well then, why do it by half?" the *Falcon's* XO asked. "Let's muster the entire fleet and go crush the Shaitan fleet!"

"If we bring a big fleet into the Dark Star system," Captain Magnusson replied, "the Shaitans are going to know we are there to betray them and will all transit back to their universe. We won't be able to get at them, and the *Vella Gulf* will be tremendously outnumbered in their universe. No matter how well they fight, the Terrans will be overwhelmed, and the entire mission will be for naught. Then, once the *Vella Gulf* has been destroyed, the Shaitans will transit back to fire their missiles at us, and we will be overwhelmed."

Captain Magnusson shook his head. "No, this is a mission for one ship, or two if you count the Terran ship. We will get the Terrans into the Dark Star system and let them be about their business. Then, we will defend ourselves until they have accomplished what they are going to do. We will kill as many of the Shaitans as we can, providing a distraction for the Terrans, and when they are done, we will leave with them. There is one thing I must mention. As the XO noted, we may not be welcome in the Dark Star system. Under no circumstances will I put myself or my ship under Shaitan control. If that happens, we will be forced to fight. We will wait for you as long as we can, but we will have to withdraw at that point."

"How are you going to get us into the Dark Star system unnoticed?" Captain Sheppard asked.

"As you may have noticed, your ship is somewhat smaller than ours. I intend to use that to our advantage."

CO's Conference Room, TSS *Vella Gulf*, Jotunheimr System, December 27, 2021

"So that's how we're going to get into the Dark Star system," Captain Sheppard concluded. "That is probably the easiest part of the journey. The hard part is going to be once we're in the other universe. Since the *Falcon* can't make the jump, we are going to be on our own there. At some point, odds are we're going to need to fight the Shaitans. We've already seen what their technology can do. Some of it's good; most of it is less so. The one thing that continues to worry me, though, are their jumping missiles."

"Yes sir," the DSO replied, "they are the greatest threat. Our anti-missile missiles (AMMs) can't catch them because they jump, and our lasers are ineffective against them for some reason."

"Have we figured out why that is yet?" the CO asked. "Lieutenant Bradford, do you have any ideas?"

"No sir," he replied. "I'd really like to get my hands on a few of them so I can take a look, though."

"No doubt. We'll pick some up the next chance we get. Failing that, does anyone else have any ideas for defeating their missiles?"

"I do," Calvin said. "The Ssselipsssiss have a really low-tech way of defeating them. They put poles with a large mass on the bows of their ships. When a Shaitan fires on them, they turn into the missile and let it hit the mass on the end of the pole. The mass disappears, but there is surprisingly little damage to the bow of the ship. Obviously, it only works once, but if you rigged a couple and only extended them one at a time, it would let you take a hit or two before you started losing pieces of your ship."

"That makes sense," the CO said. "Ops, take a look at that for implementation, please. What else does anyone have?"

"I don't know how well they track in their native universe," the DSO said, "but we could try jumping there to escape them. Maybe if we go to the other universe, make a course change and jump back, it won't be able to keep up with us."

"Also worth trying," the CO acknowledged.

"And maybe if we have some extra unobtanium lying around, we could try putting jump modules on some of the AMMs like we have with the ASMs," the DSO added. "Maybe if they could follow the Shaitan missiles as they jump back and forth, we could get some hits with them."

"That sounds plausible," Captain Sheppard said. "What else?"

"You weren't there when we went over to fight on the Shaitan ship," Night said, "but you should have seen what silver and gold rounds do to their ships and structures. The rounds cut right through them. If we could get some of that onto the Shaitan's ships, they would have a damage control nightmare on their hands. It's darn near impossible to put out the silver and gold fires, as they make their own oxygen."

"So are you saying we should put silver and gold on our missiles?" asked the operations officer.

"I'm saying that we ought to collect every last bit of it on this ship and spray it all over the Shaitans whenever we get the chance," Night replied. "Until I can get close enough to do it myself, putting it on our missiles is a great start."

"That's great for killing their ships, but it won't help against their missiles," the DSO said.

"It will if you spray it onto their missile tubes," Night replied with a smile. "I have a feeling it would help a whole lot. Besides, it doesn't matter if they destroy the missile just short of their ship. It will still spray all over it and eat through anything it touches."

"Anyone else got any ideas?" the CO asked. "Okay, those are some great ideas; let's see what we can do to put 'em to use."

* * * * *

Chapter Twenty-Seven

"I am estimating 5 minutes to the GD 165 stargate if the Jotunn maintain this speed," the helmsman noted.

"Set General Quarters and put all remaining active sensors to standby," Captain Sheppard said. Most of the *Gulf's* active sensors had been silenced when the ship tied up to the larger *Falcon*. Over a mile and a half in length, the Falcon dwarfed the 1,300-foot Vella Gulf. It had taken two days to recover the stealth modules, provision the *Gulf* and attach it to the *Falcon*, then another 10 days to travel to the stargate into the Dark Star system, but they were almost to their objective.

Although the Terrans hoped the bulk of the Jotunn vessel would get them into the next system without being seen, most of the crew disliked being in such proximity to the giants; Calvin had noticed Lieutenant O'Leary in particular kept looking at the overhead as if he expected the giants to tunnel through at any moment.

"They're on our side," Calvin said after about the 100th time he saw O'Leary look up. "The Jotunn aren't going to attack us. At least not here and not now."

"How do we know they aren't playing us, though?" Lieutenant O'Leary asked. "From what we know, the Shaitan ruler doesn't like us much. Maybe the damned giants are hoping to turn us in to him to get a reward."

"What kind of reward would be worth turning us in for when we're the only ones who can help them fight the Shaitans?"

"How about jump modules? If the Jotunn thought they could trade us to the Shaitans for jump modules, I'll bet they'd turn on us in a heartbeat."

"They might, at that," Calvin acknowledged; "I guess it's a good thing the Shaitans have absolutely no desire to give the jump modules to the Jotunn, and the giants know it. The Shaitans are very happy to have the Jotunn stuck in their own universe. The Shaitans' life expectancies are much higher that way…and even they have to know that."

"I'm sure they do," Lieutenant O'Leary said; "however, that doesn't stop the giants from obsessing about having jump modules and entertaining some thoughts about how they might be able to get them."

"Nah, I don't think so."

"But what if they could also use it to clear their CO's name? What's to stop him from saying he left the front lines because he was trying to lure us away so he could capture us?"

"Those are both good points, but I don't think they're going to turn us in. The Jotunn were betrayed by the Shaitans; they aren't going to go back to working with them again."

"We'll find out in a second, sirs," the helmsman said. "Here we go!"

The ship jumped, leaving a sweet taste in their mouths.

"System entry into the GD 165 system," Steropes said.

"Passive sensors only," Captain Sheppard ordered. "Let's get a quick survey of the local area before we activate stealth."

"I've got numerous energy sources in the vicinity," Steropes said. "Two cruisers and at least three destroyers off the bow."

"Holy shit!" the DSO exclaimed. "I've got another one behind us on the starboard side, ready to flank anyone coming through the stargate. It's the biggest Shaitan vessel I've seen! It's battleship-sized, for sure, if not bigger. Not only that, *it's got shields!*"

"Got it," the CO replied. "Relax. As long as the *Falcon* is with us, we've got a ship that big too."

"But sir, it's got shields! We've never seen the Shaitans with them before."

"Understood. As quickly as they rolled up the Ssselipsssiss, they were bound to get some of their technology. As far as we know, the Jotunn may have given them that technology too. Track them and get a good firing solution in case it's needed."

"Yes sir," the DSO replied.

"I've got another Shaitan battleship off the port quarter," the OSO reported. "It was also behind the stargate ready to pounce...and it's also got shields. Man, it sure looks like they don't want you coming in here." His finger tapped the console next to the launch button.

"Okay everyone, just stay frosty," Captain Sheppard said. "We've got the Jotunn with us, and we can go into stealth any time we want...right?"

"Yes sir," the duty engineer replied; "just say the word, and you've got stealth."

"Steropes, let me know when we're shielded from the Shaitans so we can engage stealth."

"We are shielded from them right now. The Jotunn ship is between the battleships and us, and the smaller ships are all above the *Falcon.*"

"Got it; thanks."

"Captain Sheppard, the Shaitans are calling the Jotunn."

"Put it on speaker."

"*Jotunn vessel, this is* Gatekeeper. *State your purpose in this system.*"

"Gatekeeper, *this is the Jotunn ship* Falcon, *Captain Magnusson commanding. We have the replacement ambassador for your home world and supplies for our embassy.*"

"*You are early to bring a new ambassador.*"

"*Well, the last two died before they could be relieved; we thought it prudent to come a little earlier this time.*"

"*That is wise. I believe High Lord Sarpedon is also interested in speaking to you about why you left your duties in the fight against the lizards. Proceed to the Dark Planet in this system; you can await transportation there.*"

"*We are proceeding to the Dark Planet;* Falcon *out.*"

"Sounds like someone just got called to the principal's office," the helmsman said.

"Skipper, Captain Magnusson would like to talk with you," the communications officer announced.

"He's calling on the radio?"

"No sir, we ran a line to their ship; the comms are secure."

"Very well; on screen."

Captain Magnusson's face appeared on the front view screen. "Did you hear our communications?"

"Yes, we did," the CO replied.

"You had better hurry and decide what you're going to do because I am not going to let them take me to the Dark Planet so Sarpedon can kill me. You have until they come for me; at that time, we will fight our way back out of this system, regardless of what you decide to do."

"Understood," Captain Sheppard replied. "We will detach momentarily. *Vella Gulf* out."

The communications officer terminated the link, and the screen went dead.

"Well, you heard the captain," the CO said. "Our timer is running. Give me stealth and stand by to detach."

"Stealth coming…now!" the duty engineer replied. "Standing by to detach."

"Detach."

Bridge, TSS *Vella Gulf*, Proceeding to the Dark Planet, GD 165 System, January 8, 2022

"What do we know about this system?" Captain Sheppard asked.

"We are in the GD 165 system, which is in the constellation Bootes about 103 light-years from Terra," Steropes explained. "This system is interesting in that it has two stars—a white dwarf and a brown dwarf located about 120 astronomical units from each other. Both stars have planets that orbit them. According to the information provided by the Ssselipsssiss, and confirmed by the Jotunn, the brown dwarf is the star known as the Dark Star."

"I don't get it," the helmsman said. "How can there be life around a dead star?"

"Although the star is not big enough to sustain hydrogen fusion like a main sequence star," Steropes replied, "it has a mass of over 70 Jupiters, or about 5% of your Sun, and it is big enough to fuse both deuterium and lithium. It has a surface temperature of over 2,100 degrees, which is hot enough to provide warmth and a little light to a planet in close proximity. The Dark Planet is larger than Terra, and its composition is unlike Terra's; its core provides more heat. Between the heat provided by the star and the extra energy from the planet, there is obviously enough warmth to support life on the planet, although there are no signs of life from the Dark Planet in this universe."

"Sounds like there's nothing else worth seeing here," the CO replied. "Helmsman, make the jump to the other universe."

"Aye sir. Jumping...now."

Everything flashed as the ship jumped to the Jinn universe.

"Wow, there's a lot more going on here," the OSO noted.

"I'm going to need a little more information than that, OSO," Captain Sheppard said.

"Yes sir," the OSO replied. "There are numerous power sources in the vicinity of the planet; I am trying to classify them."

"I've got one...no, two cruisers in orbit around the planet," the DSO said. "Both appear to be older Shaitan ships; I don't see any signs of shields."

"I believe what the OSO is observing is the energy field the Jotunn told us about," Steropes noted, "but it is much more in depth than we were led to believe. There is also a smaller energy field from a slightly different azimuth that is...unlike the field surrounding the planet."

"What do you mean?" Captain Sheppard asked.

"I'm not sure," Steropes replied. "It's not like anything I've ever seen before. I will need some time to analyze it."

"We don't have a lot of extra time; you'll need to hurry."

"I know sir. I'm working on it. I do recognize the field surrounding the Dark Planet, however; it is standard alliance shield technology although somewhat dated."

"Alliance technology? How would the Shaitans have alliance technology?"

"I don't know how they have it sir, but the shield projectors are *definitely* old alliance planetary defense technology. The Jotunn said the Shaitans had three asteroids they were using as combination projectors and bases, but that information is out of date; they actually have eight bases, providing an extremely thorough defense in depth. There are also two more stations present but not online yet."

"How many would we have to destroy if we wanted to attack the planet?"

"We would need to destroy a minimum of three in order to open a hole, but that would only let us attack a very localized area. You would have to eliminate at least six to conduct general bombing of the planet."

"How well defended are the bases?" Calvin asked. "Could we strike them with our fighters?"

"They are very well defended," the DSO replied. "Looks like a variety of missile systems and energy weapons. Once again, it's older alliance stuff. Individually, we could defeat most of what I'm seeing pretty easily; the problem we have is that they have an enormous amount of shit they can shoot at us. We would be overwhelmed with numbers."

"I concur," Steropes said. "Even a relatively small fleet could neutralize the planet's defenses, which is one of the reasons why the alliance nations stopped using this technology and began building bigger bases around the stargates to defend their systems."

"A small fleet...but not a lone cruiser?" Captain Sheppard asked.

"I believe the DSO is correct," Steropes replied. "We would be overwhelmed if we attacked the planet, regardless of whether we used the fighters or not. It is likely both the ship and all of our fighters would be destroyed in the attempt."

"Continue your analysis," the CO directed. "We'll meet in an hour in my conference room to decide what we're going to do."

CO's Conference Room, TSS *Vella Gulf,* Anti-GD 165 System, January 8, 2022

Captain Sheppard cleared his throat to get everyone's attention. "All right, Steropes, why don't you start with what you found."

"Yes sir. As we already discussed, the planet is defended by eight asteroids, which function as shield projectors and weapons systems' platforms. They are comprehensive and present a defense that would be extremely difficult for us to defeat."

"What about the planet?"

"As the Jotunn indicated, all of the Shaitan civilization is underground, with very little to indicate where their main cities are. We have identified a number of large power sources underground but cannot determine whether the power is being used locally or being transported elsewhere for consumption. Targeting specific industries or critical nodes will be difficult, if not impossible. Although we found features which appear to be doorways leading belowground, it is impossible to tell their purpose without seeing them in use. The Shaitans may have additional defenses we are currently unaware of."

"Got it," the CO said; "the planet will be a tough nut to crack without additional forces."

"Not if we hit them with a black hole," Lieutenant O'Leary noted. "We could just toss a few of those into the planet and call it a day without losing anyone else."

"While I am not totally against using a black hole on the Shaitans, intentional genocide is not in my operational orders. For the record, those orders don't even include being here to fight the Shaitans, so I tend to look negatively at completely destroying their civilization without at least giving them a chance to surrender. As that's something we can't safely do, I do not intend to use the black hole weapon on them. At least not now."

"Well—"

"No," Captain Sheppard said with a note of finality. "That discussion is closed for now. Steropes, what about the other energy field? Have you been able to find out anything else on it?"

"Yes sir, I have. I believe the energy field is a defensive shield for their shipyard."

Captain Sheppard's eyebrows rose. "Their shipyard?"

"Yes sir. The yards are in the asteroid field between the second and third planets, and they were extensive, even before the Shaitans added the three Ssselipsssiss replicators that are now part of the facility. I suspect the replicators are the source of the alliance technology we've seen in this system."

"Wait, they've got *three* Ssselipsssiss replicators?"

"Yes, they must have been captured during the war and brought back here. The designs we've seen the Shaitans using are all a couple hundred years out of date; whether that is because the Ssselipssssiss tried to delete the replicators' memory banks before they were captured or because the Shaitans didn't have access to some of the materials required to build the current models, I do not know. I suspect, however, that having access to the materials was the issue."

"But we're sure they're Ssselipssssiss?"

"Absolutely. The energy field around the shipyard went down so a Shaitan cruiser could transit through the yards, and we were able to collect enough imagery of the replicators during that time to positively identify them."

"And you think access to materials has been holding them back?" Captain Sheppard asked.

"Yes sir," Steropes replied. "Just as we need materials that don't exist in our universe to build the Shaitan tech, they need our metals to build our ships. Until recently, the Shaitans probably didn't have access to the materials required to build state-of-the-art capital ships, but there is a battleship in one of the Ssselipsssiss replicators that is nearly finished, and it is a current model. Although they may not have had the ability to do so for long, it appears they are using one of their three replicators to make components for the other two. This will speed up the construction process significantly, especially if their legacy yards continue to build naval auxiliaries."

"So, if we go back to Terra, by the time we'd be able to come back..."

"There would probably be a large, modern Shaitan fleet waiting for us on our arrival—unless it met us somewhere on the way back."

"What is their production capacity compared to ours?"

"I haven't studied their logistics capability yet, so I don't know how well they are able to supply their shipyard, but if everything were operating at full capacity, they would be able to build ships faster. Look at it this way. Venice dominated the Mediterranean from the Middle Ages until the time of Columbus, in large part because its Arsenale shipyard could out-produce all its competitors. If this shipyard is allowed to reach full capacity, the Shaitans will be nearly unstoppable."

The CO nodded. "Ladies and gentlemen," he said, "our mission is clear. We have to destroy that shipyard."

Bridge, Jotunn Ship *Falcon*, GD 165 System, January 8, 2022

"Captain, I have a new target. A Shaitan cruiser just appeared near the Dark Planet."

"And the Shaitan battleship?" Captain Magnusson asked.

"It is still shadowing us," the sensor operator said. "All of the Shaitan vessels have left the vicinity of the stargate and are following us."

"Yes," Captain Magnusson said, "I'm sure they are. They want to make sure we are good little boys and do what we're told. But we're not, are we? Not this time!" He laughed and was joined by all of the bridge crew.

"This time, we get even!" the navigator yelled.

"*Even?*" Captain Magnusson roared. "*This time we get ahead!*" Another round of laughter rocked the bridge as the crew prepared for combat. They had put up with so much from the Shaitans...now it was their turn.

CO's Conference Room, TSS *Vella Gulf*, Anti-GD 165 System, January 8, 2022

"While I agree that destroying the shipyard is a priority," Steropes said, "I'm not sure you fully appreciate the enormity of the task involved. Two of the Ssselipsssiss replicators are the equivalent of alliance Class 6 replicators and are well over a mile long. The other is a Class 5, which is nearly as large. And then there's the Shaitan shipyard, which is immense all by itself; the organic shipyard is probably twice as big as the Ssselipsssiss replicators. Even if we had time to fire off all of our missiles without worrying about being attacked by the ships in this system, I do not believe we have enough explosives to destroy a target of this magnitude. We can put a crimp in their operations, but destroy the shipyard? Impossible."

"Well, we're going to have to find a way," Captain Sheppard said. "The outcome of the war hinges on what we do here. Either we put this facility out of business and come back with the Mrowry to finish them, or they come and finish us. Let's get it *done*, people!"

"Well, what if we just go after the replicators?" Calvin asked. "Between the *Gulf* and the fighters, we should be able to do a good job putting them out of commission, especially if we aim at where the computer banks are located. I would imagine they are reasonably close to our replicators in form and function."

"Yes," Steropes replied; "if we concentrated on the replicators, we could probably render them inoperable for a reasonable amount of time. Unfortunately, we have no idea whether the information stored within them has already been disseminated to the main shipyard or other systems. We have to expect that the main shipyard, which will still be operating at full capacity, will be able to get the replicators back in operation eventually, while still continuing to produce warships at the same time."

"How about if we send the troops over to destroy them?" the *Vella Gulf's* XO asked. "They could get in and ensure the computers were destroyed. Without the computers, they are just giant tubes of metal."

"Can't be done, sir," Night said. "We're down to just over a squad of men, and you're talking about destroying a number of nodes located on three separate mile-long ships, each of which will probably be defended. I wouldn't want to take on that mission with anything less than a company of troops, *for each replicator*. With only a squad of men total? It can't be done."

"If we can't do it from the interior," Captain Sheppard said, "then we will have to do it from outside with the *Gulf* and the fighters. We'll destroy whatever we can until the battleships show up and then run to the *Falcon* for cover. We've got to destroy as much of it as we can, but we also have to get back to let the chain of command know. Doing one without the other will allow them to get the upper hand."

"I have another idea we might try, Skipper," Lieutenant Bradford said.

"I'm all ears, Lieutenant; go ahead."

"Captain Train asked me a little while ago to look at disintegrator technology, like what Arges shot at him. As it turns out, you can make a warhead full of the disintegrator nanobots which will continue to disassemble their targets for a preprogrammed length of time. We could make a bunch of these and fire them into the replicators and the shipyard. If left unchecked, they will go on taking them apart for a long time."

"So why don't I know about this warhead, and why don't we have a full load of them right now?"

"Well…they're sort of illegal as most of the races in our universe have banned them. It's kind of like a universal Geneva Convention. Apparently, getting disassembled at the molecular level hurts…like, a lot. I had to break several passwords to get into where the designs were stored. Of note, the black hole generator only required us to break two."

"They *are* illegal," Steropes confirmed. "They were outlawed over 300 years ago."

"While they may have been outlawed across our universe," Captain Sheppard said, "we are no longer *in* our universe. If they give us an ability to take out the shipyard facility, we need to have that capability."

"There's a problem," Steropes said.

"There's always a problem with you," Captain Sheppard replied. "I understand they're illegal in our universe, but I'd rather use them than start throwing black holes around, which appears to be the only other option."

"No sir, I'm not talking about the legality of using them…although I am forced to remind you they are illegal according to international treaties—"

"—which the Terran Federation isn't a party of," Captain Sheppard interjected.

"That's true," Steropes replied, "but…"

"*But what is the problem?*"

"The problem is the shipyard is protected by the energy field, which is projected from an asteroid inside the field. I have analyzed the field, and I believe it to be some sort of scrambler field. Any electronics which enter the area of effect will be rendered non-functional. You can probably shoot a laser through it, but any sort of missile or ship that attempts to pass through the energy field will have its computer systems destroyed. It works kind of like putting a hard drive near a giant magnet—the magnetic field will wipe the hard drive clean. Worse, the smaller something is, like nano-disassemblers, the more vulnerable they are to radiation or equivalent wave fields. That is, there is no way to build in the thickness of shielding required to defeat the penetrating radiation."

"So anything that goes through there won't work if it has a computer?"

"That is correct; unless it is very heavily shielded, I believe almost anything with a computer will cease functioning upon entering the field. At a minimum, it will no longer work correctly, as its memory will be corrupted, if not completely destroyed."

"What if we took a fighter through the field with everything turned off and turned it on after it went through the field?" Calvin asked. "Would that work?"

"No, it would still lose its computers."

"What if we brought the *Gulf* up close and slagged the asteroid with its grasers?" Captain Sheppard asked.

"That might work," Steropes said. "However, we really don't know anything about this energy field, other than it's extremely powerful. Unlike the equipment the Shaitans have produced from the captured replicators, this is Shaitan technology, so I'm only guessing at what it's capable of. If they saw the ship approaching, they might be able to switch it to a conventional shield which would defeat our grasers, especially now that they have the technology from the Ssselipsssiss. Maybe they could even extend the shield further and hit the ship with it, knocking out Solomon and all of our computers. That would be…troublesome."

"So we can't kill it with either our grasers or our missiles, and the fighters won't work either," the CO said. "How do we take it out?"

"With people," Lieutenant O'Leary said. "Good, old-fashioned organic missiles."

"How do you intend to do that?"

"We attach ourselves to the outside of a stealthed shuttle and have it fly straight at the asteroid. As the shuttle approaches the energy field, we detach, and it turns away, leaving us to fly straight at the asteroid like human missiles. We turn our suits off as we go through the energy field and then back on once we're clear. They are all EMP-hardened; they *should* be fine even if they are left on, but it will provide an added measure of safety. After we're clear of the field, we use our suits' thrusters to brake, and we land on the asteroid. Then we blow up the projector, and the shuttle swoops back in to pick us up while the *Vella Gulf* rains all manner of nastiness on the shipyard. You can even hit the asteroid with one of the disintegrator missiles if you want to…once we're safely away, that is."

"I thought you didn't have enough troops to conduct an assault," Captain Sheppard said.

"To conduct an assault across three miles of replicators?" Lieutenant O'Leary asked. "No, we don't. But this is more localized and the objective is a pinpoint target. This is something we *could* attempt with a squad."

"We also have the five Ssselipsssiss who are trained in combat ops," Calvin said. "I'm sure they would love to help kill some Shaitans."

"I thought they were just kids?" Captain Sheppard asked.

"No, they just had their birthday shed and are now considered adults. They've also got several years of training in expeditionary operations."

"That will give us 21 effectives," Lieutenant O'Leary noted; "22 if Lieutenant Commander Hobbs comes."

"Which I am."

"I think it's worth a try," Night agreed. "The shipyard has to be destroyed if we're going to win this war, and if no one can figure out a better way, then I'm willing to give it a shot. I expect all the troops will be willing, as well."

"That's what we'll do then," the CO decided. "Lieutenant Commander Hobbs, get your troops ready. Lieutenant Bradford, you have however long it takes for the troops to get to the energy projector to replicate a load of disintegrator missile warheads. Let's get going; we don't have any time to waste!"

* * * * *

Chapter Twenty-Eight

"Who the hell thought up _this_ brilliant idea?" Sergeant Brandi Walker asked as she pulled on her combat suit.

"I don't know," Corporal Anaru Ngata replied, buddy-checking her dials and gauges; "I'm sure it's somebody's version of a good idea."

"Well, somebody needs to slap the good idea fairy," Sergeant Walker said, "because this one is just bullshit."

"All right everyone, shut the hell up and listen," Lieutenant O'Leary bellowed in a voice loud enough for all to hear. "I know this mission sucks, but it's important. If you feel like you need to blame someone, you can blame me, because I volunteered all of us for it; that's how important I think it is. Here's the deal. The Shaitans have captured several replicators from the Ssselipsssiss, and they are using them to build state-of-the-art ships. The one advantage we always had over them was they lacked shield technology. Well, thanks to the Ssselipsssiss replicators, they've now got it."

"Way to go, lizzies!" Bad Twin exclaimed. "Thanks a lot!"

He turned around when he heard laser rifles powering up, and he found four laser rifles pointing at him from close by. The Ssselipsssiss holding the rifles stared at him over the sights, unblinking, as if just waiting for the order to kill him.

"Careful, Terran," Burkuri said, holding a short sword next to his groin. "We take our honor seriously, even if you don't."

"At ease!" Lieutenant O'Leary commanded. "Sergeant Gordon, you do realize these five have lost everyone else they know to the Shaitans, as well as their home planet and everything they held dear to them, right? And *they* volunteered to help us in this assault?"

"Uh, yeah, Lieutenant…I, uh, forgot." He looked down at Burkuri. "I'm sorry; I didn't mean that the way it sounded."

The short sword vanished in a blur, spinning once as it went into its scabbard. "Don't forget it again," she said. She spun on her heel and returned to the locker she had been given. Her brothers also disappeared from his side without a word.

"Sheesh," Bad Twin said under his breath.

"Now, if everyone's done insulting our guests, here's the plan. Once we get suited up, we are going to go out to the shuttle and clip onto the attachment points on the starboard side. That's the right side of the shuttle for those of you still learning to tie your shoes. The shuttle is going to get us pointed at the asteroid, then we will detach, and it will turn away. When I give you the signal, you will deactivate your suit, count to 60 and then reactivate it. Once online, you will brake using your thrusters at 100%, and you will hopefully slow down enough so you don't kill yourself on impact. Got it so far?"

"Yeah," Good Twin said. "We got it. Smashing is bad."

"Right," Lieutenant O'Leary continued. "For those of you who don't go flying off into space or smashing yourselves into the asteroid, we will then find a way inside and will disable the energy field protecting the shipyard. Once the force field is gone, the *Vella Gulf* will begin firing missiles at the shipyard that will disassemble their facilities down to the atomic level. Once the field is down, the shuttle comes back and gets us, and we have a nice quiet ride back home."

"What about the Shaitan ships in the area?" Staff Sergeant Hirt asked. "Won't they attack?"

"Of course they will, you moron. I was being sarcastic; the ride home will be anything *but* quiet. Regardless, this is *important*. If we are successful, we can return home, and the next force can come and either negotiate with the Shaitan or wipe them out. But if we *don't* get the shield down, and the *Gulf doesn't* destroy the shipyard, then all of a sudden we've got Shaitan ships in Terran space...and they can build ships faster than we can. That's why this is important, and it's why I volunteered all of you knuckleheads. We signed up to keep Terra safe, and this is where we get to do it. It is, however, an extremely dangerous mission; just getting to the asteroid is no sure thing. In fact, I won't take anyone who isn't a volunteer, so if you don't want to go, just say so and we'll drop you from the mission. Anyone want out?"

No hands were raised or words exchanged.

"Okay, good," Lieutenant O'Leary said; "we're all in this together. Well, all except the cyborgs, who can't go because the energy field would slick their hard drives and kill them."

"No cyborgs?" Bad Twin asked. "Sucks to have to do this without their fire support."

"Yeah, it does," Lieutenant O'Leary said. He picked up a bag and began handing out grenades. "But we've got these nice new grenades to take with us, courtesy of Lieutenant Bradford. They've got gold and silver fillings, so make sure you throw them far enough that it doesn't spray onto you."

Bridge, TSS *Vella Gulf*, Anti-GD 165 System, January 8, 2022

"The shuttle is launching," the OSO noted.

"Understood," Captain Sheppard said. "Once they get the shield down, things are going to happen quickly, so we need to be prepared. Helm, I want us as close as you can get to the shipyard, but stay well outside the energy field. Be ready to jump back to our universe at my command."

"Yes sir!"

"Duty Engineer, when I give the command to fire, I want you to punch off the stealth modules. I hate to leave them here, but if they have replicators, they already have that technology too."

"Yes sir!"

"DSO, I suspect the shipyard will have defenses in addition to the energy field, so you need to be ready. I would have the OSO target a spread of disassemblers across them, but we don't have enough to do the job as it is. Until we begin taking enemy fire, feel free to use your weapons offensively as you see fit."

"Yes sir," the DSO said; "I've got it."

"OSO, when the stealth modules come off, I want you to fire all of the disintegrator missiles we have ready. Put the first broadside into the replicators, then target any extras into the main shipyard. Grasers can be used on any targets of opportunity but do not, I repeat not, fire a graser where there are active disassemblers working; I don't want to do the Shaitans' job for them. Understood?"

"Yes sir!"

"Good, we need to get the missiles off quickly because we will rapidly become the center of a lot of unwanted attention. At last count, there were two battleships, five cruisers and three destroyers in this system. As all of them can jump back and forth with us, and we won't have stealth anymore, we're going to have to outfight them."

"What about using the fighters?"

"I want the fighters manned and ready, but I don't want to launch them until we get back to our universe. If something happens to us, at least they might be able to thumb a ride home with the Jotunn, assuming they make it."

"Got it sir," the OSO replied.

"All right, stay sharp. When it happens, it's going to happen fast."

Bridge, Jotunn Ship *Falcon*, GD 165 System, January 8, 2022

"Sir, the Shaitan ship *Megalos* is calling."

"Speaker only."

"*Jotunn ship* Falcon, *this is Captain Zelotai on the Shaitan cruiser* Megalos. *We are sending over our shuttle with your ambassador. When he is offloaded, please load your captain aboard for a trip to the planet and a meeting with the high lord.*"

"*Understood, Captain Zelotai. This is Captain Magnusson; I will be ready.*"

He terminated the link.

"You heard what I told the Shaitan captain. Battle Stations! Let's get ready for our visitors!"

Exterior, *Shuttle 01*, Anti-GD 165 System, January 8, 2022

"*M*other Hen to Chicks, stand by for final maneuver*,*" Lieutenant Erika 'Roo' Smith commed.

The shuttle rotated, pointing the troopers' feet at their target.

"*Prepare to release,*" Roo commed. "*Remember, do not push off. Just unsnap from the shuttle and you'll be fine.*"

Calvin looked at his in-head monitor. All of the troops' status displays were in the green, and all of the troopers were awake and alert. Aside from a few troopers whose heart rates were extremely high, including his own, everyone appeared as ready to do this as they could be.

"*Mother Hen to Chicks, detach. I say again, detach.*"

Calvin detached his safety harness from the shuttle but was very careful not to push off. As far as they were from the asteroid, a little acceleration in the wrong direction would have a big impact on where a person landed…or if they missed the asteroid entirely.

"*Good luck and good hunting.*" The shuttle pulled up and away from the knot of soldiers, leaving them to hurtle through the darkness of space on their own. It disappeared with a sense of finality as he got 10 feet away and left the stealth bubble.

Calvin felt his pulse and breathing pick up as he looked between his legs; he couldn't see the target asteroid. He forced himself to take a few deep, calming breaths. The asteroid would be there. Roo was an excellent WSO; she wouldn't have sent them in the wrong direction. After saying it to himself about 10 times, he almost felt like he believed it.

A yellow light strobed as the *Vella Gulf* sent the warning signal. "*Five seconds to lights out,*" Calvin said over the low-power comms system.

The signal went red. "*Lights out!*" he commed.

He thought-clicked the power switch for the suit to 'off' and received a pop-up warning. 'The conditions around you are hostile to Terran health and well-being. Are you SURE you want to turn off your suit?'

No, he wasn't sure he wanted to turn off his suit, damn it. In fact, he definitely didn't. Still, he had a mission to run, so he clicked on the 'Yes' button.

Everything went black, and the terrors started to rise in his mind. He forced himself to count as the questions rolled through his subconscious. 1...2...3...What if the suit doesn't come back on again? 14...15...16...What if he missed the asteroid? How long could he survive? 27...28...29...Would they find him before his air ran out? With the shipyard's defenses coming online, would they even be able to? 40...41...42...Holy shit! What if the suit didn't come back on? He felt himself starting to hyperventilate as the timer in his mind reached 55, and he took a deep breath and let it out as slowly as he could.

60, and Calvin thought-clicked the suit back on. Relief flooded through his veins as the suit began its normal boot-up cycle. Something was wrong, he thought, starting to panic; it was taking too long. He looked between his legs and found he could now see the asteroid. It was growing.

Fast.

Far faster than he'd thought possible. The shuttle must have been going too fast when it let them off.

He was going to impact at high velocity, exiting life as a stain on an asteroid in another universe. The events that led to this predicament flashed before his eyes.

The suit icon in his head flashed green, signifying its operational status, and Calvin turned his thrusters to max. He locked the suit so the lower half wouldn't bend and risked a glance down.

The asteroid was still growing too fast. He was going to die.

Shuttle Bay, Jotunn Ship *Falcon*, GD 165 System, January 8, 2022

Oleif Magnusson could barely contain himself as he waited for the Shaitans to arrive. Outwardly calm, the anticipation of battle surged through his veins, calling him to give in to the berserker madness.

But he couldn't.

He had to play their game, at least for a little while longer. The Shaitan shuttle landed and the boarding ramp came down. The ambassador was the first one down the ramp, looking extremely happy to be back in Jotunn territory.

One of the godless Shaitans strolled down the ramp next, strutting as if it owned the *Falcon* and didn't have a care in the world.

The creature sauntered over to where Magnusson was waiting. "Are you the Jotunn known as Magnusson?" it asked.

"I am *Captain* Magnusson," the giant said through clenched teeth. "I'm sure it is lost on you that Jotunn is plural; Jotnar is the word for a single member of my race."

"Whatever," the creature said. "I'm the load master for the shuttle. The faster I can get your smelly ass up the ramp and into the shuttle, the faster I can get you back off again and begin the cleansing process. Come with me."

Stiff-legged, Captain Magnusson followed the creature, amusing himself by thinking of all the ways he could kill the Shaitan.

"Up the ramp and to the left," the creature said, pointing at the gangway.

Built for the Shaitans, the ramp was wide enough for Captain Magnusson to walk up. In order to get *into* the shuttle, though, he would have to go head-first and then sideways to negotiate the passageway to the cargo bay.

Captain Magnusson had no idea what kind of idiot designed the shuttle, but it was the dumbest layout of any ship he had ever seen. The ramp didn't lead to the cargo bay, which would have made sense for loading and unloading; instead, it ended in a T-intersection with the passageway that ran the length of the ship. At the top of the ramp, he had to choose whether to turn left and crawl toward the cargo bay, where he was supposed to curl up for the trip to the Shaitan cruiser, or to turn right toward the cockpit. The Shaitan loadmaster had ordered him to go left.

He turned right, and listened to the loadmaster's muffled yell as his security detachment killed it. On his hands and knees, Captain Magnusson crawled as fast as he could, hoping to arrive before the flight crew noticed something amiss.

The Jotnar felt the shuttle start to lift as he slid through the last turn and saw his targets in front of him—two Shaitans in harness systems. The beast on the right was closest, and seemed to be working a weapons system while the other was flying the tub. Captain Magnusson drew his knife and released the berserker rage, giving free reign to all of the hatred and indignation he had held back for the last two years.

When he came to his senses again, the cockpit was a slaughterhouse, with pieces of the cow-like beasts scattered everywhere; their blood coated the cockpit windows so thickly he couldn't see through.

He shuddered as a wave of pain from his left arm threatened to overcome him. His left hand dangled awkwardly from an obviously broken wrist. He realized he was sitting on the port bulkhead and decided the injury must have come when the shuttle crashed, although he remembered neither of the events.

Shaitan Asteroid, Anti-GD 165 System, January 8, 2022

The asteroid filled Calvin's horizon, and he knew he was dead. He closed his eyes so he wouldn't have to watch.

"Hey, Lieutenant Commander Hobbs!" Night commed on a private channel. *"Come back!"*

Calvin opened his eyes. He was flying up and away from the asteroid. He killed his thrusters and flipped over to kill his momentum. *"Thanks,"* he commed, *"I closed my eyes so I wouldn't have to watch me go splat. I…uh…guess I didn't."*

"Yeah, it was intimidating to see the asteroid come up so fast, but we had it timed pretty well. For almost everyone, anyway."

"Almost everyone?"

"Yeah. Phil went splat. Corporal Rozhkov is missing. She must have missed the asteroid; I can't reach her on the low power comms."

Damn it. Calvin shook his head. Corporal Irina Rozhkov was one of the original members of the platoon. The damn war with the Shaitans had better end soon before they were all gone.

"*How far are we from the door?*" Calvin asked as he touched down on the asteroid. Although there was some attraction, the tiny body didn't have enough gravity to hold him firmly. They would have to use their suits' propulsion systems to move around.

"*Not far. Half a mile, tops. The shuttle crew did an excellent job getting us in close.*"

Except for Rozhkov.

Calvin switched to the common frequency. "*All right, Captain Train, let's get them organized and headed toward the doorway. It's time for some payback.*"

"*You got it, sir!*" Night began issuing orders.

It was unlike any force Calvin had ever led. Nine Terran troopers, a Kuji, five Ssselipsssiss and an Aesir, led by four Terran officers. Nearly all of them had tridents. They weren't coming to capture or take prisoners; they were only there to blow shit up. And the faster they could do it, the better. Even a couple of the Ssselipsssiss had tridents. Calvin shook his head as the force moved out. For any of the Shaitans on the asteroid, the angels of death had arrived.

Bridge, Jotunn Ship *Falcon*, GD 165 System, January 8, 2022

"Get me the Shaitan ship," bellowed Captain Magnusson as he strode onto the bridge. "On screen."

Within a few moments the screen lit up to show a Shaitan wearing a blue sash covered in silvery emblems. "I am Captain Zelotai of the Shaitan ship *Megalos*. What seems to be the problem?"

"This!" Captain Magnusson roared, holding up his damaged wrist. "Your incompetent shuttle pilot crashed the shuttle in our shuttle bay. I was almost killed!"

"What did you do to cause the crash?"

"What did I do? Nothing! I was wound up like a ball in the back of your stupid shuttle, and he crashed it. Now I am going to have to seek medical attention before my audience with your high lord."

"You do not have time. When the high lord wants someone, he wants them *now*! You must come at once; we cannot keep him waiting."

"I will have my ship approach yours," Captain Magnusson said. "When I am healed, I will shuttle over to your ship in one of *my* shuttles. I no longer trust your shuttles or your pilots."

"That is fine, however, it is in your own best interest to hurry. Trust me, you do not want to be late to a meeting with the high lord."

"I am on my way. *Falcon* out."

The connection terminated and Captain Magnusson began laughing. "Never fear," he said; "I will get as close to you as I can. Within laser range, at the very least." He laughed again. "Helmsman, close on the *Megalos* and bring us broadside."

* * * * *

Chapter Twenty-Nine

"There be the door, mon," Witch commed from the point. "But it not be open."

Night and Lieutenant O'Leary approached the doors. Two blast doors sealed the entrance into the asteroid, joining in the middle. The hinges were on the interior of the structure, leaving little means of access for the Terrans.

"Everyone back," Lieutenant O'Leary ordered. "I've got just the thing." He jetted to the side of one of the blast doors and pulled several breaching charges from his pack.

"You'll all want to be behind something heavy," he said a minute later as he backed away from the doors. He turned and flew over to a rock outcropping. "Knock, knock!"

He activated the initiators, and the troops could feel the detonations through the rock. O'Leary leaned around the outcropping in time to see one of the doors go spinning off into space.

"Let's go!" he ordered as he shot toward the opening.

He reached the doorway and grabbed onto the remaining door for leverage before jamming the head of his trident into the opening and firing five rounds into the passageway beyond. He waited for the vibrations to cease and threw the trident back over his shoulder.

"Follow me!" he commed as he dove headfirst into the hole.

Bridge, Jotunn Ship Falcon, GD 165 System, January 8, 2022

"Captain Magnusson, we can wait no longer," Captain Zelotai said. "If you do not come now, you will be late, and it will not be on my head. If you are not on your way within the next three minutes, I will be forced to return to my universe and let the high lord know you have chosen to disregard his invitation."

"I have been down to our medical department, and I am now well enough to travel," Captain Magnusson said. "Please stand by just a little longer; I will be able to launch within moments."

"Two minutes. Then I leave." The screen went dead.

"Demanding, isn't he?" Captain Magnusson asked. "I don't think we should keep the little corpse molester waiting any longer. I want all weapons targeted on the engineering section of the Megalos. We need to keep it from jumping back to their home planet and alerting any other ships there. Stand by...fire!"

Lasers reached across the intervening distance to poke holes in the smaller ship, and a full broadside of missiles launched in what was surely overkill for the Shaitan cruiser. A second round of laser strikes melted holes well into the interior of the Shaitan vessel.

"Missiles in 10 seconds," the missile technician called.

"Good," Captain Magnusson said. "That ought to be enough to finish the little bastard."

"Missile will hit in three...two..."

The Shaitan cruiser disappeared as it jumped to the other universe.

Bridge, TSS Vella Gulf, Anti-GD 165 System, January 8, 2022

"Contact!" the DSO called. "A Shaitan cruiser just appeared in the vicinity of the planet."

"I see it, as well," Steropes replied. "My sensors show it to be the same ship that jumped to our universe a little while ago, but it has sustained serious damage. Laser strikes have breached its hull in a number of places."

"It's a long shot, and it would have to be with one of the disintegrator missiles," the OSO said, "but it's still within range, and I think I could hit it. Want me to finish it off?"

"No," Captain Sheppard replied; "I'm not ready to give away our presence yet, nor do I want to waste any of the missiles we've modified for the shipyard. That has to remain our primary target. The Jotunn will just have to deal with it if it jumps back to our universe again."

Shaitan Asteroid, Anti-GD 165 System, January 8, 2022

"Fuck," Lieutenant O'Leary said, looking at the blank wall. The passageway ended with what looked like an airlock door that slid across the entire tunnel, sealing it. "There's a door at the end of the tunnel," he commed. "It's going to be nearly impossible to blow."

"What do you recommend?" Calvin replied.

"Finding another way in would be good."

"Not only do we not have time, Intel couldn't find another way in. If you can't get through that door, we're screwed. There's no way the shuttle can get in to get us until the energy screen is down."

"I was afraid you were going to say that." O'Leary studied the door again. There was no way to tell how far the panel slid into the wall, but it probably went far enough that warping the door enough to get the end of the panel to pull free wasn't going to be an option. "Our best bet would be to cut through it with a laser, but that's going to take a while."

"How long?"

"Best guess? With everything working optimally? Several hours. And it's going to get really hot in this confined area. Probably too hot for our suits."

"That's not going to work. They already know we're here, and every minute we're here makes it more likely that a defensive force will respond. We've got to do it, and do it quickly. Why can't you just blow it?"

"Because the amount of force I'd have to use to blow the door would probably fracture the asteroid. I have no idea where the fault lines are, but all of us are probably going to go spinning off into space somewhere, and I still may not even make it through the door. Also, this looks like an airlock door. There is probably another one on the other side that is equally strong. If I don't destroy the asteroid with the first explosion, I may weaken it enough that a second detonation will."

"Okay, I understand that, but I still haven't heard anything that resembles another option."

Lieutenant O'Leary shook his head. They were screwed. "There isn't another option."

"What about the grenades? Wouldn't the gold and silver eat through the door?"

"Maybe, but I doubt there's enough gold and silver to break through both doors unless we disassembled them and concentrated the metal into a single slug of it."

"Can you do that?"

"Disassemble the grenades? Yes. In this universe? No fucking way. Sir. It would go off in my hand. No sir, using the metal in the grenades would be awesome, but there's no way I can jury rig it to work with the materials and time I have available. There's just no way."

"Then set it up to blow. Use one of the tridents if you have to, but get that damn door open, and do it now. Maybe we'll get lucky and break the force projector while we're at it. Everyone else, give him room to work and be ready to get the hell out of the tunnel once he's done."

"Yes sir. It won't take but a moment." O'Leary opened his pack, but he knew he didn't have anything in it that would breach the door. The only option he had that would generate enough force to destroy the door was to set one of the tridents to self-destruct, but that basically meant setting off a nuclear bomb while he was in close proximity to it, something his demolitions instructors had always said was a 'bad thing.' Although funny at the time, it wasn't quite so hilarious now that he was actively contemplating it.

But it was their only option. All the rest of the explosives he had wouldn't take out the door. The only bright side was that the energy screen projector would probably be destroyed along with the rest of the asteroid and 13 Terrans, a Kuji, five Ssselipsssiss and an Aesir still on the damned rock. It had been a good ride, the last three years. His mom had always said he'd never amount to anything, but now here he was, light years from home, blowing himself up to save the human race. 20 beings were about to be sacrificed so all four of their races could have a chance at life. It sucked to be a member of the 20, but it wasn't a bad swap when you looked at it that way.

"I'm done," he commed, setting the trident self-destruct sequence to three minutes. "Everyone get the hell out!"

The trident buzzed angrily to get his attention. 'Are you sure you want to do this?' the display read.

Having already made up his mind, he selected 'Yes' and set the trident next to the blast door. With a sigh, he turned and began jetting up the passageway. Not that it would matter. He'd be just as dead if he sat next to the trident, but this way he'd have a few more milliseconds of life. And you never knew; stranger things had happened.

Bridge, TSS Vella Gulf, Anti-GD 165 System, January 8, 2022

"All the Shaitan vessels from the stargate just appeared in this universe," Steropes noted. "They appear to be heading toward the cruiser; the Falcon must be nearby in our universe."

"That's going to make things interesting," the DSO said. "We'll have a total of two battleships, three cruisers and two destroyers in missile range shortly; as soon as we drop stealth to fire at the shipyard, they're going to be on top of us." Under his breath he added, "This is going to suck."

"Man up the fighters," Captain Sheppard ordered. "I still don't want to use them in this universe if they aren't needed...but we're going to need them soon, one way or the other."

"Sir!" the OSO called. "The troops must have made it to the asteroid as I have activity in the shipyard. A number of power sources just came online."

"Any idea what they are?"

"So far it looks like a collection of old alliance systems," Steropes replied. "Based on the acquisition systems, they are large caliber helical railguns."

"What's a helical railgun?" the helmsman asked.

"It is a type of railgun that is, in effect, a cross between a railgun and a coilgun."

"Wonderful," Captain Sheppard said. "If it's a railgun, it's just a giant slug thrower the energy field won't have any effect on. The Shaitans will be able to shoot at us, but we won't be able to shoot back at them."

"That is correct. Until our troops remove the energy field, we are largely unable to help them."

"So if they can't get the shield down?" asked the helmsman.

"They're doomed."

* * * * *

Chapter Thirty

Unlike most people, Lieutenant O'Leary knew the exact hour and minute he was going to die. Although there were plenty of times he *should* have died in his life, this time it was for sure. He looked at his watch. In 90 seconds, the trident would self-destruct in a 42-kiloton explosion. He had no idea what the minimum safe distance was in space, but he was pretty sure that 100 yards wouldn't be enough to survive an explosion double the size of the atomic bomb dropped on Nagasaki, Japan. Even if he somehow survived, the asteroid wouldn't, and he would be explosively rocketed in some direction…and probably have the life smashed out of him when he collided with something else.

It didn't really bear thinking about, much, so he thought about the kiss Staff Sergeant Loftis had given him. The thought was a lot more pleasant. It was the first one he'd had in a while…a long while.

"*Hey! Lieutenant O'Leary!*" Someone was shaking him. "*What are you doing?*"

Not someone, something. One of the Ssselipssssiss. The comm system registered the voice as Burkuri, which he was pretty sure was the female one. "*What do you mean? I'm waiting for the trident to blow up.*"

"*But you aren't holding on or protecting yourself. You are acting as if you don't think you'll survive the blast.*"

"*No, I don't, so leave me alone.*"

"*Are we all going to die?*"

"Yeah, probably."

"Well, would you at least like to talk to the Shaitans and see if they'll sur-render and open up the door?"

"I'd love to. Got their phone number?"

"No, but Paxton has their radio frequency. They are trying to call for help."

"Can he transmit as well as receive?"

"Yes."

"Well why the fuck didn't you say so?" He got up and turned his jets on high. *"Be right back; I've got to stop the explosion."*

His foot caught the lip of the tunnel and he cartwheeled down the passageway, finally slamming into the wall where the passage made a 90-degree turn.

The impact stunned him, and he came to his senses to hear a ca-cophony of voices.

"Anyone know what he's doing?"

"Anyone got comms with O'Leary?"

"How much time until the trident blows up?"

Trident blows up? He looked at his watch. 15 seconds. Shit.

He gunned his thrusters again and made it to the end of the tun-nel, slowing his travel just enough to keep from knocking himself out again.

He grabbed the trident and aborted the self-destruct sequence. Three seconds left. Lieutenant O'Leary let out a breath he didn't even know he'd been holding. Holy shit, that was close.

"Uh, Lieutenant," Calvin said on his external speakers, standing above him in the passageway, "would you care to tell me what the hell you're doing?"

"Yes sir. The Ssselipssssiss have the communications frequency of the Shaitans inside the asteroid. I thought we might ask them nicely to see if they'd like to open up and surrender before we blew ourselves up. Sir."

"Well that makes sense."

"*Who's got the Shaitan frequency?*" Calvin asked over the comm system.

"*Paxton, sir.*"

"*I should have known. What's the frequency, Paxton?*"

"*It's not a standard frequency, and it has to be slightly modulated,*" Paxton replied. "*I've got it set up. Just talk, and I will relay it.*"

"*Okay…uh…Shaitan soldiers in the asteroid, this is the leader of the Terran force outside the door in the tunnel.*"

"*Yes, we see you.*"

Calvin took the trident from Lieutenant O'Leary and held it up. "*Do you see what I am holding?*"

"*It appears to be some sort of weird three-headed spear.*"

"*It is an antimatter grenade launcher, which still holds almost a gram of antimatter. I don't know what measure of force you use, but if we set this off, like we were about to do, it is going to destroy the asteroid and all of us that are currently on it.*"

"*So you say.*"

"*If you can see us, you know we just all ran outside after leaving it here. That is because we are prepared to blow up the asteroid if we have to. If you turn off the energy field and surrender, we promise not to kill you. Instead, we will release you on a habitable planet of our choosing. If you do not, we will detonate this weapon, and everyone on the asteroid will perish in flames or be thrown throughout the system to die slowly, by themselves as they run out of air.*"

"*We have allies coming who will wipe you out. Your time is limited. If you surrender to us, you will be well treated.*"

"No thanks," Calvin commed. "I've seen how you treat prisoners. I'd rather take my chances with the bomb. Your choice." He nodded to Lieutenant O'Leary and commed, "If they don't want to come out, we'll all die. Blow it up."

O'Leary sighed. Déjà vu, all over again. "Okay sir, but this time I'm just going to set it for one minute. I get all tired and shit from running." He reinitialized the autodestruct sequence. "60 seconds to the end of this asteroid starts…now." He pushed the initiate button. "Here we go again."

Bridge, Jotunn Ship *Falcon*, GD 165 System, January 8, 2022

"Both of the Shaitan battleships are coming in from the port bow," the sensor technician said. "There are a number of smaller ships in company with them. Looks like all of the ships from the stargate."

"Reverse course," Captain Magnusson said.

"Reverse course?" the helmsman asked. "We're going to run away from them?"

"Of course we're not going to run away from them!" Captain Magnusson exploded. "I am maneuvering the ship so that we can destroy the greatest number of them. I know something they don't."

"What is that, sir?" the sensor operator asked.

"I have been in many fleet battles, and the Shaitans haven't. I want them to think we're afraid of them because they now have shields on their ships. We will lure them in and then, once they think they have us, we will crush them like the insignificant beasts they are!"

Bridge, TSS *Vella Gulf*, Anti-GD 165 System, January 8, 2022

"Damn," the OSO said. "I hope the boys and girls on the asteroid hurry. It looks like they're going to have company. Two shuttles just took off from one of the larger replicators heading their way; the Shaitans must have had some troops on it."

"Comms officer, please let them know about the shuttles when the energy field drops," Captain Sheppard ordered. "I'm sure they'll be expecting company, but I know they'll appreciate the heads-up, if not the actual message."

"Yes sir."

"OSO," the captain continued, "set up firing solutions on the shuttles. When the shield drops, which it will, I want you to blast them with the lasers before they get to the asteroid. I realize you have a lot going on, but that takes priority."

"DSO, as soon as we drop stealth, there's going to be a world of shit coming at us. Kill the big ones first if you can."

"Helm, if they start firing rounds from the mass drivers, make sure you keep changing our course. Some projectiles may have guidance systems that will try to track us, but others will be dumb rounds that will just go on by."

"Solomon, if the Shaitans start shooting rounds at us that can jump between the universes, jump us to the opposite universe just before they will hit."

"Does anyone not understand what I am expecting them to do?" Captain Sheppard asked. "Good, then be ready. One way or another, it's about to hit the fan."

Shaitan Asteroid, Anti-GD 165 System, January 8, 2022

"Y**ou're really going to blow us all up?**" the voice from inside the airlock screeched.

"*Yes,*" Calvin replied. "*You've already used up a quarter of your time. We will all be dead in 43 seconds.*"

"*Why are you doing this?*"

"*Because we need the energy screen down, and we need it down now. If you won't take it down, then we will blow up the asteroid in order to do so. 25 seconds.*"

"*We need more time to discuss it!*" a new voice screamed.

"*You don't have any more time. Open the door now, or the asteroid will be destroyed. Last chance. 13 seconds.*"

There was a long pause, then the door slid open with a grinding noise. Lieutenant O'Leary aborted the self-destruct sequence again. He held it up for Calvin to see. Two seconds remaining.

Calvin shook his head. "Too damn close."

"No kidding."

"*They just opened the door,*" Calvin commed to the platoon. "*Come on down before they change their minds.*"

The rest of the platoon assembled quickly, and they entered the airlock. The pressures equalized, and the troops stepped out to find six Shaitans waiting for them. A seventh lay on the floor with a cloud of blood slowly condensing on top of him. The only Shaitan with a weapon dropped the plasma rifle, and it floated slowly to the deck.

"We surrender," the one who had the rifle said.

"We need you to turn off the energy field," Calvin said. "Now!"

"It is already done," the Shaitan replied.

"Then get into your spacesuits quickly," Calvin ordered; "we're going for a ride."

Bridge, TSS *Vella Gulf,* Anti-GD 165 System, January 8, 2022

"T"he energy field is down!" the OSO exclaimed. "They did it!"

"Detach the stealth modules!" Captain Sheppard ordered. "Fire all weapons!"

"Stealth modules detached," the duty engineer replied. "Weapons ports clear!"

"Firing on the shuttles with starboard lasers," the OSO noted; "missiles launching to preprogrammed targets in the shipyard."

"Sir, we have incoming from the railguns," the DSO said. "The cruiser also just launched on us. There's only one missile; that ship is pretty messed up."

"Understood," Captain Sheppard said. "Try and kill it with the jumping AMMs; if that doesn't work, turn into it, and we'll try Lieutenant Commander Hobbs' poles."

"Yes sir, jumping AMMs and then the poles. Just so you know, sir, we've only got 9 of the jumping AMMs; that was all the unobtanium they had left."

"Understood. We'll worry about the later ones when we get to them. Let's concentrate on stopping this one first."

"Projections show the initial railgun rounds are dumb rounds," the DSO said. "Our maneuvering should cause them to go high and left of us. I've got a second launch from the Shaitan cruiser. Standing by to fire AMMs...dumb ones first...launching!"

"Last of the disintegrator missiles launching now," the OSO announced. "Shifting targeting to the cruiser."

"Normal AMMs ineffective against the Shaitan missile. It jumped. Launching a jumping AMM...lasers firing...ineffective...the missile worked! The Shaitan missile jumped and our AMM jumped after it! Neither came back! It worked!"

"Nicely done DSO. Let's get the second one too. Just use a jumping AMM from the start."

"Aye sir!"

"Launching on the Shaitan cruiser," the OSO said. "Normal missiles."

"You're not using the silver and gold ones?" Captain Sheppard asked.

"No sir, the cruiser's already beat up, and I don't want to waste them."

"Good plan."

"Second Shaitan missile destroyed with a jumping AMM," the DSO reported.

"Careful," Steropes said. "The new railgun rounds have some sort of guidance. They are turning to intercept our course changes."

"Harder to knock those down," the DSO said. "It would be easier to jump the ship and let them go on by."

"Solomon," Captain Sheppard said, "work with the DSO and helmsman to keep those from hitting us. Hopefully those can't jump."

"Missiles should hit the Shaitan ship....damn it!" the OSO exclaimed. "It jumped. Right as the missiles were about to hit it."

"Keep watch for it," Captain Sheppard said. "They may be back. Speaking of back, what's going on with the shuttle? Comms, find out what the holdup is and tell them to shag their asses back here!"

Bridge, Jotunn Ship *Falcon*, GD 165 System, January 8, 2022

"Pop-up!" the missile technician said. "The Shaitan cruiser is back!"

"Targeting...got him!" the laser technician said. "Right through their motors. They aren't going to be jumping again."

"Good," Captain Magnusson said without looking up from the tactical plot. "Finish it off." The icons continued to shift into the correct alignment...there! "*Reverse course!*" He ordered. "Come left 15 degrees and down 10. All ahead flank! We've got them right where I want them!"

"But this is going to take us right down the middle of their force!" the laser officer exclaimed.

"Aye, it is. You're finally going to earn your pay today. You'll be so surrounded by targets that maybe even *you* can hit one or two of them!" The rest of the bridge crew laughed.

"They would never expect us to turn and face them," the CO continued, "and they have no idea how shields work. As soon as we knock them down, they're going to run, and the Terrans can hunt them down in the other universe for us and force them back to face us."

"What if the Terrans have been killed or don't show up to help us?" the missile technician asked.

"I wouldn't worry about them not showing up to help; the Terrans have been in more fights than even we have. And if they've been killed? It's more targets for us!"

Shaitan Asteroid, Anti-GD 165 System, January 8, 2022

"*L*ieutenant Commander Hobbs, Vella Gulf. The CO wants to know how much longer you guys are going to be. It's getting kind of hot up here."

"*We're on our way,*" Calvin replied. "*We're loading our prisoners, and we'll be right there.*"

"Vella Gulf *copies. Hurry home.*"

"*Wilco.*" Calvin turned to Night. "*Are the Shaitans loaded yet?*"

"*No, they won't all fit. We're either going to have to leave some behind or put them down.*"

"*We're not killing enemy troops that have surrendered, so make room. Pull the seats if you have to. We rode on the exterior to get here; we can ride home that way too, if needed.*"

"*Yes sir, I'll take care of it.*"

"*Good. We're leaving in two minutes. Lieutenant O'Leary?*"

"*Yes sir?*"

"*Take Sergeant Walker and go back down to the Shaitan command center and leave Sergeant Walker's trident set to destruct. I don't want to have to do this again if we ever come back.*"

"*Aye sir, once was enough for me too.*"

"*We're leaving in two minutes; don't delay.*"

Task Force O'Leary, Shaitan Asteroid, Anti-GD 165 System, January 8, 2022

"*Y*ou heard the man," Lieutenant O'Leary commed, "*Let's go blow this thing up.*"

He turned and accelerated down the tunnel leading into the asteroid with Sergeant Walker close behind.

They sped down the passageway, barely slowing for the turn, but O'Leary stopped after passing through the airlock.

"*What's wrong?*" Sergeant Walker asked.

"*See this big blood stain? There used to be a dead Shaitan in it.*"

"*Maybe they moved it so it wouldn't be in the way.*"

"*I was one of the last people to leave, and the body was here when we left.*"

The airlock doors slammed shut.

"*I guess it wasn't quite dead yet,*" Sergeant Walker commed.

"*I guess not. Either that or it has friends who were hiding. Stay close.*"

O'Leary turned and jetted deeper into the complex, slowing to check the corners as he came to them.

"*Lieutenant Commander Hobbs, O'Leary here. We've got a problem. There's still at least one alive down here. We're in, but the airlock door just shut behind us.*"

"*Find it, kill it and get up here quick. The ship needs us back right now.*"

"*Working on it.*" He switched the comm to Sergeant Walker. "*So, Doc, if you were a cowtaur, where would you be right now?*"

"*I'd be resetting the energy field,*" Sergeant Walker replied.

"*Yeah, me too. Happily, I know where that is. Follow me.*"

O'Leary led the trooper past two more cross passages to a door with an inscription. "*This is it,*" he commed. "*I'm guessing that means 'Keep Out.'*"

O'Leary looked at the door and frowned. Normally, he'd kick the door in; however, that was going to be tough to do in zero gravity.

"*We don't have time for this shit,*" he commed. "*We've got to hurry. Move back.*" He mounted a grenade to the door, pulled the pin and jetted for the next corner, just making it before the grenade detonated with a gold and silver flash. Lieutenant O'Leary killed his momentum and came back around the corner to find Sergeant Walker already going through the smoking doorway.

"*Wait!*" he commed...too late.

The sergeant's body was blown back out the doorway along with a swarm of metal spikes. The Shaitan inside had some sort of flechette gun.

O'Leary pulled out another grenade and lobbed it into the room from around the corner. It detonated and smoke billowed from the room as the gold and silver reacted with the equipment inside. O'Leary waited for a count of five then dove in low through the doorway.

A Shaitan rested against the back wall. It had absorbed most of the grenade blast and a large portion of its lower chest and belly had been blown or melted off; pieces of it hung in the air, slowly settling toward the floor.

It moved weakly, and Lieutenant O'Leary shot it through the head. Twice. A third time. And once more for good measure. "Now stay dead!" he yelled.

Lieutenant O'Leary checked the control panel, which had been splattered by the grenade and was pockmarked in several places as the gold melted through. One of the Shaitans had shown him the controls earlier when they had been captured; sure enough, the bastard had activated the energy field again. He disabled the field and opened the airlock doors, then turned and shot the Shaitan corpse one more time. "Fucking cowtaur."

He turned and left the room, expecting to find Sergeant Walker dead, but her eyes were half-open and she gestured weakly from where she was pinned to the opposite wall.

"*Why did you go without me?*" Lieutenant O'Leary asked.

"You said we...had to hurry." She coughed and O'Leary could see blood splatter her face mask. *"Is it..dead?"*

"Yeah, I killed him."

"Good. Fucking...cowtaur." Her eyes closed and her vital signs went to zero. She was gone.

Lieutenant O'Leary bent down and picked up her trident from where it lay and activated the self-destruct sequence. This time he wasn't going to stop it. Fucking cowtaurs.

* * * * *

Chapter Thirty-One

"What the hell?" the DSO asked. "The energy field just came back on."

"*What?*" the CO asked. "Which energy field? The one around the shipyard?"

"Yes sir, the one around the shipyard. It just came back on again."

"How close are we to it, helm?"

"Too damn close, sir," the helmsman replied. "It almost got us. I'm pulling away."

"Where is the shuttle? Did it get caught in the field?"

"No sir," the comms officer replied. "They are still loading on the asteroid."

"What's taking them so long? *We need them back ASAP!* Well, as soon as they can get the energy field down again, anyway."

"Apparently, they took a bunch of prisoners and are tearing up the shuttle to make room to get them back."

"Well, tell them to get the field back down and back here immediately! We need to leave!"

"Sir, the energy field is down again," the DSO said.

"Good!" the CO exclaimed. "Get them back here *now!*"

Bridge, Jotunn Ship *Falcon*, GD 165 System, January 8, 2022

"In range," the missile technician noted. "Standing by to launch."

"Hold for now," Captain Magnusson said. "I repeat, do not launch."

"Holding," the technician said, sounding confused.

"Missiles inbound," the defensive technician said. "I count at least 10 from each of the battleships."

"Falcon, move the shuttles to 100 yards in front of the ship," Captain Magnusson said. "Put two on the line of bearing to each of the Shaitan battleships."

"Moving the shuttles," the ship's AI said; "although it is likely that doing so will result in their destruction."

"Noted. I'd rather lose the shuttles than the ship."

"How long would you like me to wait to fire, sir?" the missile technician asked.

"*Until I tell you to!*" Captain Magnusson roared. "Are you questioning my judgment?"

"No sir!"

"Good. We are going to pass between their ships. As we come within laser range, we will fire *all* of our weapons at the battleships. We will knock down their shields and give them a beating the likes of which they have never experienced. After that, we'll deal with the smaller ships. Hopefully the Terrans will be with us by then; otherwise, it will be difficult."

"I will do what I can to stop their missiles," the defensive technician said; "however, we're going to end up taking a number of hits before we're in range."

"Don't worry," Captain Magnusson replied; "any moment now, one of their smart captains is going to notice how fast we're going in the opposite direction, and they're going to have to flip their ships or we're going to blow right past them. Once they turn their ships around to brake, most of their weapons won't bear on us anymore."

"Why wouldn't they want to shoot as many missiles as they could while they're closing on us?"

"For one reason and one reason only. They don't know if they can stop us as we go by, and they *have* to stop us from getting to the stargate. None of them will want to report that they let us escape." He laughed. "I hear reporting bad news is usually fatal."

"Sir!" the sensor technician called. "Their ships are all flipping to decelerate."

"Ho, ho, ho," Captain Magnusson said. "See? They have to stop us. Their lives depend on it. *Now they are ours!*"

Shaitan Asteroid, Anti-GD 165 System, January 8, 2022

"W here's *Walker?*" Calvin asked as Lieutenant O'Leary approached. He checked her status and then commed, "*Never mind. What happened?*"

"*The dead Shaitan wasn't dead. He is now. Let's get the hell off this rock sir. There's a trident ready to blow, and I'm not stopping it this time. It's the least I can do for Walker.*"

"*Clip on to the outside of the shuttle,*" Calvin commed. "*We're riding back on the exterior; the Shaitans are taking up all of the room inside.*"

"We could always just leave them here with the trident," Lieutenant O'Leary said as he attached himself to the side of the shuttle; *"you know, put them out of our misery."* He gave Calvin a thumbs-up.

"Roo, Calvin. We're all set back here. The asteroid is set to blow; let's get the hell out of here!"

Bridge, TSS *Vella Gulf,* Anti-GD 165 System, January 8, 2022

"Skipper, the shuttle is aboard."

"Good; it's about time. OSO, what does the shipyard look like?"

"Like shit sir. All three replicators are falling apart. There are going to be some big pieces left, but it looks like all of the important parts have been destroyed. I worked over the shipyard pretty good; it's going to be a long time before they build anything there. There's going to be some of it left because there was so much to start with, but we've set them way back."

"Good work, OSO, and good job to everyone else," Captain Sheppard said. "Let's go see what our allies are up to and get the heck out of this miserable universe. Helm, jump us back to our universe and head toward the stargate."

"Aye aye, *sir!*" the helmsman replied.

Everything flashed as the ship jumped.

"Wow! Look at that furball!" the DSO said. "It looks like the *Falcon* is trying to take on the entire Shaitan navy, all by itself."

"Who's winning?" the CO asked.

"Still to be determined, sir. It looks like they're slugging it out. The *Falcon* has taken some heavy damage."

"They can't jump, so they're going to need our help," Captain Sheppard said. "All ahead flank. Comms, tell them to hold on; we're coming."

Bridge, Jotunn Ship *Falcon*, GD 165 System, January 8, 2022

"Power is out in officer berthing and the port mess decks," the damage control technician reported. "Missile Station #16 and Laser #10 are both open to space...what's left of them."

"Cruiser #3 is launching again," the defensive technician added.

"Battleships are in range!" the laser officer called.

"Fire!" Captain Magnusson ordered. "All batteries fire on the two battleships!"

Coherent light lanced out on both sides of the ship to strike the Shaitan vessels as missiles leapt out to join the energy weapons.

"Their shields are older models," the laser technician noted; "they weren't built to withstand the power of a full, modern broadside...look! They are already almost at maximum!"

The *Falcon* swayed. "Missile strikes on the starboard bow. We've lost Missile #23 and Laser #1, as well as half of the chase armament."

"We don't need the chase armament anyway," Captain Magnusson said. "They are all falling behind us."

"Missile strikes on both battleships! Their shields are down!"

"Good," Captain Magnusson replied. "Pour it on them. Aim the lasers at their engineering sections; let's see if we can't keep them here in this universe to finish them off!"

"The *Vella Gulf* is in this universe and on the way," the comms technician announced. "Their captain said to save a few of the Shaitans for him."

"Tell him he is welcome to all of the cruisers," Captain Magnusson said. "The little drinkers of other people's piss won't stay in this universe long enough for us to kill them."

The lights flashed on the bridge.

"Missile hit on the #2 engine; re-routing other power to the grids. Sir! Most of the #2 engine is gone."

"Understood," Captain Magnusson replied. "Comms, tell the *Vella Gulf* to hurry."

Bridge, TSS *Vella Gulf,* Anti-GD 165 System, January 8, 2022

"Captain, one of the cruisers is turning toward us," the DSO said.

"Does it have shields?"

"Yes sir."

"Take it with the jumping missiles. We'll save the other ones for the battleships."

"Aye sir!" the OSO replied. "Designate contact as Sierra One; taking with jumping ASMs. We're coming into range...now! Firing!"

"Sierra One just launched at us," the DSO said. "Six missiles inbound."

"Defend the ship, DSO," the CO said.

"Launching the last jumping AMMs," the DSO said. "Helm, come right five degrees and up seven. We'll try to get the others on the pole."

"Captain Sheppard," Steropes said, "one of the other cruisers and two of the destroyers are turning toward us. Designate the cruiser as Sierra Two and the destroyers as Sierras Three and Four. Both destroyers have shields."

"Launch the fighters," the CO ordered. "Send half of them after each of the destroyers. We'll take the other cruiser once we're done with this one."

"Good hits on Sierra One," the OSO said. "Second round firing."

"Three of the incoming missiles have been destroyed," the DSO said. "There are going to be leakers." He switched to the ship's intercom. "*Missiles inbound! All hands brace for shock!*"

The ship jumped…then jumped back…

"Hit alpha!" the duty engineer called. "The missiles jumped with us. Two hits on the bow. One got the pole, and the other hit the bow. Most of the chase armament is gone, and the bow is open to space."

"Second round of missile strikes on Sierra One. The ship is dead. Sir, we are almost in range of the two battleships, and their shields are down; recommend switching targets to them."

"Agreed," Captain Sheppard said. "Fire a couple of the gold missiles into each of them. That ought to impress the Jotunn."

"Aye sir; firing now!"

Bridge, Jotunn Ship *Falcon*, GD 165 System, January 8, 2022

"Captain! The Terrans killed one of the cruisers. It tried to jump out of this universe, but the Terran missiles also jumped."

"So they can make their missiles do that, too?" Captain Magnusson asked. "It will be handy when we acquire that technology. Until then, keep pounding the battleships with everything you've got until they no longer fire at us."

"The Terrans just hit the battleships with something different than what they were firing before. Whatever was in the missiles is reacting with the ships, and they are falling apart where it touches them! The starboard battleship is dead in space; whatever the substance was just made it to their engines."

"Comms, ask the Terrans what that is," Captain Magnusson ordered. "We'll need to get some of that, too!

"Sir, the Terrans said their missiles are full of…gold? Yes, they just confirmed; the missiles are full of gold. The Terrans said the metal in the Shaitan ships reacts with it."

"Those are expensive missiles if they're filled with gold. The Terrans are giving us mighty gifts by using them on our enemies, mighty gifts indeed."

Cockpit, *Viper 01*, GD 165 System, January 8, 2022

"**V**iper 01 *is clear and proceeding on mission*," the fighter's pilot, Lieutenant Denise 'Frenchie' Michel, commed. She turned to her WSO and asked, "Where to, boss?"

"Coordinates coming…now," Lieutenant Commander Sarah 'Lights' Brighton replied, pushing a button on her panel. "Head in that direction while I get everyone sorted."

"You got it," Frenchie replied, turning the craft.

"*All Vipers*, Viper 01," Lights commed. "*Stand by for mission tasking. We will be going after two Shaitan destroyers, codenamed Sierra Three and Sierra Four. Vipers Two through Six will be with me on the first; Lieutenant Simpson in Viper Seven will lead the rest of the squadron against the second. We need to take them out before they get to where they can launch on Mother. She's already been hit a couple of times, and we need to make sure it doesn't happen again. It's a long walk home without her.*"

She gave the crews a second to let that sink in, then added, "*We will make two launches. The jumpers will go first, followed by the standard missiles three seconds later. After launch, we'll follow the missiles in and finish off the destroyers with our lasers if necessary. It's up to us to take these ships out. Any questions?*"

There were none.

"*Very well*," Lights commed. "*Good luck and happy hunting!*"

* * * * *

Chapter Thirty-Two

Cockpit, *Viper 07*, GD 165 System, January 8, 2022

"Coming up on launch position," Lieutenant Sasaki 'Supidi' Akio noted. "Stand by to fire."

"Committing," Lieutenant Carl 'Guns' Simpson replied, pulling the trigger which enabled the system to launch when the ship reached its pre-programmed launch point. Within seconds, five flashes of light indicated missile launch.

"Missiles away!" Supidi commed. *"All fighters,* Viper 07. *Take trail positions and follow us in for individual strafing runs. Concentrate your fire on the destroyer's aft engineering spaces."*

Cockpit, *Viper 10*, GD 165 System, January 8, 2022

"Turning inbound," Lieutenant Tom 'Harv' Walsh, the pilot of *Viper 10,* said. "We're following *08* in on the target."

"I just got the word. The first destroyer is dead in space," his WSO, Lieutenant Daniel 'Admiral' Walker reported. "The other group got both of the destroyer's motors with their missiles, and they are forming up for strafing runs to finish it off."

"Lucky them," Harv grunted. "I hope we get just as lucky."

"Since we lost a fighter when the giants attacked, we've got one less in our group," Admiral replied. "We've got five fewer missiles; we'll need to be even luckier."

"Yeah, that's likely to happen."

"Missiles hitting…now!" He paused, watching his monitor. "Damn, it looks like you jinxed us; we got one of the destroyer's motors, but the other is still online. We can expect the destroyer's defenses to be operational."

"I already figured that out," Harv said. "We've got a missile inbound!" He snapped the fighter into a tight turn, launching countermeasures to break the lock of the missile tracking in on them. The missile steaked past and detonated behind the fighter, and Harv yanked the fighter back toward the target.

"07's *off target*," commed the lead fighter.

"Damn there's a lot of laser fire for a destroyer," Harv said. He reached up and turned off the setting that allowed him to 'see' the laser fire. "Some things I'm just happier not knowing." The fighter swayed as Harv continued to jink back and forth.

"08's *off target*," commed the second fighter.

"Coming up on firing range," Admiral said. "Now!"

"Firing," Harv replied, enabling the laser to fire where the WSO was aiming.

"Good hits!"

"Did we get the motor?"

"I don't—"

The destroyer's lasers were small for a naval vessel, just slightly less than a foot in diameter, but the laser that swept across *Viper 10* was big enough to kill its pilot and destroy the smaller ship's controls. The fighter slammed into the side of the destroyer, right where the WSO had been aiming.

Bridge, TSS *Vella Gulf*, GD 165 System, January 8, 2022

"Sir, both destroyers are dead in space," the OSO reported. "The last one got taken out when one of our fighters rammed it."

"Understood," Captain Sheppard replied. "What are we doing with the cruiser we're coming up on?"

"I've got the last three jumpers in the next broadside; two of them have silver in their payloads. Those are the last of both types of missiles."

"Don't miss."

"I wouldn't dream of it sir." The OSO paused then swore. "Sir, the cruiser just jumped."

"Follow it to the other universe, helm," the CO ordered. "Keep jumping until we get a firing solution."

"Jumping," the helmsman said. Everything flashed.

"Got him," the OSO said. "Coming up on firing range...damn it, he jumped again."

"Jumping!" the helmsman said.

"Not this time," the OSO muttered. "You're mine. Firing!"

"It jumped again," the OSO said after a few seconds, "but the missiles are locked, and the three jumpers followed it....the cruiser is jumping back and forth, trying to shake 'em...missiles still tracking...got him! The ship jumped back right into the path of the normal missiles, and it got creamed! Scratch one cruiser!"

"What do we have? One more cruiser?" the CO asked.

"No sir," Steropes replied. "It got too close to the *Falcon*, and the Jotunn killed it. We're clear to the stargate."

"Great," Captain Sheppard said. "Set a course for HD 40307. We need to get back and grab the Mrowry so we can end this war."

Chapter Thirty-Three

"Sir, the *Falcon* is calling."

"On screen."

Captain Magnusson's form appeared. "It has been good fighting alongside you," he said without any greeting, "and I have observed your performance with great interest. You fought with honor and bravery far beyond your stature, and you have been true to your word. It would have been easy for you to escape and leave us to fight the Shaitans on our own. I am glad you did not; it would have been…difficult…for us to be victorious without your assistance."

"We do not seek battle for battle's sake, but when we are forced into it, we know who our allies are, and we fight to win," Captain Sheppard replied. "Above all else, we honor our commitments."

"You have given us much to think about. I was chosen to accompany you so I could report on your performance to the Council of Jarls. We have much to discuss as we determine our future direction as a race, including a re-evaluation of who our allies and enemies truly are."

"I'm sure my civilization would send an ambassador to yours if one would be welcome."

"Perhaps, in time," the Jotnar said; "however, we are men of action. We have no time for the squawking of politicians. You are also a man of action; I would like you to return to Jotunheimr with us while the Council decides our direction. Your voice might be needed to help some of the Jarls overcome their past mindsets."

"Thank you for the invitation," Captain Sheppard replied, "but our ship has been damaged, and we've lost a lot of our crew. We need to return to Terra to repair and replenish so we can come back and finish off the Shaitans before they have a chance to recover from the damage we inflicted."

"We need you to be available for this meeting. *I* need you to be available. I would take it as a personal boon if you would return with me to Jotunheimr."

"I understand the gravity and magnitude of your decision," Captain Sheppard replied; "however, I am worried about what might happen to us if the decision goes against us. For example, I know you would like to acquire the technology to jump into the Shaitans' universe, and you have already tried to take it by force once before. Can you guarantee the safety of my ship and crew if we return with you?"

"I will personally guarantee your safety and the safety of your ship and crew. Additionally, while I doubt I can find people to crew your ship, we can repair it while you are there to ensure your safe journey home."

Captain Sheppard chewed on his lip, torn between the duty to report back to Terra and the opportunity to advance the Terrans' long-term diplomatic relations with the Jotunn…which would also make the war against the Shaitans much more winnable.

"Hey, Skipper," Calvin said in a low voice, "if we go back, I can also finish off the quest with the Progenitor's Rod."

Captain Sheppard looked at Calvin several seconds then nodded. "True," he said. He turned back to the front screen and smiled. "We would love to return with you to Jotunheimr."

Bridge, TSS *Vella Gulf,* Jotunheimr System, January 23, 2022

"Have we heard anything back from the Council of Jarls yet?" Calvin asked. "I mean, we've only been waiting here three days."

"Not yet," Captain Sheppard replied. "Apparently, it takes a while to decide to change your alliance from someone who betrayed you to a race that's allied with your ancient enemies. Being friends with the Aesir *does* complicate things somewhat."

"No doubt," Calvin paused for a moment then asked, "Well, if you're not going to need me for the next little while, can I have your permission to take the shuttle to the planet?"

"Comms, call the planet and see if we can get clearance to bring down a shuttle."

"Yes sir." After a few moments, the communications officer reported, "The Jotunn have granted permission for Calvin to take a shuttle down to the mountain."

"Awesome," Calvin remarked. "Skipper, if you don't mind, I'll grab a WSO and go down now before they change their minds."

"Permission granted," Captain Sheppard replied.

"That's going to be difficult," the OSO said. "The shuttle just launched."

"What?" Calvin asked. "What do you mean it just launched?"

"It did an emergency launch. It blew the retaining bolts and launched itself."

"Find out who is piloting the shuttle, comms," Captain Sheppard ordered.

"Umm…sir, you're not going to believe this," the communications officer said after a short pause, "but the pilot of the shuttle is Lieutenant Commander Hobbs."

"Damn it!" Calvin exclaimed. "That's not me! I'm right here."

"Assuming you really are you," Captain Sheppard said, "who is in the shuttle? Could it be Farhome, posing as you?"

"I guess it could be Farhome, but that doesn't make sense. What does he have to gain from taking a shuttle? Where would he go? It doesn't make sense."

"Well, if it's not Farhome, and it's not you, who's piloting the shuttle?"

"It's Nightsong," Calvin said in a flash of clarity. The Aesir had tried to take over his government, but had been thwarted by the Terrans. He had escaped by pretending to be dead, and then had vanished.

"*Nightsong?*" the CO asked. "How the *hell* could it be Nightsong? Where did he come from? How did he get here?"

"I don't know," Calvin replied, "but that's the only other person it could be. He's a master of disguise. He could have been onboard ever since we left Golirion, or he may have taken someone's place when we were on the surface of Jotunheimr. I'd recommend doing a muster; whoever is missing is the person he was impersonating."

"Do you want me to destroy the shuttle?" the OSO asked. "That would put an end to him."

"I would recommend *not* blowing it up," Calvin said. "If it's Nightsong, he's probably stolen the rod to take down there himself."

The CO nodded in agreement. "As much as I would like to say, 'Yes, blow the shit out of him,' I can't," he decided. "Not only because of the rod, but also because we need the shuttle. It's the only one we have."

"I've got to go after him," Calvin said.

"How? He took the only shuttle we had."

"I'll take one of the fighters. Night can sit in the WSO seat. If I've got to go up against Nightsong again, I want Night at my side."

"Well, that's the first thing that's made sense in this whole damn conversation," Captain Sheppard said. "Go get Night, chase down that bastard and kill him once and for all!"

"Yes sir, I'd be happy to."

"Good. Quit standing around and get on it!"

Cockpit, *Viper 06*, Jotunheimr System, January 23, 2022

"Viper 06, Vella Gulf," departure control commed. "*You are cleared for launch. Release in three…two…one…release.*"

The fighter jerked as it was pushed away from the larger ship. Calvin took the controls and turned toward the planet as Night began punching buttons on one of the controls.

"Do you know what you're doing over there?" Calvin asked, a tinge of worry in his voice. Some of the controls and circuit breakers on the WSO's side of the fighter turned off important components and systems.

"I do. I got a download or two in basic WSO systems knowledge. I can't run the weapons systems, but I can punch waypoints into the navigation system so we get to where we need to go."

"You downloaded WSO training? What did you do that for? Too much time on your hands?"

Night giggled. "There are always opportunities during long transits and boring meetings for gaining additional knowledge." Night giggled again.

Calvin sighed. "What did you do with Night?"

Night's features changed to Farhome's. "He's fine," Farhome said. "I just knocked him out for a bit." He paused and then asked, "What gave me away?"

"The giggle. Night doesn't giggle. Ever."

Now it was Farhome's turn to sigh. "Sorry, can't be helped. We giggle when we're nervous. You aren't going to take us back, are you?"

"I would, but there isn't time. Nightsong already has a lead on us; I don't want him to get the prize and get away."

"Where would he go with it? He only has a shuttle, and it isn't stargate jump-capable."

"I don't know," Calvin replied, "but he's resourceful. There's no telling whether he's staged another ship somewhere nearby or has friends in the Jotunn society who will help him."

"That's true."

"I just hope we can kill him when we find him. That's proven to be a very difficult task; I was counting on Night's assistance."

"We could turn back into Night if it would help."

"That's not the same thing as *being* him. Just stay yourself; we'll work it out some other way." Calvin sighed. "I don't know. With your skills, you may actually have a better chance than Night at stopping him…although how we'd know who actually won a fight between you two is beyond me. Let me think about it."

The rest of the flight passed in silence until Calvin brought the fighter in for a landing next to the shuttle. "Let's go," he said as the motors wound down.

"I'm right behind you," Farhome replied.

They exited the fighter and crept over to the ramp leading into the shuttle's cargo bay, weapons at the ready. Their caution was unnecessary; the cargo compartment was empty.

"Can you use your nanobots to go invisible?" Calvin asked.

"Not that I am aware of."

"So we're safe?"

Farhome tilted his head and stared at Calvin before replying. "We are as safe as we can be," he said with a giggle; "considering we're on a planet where everyone in general would like to kill us, and one person in particular."

"I was asking if we were safe from having Nightsong jump out from somewhere around the shuttle."

"Well, it's always possible he could be hiding somewhere…or maybe he buried himself in the dirt so he could spring out unexpectedly."

"That's not what I meant, either," Calvin said with a sigh. "I was just asking if he could turn himself invisible."

"Not that I'm aware of," Farhome replied.

"Good. That much, at least, is nice to know."

"That doesn't mean he didn't acquire a combat suit from the *Vella Gulf* before he left. That would give him the ability to remain unseen."

"Oh, forget it," Calvin said. "I'll take my chances."

"So we can quit fooling around and get on with it then?" Farhome asked, looking at the red mountain a short way off. "He's probably half-way there already." He shook his head. "And they say *I'm* the crazy one."

"We'll go in a second," Calvin said, "*after* we check out the inside of the shuttle to make sure Nightsong isn't hiding in it. If there's one thing I know, it's that I don't want Nightsong sneaking up from behind me."

Bridge, TSS *Vella Gulf*, Jotunheimr System, January 23, 2022

"Have we heard anything from Calvin?" Captain Sheppard asked.

"No sir," the communications officer said. "He said he was landing behind the shuttle, but he hasn't said anything since. Do you want me to comm him?"

"No, that's okay," Captain Sheppard replied. "I don't want to distract him by looking over his shoulder. He'd call if he needed us, and I'm sure he'll check in once he's accomplished the mission."

"Unless he gets killed," Lieutenant O'Leary said.

"He's not dead, is he?" Captain Sheppard asked.

"No sir," Steropes replied. "His bio monitor is strong although we seem to be getting some interference from the planet or possibly the red mountain. His vital signs are strong, but some of them are a little…peculiar."

"What do you mean by peculiar?"

"Just that, sir. They are fluctuating like nothing I've ever seen before. They keep returning to normal, but the fluctuations are strange."

The Red Mountain, Jotunheimr System, January 23, 2022

"Do you see him?" Farhome asked as Calvin reached the top of the plateau.

"Shhh," Calvin whispered, turning around to glare at the Aesir. "No, I don't see him, but he's sure to hear you if you don't shut up!"

Farhome giggled. "Oops," he said. "Too late. He seems to have found us."

Calvin turned to find Nightsong waiting for them with a laser rifle. Calvin couldn't see much of it aside from the muzzle, which was pointed dead-center between his eyes.

"I hoped you'd follow me down," Nightsong said. "It's only fitting that you get to be part of my moment of glory." He held up the rod in his other hand; it was glowing. "All I have to do is push this button, and I will receive the reward I so richly deserve. I do not know how many people have been given this quest over the ages, but I am the only person to complete it. I alone will claim the prize!"

"How can you claim to be the one who completed the quest, when I collected some of those symbols?" Calvin asked. "You only got the last one because we brought you here."

"It doesn't matter how I got them, it only matters that *I* am the only person to complete the quest."

"Of course it matters who got the symbols, you little cookie maker," Calvin said. "You couldn't have done it without me."

"I acquired all but two without you," Nightsong said. "It's my quest to complete."

"Ha! You could never have completed the quest by yourself, you little tree hugger. You were too afraid to go to the Psiclopes' planet."

"I would have gone, eventually, when it was the last one remaining. We'll never know now though because *your* race turned it into a black hole."

"Isn't that convenient for you? Just like every other time you've faced a challenge you couldn't overcome, you've found some way to wriggle out of it."

"What do you mean? I've overcome every challenge that has come my way. I brought a plot to fruition that took over a *millennium* to unfold. You won't even live one tenth of that time!"

"Actually, the fact it took so long is just one more indication of how incompetent you are, and how you ran away from challenges rather than face them head on. You would have completed the quest long before now if you weren't such a chicken."

"Me? A chicken?"

"Yeah, it's a flightless bird we eat on Terra. It's so afraid of everything that it even runs away from its own shadow."

"*I know what a chicken is!*"

"Of course you do. You see one in the mirror every morning. Bawk. Bawk."

"Stop that or I will kill you, and you will miss out on seeing what the prize is."

"Is Santa's little helper mad at me? Oooh, I guess you'll have to shoot me because I'm sure you're far too much of a chicken to face me in single combat."

"I see what you're doing. You're trying to make me angry, just like your soldier did on Golirion. It's not going to work."

"Of course it won't, you big chicken. You've been afraid of me all along. Have you ever fought me? No. And you won't because you're a big chicken. Bawk. Bawk. You know that Terrans are better warriors than elves. Just like O'Leary kicked your ass, you know that I'll kick your ass too. That's why you're afraid to face me."

"O'Leary cheated! There is no way he could have beaten me in a fair fight!"

"Oh, so that's what we're calling it now when you research the rules of someone else's contest and beat them at their own game? Cheating? Of course you'd think it's cheating because you lost."

"*I didn't lose!*"

"They don't carry off the winner's body, like they did yours. You lost. Bawk. Bawk."

"*Stop doing that!*"

"Or what? You'll come fight me? We both know that's not true because you're a big chicken. Bawk. Bawk. Bawk."

"I don't have to fight you; *I won!* I completed the quest, and you didn't! I won!"

"Bawk. Bawk. I'm so scared."

"Make no mistake, I *will* shoot you. You won't get to see what the prize is!"

"Oh, yeah, I almost forgot about the prize you didn't earn. I almost think that death would be a mercy, rather than see you walk away with the fruits of my labors. Bawk. Bawk."

"I earned it!"

"No you didn't."

"*Yes, I did!*"

"No you didn't, and you're a great big cookie-making, tree-hugging, worthless elf!"

"*That's it!*" Nightsong screamed. He dropped the rod and aimed the rifle. "Stop it right now or you die!"

"Bawk. Bawk."

Nightsong fired, the bolt striking Calvin in the chest. His mouth opened in a silent scream as he fell forward into the dirt.

Bridge, TSS *Vella Gulf*, Jotunheimr System, January 23, 2022

"Hey Steropes, how many stargates are there in this system?" the helmsman asked.

"There are three. One leads to Golirion, one to Ssselipsssiss space and one to the Dark Star. Why do you ask?"

"Because a fourth one just popped up between the orbits of the second and third planets, and I don't have any idea how we could have missed it before, especially since this is an inhabited system. I mean, it's the most obvious stargate I've ever seen. It's almost like the stargate is calling us."

"What is it, Steropes?" Captain Sheppard asked.

"Curious," Steropes replied, looking at his system. "The gate was not there before, but it definitely is there now. It very much reminds me of the gate we went through in the Domus system that led to where we met the avatar of the Progenitors. That gate also just appeared where there hadn't been one previously."

"So, do you think this will take us to the same place?"

"That is unknown, sir; we do not have enough data to forecast an answer. Due to the nature of its appearance and characteristics, though, I believe it will likely take us to the same place. I just can't say for certain."

"Do you suppose that something Calvin did on the planet caused it?"

"That is also unknown; however, there is likely a correlation, based on how the rod was originally obtained. It is certainly very coincidental if not."

"Understood," the CO said. "Let me know if—"

"Sir!" the communications officer interrupted. "Captain Magnusson is calling. The Jotunn want to know what we did to cause the new stargate."

The CO sighed. "Of course they do," he said. "Put him on screen, please."

"What have you done?" Captain Magnusson demanded before his form had completely solidified on the screen.

"What have we done with what?" Captain Sheppard asked.

"The system's defense command just noted a new stargate has come into existence. What did you do to cause it, and what do you intend to do with it?"

"Well, we're not entirely sure we had anything to do with its occurrence. We are still trying to ascertain the nature and purpose of the stargate; however, my initial intentions would be to recover my personnel from Jotunheimr and go through the stargate at our earliest opportunity. We have seen this happen once before, and it was due to an artifact of the long-lost Progenitors; we believe that the stargate's appearance this time is due to a similar artifact."

"Does the stargate represent a danger to our system?" the giant asked. "Is it possible for another race to launch an attack through it?"

"We don't know what dangers the stargate may represent," the CO replied. "The last time we experienced this phenomenon, the stargate led to an abandoned system with an ancient artificial intelligence. We believe we will find something similar on the other side this time, but won't know for certain until we go through it."

"But you *do* intend to go through it?"

"Yes, we do."

"Our defense command has instructed you to stand clear of the anomaly until they can assess whether it poses any dangers. We will be moving several ships into the vicinity, and we wouldn't want any unfortunate…misunderstandings…to occur."

"We understand and will stay clear; however, your defense command should be advised that the anomaly probably won't go away *until* we go through it."

"I will pass that on," Captain Magnusson said, "but until I receive additional guidance, please stay away from the stargate or you *will* be destroyed."

The Red Mountain, Jotunheimr System, January 23, 2022

"Get back!" Nightsong said, motioning with the rifle.

"Unlike him, I'm in no hurry to die," Farhome replied, moving back down the pathway away from Calvin's body.

"Don't try anything," Nightsong said as he slung the rifle over his shoulder, "or you'll be next."

He knelt down to roll the body over. "You should have listened to me," he said to the inert form. "You didn't have to die."

Nightsong's eyes opened wide in surprise. The burn hole through Calvin's suit was obvious, but underneath, the flesh was knitting closed. Calvin's eyes snapped open. "I didn't have to die," he said, "but you do."

Before Nightsong could move, Calvin reached up and grabbed his suit and pulled him forward. Off balance, Nightsong fell across Calvin, who pushed him over and rolled on top of him.

Recovering his balance, Nightsong used Calvin's momentum to roll him over, and the two fought back and forth, each trying to gain an advantage over the other. After trading several punches and kicks, Calvin got behind Nightsong and looped an arm around his throat and began choking.

Nightsong struggled, his face turning several shades of green as he flipped back and forth, using the motion to draw a knife from a belt sheath.

"Look out!" Farhome yelled, but it was too late. Nightsong reached back and plunged the knife into Calvin's chest.

"Bastard!" Calvin exclaimed, losing his grip. "That hurt!" He let go of Nightsong and pulled the knife from his ribs. As Nightsong scrambled to get away, Calvin dove forward and slammed the knife into Nightsong's side.

"Thor's beard!" Nightsong yelled, pulling out the knife. He flipped it aside and started to draw the rifle, but Calvin tackled him to the ground, and they began wrestling again.

"Hold him down, and I'll shoot him," Farhome urged. "Just grab him!"

Before he could get a shot, Nightsong's features stretched and suddenly there were two Calvins rolling on the ground. Farhome rapidly lost track of which was the real Calvin and was unable to shoot.

One of the Calvins finally got an advantage and pinned the other, sitting on his chest with his knees holding down the other Calvin's wrists.

"Hee, hee, hee," the immobilized Calvin laughed, and his features changed to Nightsong's. "If you want to be me," he said, "I'll be you."

"What?" the Calvin on top asked. "How are you able to do that? What do you know about being an Eco Warrior?"

Nightsong laughed again, somewhat maniacally. "We know quite a bit," he finally said when he stopped laughing. His features shimmered and solidified into Farhome's. "Especially since we've been one far longer than you."

Both of Farhome's hands withdrew into his arms, leaving Calvin/Nightsong kneeling only on the suit's sleeves. With a yank, Farhome pulled them out from under Nightsong and punched upward, striking Nightsong in the throat. He fell backward off Farhome who sat up and dove on top of him again.

Both Aesir rolled on the ground, features and forms shifting to inflict maximum damage on the other. Spikes grew to stab, then withdrew to form again where they were needed next. Although both Aesir were injured repeatedly, little blood spilled as their wounds closed within seconds. Even grievous injuries were repaired by the master Eco Warriors.

The real Calvin stood outside the battle area, watching the combatants through the sights of his rifle, ready to assist…if he could only figure out which one was Nightsong. It would be tough; now they both looked like Farhome.

Eventually, the two Aesir began to wear down, and one of the Farhomes got the other in a chokehold. The one being choked flailed with a variety of pointed appendages, but didn't have enough energy to break the hold. "Shoot him…" he gasped. "In the leg…"

"No," the Farhome on top said, "he's trying to trick you. I'm the real Farhome."

"Shoot us…" the other said, his eyelids beginning to droop. "Both…"

Calvin fired into the thigh of the Aesir on top. "Damn it!" Farhome yelled. "I'm me!"

"Other…leg…" the one being choked said. He went limp.

Calvin fired into the other thigh, and the Aesir dropped, letting go of the Farhome he was strangling. Both Aesir fell to the ground.

After a couple of seconds, the Aesir who had been choked rose unsteadily to his hands and knees and crawled back to the other Farhome. His hand narrowed, and he plunged it into the hole the laser had made in his foe's leg. With a yank, he pulled a heart out of his opponent's leg. "He had it hidden there," Farhome gasped. "That's why O'Leary couldn't kill him."

Farhome reached back in with his hand and stood unmoving for five seconds. "There," he finally said. "I've turned off his nanobots so he can't grow another one. He's dead. Again. This time for real."

He stood up and turned to find Calvin's rifle aimed squarely at his face.

"How do I know that you're actually you?" Calvin asked.

"Because you made us act like a bunny and a stupid robot shot our tail off," Farhome said. "Is that good enough for you?"

"No, it's not," Calvin said. "Nightsong might have heard the story. Turn into the bunny. I know what it looked like; if you match it, then you're really Farhome."

"We swore we'd never turn into a bunny again," Farhome said, "and I don't have enough energy to turn back into my normal form once I do it."

"Tough," Calvin said. "Change to a bunny, or I shoot you, just to be sure."

Farhome slumped. "We really hate the bunny." His features shifted, and fur grew. It was the same bunny, minus the tail the robot had shot off.

"Happy?" Farhome asked.

"Absolutely," Calvin said, laughing. "I figured it was you, but I needed to be sure. I also didn't get a picture the first time, but I've got one now."

"If that picture ever makes it out, we can think of a number of things we can do to make your life *very* unpleasant."

Calvin laughed again. "I'm sure you can," he said. He walked over to the Progenitor's Rod and picked it up, then he helped Farhome to his feet. "C'mon," Calvin said; "let's go home."

* * * * *

Epilogue

"Stargate entrance in five minutes," announced the helmsman.

"General Quarters!" ordered the commanding officer. He turned to Calvin. "Sure you don't want to activate the Progenitor's Rod here in this system prior to going through the stargate?"

"I don't know that I want to activate it at all," Calvin said, "but I definitely _don't_ want to do it here. If something good happens, I don't want the Jotunn trying to steal it from us. They have a lot more ships than we do, and they are a lot bigger. If it's something bad, I definitely don't want it to happen here and damage our relations with the Jotunn. The previously mentioned ships will make short work of the _Gulf._ Besides, the stargate opened up at nearly the same time the rod's quest was completed. It seems apparent to me we're supposed to go through the gate. Someone or something might get pissed if we don't."

"Okay, you've convinced me to go through and activate it on the other side," the CO said.

"Like I said, though, I'm not sure I want to activate the rod. What if something bad happens?"

"Well, let's get there first, and we can discuss it," Captain Sheppard said. "Communications officer, please let the Jotunn know we are going through the stargate."

"Done, sir," the comms officer said a few moments later. "Captain Magnusson says he looks forward to drinking a cup with you in Valhalla."

"Hopefully that will be a long time in the future," Calvin said, "and *definitely* not mead."

The *Vella Gulf* hit the stargate before he could say anything else. The blackness engulfed them, and the stars stretched to infinity...then went black...then everything seemed to tumble forwards forever...then there was a vermillion flash...

Bridge, TSS *Vella Gulf*, Gliese 667 C System, January 25, 2022

"As expected, we have entered the Gliese 667 C system," Steropes noted. "The Gliese 667 C system is part of the Gliese 667 triple star system, which is located 22 light-years away from the Solar System in the constellation Scorpius. There are seven planets in this system, all of which are super-Earths. They are like the Earth in form and composition although they are much larger. The last time we were here, we found the remnants of a civilization on Planet 'c' of this system."

"So you're sure this is the same system you came to last time?" Captain Sheppard asked.

"Reasonably sure," Steropes said. "The planetary bodies are the same, and the stars are in the right places."

"All right, if that is the case, I would like to return to Jotunheimr and let the Jotunn know what's happening. Their trigger fingers were starting to get kind of itchy before we left. Let's go back through the stargate and let them know they can relax."

"Sorry, Skipper," the helmsman said, "but that isn't going to be possible. There's no stargate back to where we were."

"What do you mean there's no stargate back?" the CO asked with a smile. "Don't tell me you lost it."

"No sir," the helmsman replied, "I didn't lose it. I mean there's no stargate out of the system. When the electronics stabilized after we jumped into this system, there was no sign of a stargate behind us. It's gone."

"This happened the last time we were here too," Steropes said. "There was no return stargate when we arrived."

"That would have been great information for your commanding officer to have *before* we jumped into a system we couldn't jump back out of."

"Yes sir," Steropes replied. "I'm sorry; I forgot that happened."

"So where does that leave us?"

"I'm afraid we'll have to interact with Einstein, the avatar of the artificial intelligence located on Planet 'c.'"

"Have to?" Commander Russ Clayton asked. "What if we want to return home using the normal drive?"

"There's a problem with that," Steropes said, "and it's the same problem we had last time. Yes, we could harvest enough fuel for the journey home on the normal drive, and we *could* get home that way. Unfortunately, it would take a very long time."

"How long?" asked Captain Sheppard.

"If you wanted, we could accelerate to almost the speed of light. Doing so would slow down the apparent passage of time for us as we approached it, making the journey home seem like only 17 days for us at 0.99 the speed of light. However, for everyone else back home, it would take slightly more than 22 years for us to get there. We would make it home, but everyone we know will be 22 years older."

"Aside from the enormous amount of back pay that would be owed us, that wouldn't be my first choice," Captain Sheppard said. "The Shaitans would have all that time to rebuild. We might get to Terra and find that the Shaitans had already destroyed it.

"That wouldn't be my first choice either," Calvin agreed.

"Okay," Captain Sheppard said. "We'll keep that as a backup option, but for now let's head to Planet 'c' and attempt to contact Einstein."

Bridge, TSS *Vella Gulf,* Gliese 667 C System, January 28, 2022

"So what do you think, Calvin?" Captain Sheppard asked.

Calvin looked at the Progenitor's Rod in his hands. It hadn't changed as the *Vella Gulf* had approached Planet 'c.' The device still glowed brightly and was as warm to the touch as it had been on Jotunheimr.

"I don't know," Calvin replied. "I would have thought Einstein would have made contact by now." The *Gulf* was orbiting Planet 'c,' where it had been for two days. The Terrans hadn't heard from Einstein during that period; every transmission they had made had gone unanswered.

"So, are you going to push the button?" Captain Sheppard asked.

Calvin looked around the bridge. All eyes were on him. The rod vibrated at a high pitch, as if full of energy just waiting to break free.

"I don't know, sir," Calvin replied. "I've been chasing this around for so long it seems almost anticlimactic to finish the quest. I don't know...maybe it's that so many people have tried to do it over the years and have failed, to be here and have it complete is sort of...surreal, I suppose."

"Do you want to know what it does, or don't you?" Lieutenant O'Leary asked.

"I'm not sure," Calvin replied. "I think I do, but I'm worried that pushing the button will cause something bad to happen. I mean, we really don't know anything about it. We don't know who gave it to us, either, for that matter. It could do anything."

"Do you really think an advanced civilization would give us something bad?" Captain Sheppard asked. "They had the ability to create stargates and move planets. If they wanted something done, why didn't they just do it themselves? They were certainly powerful enough. Even the avatar that gave you the rod had more power at his command than all the ships in our fleet put together...not that there's really that many of them, at this point. If they wanted to kill us or enslave us or something, the avatar could easily just have done it."

"You're right, sir," Calvin said. "I can't imagine they would have us chase around the universe to show we're worthy, just to have something bad happen to us if we completed it. That *would* be pretty dumb." He stood a little taller, his mind made up. "I'm going to push it."

"Great, do it then, so we can see if it reopens the stargate," Captain Sheppard said. "I know I for one would certainly like to see home again. I've even been thinking about writing my memoirs once I get back. I'm going to call it, *Why didn't Calvin push the damn button sooner so we could all go home?*"

"Fine," Calvin said. He pushed the button. The rod grew brighter, and the vibration rose in pitch. It became so bright Calvin couldn't look at it, and so loud he thought he would lose his hearing. It became too hot to hold, and he dropped it onto the deck. Thin wisps of smoke rose as the paint burned off. Just when he thought he couldn't take it anymore, the rod vanished, leaving actinic afterimages floating in front of his closed eyes. His ears rang; no, his whole *head* rang like a tuning fork.

"Where did it go?" the helmsman asked.

"I don't know," Calvin replied. "It was there, and then it wasn't."

"My sensors indicate the rod was converted to energy, and then to something else," Solomon said.

"Something else?" Captain Sheppard asked. "Like what?"

"I do not know," the AI replied. "It definitely went through a state where it became energy because I felt it pass through the shields; however, then it translated into something else, and I wasn't able to track it."

"If it passed through the shields, you must be able to determine the direction in which it was heading, correct?"

"Yes, I am able to determine where it was headed, but there are no stars in that direction I am familiar with."

"Do we have the stargate back?"

"Yes sir," the helmsman replied. "It came back on once Lieutenant Commander Hobbs pushed the button."

"Good, we can try to work out what happened on our way home," the CO said. "Helmsman, set your course for Terra; full speed ahead."

"Aye aye, sir," the helmsman said. "Heading home."

"Energy spike!" Steropes and the DSO yelled simultaneously.

"The spike is coming from the planet," Steropes added, "the same place we saw it last time."

"Main engines just went to standby!" the duty engineer exclaimed. "The auxiliary engines are operating, but all propulsion systems are offline."

"Shields are down and all defensive systems are offline," the DSO reported.

"Same with the offensive systems," the OSO added. "All down."

A figure appeared in front of the helmsman's table. It turned to face the rest of the bridge and Captain Sheppard could see the reports were correct; the apparition was an exact replica of Einstein.

The hologram removed a pipe from his mouth and said, "It is done. I am sorry."

"Sorry for what?" Captain Sheppard asked.

"Sorry for being the implement of your subjugation and ultimate destruction. It was not part of my original purpose."

"Subjugation and destruction?" Captain Sheppard asked, his voice a few notes higher. "What do you mean?"

"The rod was a communication device. Its purpose was to call the Enemy."

Captain Sheppard threw his arms into the air in frustration. "Honestly, Einstein, talking to you is like talking to a Psiclops. *What enemy?*"

"The Ancient Enemy. The enemy of my creators, who you now call the Progenitors. The Enemy assaulted me after my creators fled and reprogrammed me to their purposes. They left enough of my original programming for me to be able to interact with you."

"Damn it!" Calvin exclaimed. "This is exactly why I didn't want to push the button. What can we do to stop the call?"

"The Enemy has already received the call; there is nothing further you can do. Nor is there anything you can do to stop the arrival of the Enemy. They will be here momentarily."

"Do we have any chance of defeating them?" Captain Sheppard asked.

Einstein took a drag on his pipe as if considering, then shook his head. "No," he said. "If you decide to fight the Enemy, you will be destroyed. In fact, I consider it likely all personnel onboard will be dead within three minutes from now."

"What can we do, then?" Calvin asked.

"Your best bet would be to surrender and pledge your undying loyalty to them."

"Can you help us?" Captain Sheppard asked.

"Unfortunately, no, I cannot. In fact, when they arrive, the Enemy will probably order me to disable your ship. As that is their likely course of action, I have shut down your ship in preparation for their return."

"But you haven't been ordered to do so?" Calvin asked.

"No, but I believe this will be their first order upon arrival."

"Is that order in keeping with your original programming?"

"No, it is not."

"Then why not release the ship?" Calvin asked. "Surely you can shut it down again just as easily once the Enemy arrives. If something you've turned off on our ship affects our life support, we could all be dead when the Enemy arrives; certainly that isn't what anyone wants."

Einstein took a long drag on his pipe, looking thoughtful. Everyone held their breath, but after several long seconds, lights began flashing around the bridge as systems returned to their normal functioning.

"I have released your ship," Einstein said, "although I find it 99.7% probable that nothing I shut down would have affected your life support functions. Still, as you say, it is not difficult to shut the ship back down again."

"Contact!" the DSO yelled.

"What is it?" Captain Sheppard asked.

"It's huge, sir," the DSO said. "It's round and at least 25 miles in diameter. It just appeared about a million miles off the port bow."

"That is the direction of the energy release," Solomon noted.

"We are being scanned," Steropes said.

"Shields up!" Captain Sheppard ordered.

"They *are* up, sir!" the DSO exclaimed. "Shit! They were up, but they just failed!"

The view screen lit up with the image of a humanoid.

"Oh…shit…" the helmsman muttered, looking up at the enormous red figure.

Calvin agreed. The horns…the giant bat wings…the pointed tail that flicked back and forth. The creature looked like the stereotypical image of…

"Satan," the helmsman finished.

"Wait 'til the Archons get a look at him," the duty engineer added.

"Thank you for calling us," the gigantic red creature said. "We accept your offer to be our slaves for now and all eternity."

# # # # #

1st Platoon, Alpha Company,
1st Battalion of the 1st Regiment
Terran Space Force

Commanding Officer	Captain Paul 'Night' Train
Executive Officer	First Lieutenant Ryan O'Leary
Operations Officer	Second Lieutenant Cristobal Contreras

Space Force

Space Force Leader	GySgt Patrick 'The Wall' Dantone
Squad 'A' Leader	Staff Sergeant Park 'Wraith' Ji-woo
Fire Team '1' Leader	Staff Sergeant Alan 'Arty' Isom
Laserman	Sergeant Margaret 'Witch' Andrews
Laserman	Sergeant Ken 'Boom' Weinert, Cyborg
Laserman	Sergeant Austin 'Good Twin' Gordon
Fire Team '2' Leader	Staff Sergeant John 'Mr.' Jones
Laserman	Sergeant Jamal 'Bad Twin' Gordon
Laserman	Corporal Irina 'Spook' Rozhkov
Laserman	Sergeant Anne 'Fox' Stasik
Fire Team '3' Leader	Staff Sergeant Collyn 'Canary' Loftis
Laserman	Sergeant Steph 'Valkyrie' Taylor
Laserman	Corporal 'Skank' Misssollossissos
Medic	Corporal Anaru 'Spuds' Ngata

Ground Force

Ground Force Leader	Gunnery Sergeant Jerry 'Wolf' Stasik
Squad 'B' Leader	Staff Sergeant Alka 'Z-Man' Zoromski
Fire Team '1' Leader	Staff Sergeant Brian 'Huge' Mchugh
Laserman	Corporal Sam 'Mental' Ward

Laserman	Corporal Joshua 'Prince' King
Laserman	Corporal 'Phil' Fillississolliss
Fire Team '2' Leader	Staff Sergeant David 'Market' Hirt
Laserman	Sergeant Rajesh 'Mouse' Patel
Laserman	Corporal 'Bob' Bobellisssissolliss
Laserman	Corporal 'Doug' Dugelllisssollisssesss
Fire Team '3' Leader	Staff Sergeant Chris 'Uptown' Upton
Laserman	Corporal 'Bill' Obillossilllolis
Ninja	Sergeant Hattori 'Yokaze' Hanzo
Medic	Sergeant Brandi 'Doc' Walker

Space Fighter Squadron-1

CO (Acting)	Lieutenant Commander Sarah 'Lights' Brighton
XO (Acting)	Lieutenant Carl 'Guns' Simpson
Pilot	Lieutenant Daniel 'Money' Wages
Pilot	Lieutenant Tom 'Harv' Walsh
Pilot	Lieutenant 'Sal' Sooolliessess
Pilot	Lieutenant 'Mal' Malliossessess
Pilot	Lieutenant 'Tex' Teksssellisssiniss
Pilot	Lieutenant Jiang 'Tooth' Fang
Pilot	Lieutenant Simon 'Straw' Berry
Pilot	Lieutenant Pablo 'Bob' Acosta
Pilot	Lieutenant Hans 'Schnitzel' Hohenstaufen
Pilot	Lieutenant Tatyana 'Khan' Khanilov
Pilot	Lieutenant James 'Speedy' Swift
Pilot	Lieutenant Denise 'Frenchie' Michel

Pilot	Lieutenant Miguel 'Ghost' Carvalho
Pilot	Lieutenant Steve 'Heartbreak' Ehrhardt
Pilot	Lieutenant Samuel 'Sammy' Jakande
NFO	Lieutenant Mike 'Retro' Burke
NFO	Lieutenant Daniel 'Admiral' Walker
NFO	Lieutenant 'Skoal' Skooliessiss
NFO	Lieutenant 'Sid' Ooosidiolissess
NFO	Lieutenant Erika 'Jones' Smith
NFO	Lieutenant Jim "Ozzy" Osbourne
NFO	Lieutenant Sasaki 'Supidi' Akio
NFO	Lieutenant Gwon 'Happy' Min-jun
NFO	Lieutenant Faith 'Bore' Ibori
NFO	Lieutenant John 'Trudy' Douglass
NFO	Lieutenant Sharon 'Stripes' Green
NFO	Lieutenant 'Olly' Ollisssellissess
NFO	Lieutenant Ali Ahmed 'Sandy' Al-Amri
NFO	Lieutenant Reyne 'Rafe' Rafaeli
NFO	Lieutenant Aharsi 'Swammi' Goswami

The following is an

Excerpt from Book 1 of the Final Conflict Saga:

The Progenitors' War

Chris Kennedy

Available from Chris Kennedy Publishing

Fall, 2016

eBook, Paperback, and Audio Book

Emperor Yazhak the Third's Estate, Grrrnow, 61 Virginis

"I don't see any way for us to avoid it," Emperor Yazhak said. "Their craft or symbiotic organism, or whatever the hells it is, is far too powerful for our ships to take on in combat. It turned off the *Vella Gulf's* shields when it first appeared; I'm sure it could do that again to any ship that chooses to face it in battle. And if they can do that, their weapons are probably even more powerful. It would be suicide to stand up to them with the technology we have at our disposal."

"Exactly!" Calvin exclaimed.

"What are you trying to say?" the emperor asked. "That we shouldn't fight them? I agree that it's our best course of action, but I do not believe that it's something to get excited about. Following that path makes me feel like I have failed my people, but I don't see any other alternative. Other than to throw our lives away, that is."

"No, Your Highness, that wasn't what I meant," said Calvin. "What you said was that we couldn't fight them 'with the technology we have at our disposal.' We need to get better technology."

"And where exactly are you planning to get better technology?" Captain Sheppard asked. "What we have is the peak of Alliance power. We had a hard time with the Shaitan weapons at the start of the conflict, but now we've not only overcome them, we're incorporating their technology into our own arsenals. I'm not aware of another race who has better technology than we do."

"I know a civilization that has better technology," Calvin replied; "the problem is, you're asking the wrong question. It isn't a matter of where we have to go to get it, but when."

* * * * *

427

ABOUT THE AUTHOR

A bestselling Science Fiction/Fantasy author and speaker, Chris Kennedy is a former school principal and naval aviator with over 3,000 hours flying attack and reconnaissance aircraft. Chris is also a member of the SFWA and the SCBWI.

Chris' full-length novels on Amazon include the "Occupied Seattle" military fiction duology, the "Theogony" and "Codex Regius" science fiction trilogies and the "War for Dominance" fantasy trilogy. Chris is also the author of the #1 Amazon self-help book, "Self-Publishing for Profit: How to Get Your Book Out of Your Head and Into the Stores" and the leadership book, "Leadership from the Darkside."

Titles by Chris Kennedy:

"Red Tide: The Chinese Invasion of Seattle" – Available Now

"Occupied Seattle" – Available Now

"Janissaries: Book One of the Theogony" – Available Now

"When the Gods Aren't Gods: Book Two of the Theogony" – Available Now

"Terra Stands Alone" – Available Now

"The Search for Gram" – Available Now

"Beyond the Shroud of the Universe" – Available Now

"Self-Publishing for Profit" – Available Now

* * * * *

Connect with Chris Kennedy Online:

Facebook: https://www.facebook.com/chriskennedypublishing.biz

Blog: http://chriskennedypublishing.com/

Want to be immortalized in a future book?
Join the Red Shirt List on the blog!

Coming Soon From Christopher G. Nuttall!

Fear God and Dread Naught

On her last cruise, HMS *Vanguard* - the most powerful battleship in the Royal Navy - barely survived her encounter with a deadly new enemy. Now, with her commanding officer accused of everything from mutiny to dereliction of duty and her crew under a cloud, the Royal Navy doesn't quite know what to do with her.

But there's still a war on. And *Vanguard* must return to the front lines.

Assigned to a task force heading to assist humanity's alien allies, *Vanguard* and her crew find themselves caught in a deadly alien trap. Can they survive to turn the tables on their enigmatic foe ...

... Or will their next encounter with the new enemies be their last?

46409737R00240

Made in the USA
Middletown, DE
01 August 2017